# Crashed

**Also by Timothy Hallinan**

The Junior Bender Series
*Crashed*
*Little Elvises*
*The Fame Thief*

The Poke Rafferty Series
*A Nail Through the Heart*
*Breathing Water*
*The Fourth Watcher*
*The Queen of Patpong*
*The Fear Artist*

The Simeon Grist Series
*The Four Last Things*
*Everything but the Squeal*
*Skin Deep*
*Incinerator*
*The Man With No Time*
*The Bone Polisher*

# Crashed

A Junior Bender Mystery

## TIMOTHY HALLINAN

CRASHED

Copyright © 2012 by Timothy Hallinan

Published by Soho Press, Inc.
853 Broadway
New York, NY 10003

Library of Congress Cataloging-in-Publication Data is available.

HC ISBN 978-1-61695-274-7
PB ISBN 978-1-61695-276-1
eISBN 978-1-61695-275-4

Interior design by Janine Agro, Soho Press, Inc.
Illustration by Katherine Grames

Printed in the United States of America

10 9 8 7 6 5 4 3 2 1

*To my supremely talented brothers,*
*PK and Michael*

# Crashed

Part One

LIGHTS

# 1
## Safe at Home

If I'd liked expressionism, I might have been okay.

But the expressionists don't do anything for me, don't even make my palms itch. And Klee *especially* doesn't do anything for me. My education, spotty as it was, pretty much set my Art Clock to the fifteenth century in the Low Countries. If it had been Memling or Van der Weyden, one of the mystical Flemish masters shedding God's Dutch light on some lily-filled annunciation, I would have been looking at the picture when I took it off the wall. As it was, I was looking at the wall.

So I saw it, something I hadn't been told would be there.

Just a hairline crack in the drywall, perfectly circular, maybe the size of a dinner plate. Seen from the side, by someone peeking behind the painting without moving it, which is what most thieves would do in this sadly mistrustful age of art alarms, it would have been invisible. But I'd taken the picture down, and there it was.

And I'm weak.

I think for everyone in the world, there's something you could dangle in front of them, something they would run onto a freeway at rush hour to get. When I meet somebody, I like to try to figure out what that is for that person. You for diamonds, darling, or first editions of Dickens? Jimmy Choo shoes or a Joseph Cornell box? And you, mister, a thick stack of green? A troop of Balinese girl scouts? A Maserati with your monogram on it?

For me, it's a wall safe. From my somewhat specialized perspective, a wall safe is the perfect object. To you, it may be a hole in the wall with a door on it. To me, it's one hundred percent potential. There's absolutely no way to know what's in there. You can only be sure of one thing: Whatever it is, it means a hell of a lot to somebody. Maybe it's what they'd run into traffic for.

A wall safe is just a question mark. With an answer inside.

Janice hadn't told me there would be a safe behind the picture. We'd discussed everything but that. And, of course, *that*—meaning the thing I hadn't anticipated—was what screwed me.

What Janice and I had mostly talked about was the front door.

"Think baronial," she'd said with a half-smile. Janice had the half-smile down cold. "The front windows are seven feet from the ground. You'd need a ladder just to say hi."

"How far from the front door to the curb?" The bar we were in was *way* south of the Boulevard, in Reseda, far enough south that we were the only people in the place who were speaking English, and Serena's Greatest Hits was on permanent loop. The air was ripe with cilantro and cumin, and the place was mercifully lacking in ferns and sports memorabilia. A single widescreen television, ignored by all, broadcast the soccer game. I am personally convinced that only one soccer game has ever actually been played, and they show it over and over again from different camera angles.

As always, Janice had chosen the bar. With Janice in charge of the compass, it was possible to experience an entire planet's worth of bars without ever leaving the San Fernando Valley. The last one we'd met in had been Lao, with snacks of crisp fish bits and an extensive lineup of obscure tropical beers.

"Seventy-three feet, nine inches." She broke off the tip of a tortilla chip and put it near her mouth. "There's a black slate walk that kind of curves up to it."

I was nursing a Negra Modelo, the king of Hispanic dark beers, and watching the chip, calculating the odds against her actually eating it. "Is the door visible from the street?"

"It's so completely visible," she'd said, "that if you were a kid in one of those '40s musicals and you decided to put on a show, the front door of the Huston house is where you'd put it on."

"Makes the back sound good," I'd said.

"Aswarm with Rottweilers." She sat back, the jet necklace at her throat sparkling wickedly and the overhead lights flashing off the rectangular, black-framed glasses she wore in order to look like a businesswoman but which actually made her look like a beautiful girl wearing glasses.

Burglars, of which I am one, don't like Rottweilers. "But they're not in the house, right? Tell me they're not in the house."

"They are not. One of them pooped on the Missus's ninety thousand-dollar Kirghiz rug." Janice powdered the bit of chip between her fingers and let it fall to her napkin. "Or I should say, *one* of the Missus's ninety thousand-dollar Kirghiz rugs."

"There are several women called Missus?" I asked. "Or several rugs?"

"Either way," Janice said, reproachfully straightening her glasses at me. "The dogs are kept in back, and they get fed like every other Friday."

"Meaning no going in through the back," I said.

"Not unless you want to be kibble," Janice said. "Or the side, either. The wall around the yard is flush with the front wall of the house."

"Speaking of kibble."

"Please do," Janice said. "I so rarely get a chance to."

"Does anyone drop by to feed the beasts? Am I likely to run into—"

"No one in his right mind would go into that yard. The only way to feed them would be to throw a bison over the walls. The

Hustons have a very fancy apparatus, looks like it was built for the space shuttle. Delivers precise amounts of ravening beast-food twice a day. So they're strong and healthy and the old killer instinct doesn't dim."

"So," I said. "It's the front door."

She used the tip of her index finger to slide her glasses down to the point of her perfect nose, and looked at me over them. "Afraid so."

I drained my beer and signaled for another. Janice took a demure sip of her tonic and lime. I said, "I hate front doors. I'm going to stand there for fifteen minutes, trying to pick a lock in plain sight."

"That's why we came to you," she said. "Mr. Ingenuity."

"You came to me," I said, "because you know this is the week I pay my child support."

Janice was a back-and-forth, working for three or four brokers, guys with clients who knew where things were and wanted those things, but weren't sufficiently hands-on to grab them for themselves. She'd used me before, and it had worked out okay. She didn't know I'd backtracked her to two of her employers. One of them, an international-grade fence called Stinky Tetweiler, weighed 300 hard-earned pounds and lived in a long, low house south of the Boulevard with an ever-changing number of very young Filipino men with very small waists. Like a lot of the bigger houses south of Ventura, Stinky's place had once belonged to a movie star, back when the Valley was movie-star territory. In the case of Stinky's house, the star was Alan Ladd, although Stinky had rebuilt the house into a sort of collision between tetrahedrons that would have had old Alan's ghost, had he dropped by, looking for the front door.

Janice's other client, known to the trade only as Wattles, worked out of an actual office, with a desk and everything, in a smoked-glass high-rise on Ventura near the 405 Freeway. His company was listed on the building directory as Wattles

Inc. Wattles himself was a guy who had looked for years like he would die in minutes. He was extremely short, with a belly that suggested an open umbrella, a drinker's face the color of rare roast beef, and a game leg that he dragged around like an anchor. I'd hooked onto his back bumper one night and followed him up into Benedict Canyon until he slowed the car to allow a massive pair of wrought-iron gates to swing open, then took a steep driveway up into the pepper trees.

But Janice wasn't aware I knew any of this. And if she had been, she wouldn't have been amused at all.

"Where's the streetlight?"

She gave me her bad-news smile, brave and full of fraudulent compassion. "Right in front. More or less directly over the end of the sidewalk."

"Illuminating the front door."

"Brilliantly," she said. "Don't think about the front door. Think about what's on the other side."

"I am," I said. "I'm thinking I have to carry it seventy-three feet and nine inches to the van. Under a streetlight."

"You always focus on the negative," she said. "You need to do something about that. You want your positive energy to flow straight and true, and every time you go to the negative, you put up a little barrier. If it weren't for your constant focus on negative energy, your marriage might have gone better."

God, the things women think they have the right to say. "My marriage *went* fine," I said. "It was *before* the marriage that was difficult."

"You have to be positive about that, too," she said. "Without the marriage, you wouldn't have Rina."

Ahh, Rina, twelve years old and the light of my life. "To the extent I have her, anyway."

She gave me the slow nod women use to indicate that they understand our pain, they admire the courage with which we handle it, and they're absolutely certain that it's all our fault. "I know it's tough, Kathy being so punitive with visitation. But she's your daughter. You've got to be happy about that." Janice put down her glass and patted me comfortingly on the wrist with wet, cold fingers. I resisted the impulse to pull my wrist away. After all, her hand would dry eventually. She was working her way toward flirting, as she did every time we met, even though we both knew it wouldn't lead anywhere. I was still attached to Kathy, my former wife, and Janice demonstrated no awkwardness or any other kind of perceptible difficulty turning down dates.

"Of course, I'm happy about that," I said. And then, because it was expected, I made the usual move. "Want to go to dinner?"

She lowered her head slightly and regarded me from beneath her spiky bangs. "Tell me the truth. When you thought about asking me that question, you anticipated a negative response, didn't you?"

"Absolutely," I said. "It's the ninth time, and you've never said yes."

"See what I mean?" she said. "Your negativity has put kinks in your energy flow."

"Can you straighten it for me?"

"If your invitation had been made in a purely affirmative spirit, I might have said yes."

"Might?" I took a pull off the beer. "You mean I could purify my spirit, straighten out my energy flow, sterilize my anticipations, and you still might say no?"

"Oh, Junior," she said. "There are so many intangibles."

"Name one."

The slow head-shake again. "You're a crook."

"So are you."

"I beg to differ," she said. "I'm a facilitator. I bring together different kinds of energies to effect the transfer of physical objects. It's almost metaphysical." She held her hands above the table so her palms were about four inches apart, as though she expected electricity to flow between them. She turned them so the left hand was on top. "On one side," she said, "the energy of desire: dark, intense, magnetic." She reversed her hands so the right was on top. "On the other side, the energy of action: direct, kinetic, daring."

"Whooo," I said. "That's me?"

"Certainly."

"Sounds like somebody *I'd* go out with."

"And don't think I don't want to," she said, and she narrowed her eyes mystically, which made her look nearsighted. I've always loved nearsighted women. They're so easy to help. "Some day the elements will be in alignment." She pushed the glass away and got up, and guys all over the place turned to look. In this bar, Janice was as exotic as an orchid blooming in the snow.

"A brightly lighted front door," I said, mostly to slow her down. I liked watching her leave almost as much as I liked watching her arrive. "Seventy-three feet to the curb. Carrying that damn thing."

"And nine inches."

"Seventy-three feet, nine inches. In both directions."

"And you have to solve it by Monday," she said. "But don't worry. You'll think of something. You always do. When the child support's due."

She gave me a little four-finger wiggle of farewell, turned, and headed for the door. Every eye in the place was on her backside. That may be dated, but it was true.

**And, of course,** I *had* thought of something. In the abstract the plan had seemed plausible. Sort of. And it had continued to seem plausible right up to the moment I pulled up in front of the house in broad daylight. Then, as I climbed out, wincing into the merciless July sun that dehydrates the San Fernando Valley annually, it seemed very much less plausible. I felt a rush of what Janice would undoubtedly call negative energy, and suddenly it seemed completely idiotic.

But this was not the time to improvise. It was Monday afternoon in an upscale neighborhood, and I needed to justify my presence. Sweating in my dark coveralls, I went around to the back of the van and opened the rear door. Out of it I pulled a heavy dolly, which I set down about two feet behind the rear bumper. I squared my shoulders, the picture of someone about to do something difficult, leaned in, and very slowly dragged out an enormous cardboard refrigerator carton, on one side of which I had stenciled the words SUB ZERO. This was no neighborhood for Kelvinators or Maytags.

Back behind the house, the dogs began to bark. They were all bassos, ready to sing the lead in "Boris Godunov," and I thought I could distinguish four of them, sounding like they weighed a combined total of 750 pounds, mostly teeth. Christ, I was seventy-three feet, nine inches from the door, not even standing on the damn lawn yet, and I was already too close for them.

Kathy, my ex-wife, has taught Rina to *love* dogs. It doesn't matter how obscure the opportunity for revenge is; Kathy will grab it like a trapeze.

Grunting and straining, I tilted the box down and slid it onto the dolly. I'd put a couple of sandbags in the bottom of the box, mostly to keep it from tipping or being blown over, but it took some work to make it look heavy enough. Once I had it on the dolly, I tilted it back and made a big production of hauling it up the four-inch vertical of the curb. Then I walked away from it so I was visible from all directions, pulled out a cell phone, and called myself.

I listened to my message for a second and then talked into the phone. With it pressed to my ear, I turned to face the house, looked up at a second-story window, and gave a little wave. The cell phone slipped easily into the top pocket of the coveralls, and I grabbed the dolly handles, put my back into tilting it up onto the wheels, and towed the carton up the slate path.

At the door, I positioned the box so the side with SUB ZERO

on it faced the street. Then I got in between the box and the door and pushed open the flap I'd cut in the closest side of the box—just three straight lines with a box cutter, leaving the fourth side of the rectangle intact to serve as a hinge. The flap was about five feet high and three feet wide, and it swung open into the box. I climbed in. From the street, all anyone would see was the box.

The door was fancy, not functional. Heavy dark wood, brass hardware, and a big panel of stained glass in the upper half—some sort of coat of arms, a characteristically confused collision of symbolic elements that included an ax, a rose, and something that looked suspiciously like a pair of pliers. A good graphic artist could have made a fortune in the Middle Ages.

My working valise was at the bottom of the box. I snapped on a pair of surgical gloves, pulled out my set of picks, and went to work on the lock. The temperature in the box was about a hundred degrees, the gloves quickly became wet inside, and—appearances to the contrary—the lock had muscles. But I didn't feel cramped for time, since I doubted anyone would suspect a Sub Zero refrigerator of trying to break into a house. After nine or ten warm, damp minutes, the lock did a tickled little shimmy and then began to give up its secrets. I dropped the final pin, tested the knob, and put on a bathing cap to cover my hair. Then I climbed out of the box, opened the door, and stepped inside.

I read continually about burglars who experience some sort of deep, even sexual pleasure at the moment of entry, as though the house were a long-desired body to which they had finally gained access. For me, a house is an inconvenience. It's a bunch of walls surrounding something I want. In order to get what I want, I have to put myself inside the walls, and then get out as fast as I can. I figure that the risk of being caught increases by about five percent each minute once you get beyond four minutes. Anybody who stays inside longer than twenty to twenty-five minutes deserves a free ride in the back of a black-and-white.

The alarm was exactly where Janice said it would be, blinking frantically just around the corner from the front door, and the code she gave me calmed it right down. The dogs were going nuts in the back, but that was where they seemed to be staying. I gave it a count of ten with one foot figuratively outside the door just to make sure, but all they did was bark and howl and scrabble with their toenails at a glass door somewhere on the far side of the house. When I was certain none of them was toting his fangs from room to room inside, I went back out onto the porch, used the dolly to tilt the carton, and wheeled it inside. Then I closed the door.

Getting in is more than half of it; in fact, I figure that a safe entry is about sixty percent of the work. Finding what you want will burn up another twenty to thirty percent, and getting out is pretty much a snap. Usually.

The house was a temple of gleam. Entire quarries in Italy had been strip-mined to pave the floors, and many young Italian craftspersons had probably died of dust inhalation to bring the stone to this pitch of polish. I was in a circular grand entry hall, maybe thirty-five feet high, dominated by a massive chandelier in what might have been Swarovski crystal, dangling by a heavy golden chain. To the right was a circular stair curving up the wall of the hall, with a teak banister that had been sanded, polished, stained, polished, varnished, polished, and varnished again.

Not for the first time, I asked myself what Mr. and/or Mrs. Huston did for a living.

Despite the museum-like grandeur of the entry, there was a homely smell that took me back years and years, to my grandmother's house. I needed a second to identify it as camphor, the active ingredient in mothballs. We don't use mothballs so much any more, maybe because we have fewer natural fabrics, but they were being used here. The odor suggested a certain strained fussiness, not an attitude that would be comfortable with Rottweilers leaving piles on the rugs.

The camphor seemed to come from my right, where a set of steps led up to the living room, so perhaps the mothballs were intended to protect the carpets. Straight ahead, a set of five steps led up to the rest of the first floor, accounting for the high front windows. The piece I had been sent for was all the way upstairs, in what Janice had described as the marital theme park.

As I climbed the curving stairway, the dogs reached a new pitch of frenzy, and I began to think about accelerating the process. Some neighbor might get pissed off and call the cops, and the cops, in turn, might wonder why the Fidos were so manic. I took the stairs two at a time.

The master bedroom was bigger than Versailles. Three things about its occupants were immediately obvious. First, they were sexually adventurous and willing to pay for it. The ceiling was mirrored, the bedspread was some sort of black fur, a shelf recessed in the wall above the head of the bed held a garish assortment of toys, lubricants, and, for all I could tell, hors d'oeuvres. There were at least a dozen little bottles of amyl nitrate under different brand names, and a crystal bowl of white powder on a mirror, with a razor gleaming beside it. Over against one wall was an actual gynecologist's table. The stirrups had sequins on them.

The second thing that was apparent was that they both thought Mrs. Huston was a knockout. There were at least a dozen large color photos of her, blond, a little over-vibrant, and seriously under-dressed, along the wall to the right of the bed. She didn't look like someone who puts mothballs on her carpets, if only because they'd aggravate carpet burn. Of course, it was an assumption that the woman wearing, in some of the pictures, no more than a coat of baby oil, was Mrs. Huston, but if she wasn't, the relationship was even stranger than the bedroom would suggest. The odd energy she was projecting in some of the pictures might have owed something to the bowl of white powder on the shelf. Even without the energy, even without the

baby oil, she had a kind of raw, slightly crude appeal that probably interested men whose tastes were coarser than mine.

The third obvious thing was that—while they might have
been unanimous in their admiration of Mrs. Huston—they had
very different tastes in art. On the far wall were five, count
them if you can bear to look at them long enough, *five* of those
flesh-puckering big-eyed children painted in the 1950s by Mr.
Keane or Mrs. Keane: waifs of the chilly dawn with dreadful
days awaiting them, days they will meet with eyes as big as
doorknobs, but not as expressive. It had always amazed me
that Mr. and Mrs. Keane went to court to establish which of
them was responsible for these remorseless reiterations of ele-
mentary-school bathos. If I'd been the judge, I'd have yanked
their artistic licenses in perpetuity and sentenced them to a lifetime twelve-step program in which all twelve steps consisted of
spending fourteen hours a day watching real children through
a foot-thick pane of glass.

By contrast, on the wall directly opposite the door was the
Paul Klee painting that was the object of Janice's client's lust.
Even at this distance, I hated it, although not as much as I
hated the Keanes. Full of thin angular shapes and flat 1950s
colors that looked like they were inspired by Formica, it looked
to me like something painted with a coat hanger. Klee despised
color in his early career, so I didn't feel so bad about despising
the ones he'd used here. I looked back at the Keanes, thinking
that when I came back to the Klee I'd like it better through
sheer contrast, but it didn't work. It still looked like a watch-
spring's daydream.

Now that I was all the way inside the room, I saw a small
surprise on the wall into which the door was set: another Klee,
this one smaller and maybe, just marginally, not as ugly. I'd been
told only about the one for some reason, and I wasted a brief
moment wondering whether to bag both of them, then rejected
the thought. I was in no position to fence a Klee. Fine art fencing

was a specialty, and a perilously risky specialty at that. I'd take the one I'd been sent to take, and let my employer worry about handing it off to someone.

The room was bright with the sun banging on the big windows, the light filtered white through semi-opaque curtains of organdy or something diaphanous. The bed was to the left, and beyond it was an open door. I slogged my way across a carpet about five inches deep and checked out the door. It led to a sort of sitting room, all mirrored, with a makeup table big enough for the Rockettes on one wall. Beyond that yawned an enormous bathroom. The bathroom, in turn, had two doors leading off it, one into a chamber built just to hold the toilet, and the other into a room that could have slept four but was filled entirely with women's clothes. There was a door at the far end that undoubtedly led back to the hallway.

I went back into the bedroom. The other door, to the right of the wall, was a closet, obviously his unless she liked to wear men's suits to spice things up from time to time. Content that I had the floor plan stored where I could find it if I needed it suddenly, I approached the painting.

God, it was ugly. I checked behind it, found no evidence of an alarm or any cute little locking mechanisms that would prevent its being lifted from the wall. In fact, it seemed to be hanging on a regular old picture hanger like the ones you can buy in the supermarket, although a little heavier. I centered myself in front of the picture, grasped the frame by the sides, and lifted it. It came up easily, weighing only four or five pounds, and I pulled it away and lowered it to the floor.

Without, as I said, looking at it.

And there it was, that circle cut into the wall.

Everything the Klee hadn't done for me, that circle did. My heart embarked on a little triple skip, my face was suddenly warmer, and I found I was breathing shallowly. The kind of reaction I would imagine a prospector might experience when he discovers that the rock he just tripped over is a five-pound gold nugget . . . but.

But Janice hadn't mentioned the safe. Presumably, therefore, she didn't know about the safe, even though the information she'd handed me was detailed and accurate right down to the alarm code.

So. What *else* hadn't Janice known about?

And at that precise moment I felt the telltale prickling on the back of my neck.

A little late, I covered the bottom half of my face with my forearm as though wiping sweat away and turned to survey the room, unfocused and trying to take it all in. There it was, at the edge of my vision, high up near the join of wall and ceiling: a little hole the size of a dime.

Well, *shit*.

Wiping my face with both hands, I walked briskly across the room, detouring around the bed and finding something on the carpet to look down at, and straight into the bathroom. In the medicine cabinet I found a travel-size can of shaving gel, popped the cap, and gave it a pointless shake. Then, edging along the wall, presumably out of sight of the little lens that was certain to be right behind that hole, I positioned myself until I was directly below it, flexed my knees, and jumped, my arm stretched above me. When the can's nozzle was even with the hole, I pushed it. One more jump, and I had a nice little billow of foam filling the hole.

I tossed the can onto the bed and charged across the room to my bag. A second later I had a hammer and a chisel and I was dragging behind me a chair that had been sitting peacefully all by itself to the right of the paintings. I shoved it against the wall with the camera behind it and jumped up onto it.

Time was *not* on my side. I'd been in the house almost too long already, but there was no choice. I had to do this, and it almost didn't matter how long it was going to take. But I was sweating for real now, my hands slippery inside the gloves.

The question with surveillance cameras, if you're unlucky enough to be caught on one, is where the images are being stored. If they're on-site and you can find the storage device, you're good to go—just take the whole thing with you. If the images are being stored off-site, then you're—

I hammered the chisel for the third time and levered it right, and a chunk of chalky-edged drywall broke off and fell to the floor and I realized I was—

*Screwed,* because it was the worst possible scenario. The lines leading away from the camera jacks were telephone cable.

So, either (1) the storage was off-site and I could give up looking for it or (2) the storage was off-site and I could give up looking for it, *and* the live feed was being watched by several not-easily-amused men who were at that very moment dispatching an armed response team.

Well, the good news was that I didn't have to waste any time looking for the storage. The bad news was everything else.

I checked the hole and found the foam starting to drip down the wall, so I just yanked the cable from the camera jacks. Then I jumped down from the chair and went back to the safe.

Since I was already in the red zone for time, I gave myself a count of sixty to get the thing open.

It took me all of nine seconds to get my bag unzipped and remove the five-inch suction cup, designed for glass but useful on smooth walls. I had to rummage to locate the second item, a Windex spray bottle filled with tap water. Two shots with the sprayer got the wall nice and wet and then I placed the cup evenly against the cut-out, centered it, and pushed it in to secure the seal. Took hold of the handle, and pulled.

The cut-out popped free like a loose cork. It had been cut on a slight bias so it was larger on the outside than on the inside, making it a snap to remove and replace. I put the whole thing down next to the painting, closed my eyes for a second in vague, generalized supplication, and opened them to look at the safe.

Fourteen seconds.

I saw nothing to diminish my enthusiasm. Expensive, yes, shiny and solid-looking, designed to inspire confidence, but nothing that a relatively talented duffer couldn't pop, and I am not a duffer. Thirty-seven seconds of gentle persuasion later, it swung gently open. Something glittered at me.

Fifty-one seconds.

The glitter put an end to my internal argument, if I'd been having one. End of whatever wispy reluctance I might have felt about going another twenty or thirty seconds. Diamonds have a way of prevailing over logic.

So I did it. I reached inside.

And as my fingers closed over the cold fire and broke the beam of light that flowed from one side of the safe to the other, I heard three things. First, the squeal of something that needed oiling as it slid open downstairs. Second, a sudden increase in the volume of the dogs' barking. Third, the sound of dogs' toe-nails. On marble.

Inside the house.

# 2

## Dog day

Diamonds in my pocket. Plug back in the wall. Suction cup in the bag. Picture under the arm. Heart in the throat.

Dogs on the stairs.

I ran to the bedroom door, dropped the picture and the bag beside it, and shoved the door with both hands to close it, but when it had only six or eight inches to go, a battering ram hit it from the other side. It was all I could do to keep hold of it. A black muzzle, richly furnished with teeth, shoved its way around the edge of the door, and I hauled off and booted its nose. The beast pulled back, and I got the door closed. I stood there with my back against it, feeling my heart carom around in my chest like a bad ricochet, and focused on counting my viable options.

I couldn't quite make it to one.

No going out the window. That would put me in the dogs' yard, with a nine-foot fence to scale. The door I was leaning against took me directly into Fangland. There was no way to get to the roof, even if I wanted to be up there, waving at the neighbors while carrying a Paul Klee painting in broad daylight. I double-checked to make sure the door's latch was fully engaged and then scurried across the room to peer into the closet, hoping for a crawl-hole into whatever passed for an attic, but there wasn't one.

The bang on the door this time actually chipped paint off the inside. It wasn't going to hold for long.

No crawl-hole in the dressing room. No crawl-hole in the room full of women's clothes. But the door from the bathroom into that room opened in, and that gave me a pale imitation of an idea. I pushed the door all the way open and left it that way. A dog slammed against the door that led from that room to the hall, so I wasn't the only one with a mental floor plan. I headed back to the bedroom, hoping to get there before the hounds of Hell knocked the door off its hinges.

As I approached the door, the snarling scaled up a couple of notches, and claws scrabbled at the paint on the other side. With all the money these people had sunk into this house, why did they choose doors that might as well have been made out of Saltines? Why did their contractors let them? Whatever happened to pride in building? Whatever happened to solid mahogany doors on heavy brass hinges? Where were the values that made this country great?

The dog, or dogs, slammed the door again. Okay, dogs: there were definitely more than one. They were growling in a kind of homicidal harmony that did little to calm me. With my body pressed against the door, I surveyed the room for something, anything, I could use.

Bad painting, five more bad paintings, photos of the Missus, big bed, fur bedspread, four pillows in black satin, gynecologist's table, shelf of, uh, marital aids.

Shelf of, uh, marital aids.

RUSH, it said on the labels, which seemed like excellent advice: two little bottles about the size of Alice's "drink me" but a lot more urban-looking. Standing right there on the shelf, next to a battery-powered something that defied sane speculation. What orifice? How? Under what circumstances? Why?

Think about staying alive. The immediate goal was to make it down the stairs in one piece, as opposed to several.

The Rush. I reluctantly stopped leaning against the door, which promptly shuddered on its hinges as I lunged for the bottles. I grabbed both of them, hurled myself back against the door, inspiring one of the beasts to actually *bite the wood* with a sound that practically folded the skin on the back of my neck. It took a couple of deep breaths to steady my hands to the point where I could unscrew the bottle tops, and then there I was, leaning against a cheap door, besieged by slavering, red-eyed carnivores, holding two bottles of amyl nitrate.

Don't think about it. Just do it.

I took one step back, propped my foot behind the door, near the edge, and opened it an inch, then held it there with my knee. This time, *two* muzzles forced their way into the crack, fangs bared, tongues lolling and drool spooling down, and from a distance of about eight inches, I threw the contents of the RUSH bottles directly at the black noses.

As the name *Rush* suggests, amyl nitrate is fast, but in my cranked-up state the dogs' reaction seemed to happen in stalactite time: first, the growls shut down, then the noses stopped shoving inward, and then I heard a series of rewarding yelps as the amyl interacted with the astonishingly sensitive nasal apparatus that guided all those teeth. The yelps scaled into the soprano range, and the muzzles disappeared. To my infinite relief, I heard nails scrabbling down the stairs.

But another dog was banging against the door to Mrs. Huston's clothes room. I picked up my bag, which weighed about fifteen pounds, and put it against the door, which I'd left ajar. Then I took a peek through the crack in the door and saw the dog about fifteen feet away, hurling himself mindlessly against the closed door. I stuck my hand out, yelled *"HEY!"* and ran like hell.

The dog hit the door as I hit the dressing room, but I could hear the door collide with my bag, giving me maybe two extra seconds, and by the time the door banged open I was most of the way through the bathroom. About a tenth of a second after I ducked behind the open door to Mrs. Huston's Palace of Clothes, the dog shot into the room at fifty miles an hour. I could see it trying to brake, putting on the skids with its rear legs, as I stepped around the door and slammed it behind me. Two seconds later, the dog's body buckled the door from the other side, but it opened in that direction, so I didn't waste a thought on it.

In the bedroom, the hallway door still yawned open, and the small area of the hall I could see was miraculously dog-free. I grabbed the painting and my bag and headed into the hall. I was five feet from the top stair when the Rottweiler in Mrs. Huston's mega-closet came *straight through the door*, just a black streak and a bunch of white wood chips.

I slung the painting, keeping it as flat as possible, at the stairs, and heard it start to bump its way down. I tossed my bag over the banister. The dog covered the fifteen feet between it and me in less time than it takes to bite your tongue, gathered itself down on its haunches, and jumped.

*I* jumped.

I jumped straight for the top of the banister, where I wind-milled my arms for a sickeningly off-balance second, and then—with the dog three feet above the hardwood, teeth first, and closing fast—I shoved off and sailed into space, twenty feet above the gleaming marble floor of the entrance hall, flailing my way through the thinnest of thin air toward the thick gold chain that supported the crystal chandelier.

And got my hands around it, but it was slick with grime, and I slid down it almost as fast as I'd been falling until I managed to hook a couple of fingers through the links in the chain. I nearly dislocated both shoulders, but it stopped me. I hung there, gasping for breath, swaying back and forth as the chandelier jingled like a full-scale carillon beneath me, and watched the dogs assemble below. The one who had burst through the door trotted downstairs to join the other two. And there they stood, looking up at me like I was a squirrel whose time was up.

And then, just to make the moment more special, another dog, big enough to take the other three like aspirin, shouldered its way into the hall with a growl so low it rattled the crystals in the chandelier. The other three backed off to a safe distance, but kept their eyes on me.

There was a little creaking sound, and the chain—and I—dropped about three inches. I reflexively looked up and was rewarded by a nice eyeful of plaster dust. Then something snapped, and I dropped another three or four inches, and it was raining small pieces of ceiling. The dogs started barking in anticipation, and why not? Dinner was about to be delivered via airmail.

An idea flashed through my mind, more like an image, really, and not a particularly persuasive one. The stained glass in the door. My feet, breaking it cleanly. My body, following my feet to land uninjured and intact, on the front porch. The dogs pouring through the broken—no, no, stow that, deal with it when it's necessary.

And what was the alternative, anyway?

I swung my legs back and forth, and, with much creaking, the chandelier and I began to travel in an arc, a huge jangling pendulum. A sound like *boick* heralded another drop—maybe a foot this time, but I was getting a pretty good swing going. I focused my eyes directly on the stained glass, visualized a clean passage through it, and, with the adrenaline-heightened vision of those about to die, I saw:

The thick chicken wire . . . running through the glass.

I had exactly enough time to think *nooooooooooooo* before the chain pulled free from the ceiling and I was plummeting downward, way too fast, with the chandelier's long icicles floating away from it below me like the world's biggest, most glittery spider, and then it hit the marble with a noise so loud it could've been heard over the Big Bang, and an explosion of crystals, crystal fragments, and crystal dust billowed out in all directions, and the terrified dogs scattered to the cardinal points of the compass as I landed on top of it all.

No time to hurt, no time to bleed. I got up, snatched my bag, grabbed the painting, opened the door, and pushed the SUB ZERO carton outside. I slammed the door shut just as the first dog hit it with all his weight, and I hauled off and kicked the door back, creating an entirely new level of canine insanity inside.

With trembling hands, I loaded my bag and the painting into the carton, tilted back the dolly, and wheeled the whole thing seventy-three shuddering feet and nine inches to the curb. It took me a couple of tries to get the rear doors of the van open, but when I did, I just upended the dolly into the back—the carton wasn't supposed to be heavy any more, anyway—and slammed the door. Then I went around to the front, got in, and leaned forward until my forehead was resting on the steering wheel.

Just as I was getting my breathing under control, something cold touched the back of my neck, and a man's voice said, "Well, look who's here."

## 3
### Hacker

The face in the rear-view mirror possessed more distinctive characteristics than you'd normally find in a whole room full of faces. The eyes, black as a curse, were so close to each other they nearly touched, barely bisected by the tiniest nose ever to adorn an adult male face. I'd seen bigger noses on a pizza. The guy had no eyebrows and a mouth that looked like it was assembled in the dark: no upper lip to speak of, and a lower that plumped out like a throw pillow, above a chin as sharp as an elbow.

It wasn't a nice face, but that was misleading. The man who owned it wasn't just not nice: he was a venal, calculating, corrupt son of a bitch.

I said, "Hello, Hacker."

"Is the painting in the box?" Hacker asked.

"What painting? I just delivered a refrigerator. I'm exploring the dignity of honest labor."

The gun pushed its way between a couple of vertebrae. "Okay," I said. "What do you think, I forgot it?"

"Sounded like a bunch of werewolves in there. And you got little cuts all over you, you know that? If I pull this gun back a couple inches, you going to be stupid?"

"I've already been stupid," I said. "I try to keep it to once a day."

"Good. Well, I can't tell you what a thrill this is. Catching Junior Bender in the act."

"For someone with your record, it must be."

"I should read you your rights," Hacker said.

"If you could."

"You ain't taking this seriously, bro."

"I'm thinking about it."

"What's to think about. I got you."

I checked the side mirrors again. Sure enough, something was missing. "Okay, you got me," I said. "But why?"

"Whaddya mean, why? I'm a cop, you're a crook."

"With no record at all. And where's your black-and-white?"

Hacker's eyes flicked away from mine in the mirror. "Somebody's prolly driving it."

"And your partner?"

"Charlie? He's got the day off." He lifted the barrel of the automatic to his face and scratched his chin with the sight. I could hear the scrape of metal over whiskers. "In fact, we both got the day off."

"Maybe I should have taken the day off, too."

"Little late for that," Hacker said.

Hope, the slut, springs eternal. "No partner. No black-and-white. So this isn't a bust."

"Oh, no," Hacker said, settling happily back on the seat. "This is *much* worse than a bust."

**With Hacker contributing** some backseat driving, I navigated down the curving hillside streets to Ventura Boulevard, a largely charmless four-lane throughway that was orphaned several decades back by the Hollywood Freeway, which parallels it, but has since developed a seedy appeal all its own as the main drag of the southern end of the San Fernando Valley. By now it was a little after four, which meant that we were bumper-to-bumper with all the people who make rush hour start early by trying to get home before rush hour. The air conditioning in the van, which I had rented for the day, couldn't have cooled a coat closet, so we had the windows open and got a chance to breathe in all the exhaust two or three hundred expensive cars can put out. It's interesting, I guess; with all the work automakers put into making deluxe cars different from the instant wrecks they sell the proletariat, no one seems to have looked into making the expensive exhaust smell better. I said something to that effect to Hacker, and got a grunt by return mail.

"So why don't you tell me what we're doing?"

"We're going north on Ventura," Hacker said.

"How'd you know I was going to be there?"

"Circles in circles."

"I don't mean to sound paranoid," I said, "but this feels just the teensiest bit like a setup."

"Change lanes," Hacker said.

"Lyle. Who set me up?"

"Like I said, change lanes. You're going to make a left in a mile or two. And don't call me Lyle."

"Plenty of time."

"You can't drive for shit. You're making me nervous."

"*You're* nervous? There I was, committing a perfectly normal burglary, if you don't count the dogs and the amyl nitrate, and suddenly I'm being kidnapped at gunpoint by a rogue cop. Where are we, Argentina?"

Hacker said, "Amyl nitrate?"

"Poppers," I said. "Surely you've heard of poppers."

"You were doing poppers up there?"

"Me and the dogs," I said. "Best way to get close to a dog."

"Crooks are different from people," Hacker said.

"You should know."

"Hey," Hacker said. "I'm no crook."

"Ah, Lyle," I said. "The line is a fine one, easier to step over than a crack in the sidewalk, and then suddenly there you are, in a brave new world and no map home."

Hacker said, "You read too much."

"Is it possible to read too much?"

"Just drive."

"Who set me up? Where are we going?"

Hacker's suit was an alarming budget plaid made up of colors that shouldn't have been in the same room, much less on the same piece of cloth. When he leaned forward, the suit flexed menacingly. "What you should be thinking about is where we're *not* going. We're not going to the station. We're not going somewhere where you'll get your prints rolled, and smile for the birdie, and spend the night on a concrete floor with a bunch of guys who smell like puke. We're not going someplace where there's a bunch of guys who want to practice their kidney punches."

"That's all very reassuring."

"Hope to shit," he said. "You gonna change lanes any time in this lifetime?"

"But, I mean, there's a certain amount of coercion here, you know?"

But Hacker had his head craned around. "You're almost clear," he said. "Just muscle your way left."

I did, to the accompaniment of a great many horns.

"See fourteen five-eighty-six?" he asked. "The black glass building just past the Starbucks. Turn into the driveway."

"Aha," I said.

"Aha what?"

"Aha, I know who sent you."

**4**

Wattles, Inc.

"You met Mr. Wattles?" Hacker said.

"Not till now. Though, of course, his reputation precedes him."

The fat, red-faced little man glanced up at me, saw nothing to hold his attention, and went back to considering the screen of the laptop in front of him. After a long moment, he rasped, "Sit." Then he hit a couple of keys as though he had a grudge against them.

I sat on something amazingly uncomfortable that someone had disguised as a couch. Hacker stood with his beefy arms crossed, leaning against the door to the outside world, which he'd shut behind us as we came in. On the other side of the door was a reception room with a battered desk in its center. Seated behind the desk to greet us when we came in had been a life-size blow-up doll, the red "o" of her mouth unpleasantly reminiscent of the circle of drywall in front of Huston's wall safe. She'd had orange hair and inflated fingers like puffy little sausages. There had been something familiar about her, although I number relatively few blow-up dolls among my circle of acquaintances.

The building was your basic 1980s medium-high rise, tall enough to give you a view but not so tall it'd go over sideways in a six-point quake. The windows faced south, toward the hills that divided the Valley from Los Angeles proper, and the address was only a block or so away from the 405 Freeway.

Wattles, Inc. was saving a fortune on office furniture. The desk Wattles sat behind was gray, battered institutional steel that someone had scraped deeply several times as though it were a Mercedes Benz parked on the wrong street. The so-called couch to which Hacker pointed me had probably seen a decade's worth of faithful service in a Motel 6 before someone hauled it to the curb because it was too big for the dumpster. I could practically stretch out a leg and tap the desk with my toe. You could have carpeted the room with a carhop's uniform.

And yet, behind Wattles some very fine dark cherry book-shelves stretched from floor to ceiling, and filling them was a whole wall's worth of California legal statutes, nicely bound and running all the way up to the last quarter of the previous year. The set that belonged to my very expensive lawyer ended with 2005. So I would have known Wattles was doing well here, even if I hadn't seen the wrought-iron gates with the big canyon house behind them.

"Nice and quiet in here," I said to Hacker.

"Keep it like that," Wattles said, abusing a few more keys. "Or go wait outside, with Dora."

"Dora."

"The receptionist."

"Does she get meal breaks?"

"Shut up."

I shut up. After a couple of minutes, one of the phones that shared Wattles's desk with the laptop lit up. It didn't do anything as vulgar as ring; it just blinked a couple of times. Wattles picked it up and put it to his ear.

Then he said, "No." He listened some more. Then he said, "Fuck you," and hung up. He had a voice that was created to say, "Fuck you," the kind of voice Tom Waits probably has when he's just woken up and he's got the flu. He went back to the computer.

I counted silently to fifty.

"Well," I said, standing up, "this has been very interesting."

"Sit," Wattles said again.

"There's a painting in my van——"

"Not no more," Wattles said. "Long gone." This time he looked up at me. His eyes were so deepset they looked like raisins someone had pushed into raw dough. "You're way past fucked," he said. "You know whose house that was?"

"Somebody named Hus—."

"You know Rabbits Stennet? You just robbed Rabbits Stennet's house." As my stomach dipped all the way to my feet, Wattles pushed his chair back from the desk, leaned back, slapped the side of his gut, and let out a one-syllable bark that I supposed was a laugh.

I nodded. "'Past fucked' is accurate."

"It's worse," Wattles said. "What you took is part of little Mrs. Stennet's prenup. It's her favorite thing in the world."

"Her pre—"

"I don't know how much you know Rabbits, but probably not much, right?"

"Right. And not eager to—"

"Well, old Rabbits didn't used to be exactly a family values kind of guy. Four wives, probably put 'em together and they didn't last six months. Took over running the hookers for the West Valley mainly so he'd always know where to find them. Used to take them four and five at a time, dress 'em up like Tinker Bell or Snow White. You know, like cartoons? Had a whole basement full of Disney costumes. It was, like, a life style choice. So when he married Bunny . . ." He broke off, looking up at Hacker. "Isn't that cute? Rabbits and Bunny."

"Cuter than hamsters," Hacker said.

"Yeah, cute." The phone nearest to Wattles flickered again, but he gave it the finger. "So when he married Bunny and she wanted a prenup, old Rabbits dug in. He figured she'd be gone before breakfast got cold, and he'd be back to the cartoons, and anyway there was no way he was going to open the door for a bunch of divorce lawyers to come through and sniff around in his finances. But on the other hand, Bunny—you seen Bunny?"

"Not in person, but I've always had a thing for women named—"

"Bunny's hot as Palm Springs. You been to Palm Springs?"

"Why ask? You're not going to let me fin—"

"Hot," Wattles said. He shook his hand as though flicking hot water from his fingers. "Bunny's hot. So Rabbits, he looks at Bunny and says, no prenup, no fuckin' way, but whaddya want? Something you can take if things don't work out. In your name, all nice and legal, you keep the paper. And she said she wanted a couple of paintings by some European guy, and you just took the best one."

"That was the *best*—"

"You know, you talk too much. Me, I like what Sam Goldwyn said. You know what Sam Goldwyn said?"

"He said, Don't say—"

"He said to a bunch of yes-men, 'Don't say yes until I finish talking.' I like that."

"It's hard to know when you're finished. Sometimes you stop for—"

"I gotta breathe. Tell you what, when I'm finished I'll say 'your turn.' Okay?"

I didn't reply. Wattles pushed down the lid of the laptop and glared at me. "Okay?"

"You didn't say 'your turn'."

I got an index finger pointed at the bridge of my nose, and Wattles got another pint of blood to the head, if the color of his face was any indication. "Don't dick around with me. I'm the only thing between you and them dogs. Rabbits gives guys to the dogs sometimes, you know? Don't answer. So you took the better half of Bunny's prenup, and she's going to be *pissed*. And when Bunny gets pissed, Rabbits loses it. Even after two years, he loses it. I don't know what she does, but she's gotta do it good. He's not ordering Cinderella or the Wicked Queen to get delivered any more, not even once, and he still gets all chesty when somebody even looks at her wrong. Oh, and you don't know the best part."

I waited, and Wattles said, "Your turn."

"What's the best—"

"Where the video footage from that surveillance camera is stored," he said.

## 5

### On the Other Hand

I looked over at Wattles, who had reopened the screen on his laptop and was glaring at it like it had stuck its tongue out at him. "Did Janice know about the cameras? Did she know—"

"Nah," Wattles said. He lifted an edge of the computer and dropped it again, as if that would improve whatever was on the display. "She didn't know nothing. She wouldn't of played if she had. She thinks hummingbirds nest in your butt."

"She hides her feelings well."

"Why do you think she chose you?" He gave me the glare I was coming to recognize as his normal expression. "There's a lot of guys. I tell her I need the smartest, and she says, 'Gotta be Junior.' I'm telling you, you're halfway home. Buy some flowers, get a haircut, you're there."

"I don't get it," I said.

"What?" He was back to the computer, and he didn't sound very interested.

"Why did you want smart? If you're going to hose some-body, why do you need him to be smart? Seems to me you'd want the dumbest—"

"You'll find out," Wattles said. His head came up, and the movement set the two lower chins wobbling. "What're you doing, Lyle? Waiting for the fuckin' film to develop?"

"He's what?" I asked, thumbing at Hacker. "Your pet policeman?"

Hacker flexed his suit at me. "I got two words for you. Three strikes."

"I don't have any strikes." In California, the three-strike law means geological time for a third felony conviction.

"You have any idea how many open burglaries I've got?" Hacker said. "How'd you like to be the way I close two of them? And this one on top of it? Can you count that high?"

"Lyle," Wattles said. "Bite one."

"Sorry," Hacker said.

"Show the man," Wattles said.

"What?" I asked. "What are you showing me?"

"Rabbits is smart," Wattles said. "Got great tech, you know? We live in the age of tech, tech's what keeps the world safe from people like us. Unless we can use tech ourselves, like me. Old cocker like me, tech don't come natural, but I learned about it 'cause I had to, and there *you* are, a lot younger than me and sitting on that shitty couch because you don't know your tech. You shoulda spotted those pinhole cameras in a minute, but no. Walk in big as life with your face showing and everything. Rabbits got himself the best. That was cute, what you did with the foam, but not cute enough 'cause the camera got your face anyway and the video's stored off-site. So you foam the camera but you can't wipe the disk or steal the machine. Problem is, we know where he sends it to. So you're screwed, and you know why?"

"Tech?" I ventured as Hacker slid aside a picture of some gauzy flowers, a half-hearted stab at Renoir, probably painted in Southern China, to reveal a good-size flatscreen.

"Tech. Like this screen. Betcha didn't know it was there."

"You win."

Wattles made a restrained raspberry sound. "Show him, Lyle."

Hacker took a remote off Wattles's desk and pushed a

button. The screen lit up. I was looking at the Stennet bedroom. The picture was bright and crisp. I could see the glitter sparkle on the stirrups.

"High definition," Wattles said, reading my mind. "Fuckin' great tech."

"It was humiliating enough to do this without having to watch it, too. I don't want to see it."

"Oh, yes, you do. Watch."

The door to the bedroom opened. Someone came through it and crossed the room to the Klee. I felt my jaw drop. Looking behind him as though he'd heard a noise, the someone carefully took the Klee down from the wall. He didn't look at the painting.

The someone weighed about 275 pounds and had a mop of blond hair like the Little Dutch Boy. He put the painting under one arm and left the bedroom, thoughtfully closing the door behind him.

I said, "I know people photograph heavy, but that's ridiculous."

The set blinked off and went black.

"You got a choice," Wattles said. "Four days from now, Friday afternoon, when Rabbits and Bunny get home from whatever king-size bed they're taking their vacation on, they're going to look where that picture isn't and then they're going to check the recorder. If you're a good boy, they're gonna see a fat guy steal Bunny's pre-nup. If you're not a good boy, I hope you're not afraid of dogs." He leaned back, slapped the side of his gut, and let the one-syllable laugh loose again.

"Who was that?"

The deepset little eyes regarded me for a moment. Then he shrugged. "Name of Ed Perlstein. Works in Saint Louis mostly."

"And he stole the—"

"And put it back," Wattles said. "About an hour later."

I sat back on the couch and wished I were anywhere else.

Working as a short-order cook in Denny's, for example, up to my knuckles in hot fat. Sorting gravel at minimum wage. "You've gone to a lot of trouble."

"You're smart," Wattles said. "Even if you don't know tech from artichokes. Janice says so. And I needed to put together something you couldn't dig your way out of." He leaned forward and put both elbows on the desk. "See, it's tricky," he said with the air of someone who's accustomed to explaining the obvious. "On the one hand, I need a guy who's smart. Somebody who can figure out which way to jump without having to read the instructions on the box. On the other hand, he's gonna get told to do something he's not gonna want to do. A smart guy, he'll figure a way to get out of it. So what you just seen, it's like a cage to keep you in as long as I need you."

I looked over at Hacker, who made a gun out of his fingers and dropped the hammer. "So tell me," I said. "Why do you need smart?"

"Before we get to that," Wattles said. "Let's get something right out on the table. Right in the middle, next to this here low-tech ashtray. I *will* give you to Rabbits. I *will* make sure the right burglar is on that hard drive. Shit, I'll come over for cocktails and watch the dogs eat you." He flicked a finger at Hacker. "Lyle?"

"He will," Hacker said.

"I will," Wattles affirmed.

"You will," I said. "I'm persuaded."

"Good." Wattles got up. It didn't make him much taller. He twisted his shoulders a couple of times, reached behind to massage his lower back, and went, "Uuhhhhhh." Then he put both hands on his belly and followed it to the window. By the time he got there, he was panting. He looked down at the street. "Nice day," he said.

"It was," I said. "Tell me what you need me to do."

"Me?" Wattles said. "I don't need nothing. I'm a broker, not a principal. You're gonna be working for Trey."

I suddenly remembered my parents' old TV. When you turned it off, the picture shrunk to a bright little dot before the screen went black. I felt my life do that. "No," I said hopelessly. "Not Trey."

"You know Trey?"

"I know Trey the same way I know the herpes virus. I've never laid eyes on it, but I've seen what it does."

"You're a lucky boy," Wattles said. "Here's your chance to see it up close."

## 6
### Not Fred

A zillion years ago, the San Fernando Valley basin held a warm saltwater sea. It's easy to imagine it as you crest the hill on the 405, and the Valley spreads itself below you. Squint a little, and you can see the ghosts of plesiosaurs swimming languidly through the smog, looking for the nearest McDonald's.

Then, a little less than a zillion years ago, the sea dried up. A bunch of history happened in other places, but not here. Eventually, some people crossed over from Asia, pronounced themselves Native Americans, and headed for California like everybody else. Then there was a wave of people who spoke Spanish and stole the land from the Native Americans, and they were followed, in the 1910s, by Anglos who invented new kinds of legal documents to steal the land from the Spanish speakers. They parceled the Valley out into millions of acres of orange groves and tomato farms, and the air was perfumed with oranges. Then the movies came, looking for the same things they always looked for: cheap land and sunlight. Warner Brothers and Universal set up shop over the Cahuenga Pass from Hollywood and started cranking out dreams for people who'd never smelled an orange blossom. With the studios came the production crews, makeup people, extras, directors, and even a few stars. Finally, the rich old guys who already owned most of downtown made it a clean sweep by buying the Valley, too. They knocked down the orange groves and plowed the tomatoes under and gave the world Instant Suburb. The stucco capital of the world.

Today, Spanish has returned: The Valley is overwhelmingly Hispanic across broad swathes of the flats, but white affluence clings to the hills south of Ventura. The water's long gone, but there's a new sea, at least metaphorically, a sea of bad money with several new species of beasts swimming through it. Lots of drug running, lots of chem labs cooking up the psychosis *du jour*, a few highly visible, emphatically for-profit religions. And, of course, the Valley is the epicenter of the American pornography industry, generating billions in phantom, untaxed dollars yearly. If you could get it all in one place and spread it around evenly, the bad money would cover the entire floor of the Valley, roughly hip-deep.

And Trey, whom I was being taken to see, was in the middle of that. *All* of it. A third-generation hood and the heir to the Valley's most diversified crime family. A finger in every poisonous pot. Maybe thirty, thirty-five, reputedly Stanford-educated, notoriously reclusive and famously icy, Trey was rumored to have paid for the emphatically fatal shooting of the family's previous top dog, Deuce, in a Korean nightclub on Western Avenue, where Deuce had an affectionate commercial relationship with a couple of hostesses. The shooter was so enthusiastic that he put more than thirty holes in Deuce and divided another couple dozen between the hostesses.

Deuce had been Trey's father.

"Left on Vanowen," Hacker said. He opened his cell phone and began pushing buttons.

I made the turn, past what has become a normal Valley strip mall: dry cleaner, Mexican restaurant, Korean restaurant, liquor store, massage parlor, check cashing outlet. Then there were pepper trees on either side of the road, old ones, trailing long green streamers to the ground.

The diamonds were hot in my pocket. Thanks to the shaving

foam over the camera's lens I was ninety percent certain Wattles and Hacker had no idea I had them, and even if I were wrong, what was my choice? I wasn't about to say hi to the dogs again and put them back.

"Hacker," Hacker said into the phone. Then he said, "Okay," and folded the phone.

I said, "I don't like chatty people, either."

Hacker grunted.

The sun was maybe twenty degrees above the horizon now, and the trees cast long shadows across Vanowen. Made me think about what the Valley had once been like.

"Right on Hadley," Hacker said. "It's a couple more streets."

"So," I said, "you're not working for Wattles. You're working for Trey."

"Yeah?" Hacker said.

"Trey's got a problem and hires you to find somebody to fix it. You go to Wattles for help. Wattles asks Janice, who says I'm smart, and Wattles sets me up."

"Think that's how it happened?"

"You tell me."

He chewed on it for a second. "More or less."

"And what do you get out of this? Trey paying you?"

"Not much."

"This is like what? A good deed?"

"What's a cop's job?" Hacker asked.

"Gee, I don't know. To ensure a good third act?"

"To cut down on crime, smartass, or most kinds of crime, anyway. Some kinds of crime, crime that don't make headlines and don't hurt too much and gets committed by generous suspects who deal in cash of small to moderate denominations, we can leave alone. It's like a fringe benefit, you know?"

"I've never heard the specs detailed so succinctly before."

"So what I'm doing right now," Hacker said, "I'm cutting down on crime."

"You want to explain how?"

"Nah. I'll let Trey do that."

**The house was** a fantasy out of Pearl S. Buck. Sprawling over maybe 10,000 square feet, it was set back from the road and shielded from vulgar curiosity by a used-brick wall, half-covered in ivy, that was at least ten feet tall. Eleven, if you counted the wrought-iron spikes bristling on top. Before laying eyes on the house, I had to stop at a gate the mysterious color of copper patina, and which may actually have been copper patina. A little iron door next to the gate opened, and a guy came out. His face and neck were thin but his suit was bulked up in a way that suggested a layer of bullet-proofing. He looked first at me and then at Hacker, containing his enthusiasm nicely. Hacker rolled down his window and said, "Lollipop," and the guy nodded and went back through his little door.

A moment later, the gates opened inward.

I said, "Lollipop? What a sweet name."

"Code word," Hacker said. "Changes every few hours. I got it when I phoned."

The drive, which was surfaced in tan gravel, wound its way through a man-made landscape of hills, ponds, willows, little Asian gazebos, and the occasional Chinese bridge. The whole thing looked like it had been copied off a dinner plate, but it was pretty in a finicky, over-managed way.

I said to Hacker, "Do I get a fortune cookie?"

"You just behave. Trey doesn't fuck around, and remember, I brought you here. You get anybody in the house upset, you're gonna have Wattles and me after you, too."

"Holy Moly." I stopped the van where Hacker told me to, to the left of the house where it wouldn't intrude on the view of Imperial China from the front windows, and we hiked back to the front door, which was standing open. The doorframe was entirely filled by a very wide gentleman of Hispanic ancestry wearing black from head to toe. The width was the product of years on the weight bench, years that had bulked his shoulders and chest and built muscles at the sides of his neck. It wasn't Gold's Gym bulk, either; it was California Prison System bulk. His shirt was one of those '60s-inspired mutants without a collar, and the gold chain around his neck was probably heavy enough to tow a car. His expression said he could eat me for breakfast without a knife and fork.

"Living room," he said. Then he backed away in front of us, doing the whole hallway in reverse as we came in. He never looked behind himself, and he never blinked: just kept his eyes fixed on mine.

I said to Hacker, "Can I say anything about this?"

"No."

At long last, the living room yawned to our left, two steps down into a sea of beige half the size of an Olympic swimming pool. A white grand piano had staked out the far rear corner, maybe fifty feet from us, and various pieces of precious and semiprecious furniture had flung themselves casually around the room. There was nothing as common as an arrangement. It looked like they might change positions on their own after everyone went to bed. There was a lot of white wood, and most of the upholstery was the soft yellow of Danish butter.

"Wait in the conversation area," the Man in Black Without a Collar said.

"The conversation area?" I asked, but Hacker had already grabbed my arm and was hauling me toward a grouping that included two eight-foot couches, a chaise fit for an odalisque, and a low coffee-table of bleached, distressed wood. I detoured left to look more closely at a very large, very skillful, and commensurately terrible oil portrait that hung between two windows. In front of a steamy, bleached-out landscape that could have been Renaissance Italy was a man with a romantically cleft chin, an impossibly perfect flop of Byronic hair, and eyelashes as long as palm fronds. He wore what looked like a silk shirt, dramatically white and just a little blousy, and a gold wristwatch that probably weighed two pounds, but his primary accessory was a heart-attack blond, all eyes and cheekbones, with the kind of bone structure that had undoubtedly made the painter start moving lights around and wishing for more talent. The woman wore a period gown, maybe 17th century, with seed pearls sewn all over the front of it. Her golden hair hung in Botticelli ropes over her shoulders, almost to her lap.

"Please," someone said. "Have a seat."

I turned to see the maiden in the painting—this time in the flesh, but wearing contemporary clothes—gracefully enter the room. She wore the 21st century as decoratively as she'd worn the 17th. The heavy blond hair was looped up and held in place by a couple of thick pins of deep green jade, and old jade, at that. She wore the kind of distressed jeans they distress by rubbing money on them and a T-shirt that said HELLO, RUST BELT! in what looked like real rust and probably cost $300. Around her slender neck was a crimson dog collar in patent leather. It fastened with a gold buckle, and gold tags dangled from it. She was barefoot. In her hand was a bottle of white wine, cold enough to sweat.

"Chardonnay, Mr. Bender?" Then she gave Hacker a bigger smile than he deserved and said, "Hello, Lyle. One for you, or do you want Scotch?"

I said I'd like the Chardonnay, and Hacker opted for Scotch. The Man in Black Without a Collar came in carrying a tray on which were three glasses and a bottle of Scotch. He carried it as though he wished it was an Oldsmobile or something else that would justify all that upper-body work.

"I'm Trey Annunziato," the blond woman said, holding out her free hand. I shook it, and she settled onto the chaise with one bare foot tucked beneath her, and patiently waited for me to finish looking at her. Up close, she was the kind of thin that's just a little more than intentional, the kind of thin that speaks to a life of boneless skinless chicken breasts, salad with dressing on the side, sashimi rather than sushi, and personal control issues. The bones of her face, perfect as they were, could have used a little softening, and the ball joints on the outside of her wrists were as prominent as marbles implanted beneath the skin. The eyes were chocolate brown, an odd contrast with the pale hair, and the whites had a faint bluish cast, like skim milk. She held up the hand with the bottle in it, and The Man in Black Without a Collar took it. "Would you do the pouring, Eduardo?" she asked. Her tone was sweet enough, but I noticed she didn't feel any need to look over at him.

Eduardo poured.

"Well, haven't we put *you* through a lot?" Trey Annunziato said. "It's just been one crook after another, hasn't it? Not Lyle, here, of course. We all know he's true to the badge."

"I'm used to crooks," I said.

"Well, of course. I mean, being one, and all. But still, most of us prefer to choose our company, and you've been hauled from place to place, I'm afraid." There was something studied about the way she moved and talked, accentuated by the semi-British construction of her sentences, even though she avoided the dread mid-Atlantic vowel syndrome. "Please, Eduardo." She held up a hand and he put a glass into it, *very* carefully, and then condescended to serve the mortals in the room. I took my glass and hung onto it, and Hacker buried his nose in the Scotch. His sigh when he lowered the glass could have blown out a window.

"So nice to see a man enjoying himself," Trey Annunziato said. Then she said to me, "How in the world did you get so nicked up?"

"I was swinging on a chandelier to escape some dogs, and the chain broke."

"Oh, well," she said. "Ask a silly question." A moment earlier, I had glanced back at the large awful painting, and her eyes flicked over to it. "What do you think of the picture?"

"I like the original better."

I got the kind of smile Pollyanna might have offered a passing butterfly, all innocent delight. "How gallant." It came out "gal-la*hnt*," "And what about *him*?" She inclined her head toward the man in the white shirt.

"You want the truth?"

With the smile still in place, she said, "Do you think I have time to sit here and listen to you tell lies?"

"He's too handsome for his own good. That kind of handsome stifles personal growth."

She leaned forward as though I were too far away for her to hear, and her eyebrows came up an inquiring quarter of an inch. "Personal . . . "

"Growth."

Trey Annunziato looked over at Hacker. The smile was down to a muscle memory, just a meaningless tilt of the lips. "What do you think about that, Lyle?"

Hacker sighted over the edge of his glass. "We talking about Tony?"

"We are, and please try to keep up."

"Tony's an asshole."

"He is indeed," Trey said. "Do you know who Tony is, Mr. Bender?"

"No."

"He's my husband." She turned her face slightly to the left and regarded me from the corners of her eyes, the angle you sometimes see in self-portraits where the painter is looking at himself in a mirror. There was nothing spontaneous in the gesture; it looked like someone had told her it was a good angle, and she'd been practicing. "As you should have surmised from looking at the painting."

"We all make mistakes," I said. "He was probably one of yours."

Her perfect eyebrows came together a fraction of an inch,

an attractive way to suggest perplexity. I was beginning to think that Trey Annunziato was one of those people who see their lives as a series of close-ups.

"Mmmmm," she said. "How candid." She rested her chin in her hand the way Charlie Rose sometimes does when he knows he's on camera. "Do you know anything at all about me?"

"As little as possible," I said. "As an intentionally disorganized criminal, I try not to get anywhere near the organized variety. I know you went to Stanford, took some sort of graduate degree—"

A nod. "Business administration."

"And I know you've been running the show since your father, ah . . ."

"Had his accident." She sipped her wine, the brown eyes cool on mine, as though she were daring me to have a reaction. "What did you expect me to be like?"

"I didn't. I never thought much about you until I was on the way over here."

"Did you, for example," she said, crossing her legs, "expect me to be a woman?"

My eyes were drawn to the fire from the diamond circlet around her ankle. "I'd heard a rumor, but Frederick G. Annunziato the Third isn't a conspicuously feminine name."

"Good old dad," she said unfondly. "He would have preserved the name if his only child had been a donkey. My older brother died when he was three, and I was the last baby my mother could have, so he just unpacked the name again and gave it to me. Nicest thing he did was not calling me Fred when he talked to me. He always called me Trey."

"That's mildly interesting," I said.

"And you're wondering why in the world I'm telling you about it." She lifted the glass to her lips and then did a good job of pretending to notice I hadn't tasted mine. "Please," she said. "Try it. I'd like to know what you think. It's the second growth from our new vineyard."

I tasted it, and then I tasted it again. "I'm not a wine connoisseur," I said, "but it's good enough to swallow repeatedly for a long period of time."

She threw her head back, shook her hair out, and laughed. The laugh might have worked if she hadn't thrown her head back. When she was through simulating affectionate mirth, she turned to Hacker and said, "You didn't tell me he was cute."

"I guess I missed it," Hacker said.

"Well," she said, leaning forward to demonstrate that she was going all frank on me. "Here I am. I'm a girl who should have been a boy, who got a boy's name, and was handed a life sentence at birth: Run the business. The enterprise, as my father always called it, was created by my great-grandfather, broadened and deepened by my grandfather, taken international and expanded exponentially by my father, and handed to me. With the expectation that I'd pass it on even bigger and more profitable than it was when I got it."

"I'm sure you'll do fine," I said, since she seemed to be waiting for someone to say something.

"I'm sure I would, too," she said. "If I weren't in the process of shutting the whole thing down."

## 7
### Junior Agonistes

The sun, most of the way down to the treetops, made a farewell appearance through the window, and projected itself into the bottom of Trey's wine glass to create a fiery little point of light there. It was so bright I had to look away from it, which at least had the advantage of giving me something to do.

"When you say closing it down," I said, "do you mean, um, closing it down?"

She said, "You could at least try to paraphrase me."

"You caught me off-balance," I said, "which is what you wanted to do."

This time she didn't throw back her head. She just laughed. It wasn't much of a laugh, maybe a two-stop chuckle, but it was about eighty percent real. "This is a quiz," she said, holding her glass up a couple of inches, which doused the miniature sun. "Where does the wine come from?"

"Your vineyards. Second growth." I sipped it again. "It's a little heavy on the tannin."

Hacker pulled his nose out of his glass long enough to hiss, "*Bender*," but Trey waved him off. She sipped and said, "Does a vineyard sound like a criminal operation?"

"Not if the wine's any good."

"At the moment," she said, "I own a vineyard, four dry cleaning shops, six Seven-Eleven franchises, a real estate holding company that controls nine office buildings on Ventura, including the one that Mr. Wattles occupies, and I just bought a chain of two-hour optometrists." She sat back. "They're called 'Dr. Simon's' now, but I want to change it. What do you think of 'Look Fast'?"

"How about 'The Frame-Up'?"

"Something that says speed," she said.

"Second Sight?"

"Too abstruse."

"Twenty/twenty in one-twenty?"

Now she was giving me a genuine grin. "Got any more?"

"Four Eyes in Two Hours?"

"Eeeewww." But the grin widened.

"This is not why you called me here," I said. "You could have asked for help naming a business without such an elaborate setup." I grinned back at her. "And while we're playing Show Me, you also own a bunch of bookie shops, a protection racket, about a third of the Mexican grass in the Valley, the hookers on the north side of Ventura for a couple of miles, a car theft operation that ships the cars to Eastern Europe, and one of the biggest porno operations in the country."

"Actually," she said briskly, "it's the biggest. And you left out quite a lot, although you're wrong about the protection and the hookers. I've offloaded both of those operations. They're no longer under the Annunziato umbrella, so to speak. The other businesses, the ones I named, not the ones you did, are one hundred percent legit. And, of course, pornography is legal, although I'm repurposing that business,"

"Re *what*?"

"Repurposing."

"Is that MBA language?"

"It is."

"Good, because it certainly isn't English."

"It means I'll no longer make the films. I'll own the things people *use* to make the films: cameras, lights, microphones, post-production equipment, even studio space. The printing presses to make the box. The DVD duplication facility, the website for online distribution. You want to make *Girl Guides Run Wild Three*, you rent everything from me."

"If there was ever a film that needed two sequels, *Girl Guides Gone Wild* is that film."

"You have absolutely no idea," she said, "how much the first two made. So much we didn't know where to put it. But I won't be filming the third one. I've sold the franchise and I'll rent the equipment. Because that's where I'm going, Mr. Bender. Within eighteen months, the Annunziatos will no longer be part of the shadow economy."

"The shadow economy," I said. "What a romantic way to put it."

"I'm in the middle of handing off the marijuana operation right now. Forty-eight hours from now, we'll be out of the dope business. The others will follow."

"Well, with no desire to offend," I said, "if that's your plan, why are you talking to a crook?"

"We're going to come to that." She turned her head and said, without raising her voice, "Eduardo." And there he was, in all his glowering Blackness, standing in the doorway in suspended animation. *Kill? Sure. Vacuum? Sure.* "Could we have some more wine, please? Another Scotch, Lyle?"

Hacker said, "You bet." Eduardo crossed the room and picked up the bottle, which was no more than eighteen inches from Trey Annunziato's elbow, and poured for her. I waved him off. Then he took Hacker's glass, dropped in a new ice cube, and filled it almost to the brim. Hacker took it without glancing up or grunting thanks, and from the look in Eduardo's eyes, what was all right for Trey was very much not all right for Hacker. He turned and left, and the room brightened noticeably.

"You're asking yourself why you're here," she said to me.

"Not at all," I said. "It's not every day I get to taste a good second growth."

"You're here because I need *someone*," she said. "So that's really two questions, isn't it? Why do I need someone, and why is it you?"

"Which one would you like to answer first?"

She scooched her rear around on the seat a little and extended an arm over the top of the chaise, not so much to get more comfortable as simply to make sure I was completely focused on her. "Let's start with why it's you. Do you remember someone named Flaco Francis?"

Whatever I'd been expecting, this wasn't it. "Vaguely."

Her smile this time was tolerant. "I'm sure it's more vivid than that. The name alone should guarantee it, *Flaco* being Spanish slang for skinny, and *Francis* being, well, Francis. According to my father, Flaco was like those white guys now who want to be black, with the watch caps and the—what do they call that awful jewelry?"

I didn't feel like playing. "I don't know. Awful jewelry?"

"*Bling*," she said. "They call it bling. If he were around now, Flaco would be wearing bling. But this was fifteen years ago, and Flaco wanted to be Mexican."

"Let's back it up a minute. Your father knew Flaco?"

"My father owned Flaco."

Suddenly several things from long ago made sense. "Did he."

"Body and soul. And you got a little tangled with Flaco, didn't you?"

"If you say so."

"No, no, no, Mr. Bender. You got *very* tangled with Flaco."

I had. "He stole something from a friend of mine."

"He stole seven Cadillacs, all brand new. Cadillacs that your friend had acquired by unconventional means. This was when Cadillacs still had some cachet. When they were bling, so to speak. And your friend couldn't very well go to the police, since they take a dim view of crooks who have a bunch of Cadillacs without pink slips. So he called you, and you figured out who took the cars and recovered three of them. And then, just to prevent retaliation, you set Flaco up on a phony burglary, and he was arrested. On Thursday, he had seven new Cadillacs, and on Friday he was sitting in jail in Van Nuys, looking at three to five."

"I remember."

"Finally. Well, since your memory has kicked in, what happened next?"

"Somebody from Flaco's posse came to me and told me Flaco had five kids and a pregnant wife, and promised to tell me where the other four Cadillacs were if I could somehow pop Flaco out of jail. He also suggested that there were lots of people willing to get even with me even it Flaco personally couldn't."

"There certainly were," Trey said.

"I had no way of knowing that. Anyway, since I had essentially put Flaco there, the guy figured I might be able to get him out."

Trey nodded encouragingly. "And you did."

"Evidence got lost," I said. "Right at the station." I kept my eyes off of Hacker, who had sat up. "And don't ask who lost it for me, because that's off-limits."

"End of the day, your friend had all seven cars back, and Flaco was a free man. And Flaco went to my father and told him the story."

I said, "What a guy."

"He didn't have much choice. He had to explain what he'd been doing in jail. My father didn't like it when his people wound up in jail."

"Understandable."

"And then there was Antoine Duvall," she said.

"Jesus Christ," I said, "What is this, *This Is Your Life*?"

"Antoine Duvall fell for the Nigerian scam, didn't he?" She

turned to Hacker. "Do you know about the Nigerian scam, Lyle?"

"Uh-uh," Hacker said. He was staring at me, trying to figure who I might know at the Van Nuys station.

"The way I understand it," Trey said, "the person working the Nigerian scam sends just thousands and thousands of people an e-mail telling them that he's an investor who got involved in a deal in some African country and ran afoul of the authorities. Some very complicated story. Right so far?"

"Right," I said.

"Anyway, the hook is an absurd amount of money—say forty or fifty million—in a bank account in whatever country. Let's say Nigeria, since that's where it started. Because the authorities have him on their bad list, he can't pull the money out. But *you* could, and if you'll do it for him, he'll pay you ten or fifteen percent. A nice chunk of money for essentially doing nothing. All he needs is for you to sign some meaningless forms, which are just there because they look official, and on one of them you list the number of the bank account to which you want these millions of dollars transferred."

"An account number?" Hacker said. "Ain't nobody going to fall for that."

"Out of the twenty or thirty thousand e-mails every month, they are going to reach, statistically speaking, three or four bona fide idiots," Trey said. "Or maybe they're old people whose judgment isn't so good. Antoine, who had worked for my grandfather, was seventy-seven, and not quite as sharp as he might have been. He responded with his account numbers and got cleaned out."

"Antoine was a sweet old guy," I said. "He baked cookies for the local fire department every week."

"And he was devastated," Trey said. "One of the problems with living on this side of the law is that there's no pension plan. No health insurance."

"And his wife," I said. "She was sick or something."

"Shirley," Trey said. "I knew her when I was little. Alzheimer's. Anyway, you took care of it."

"I can't take the credit. A kid did most of the work. But Antoine had a friend who was a mentor of mine, a burglar named Herbie. Herbie told me about it, and I met Antoine and Shirley, and I got really pissed off. So I got it back for him."

"And some extra," she said.

I shrugged.

"Antoine told my father what you did, but he didn't understand *how*."

"I reverse-engineered it," I said. "I knew a fifteen year-old kid, a girl, who could make computers leap through rings of fire while they sang arias from Verdi. So we set up a virtual bank, the Bank of US, that was really nothing more than an invisible forwarding link to a real account with a few thousand bucks in it. Then we sent responses to the con man's e-mail as though it had been sent to us, with the number of the phony account. The second he hit the link we'd set up, which was on our own computer, we followed him, electronically I mean, to the account he was transferring to. The kid hacked the bank the con man was using and found that he'd set up a couple of linking accounts at the same bank. We cleaned them all out and then we sent him an e-mail from a phantom mailbox saying the next time he tried to pull the scam he'd lose more than just money."

"Like what?" Hacker asked.

"I think the right hand was mentioned."

Trey was back in the chin-on-hand pose. "And you gave Antoine how much?"

"I don't know," I said uncomfortably.

"All of it, I believe," she said. "About two million. He'd only lost three hundred thousand."

"Pain and suffering," I said. "Antoine was a nice old guy."

"So the long and short of it," Trey said, "is that my father had heard both these stories, and he told me about you. He said you were a smart guy and I should keep track of you in case I ever needed you."

I held up both hands. "Hold it. I thought you went to Hacker here, and then Hacker went to Wattles, and—"

"All true," she said. "I told you that my father suggested I keep track of you, not that I succeeded in doing it. You're a hard man to find."

"Not hard enough, apparently."

"By dumb luck, I went to people who knew where you were. When Lyle told me your name, I thought, well, here's virtue rewarded. I'm trying to go straight, and I get the very man I need. A man my father called *smart*. My father didn't exactly throw compliments around."

"If I were smart," I said, "I wouldn't be sitting here."

"Where did you go to school?"

"Here in the Valley," I said, although it wasn't true.

"Cal State Northridge?" A faint wrinkle of distaste briefly shortened her nose by a hundredth of an inch or so. Not enough ivy for a Stanford post-grad. "What did you take?"

"Nothing," I said. "But it was a great place to meet girls."

The tendons in her neck were suddenly tight. "Mr. Bender, I am asking about your education."

"And I'm avoiding answering you."

Hacker said, "Answer the lady."

"Lyle." It was a snap, but she sweetened it with a smile. "When I want basic muscle, I'll request it."

"Sorry," Hacker said.

"Mr. Bender? I'm prepared to believe you're an unusual man. But I strongly believe that higher education trains the mind. It's not a matter of *what* you learn, it's that you learn *how* to learn. Given the way your mind seems to work, I'm curious about your education."

"I read a novel," I said.

She tried to put her glass down without looking and missed the table. "You . . . read a novel."

"In the one class I attended regularly, Modern American Literature. The novel was called *The Recognitions*."

"One novel," she said, as though she was trying to make sense out of the words.

"It was written by a guy named William Gaddis, back in the fifties. Came out, no reviewer knew what to make of it, and it sank without a ripple. Maybe the greatest novel of the twentieth century."

She grabbed the bottle and poured her own wine this time, ignoring the sound of Eduardo tripping over his feet to get into the room. "I have to confess that this *is* a disappointment," she said. "One novel? I don't care if it's *War and* fucking *Peace*. One novel?"

"With all due respect to your wonderful degrees," I said, "a lot of people come out of college too dumb to exhale. I gave myself a better education out of *The Recognitions* than any college on this coast, including Stanford, could have offered."

"That's quite a claim."

"You haven't read it. It's roughly a thousand pages long, and it's about everything in the world. But most of all, it's about forgery and faith, and between those things you can crowd most of life. I read it in five days, pretty much around the clock, and then I went back to the beginning and started taking notes. I got though the first hundred and fifty pages, writing all the time, and then I got every book I could get my hands on about the things Gaddis talks about in those pages."

She had angled her head slightly to one side by way of demonstrating that I had her ear. "For example."

"Spanish monasticism. The Gnostics. Authorship of the New Testament. The Flemish masters, especially van der Goes and van Eyck. The music of Pergolesi. Inherent vice—that's the tendency of certain artistic materials to deteriorate over time, the way most frescoes eventually peel and chip. The Catholic

Church's use of fictitious martyrs to convey the faith. The international trade in art forgery. How to mix seventeenth-century pigments. Greenwich Village society in the early fifties. The spatial organization of triptychs. The symbolism of the elements in a painting of the annunciation—with your last name, that might interest you. And about fifty other things. And I had eight hundred fifty pages to go."

I drained my wine, reached past her, and poured myself some more. She watched me, her mouth drawn in at the corners and her eyes on my hands. "And this continued," she finally said, "for how long?

"About five years. Some books led me to other books. Other topics. The Spanish Inquisition, for example, led me to the Jewish diaspora, which led to a million things, including the invention—speaking of your new chain of opticians—of eyeglasses. Did you know that Spinoza ground lenses all his life?"

"Do tell," she said. "Maybe I should call it *Spinoza's.*"

"And then I did the same with *Moby-Dick,*" I said. "That leads you to an entirely different world of stuff."

"A wetter one, certainly."

"For the last three or four years, I've been working out of a seventeenth-century Chinese novel called *The Dream of the Red Chamber.* Just to get away from the Western tradition."

"And what, of any possible practical use, could you get out of that?" she said.

"Your hairpins," I said. "They're seventeenth century, probably from a tomb near Nanjing. And the Chinese government would like them back."

For a count of three or four, she just looked at me as though I were a trinket she was thinking about buying. Then she reached over, picked up the bottle of wine, and topped up my glass.

"So," I said, "I may not be a whiz with spread sheets, accrual accounting, and business plans, but I'm not Barney Flintstone, either."

"No," she said. "No, you're not." She put down the bottle and her glass, and clapped her hands twice, and Eduardo shot into the room as though he were propelled by a slingshot. Without turning, Trey Annunziato said, "Eduardo. Bring us some food."

# 8

## Snor-Mor

"So I got a chance to watch Hacker eat," I said. "Not an experience I'm eager to repeat."

"Hacker," Louie the Lost said. "What a fuckin' guy. Sets like a new global asshole standard."

"He holds his spoon in his fist, like a three-year old, and scoops straight out of the serving bowls, like he's trying to keep anyone from having to wash his dish. And in the meantime, there's Trey at the other end of the table cutting peas in half and looking like she'd prefer to be at a hummingbird feeder. One of the odder meals of the week."

Louie leaned toward me, took another look at my face, and winced. "If I'd seen how banged up you was this morning, I'da bought a bunch of stock in Johnson and Johnson."

We were sitting at the tiny, cigarette-scarred table in room 204 at the Snor-Mor motel on Sherman Way, my current address. I pretty much live in motels, and while the Snor-Mor—with its sagging beds, flyspecked mirrors, and thriving trade in one-hour rentals—would barely earn a single star in the Bender Blue Book of Dumps, it's a place no one would look for me unless they knew which website to check and which name I was posting under. There are maybe half a dozen people who know the FIND JUNIOR rules, and Louie was one of them.

Louie was a top-rated wheelman until he took a memorable

wrong turn after a jewel heist about six years back and wound up rattling around in Compton in this big Lincoln town car, four jacked-up white guys inside, everyone outside black and staring in at them, and about 600 K in diamonds in the trunk. They made it out somehow, and Louie got off easy—ended up with nothing more permanent than a nickname and a change of jobs. He's still a good driver, and at the moment I needed a good driver.

Louie put the butt of his cigar in the center of his mouth, looked crosseyed down at the coal for a second, and then inhaled. "So somebody's sabotaging Trey's movie," he said, in a cloud of blue smoke. "And you're like her cop or something, got to figure out who's the bad guy."

"It feels odd to me, too."

Louie burped. "Fuckin' Mexican food," he said. "Don't know why I eat it. It's like *here I am again* every ten minutes for the rest of the night."

"You have no idea," I said, "how sorry I am for you."

"Yeah, yeah. I know. You got a real problem, and I'm gassing at you about enchiladas. Here's one of the things I don't get. This movie that somebody's trying to fuck up, it's a hand-job flick, right?"

"To hear her talk about it, it's *The Birth of a Nation*."

"Yeah? Didn't see that one. But, come on, there's only so much money there. It's not like ten years back. Right now, those things have a shelf life shorter than an oyster, and then they're all over the Internet. Only way to make enough money to fold is to crank out a couple or three a week and keep them cheap. Don't sound like an empire-saver to me."

"Well, she thinks it is. And she's going to make the movie even though she wants to close down the porno operation. Sort of a final climax, if you'll forgive the expression. She thinks it'll make millions that she can use to finance everybody's transition to the straight life. She's in a rough place, Louie. She's putting all these extortionists into legitimate collection agencies, loan sharks into payday check-cashing operations, car thieves into auto mechanics' shops, and I don't know what else. Stuff that'll pay off in the long run, but probably not right now. And these guys, I'd imagine, are sort of *happy* being extortionists and loan sharks. It's what they know, you know? Break a kneecap, steal a Porsche. Go home early and kiss the little woman. Or the little man, I guess. It's part of their identity, like former presidents. What are they going to do when they can't dial the red phone any more? These guys feel the same way, on a lesser scale, probably."

"Feels big to them, though," Louie the Lost said.

"To make it worse for her, she's the first woman to run the operation. They already didn't like it, and now here she is, saying, okay everybody, time to join the chamber of commerce."

"And then there's her dad," Louie said. "He was a popular guy. Some guys would like to do her just for that."

"I think that cuts both ways. Yeah, they liked the old man. But they've got to figure, if she's icy enough to gun down Pops, she's not going to be real slow about taking out anybody who gets out of line. Do you know about the dog collar?"

Louie's eyes went into soft-focus. "Ohh, man, I knew a chick once, wore a black leather—"

"It's red," I interrupted. "Bright red, impossible to miss. And it's got three tags, solid gold, hanging off it."

With some reluctance, Louie let the memory pass. "Tags?"

"Three tags, three names. To hear her tell it, each of them is someone she aced personally. They jingle when she walks. So I think she's maybe overcompensating a little, but it's a pretty clear message: *I'm a girl, but don't get silly.*"

Louie eyed the cigar, now shorter than his thumb, with what looked like profound regret. I thought for a moment he was going to kiss it goodbye. But then he smashed it flat in the pumpkin-colored salad bowl he was using as an ashtray, leaned to the window, and pulled back the greasy curtain an inch to peer outside. The bright red on-off neon sign that said SNOR-MOR hit his face, making him look intermittently demonic.

"Your company. They're still out there."

"And likely to stay, until we do something about them."

Louie let the curtain drop. "Did you like her?"

"Like her?" I pushed my chair back, took the salad bowl into the tiny bathroom, and flushed the corpse of Louie's cigar. When I came back in, he was doing that finicky little trim thing to one end of a new one. "She's not someone you like or don't like. She's Mount Rushmore with hair. She doesn't do anything on the spur of the moment. You get the feeling that people have been studying her for reactions for so long that she practiced a bunch of them in front of a mirror, so nobody will bury her prematurely. I think she's got a body temperature in the low sixties."

"On the other hand," Louie said.

"On the other hand, what?"

He pulled out his lighter, a miniature silver propane tank, and flicked it, producing a blue flame an inch long and as sharp as a needle. "If there wasn't something on the other hand, you wouldn't of got up and gone in the bathroom."

"On the other hand, she's trying to do something that could get her killed. Maybe will get her killed, in spite of all the show she puts on. And, you know, it's not a bad thing to try to do. The guys are going to bitch about it, and maybe try to cap her, but their wives and kids—sorry, or husbands and kids—are going to breathe a lot easier knowing that their significant other isn't going to wind up doing fifteen to twenty pumping iron behind razor wire and getting ugly tattoos."

"I guess," Louie said. "Gonna be a lot duller, though."

"And she's doing what she can to avoid getting capped. She's living behind metal gates, surrounded by a bunch of try-me guys wearing Valentino Kevlar. Her car's been bulletproofed. But she can't control what's going on around the movie, and she's made it the big symbol of the transformation. That's what she calls it, the transformation. Also, she's smart, and I like smart. After she gave me the whole Hallmark version of the transformation, complete with the string section, about living on the right side of the law and sleeping well at night, and all the wives and husbands who won't have to wait up every night to see whether Thuggo comes home on a slab, she told me the real reason. You want to hear it?"

"What am I gonna do?" Louie said. "Stick my fingers in my ears? Go outside?"

"She said, and this is pretty much a quote: The government's not going to be worrying about terrorists forever. And when it's not, all the new laws saying nobody has the right to privacy or untapped phone lines or unread e-mail, all that stuff is going to get turned on *us*. And she plans to be as clean as a whistle by the time that happens. A hundred percent legal, tax-paying, highly diversified multi-millionaire."

Louie said, "Yikes."

"That's pretty much what I thought. So she's cold and she's smart and she's willing to try to do something that's going to be dangerous as hell for her. So, yeah, I kind of like her."

"I don't know how smart she is," Louie said, "if she thinks she's gonna pay for all this with a skin flick."

"Not one, three. And what she's selling is the idea that these are going to be the biggest one-hand movies ever made, and they're going to earn millions and millions of dollars, and those dollars are going into a retirement fund and a health care plan, if you can believe that, for all these thick-necks who are suddenly teaching Sunday school. She calls it a trilogy, like it has a Dewey Decimal Number or something. It's supposed to produce a big fat legal flow of porno dollars, and it all gets salted away to secure the future of her guys. And girls."

"This is seriously cracked," Louie the Lost said. "This ain't

1970. These days, everybody's seen everything. What kind of peepshow can earn that kind of money?"

"She's got a star," I said. "Name doesn't mean anything to me, but it seems to put everyone else in the drool zone."

"Let's hear it."

"Thistle Downing."

Louie the Lost bit his cigar in half.

## 9
### Thistle

Life is definitely not fair. First I had to watch Hacker throw food at his mouth, miss with about half of it, and chew openmouthed on the stuff that found its way in. Then I had to watch Louie cough and spit and pull long dark shreds of wet tobacco off his tongue. When he was finished, he had brown lips and there was a pile of something in front of him that looked like used carnitas. I decided to skip dinner.

"Thistle *Downing*?" he finally said. "You're shitting me."

"Okay," I said. "Means something to you, too. But not me. There's something familiar about the name, but I can't place it."

He shook his head pityingly, as though I were the only guy in Turin who'd never heard of the Shroud. "You ever steal a TV?"

"No. Too big, no resale value."

"You live in these fucking motels," he said. "Take a look around. Tell me what the second-biggest piece of furniture is."

"I use it to put my spare change on."

"Well, if you turned the damn thing on, you'd know who Thistle Downing is." Louie looked at the remnants of his cigar and dropped it, with a surprising concentration of disgust, into the salad bowl. "But . . . but . . ." His head was shaking back and forth and he was practically spluttering. "They can't put *Thistle* into that kind of movie. They can't."

"Why not?"

"It's—it's *sick*. Diseased, perverted, just wrong." Louie is a short, stout guy who has a fat, cheerful little face that's mostly forehead, and a dark Mediterranean complexion, and he generally looks like a happy olive. But he was actually flushed with indignation, and his lower lip was quivering. "They *can't*."

"Louie," I said. "You're acting like she's your kid sister."

"She is," Louie said. "She's *everybody's*—wait, wait." He looked at his watch and then looked at the TV. "Does that thing work?"

"I have no idea."

"You ain't *never* turned it on?"

"To tell you the truth," I said, "it never occurs to me."

"You're missing a lot."

"It keeps me up nights."

"Something wrong with you. Does this place get The *TV Channel*?" He got up, grabbed the remote and pointed it at the television.

"I don't know. I suppose it gets a bunch of them."

"No, no. The *TV Channel*. It shows, it shows . . ." He was punching buttons on the remote, flipping past earnest newsreaders with neon makeup on their faces; the newest retrohip-inverse-ironic cartoon series; a bright orange Bob Barker, undoubtedly the oldest life form on the planet; and some justpossibly-not-entirely-naturally-well-endowed young women on a beach, empowering the hell out of themselves by wearing red bikinis. Then Louie stopped, frozen into immobility, the remote pointed like a magic wand at a completely unironic living room from the 1990s: couch, tables, bay window, stairs to the second story in the background, a room like a million I burglarized back then, when the words "twentieth century" sounded current. Everything on the screen, from the furniture to the lighting, looked cheap and slapped together in that way that—even to a non-TV watcher like me—says "sitcom." And nothing about that impression was contradicted by the room's sole inhabitant:

a slender middle-age man who was standing next to the coffee table with a dinner platter glued to each hand. He was trying a bit over-desperately to get them off, and the electronically
enhanced audience was finding it mechanically hilarious.

"This is the one about the cheese," Louie said, sitting on the
end of the bed. "Watch."

"The one about the—"

"Cheese," Louie snapped. "Forget it, it doesn't matter. *Here's*
what matters."

The director cut to a door stage right that opened about
six inches, and a girl of eleven or twelve peered apprehensively
into the room. Light brown hair above uptilted eyes with lots
of intelligence in them. The word that came to mind was *elfin*.
She registered the man with the platters on his hands, and her
shoulders came up to her ears and she squeezed her eyes closed,
and with those two simple movements she somehow conjured
up someone whose deepest wish was to shiver herself into mol-
ecules and disappear forever from the face of the earth.

The laughter this time didn't sound enhanced.

"She's good," I said.

"She's great," Louie said. "*That's* Thistle Downing."

On the screen, the man with the platters stuck to his hands
caught sight of the girl behind the door and waved her angrily
into the room, the platters making glittering arcs through the
air. She came in, but walking as though she was heading into a
ninety-mile an hour wind. It seemed to take every muscle in her
body to travel four steps. I could almost see her hair blowing
behind her.

"How does she do that?" I asked.

"She did that or better every week," Louie said, without taking his eyes from the screen, "for eight years."

The man was shouting accusations and waving his arms. The
words seemed to have actual weight as they struck the kid called
Thistle, and automatically, in self-defense, she brought her hands

up, palms out. Some primitive special effect created a current of blue ectoplasm or something from her hands to the platters, and suddenly they were piled high with cubes of cheese.

People laughed like God had just stepped on a banana peel.

The doorbell in the TV living room rang. Thistle and the man both looked at the door. The man's panic was minimum-wage acting, but Thistle's went all the way to her socks.

"See," Louie said, completely absorbed, "she can't control her powers yet."

"Her powers?" I said, sitting next to him and leaning toward the screen. "That's her father? The geeky guy?"

"Yeah. Like the third actor to play the part. Nobody could handle working with Thistle. Standing next to her, they all disappeared. They put in a year or two, stashed some money in the bank, and quit."

On the screen, Thistle Downing crossed the room, dragging her feet like her shoes were made out of cement, and opened the door. A stuffy-looking older man barged in, accompanied by his wife, an imperious woman of stately carriage wearing one of those fur pieces made up of small animals biting each others' tails. The older man handed Thistle his coat without even looking at her, and when it landed in her hands it turned into a little boy's sailor suit with short pants. Thistle's eyes filled half her face, and she whipped it behind her. In the meantime, her father had collapsed on the couch, bending forward awkwardly to put his hands, with the platters attached, at table level. The older man, apparently Thistle's father's boss, sat down and began taking handfuls of cheese. Mrs. Boss claimed the armchair and gave Thistle a disapproving look. Thistle summoned up a hopeful smile, and the woman turned away with her nose in the air, and then Thistle, in one uninterrupted ten-second arc, took the painful smile to an expression of pure horror as one of the animals around Mrs. Boss' neck lifted its head, winked at her, and bared its teeth.

"Turn it off," I said.

"This is the good part," Louie said as the mink, or whatever it was turned its head to eye the neck it was draped around.

I took the remote out of his hand and turned the set off. "That's her?"

"That's her. Hottest thing in America from the time she was eight until she was maybe fifteen, when she quit the show. Grew up in my fucking living room. I never missed her."

"What happened?"

Louie got up and went to the window, using one finger to part the curtain. "They're still out there." He turned back to me. "She grew up, I guess. And no show lasts forever. Some of the papers, they said she gave people a hard time the last couple of years, but you know? She was worth it. She'd been working since she was way little, carrying the whole thing, and she probably got fed up." He looked with some longing at the dark screen. "She was something, though."

Looking at my own reflection in the screen, I could still see the child, see her uptilted features and bright, intelligent eyes. "How old would she be now?"

Louie screwed up his face. "Twenty-two, twenty-three. She got seriously beautiful when she was fourteen, fifteen, toward the end. You know, you don't think of beautiful girls as funny. But she was. She could do anything. Shit, she coulda played that Shakespeare guy."

"Hamlet?"

"That's the one."

"A funny Hamlet is probably a good idea. But she didn't."

"I think there was drugs," Louie said. "You know, back then people sorta left stars alone, not like it is now where you're looking up their skirts and up their noses all the time. But I think she was getting loaded and screwing up. She got fired off some movie, I remember that."

"Thistle Downing," I said.

"Whydya turn off the TV?"

"I didn't want to see any more. I didn't want to see how good she was."

"What you didn't want to see," Louie said, nailing it, "was that she was a little kid."

"Louie. You said it yourself. She's in her twenties by now."

"For me and about two hundred million other clowns, she'll *always* be a little kid. That's what's so wrong with this." He pulled out one of the wooden chairs at the table and plopped himself down on it as though his own weight was too much for him. "The guys who go see this or buy it on DVD, they'll be paying to see that little kid. There oughta be a law."

"She's twenty-three," I said. "I don't think there is."

"Well, there oughta be. This is just fuckin' wrong. And you know it."

I went and sat across the table from him. "I do," I said.

"And maybe I missed this," Louie said," but how, exactly, are you going to be involved?"

"Trey believes the movie is being sabotaged. I'm the smart guy who's supposed to figure out how and by whom, and keep things on track."

"In other words," Louie said, "you're supposed to make sure it happens."

"I am." Suddenly my daughter Rina's face flashed in front of me, not much older than the child I'd just seen on the television screen, and I blinked it away.

Louie laced his fingers together on the table, avoiding the pile of loose wet tobacco, and stared at me. Finally, he said, "You gonna do it?"

"There's Rabbits," I said.

"Rabbits," Louie said, nodding. "Rabbits is definitely something to keep in mind."

"I don't think I'm in much danger of forgetting about him."

Louie nodded again and let his eyes drift down to the table.

He seemed to be working something through in his mind. Louie was a slow thinker, but a long one. And when he went into thinking mode, I always had to remind myself that, friend or not, Louie the Lost was a crook. It was not safe to bet the farm, or even the back forty, on which side of his mental coin would land up. Whichever side it landed on, he kept it to himself. "So," he said at last. "What now?"

*Now* was something I could deal with. "Let's see if we can't screw with my followers."

## 10
Firebird

The Snor-Mor was built on the classic California motel plan: a two-story stucco "L" edging a parking lot. The car that had followed me from Trey's was parked not in the lot, but about three spaces back, on the near side of the street, so it would be in position to pick me up if I went out to the Safeway or to burgle Aladdin's cave. The car was a heap, an old Chevy that looked like it had been thrown off the top of Pike's Peak and bounced all the way down. A few dents had been half-heartedly pounded out and primer applied. Altogether, the car couldn't have been more conspicuous if it had been a giant chrysanthemum.

The Chevy had picked me up as I drove Hacker out of Trey's Chinese theme park. Acting on the assumption that anything I knew and Hacker didn't was probably a plus, I kept my eyes off the rear-view mirror except when there was a reason to check it out. And the Chevy was always there, lumbering along one or two cars behind me, trailing the dark-colored smoke that makes mechanics so happy. Two heads were visible through the front windshield, but they never got close enough for details, except that one of them rode really low, sitting way down on his or her lungs so that only about half of the face was visible over the dash. The position seemed so furtive that I wondered whether it was a face I'd recognize.

So after I dropped Hacker around the corner from Rabbits'

mansion, now filled with dogs, I took it nice and slow downhill so they could keep up, and when I got into the room, I'd called Louie.

What with eight or ten changes of sheets on some of the beds every day, the Snor-Mor wasn't quite in the Ritz-Carlton league, but it had my two minimum deliverables: a king-size bed, since I'm almost six-four, and some adjoining pairs of rooms with a door linking them, probably intended for moms and dads whose kids were too old to sleep in the same room but too young to want to sneak out on their own. The situation, in other words, that Kathy and I would be in with Rina if we were still married. So the watchers had seen me go into room 204, and twenty minutes later, Louie had gone into the room next door, 203, which I'd left dark. He'd pretended to screw around with a key while I opened the door from the inside, backing out of sight as he came in, and then we'd turned on the light.

"Around the block, right?" Louie said as I followed him into 203.

"And about five or six cars back," I said. I turned off the light and counted out loud to three, and Louie went out, pulling the door closed behind him. I heard his steps on the stairs, and a minute later the eight-cylinder roar of the reconditioned Pontiac Firebird he'd chosen for the night's work. Like a lot of crooks, Louie was both a conservative and a patriot. With eight or nine cars stashed in various garages, available for very short-term lease to any thug who needed one for the night, he'd never once bought Japanese.

Persuading myself I just needed to give Louie some time, I turned the television back on, sat on the end of the bed, and watched the end credits of the show, behind which Thistle Downing scraped some imaginary bubble-gum off the sole of her shoe and then tried to get rid of it after it got stuck between her thumb and index finger. She must have found eight ways to approach it in ninety seconds. I had a feeling they just gave her the basic idea, told her how much time they needed for the credit roll, pointed the camera at her, and turned on the tape while she made the whole thing up on the spur of the moment. She finally returned the gum to the sole of her shoe, which accepted it immediately. Then she limped out of the room, the shoe sticking to the floor at every step. The camera froze her as her foot came right out of the shoe and her sock fell off.

And Louie was right. She was a couple of years away from being beautiful.

So was my daughter.

I wasn't feeling very good about myself.

I shook it off and grabbed the keys to the rented van, which I needed to return, but that could wait. I could have taken my own car, but it probably would have confused my followers. They hadn't seemed very good at tailing, and I didn't want to drive around looking for them if they got off to a bad start and made a wrong turn or something. I stepped out onto the second-story walkway, the July heat still hanging around to surprise me, stood there for a minute to make sure I'd been noticed, and trotted on down the stairs.

When I nosed out onto Sherman Way, I saw the two of them duck down, thereby fracturing Rule Number One: *Sudden movement attracts attention*. Way behind them, halfway back to the corner, I saw Louie's black Firebird idling in front of a bus bench. I waited until there was a nice big safe space between me and the nearest oncoming car, and pulled out.

Bingo, headlights behind me. And behind that, Louie's headlights. All we needed now was some paparazzi trailing us to make the motorcade complete. The DON'T WALK sign at the intersection ahead of me began to blink, so I lifted my foot from the accelerator and waited for it to go yellow. As I slowed for the red, my cell phone rang.

"Are these guys smooth, or what?" Louie asked.

"You mean, aside from how close they're sticking?"

"They got an expired plate. Talk about amateur hour."

"Well, they've been with me since about four o'clock, so it's amateur night."

"Long as we're talking, I got a nice clean Cadillac Escalade you might like. Only about 28K on it, and I could let you have it for twelve or thirteen thou."

"Twelve, or thirteen?" I asked, trying to dodge the reflection in the rear-view mirror. In addition to everything else, my followers had their brights on.

"Thirteen," Louie said.

"What happened to twelve?"

"That was a figure of speech."

The light changed, and I accelerated, slowly and deliberately, into the intersection. My little parade trailed along behind me.

"You said *clean*," I said. "I see that in the used-car ads all the time. What does it mean?"

"*Clean* means the front end is still on and it's got four wheels. *Real clean* means it wasn't trucked up from New Orleans after spending six weeks under water."

"I don't know," I said, putting on my turn signal and tapping the brakes to get my followers' attention. I did a hand signal, too. "I've never seen myself in a Cadillac."

"You got a negative self-image, you know that?"

"I could introduce you to a girl named Janice, and you guys could talk about it."

"Alice would love that." Alice was Louie's famously possessive wife, who seemed to think her husband, all five feet of him with his eight-inch comb-over, was the world's only serious competition to Brad Pitt. "You're turning, huh?"

"How'd you know?"

"You got that fuckin' thing blinking about three hundred yards is how."

"Coming up. I'll turn right—"

"Thanks for the tip."

"—and then go a couple of blocks, then make a left into Westwind Circle. You know what to do."

"I knew what to do when I was twelve."

"Here goes," I said, turning.

Louie said, "Whee."

The people who built the Valley's housing tracts were infatuated with circles, streets that end in a nice, decorative, round dead-end with the houses facing each other across it. The thinking was that a circle meant no through traffic, so kids could play safely, people could keep an eye on each other's houses, and there was less likelihood of drive-bys by members of minority groups. Now, of course, the minority groups live there, driving by to get into their garages.

The nice thing about Westwind Circle, from the perspective of this particular exercise, was that it didn't *look* like a circle. It dog-legged right before the circle became visible, although I was beginning to think the people behind me would have dutifully followed me into a ten-foot long cul-de-sac with DEAD END blinking in red neon on the corner. It was almost enough to make me feel guilty about tricking them. Still, something worth starting, as my mother always said, was worth finishing. And anyway, it was taking my mind off of Thistle Downing.

I turned right, did a nice slow putt-putt until the dogleg, and then accelerated around it. I was sitting there at the curb, facing out, by the time the Chevy entered the circle, hurrying to keep up. It slowed as the driver undoubtedly surveyed the situation, and then it stopped. The car sat there, idling, with its brights still on, and then the tail-lights lit up as the driver put the car into reverse. But suddenly Louie's black Firebird was pulled across the road, blocking the way.

They had nowhere to go.

I got out of the van.

The Chevy backed up a few feet and stopped. Then the front tires turned toward my right, almost ninety degrees, and the car jumped forward with an ululating squeal that probably came from a loose fan belt. The car turned sharply, crossed the circle, jumped the curb, and hopped the sidewalk onto someone's nicely maintained lawn. Then it cut back toward the opening of the circle, so it was facing out. Suddenly, it stopped as though it had hit a glass wall. The engine revved, and the car went forward about two inches and stopped again, before going back a couple of inches and then forward again. I couldn't see any mud or sand, but it looked very much as though the rear wheels were stuck in something.

I started walking, and the driver stopped gunning the engine. All of a sudden I wished I were carrying a gun. I stopped, thinking about it. I had no idea who was behind that wheel, and while whoever it was had no serious tailing skills, that was no guarantee that he or she wouldn't be very good at shooting someone. Different people have different talents.

Oh, well. I held both hands up, palms out, about hip-high. At least I could reduce the odds they'd shoot in what they thought was self-defense. The car rocked forward and back one more time, and subsided. Still stuck, apparently.

It seemed to take three or four minutes for me to cross the circle, although it couldn't have been more than thirty seconds. I moved to my right to get the headlights out of my eyes, and kept coming. When I was about eight feet away, two faces turned toward me, and I stopped cold.

*Girls.* The driver was, to be generous, fourteen. The passenger, whom I had thought was sitting way down in the seat, had in fact been sitting bolt upright. She was eight if she was a day. As I stood there, recalculating everything about the encounter, the driver slowly nodded: once, twice, and then a third time.

On the third nod, two left hands came up in perfect unison with the middle finger extended in the universal blow-off salute, and the car's rear wheels spun, throwing someone's nice lawn and dirt in an arc ten feet long. The Chevy leaped forward, plowed through a hedge, knocked over a mailbox, clipped the rear of Louie's Firebird, sending it into a half-spin, and burned rubber into the night.

**11**

Candles

Louie and I left the scene within ninety seconds in the van. The Firebird wasn't drivable, but there was nothing in it to trace it to Louie. Porch lights had been snapping on all the way around Westwind Circle, and I could hear sirens in the distance.

"I *liked* that car," Louie said. "Put a lot of work into that engine."

"Other engines will manifest," I said poetically as I looked for flashing red lights. "Engines abound."

"Fuck that noise," Louie said. "Detroit iron, eight cylinders. That stuff don't grow on trees." He sucked on his teeth, then laughed. "They gotcha, didn't they, with that *ohmigod my car's stuck* routine."

"Yes, Louie. If it helps to comfort you for the loss of the Firebird, they got me." I cut the wheel sharply left to get us onto a through street.

"Who were they?"

"Mexican guys. Never saw them before." I was not about to tell Louie that I'd been suckered, and his favorite car destroyed, by a couple of girls whose combined ages would barely let them buy a drink.

"Were they carrying?"

Colored pencils, maybe, I thought. A three-ring notebook or

two, cocked and ready to fire. "If they were, they didn't point it at me."

"Didn't have to. You did everything except offer them a push."

We turned onto Sherman Way. "Sorry about the car," I said.

"Aaaahhhhh," Louie said. "It was almost worth it. You standing there with your hands up while they hit the booster rockets." He laughed again. "Guy drove like a fuckin' teenager," he said.

I said, "Didn't he." I dug into my front pocket and brought my hand out with diamonds dripping from my fingers. "I figure this is worth thirty to forty, fenced. Take it, and we'll call it even."

Louie took the necklace and turned it over a couple of times, checking the backs of the settings. "That's a lot better than even. I'd owe you. This good, you think?"

"Good enough to be all by itself in a wall safe."

"Yeah?"

"You might want to fence it carefully."

He turned to look at me, all the colored lights of the street blazing in the diamonds' cold crystalline hearts as they hung from his hand. "*Whose* wall safe?"

"Well," I said. "Rabbits Stennet's. It belongs to his wife."

"Holy shit," Louie said, practically throwing the necklace at me. "Bunny's? Get it away from me." He rubbed his hands together as though to wipe off any traces of contact. "If I fenced that thing in Timbuktu, Rabbits would know."

"Nice piece," I said.

"I ain't met her, but that's what everybody says."

"I meant the necklace."

"Yeah, and it might as well be radioactive."

I checked the mirror, just in case. They weren't behind me, and I found I missed them. "So I'll use it as a paperweight," I said.

**Just to be** on the safe side, I checked into a Travelodge in Encino. I doubted that *the girls,* as I was coming to think of them, were likely to come around and kick in my door, but they knew where I'd been sleeping. I don't usually let people know where I'm sleeping.

Not that I did much sleeping that night.

I'd seen a lot of lighted windows, on both sides of the streets we'd driven down, and glowing in the houses that looked onto Westwind Circle. Lighted windows aren't my favorite thing, although I can usually deal with them. There's something about those warm yellow rectangles, with the unavoidable implication that there are families inside, still whole and complete, safe and comfortable, living by the rules and loving each other. I know it's not always that way, I know that terrible things can happen in a lighted window, but that's not what I see. What I see is one of the candles that holds the world together. When the world seems to be running along as it should, which it is most of the time in the part of it I'm lucky enough to live in, I sometimes think of it as held together by millions of people just doing their best, looking out for each other, keeping their promises. Nothing heroic, nothing dramatic, just plain everyday goodness. And when I'm thinking this way I see the structure of the world as an enormous palace made of light, with the walls and floors and ceilings held in place by the energy from millions of candles, and all those candles are in the hands of people who are doing the things they should, the little tiny things they told each other they'd do. And I'm somewhere outside, looking for a dark window I can break in through.

Especially since the divorce.

Like I say, I can usually deal with it. But in the Travelodge's king size bed that night, I had Thistle Downing on my mind, and it didn't make me feel even a little bit like someone carrying a candle.

**"Three Wishes," Rodd** Hull said, so proudly he might have thought of it himself. "Three films, one film for each of the wishes. Taken together," he said, framing the rectangle of a motion picture screen with his thumbs and index fingers and panning the room with it, "taken together, they comprise a complete arc in the life of a modern-day woman. An arc that takes her from repression to empowerment." He sat back, picked up a paper cup full of coffee with his pinky extended, and waited for people to fall out of their chairs.

I said, "Wow."

"Get to basics," Trey Annunziato said.

Rodd Hull looked disappointed. He wore a photographer's vest with more pockets than a pool table, a meticulously wrinkled linen shirt, and jeans that had been pressed to a razor-sharp crease. Around his neck was a lanyard dangling one of those incredibly expensive little viewfinders that cameramen sometimes wear when they're not sure everyone on the set knows how important they are. Rodd Hull, I had learned on Google the previous evening, had once received an Emmy nomination for daytime drama, which I guess meant soap operas. He was obviously determined to see this as a step up.

"Actually," I said to Trey. "I'd like at least to get the framework. The main, um, story elements, the other characters, sort of who's who. Might help me see the production's weak spots, from a security perspective. Maybe anticipate problems."

Trey looked at her watch for the fourth time in the ten minutes we'd been in the room. "It's your morning," she said. "Did you know that Rodd almost won an Emmy?"

I expressed suitable awe and amazement, and Rodd got to practice looking modest.

"What's so thrilling," Rodd said, only slightly grimly, "is that we're using an entirely new modality to tell the story. Sex. When you think about the women's movement, it's obvious that it's always been basically about sex. The great metaphor: *Woman on the bottom*. It applied to everything, but it began in the bedroom."

"Not in my bedroom, it didn't," said Tatiana Himmelman. Tatiana, four feet tall, three feet wide, wearing a well-waxed flattop and jeans festooned with chains, was the production supervisor, the person responsible for making sure that everything necessary to the day's filming was in place: performers, props, set elements, crew, everything. In other words, she did the actual work.

"Let's not think about your bedroom, Tat," Rodd Hull said. "It's just too grim."

"As opposed to yours, Rodd," Tatiana said, "which uses the old set from *Romper Room*."

Trey said, "Children. Play in a time-efficient manner, please. We have a movie here that's already two days behind schedule, and every day costs me about twenty-one thousand dollars." She got up and went to the chalkboard at the front of the room, which was actually a three-walled set built to impersonate a high school classroom for reasons I preferred not to speculate about. Tatiana and I were crammed into desks in the front row while Rodd Hull sat on the edge of the teacher's desk in front of the chalkboard. Trey, wearing a golden dog-collar today, along with a pale yellow silk business suit that would have turned heads at a Braille convention, had been leaning against a wall until the squabbling prompted her into motion. Three of her hard guys, one of whom was Eduardo, bristled at the world in the corners. All of them bulged in the obvious places. Eduardo was obviously thrilled at being taken for a walk. He was wearing black leather gloves as though to conceal the tiny biceps in his fingers.

Trey picked up a piece of chalk and said, "Here are your basics." She drew three horizontal lines on the board, each about two feet long, stacking one above the other, but staggering them so that the second line began below the one-quarter point in the top line, and the third line began a quarter of a way into the second. Next to the top line, Trey wrote, "First Wish." She wrote "Second Wish" next to the second line and, apparently getting impatient with the process, put the number "3" next to the bottom line. "This is our time line," she said.

It looked like this:

"First Wish"      _____

  "Second Wish"      _____

    "3"                     _____

"Each of these lines is one of the movies," she said. "The staggered lines represent start dates. You can get plot details and arches—"

"Arcs," Rodd Hull said.

"I'm paying for them," Trey said, "and I'll call them whatever I want." She waited to see whether Rodd would respond, but he found something that needed to be viewed through his viewfinder, and he viewed it.

Trey drew a dot roughly in the middle of the top line. "This is about where we'll be tomorrow morning, roughly nine weeks into the process. We've used all the time until now getting the scripts right, doing the schedules and the budgets, developing the graphics for the titles and the ads, because we're going to start advertising this movie long before we finish shooting it. We've hired Todd—sorry, Rodd—and Tatiana, and all the other talented people who will actually make the films. We've cast all the secondary parts, even the crowd scenes. And we've shot a bunch of second-unit stuff—cars in motion, the outsides of buildings, some scenes that don't have our star in them. And finally, we've done some doubles work, by which I mean using a double for Thistle, wearing Thistle's wardrobe—mostly shot from the back, walking on sidewalks, going through doors, getting onto elevators, and so forth." She lowered the hand with the chalk in it and looked over at Rodd. "What have I forgotten?"

"Nothing whatsoever," Rodd said. "Absolutely nothing. Brilliant, just brilliant."

"We also designed and built the sets," Tatiana said without

a glance at Rodd. "We identified and locked the locations. We leased the equipment we're shooting with. We hired the publicist and the still man."

"Thank you, Tatiana," Trey said. Then, to me, she said, "And all of that hasn't given us one second of what we're all here to do, which is to get a single frame of film on Thistle Downing. And here's where it gets hairy."

She put the chalk on the dot in the top line and drew a vertical straight down so it intersected the other two horizontals. Then she measured off about another eight inches, made another dot on the top line, and drew another vertical line straight down.

Now it looked like this:

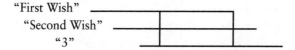

"First Wish"
"Second Wish"
"3"

"This is it," she said. "This little bit of space between those two vertical lines. This is the twelve-day period when we live or die. This period, which begins *tomorrow morning*, everybody, is the window of time during which we have Miss Thistle Downing in our sights, and I mean that literally. She's going to be here, she's going to be babysat every second of the day and night, and she's going to work her ass off, twenty-four hours straight, if necessary. And when we see the last of her, right about *here*"— She tapped the top of the second vertical line—"we'll be finished with every scene she does in all three movies."

"Why stack it like that?" I asked.

"Because," Rodd Hull said, "Miss Downing is a piece of work the likes of which you have never had to experience, if life has been kind of you. Remember that cute little kid? Well, forget about her. What's going to walk in here tomorrow morning is the kind of thing that makes Catholic priests think about exorcism. Which is not to say," he added hurriedly, with a nervous glance at Trey, "that she isn't beautiful. Made up just right, shot carefully, lighted perfectly, with lots of soft-focus in the close-ups—the *facial* close-ups, anyway—people will recognize her."

"What about that sore on her lip?" Trey demanded.

"The good news is that Doc says it's not herpes. The bad news is that it's going away at its own rate, which is slower than we'd like. So for the first couple of days, she's Claudette Colbert."

Trey said, "Who?"

"Movie star from the thirties and forties. She was pathologically convinced that the left side of her face was her good side. People called her right profile 'the dark side of the moon.'"

"It's not that bad," Tatiana said. "Poor little chickie, she's taking in like exactly zero vitamins. I'm not surprised she's got a couple of sores here and there."

"A little sunlight wouldn't hurt, either," said Rodd Hull. "She probably hasn't seen her shadow in years."

"Well, just stop piling on," Tatiana said. "She's not, like, dead, you know. You think she won't pick up on this attitude? Anyway, there's more talent scattered on the floor after she gets her hair cut than you've demonstrated in your entire career."

"Well, of course, she's our little *star*," Rodd Hull said, his eyebrows practically at his hairline. "We'll strew petals at her feet."

I was well into developing a strong dislike for Rodd Hull.

"Good idea," Trey said. "Tatiana. Tonight send a couple of gnomes to three or four flower shops. Tell them to buy the oldest flowers in the place, the stuff that's going to get tossed. They should try to get a deal. I want those flowers stripped of petals, and I want those petals in buckets—no, in big gift boxes—at 8:30 tomorrow morning. Eduardo," she said. "Make a note for me to find out about the profitability of flower shops, maybe a change of pace for dope dealers. We can build a chain. What should we call it, Mr. Bender?"

"Todd, I mean Rodd, here, already named it," I said. "Petals at Her Feet."

**12**

Tatiana

"It's about what you'd figure," Tatiana said. She was folding a restaurant napkin into a tight, tiny square. "Take an eighteen-year-old girl, give her no education because she worked six days a week from the time she was seven until she was fifteen. Make her as sensitive as a fern, and throw in an absolute beast of a mother who's trying to rip her off and a brother who hates her because she's famous. Then give her an almost unlimited amount of money and no one to say no to her. Dig up a crowd of parasites, some of whom are her relatives, to sue her for big chunks of the money. Add unimaginable amounts of cocaine, methedrine, ice, and, for all I know, heroin, and a bunch of bloodsucking motherfuckers who pretend to be her friends so she'll keep buying dope for them. Let her trust them and believe they care about her, so they'll be able to break her heart when the money runs out. Close the doors on all that and leave it to cook for five years. Then let her stagger out into the sunlight, broke, friendless, strung out, and unable to tell up from down. Uninsurable in an industry that won't cut a fart without taking out a policy. Bingo: You've got Thistle Downing."

"This year's model," I said.

"That fucker Rodd," she said. She tore the napkin in half. "Goddamn television directors. What have they got? The best technical crews and the best journeyman actors in the world.

Pretty good writing, as good as they could appreciate, anyway. And it's all about *them*, the genius directors. They're fucking *auteurs*. D.W. Griffith, Murnau, von Stroheim. Nobody as vulgar as Hitchcock or Spielberg."

"I'd like to feed him his viewfinder."

"He's too dumb to know that Thistle, whatever shape she's in, is the most talented person he's ever been in a room with. If she hadn't fucked herself up, she could be one of the biggest stars in the world. I mean, she could have been on a career path that would have kept her working until she was eighty. Instead, here she is, doing . . ." She crumpled the napkin with both hands and threw the wad over her shoulder, and went, "Puh."

We were at a coffee shop on Ventura, about a mile from Palomar Studios, the complex Trey had bought and was using for *Three Wishes*. Trey had gone back to adding assets to her newly legitimate empire, and Rodd was probably looking at his reflection through the viewfinder. A couple of people from the crew were due to join us and bring me up to speed on what had been happening, but Tatiana was still steaming from the encounter with Rodd.

"And what's with that second 'D'?" she said, loudly enough that people were looking at her. "One isn't enough? Maybe we ought to pronounce it that way. Hi, Rod-d. Morning, Rod-d. Or start doing it to other words. That's rid-diculous. Sorry, Rod-d, I d-didn't hear you. Honestly, Rod-d, d-don't you think that's red-dund-dant?"

"Do it with other letters," I suggested. "F-frankly, Rod-d, I d-don't give a d-damn."

Tatiana started to laugh, and then cut it off. "Why do I trust you?" she said, leaning forward across the table to look at me more closely.

I'm not actually fond of being looked at closely, but I held my ground. "Got me. Why shouldn't you?"

"I don't know anything about you." She picked at a cuticle,

and I noticed that they'd all been worked ragged. "This movie, if you can call it a movie, has more intrigue behind the cameras than the Italian Renaissance. I know you're with Trey, who I sort of like, but as we all know, she's made out of ice. I guess I don't know which side you're on."

"If there's a side that wants to see Thistle treated like a human being, that's the side I'm on."

"That's better than nothing," she said. "Rod-d would run over her with a truck if he thought it would cap a scene."

"And you don't like that."

"I like talent. There's never enough of it. I grew up with her. On TV, I mean. She's one of the best things I ever saw, and she did it week after week, up to those last couple of years."

"What happened then?"

She shook her head. "I don't know. She ran out of steam. She'd been, and I hate to use this word because nobody ever means it, but she'd been unique. Even the last couple of years, she was better than most actresses on their best day. And then there's the movie itself. It's bad enough that she has to be making this piece of shit without her being treated like a bagged-out crack whore."

"I'm with you."

"Not that it's a *total* piece of shit," she said. "I'll give it to Trey. I've worked on real porno, and this isn't it. I mean, she got an actual writer, she got Rodd, who, for all that he's the dickwad of the century, has directed some good actors. She got a cameraman—camerawoman, I mean—Lauren Wister, who's shot a couple of independent features, and I think it'll be easier for Thistle with a woman behind the camera. And the second-line people—me, Craig-Robert, whom you'll meet in a minute, a bunch of others—well, we're pretty good. Trey's probably dropping five, six million on this thing. The average budget for porn is lower than most home movies."

"That's one of the reasons Trey's wound so tight," I said.

"But even with all that money, and people who know how to do their jobs, the thing that scares me senseless—" She broke off and looked past me, and I turned to see two people come in to the coffee shop, one a worried-looking young woman in her early twenties and the other a play-it-to-the-rafters African American queen with orange hair and honeybee yellow lips, wearing a kelly green semitransparent scarf that swirled around him dramatically as he made what was, apparently for him, the newest in an unending succession of grand entrances.

"How astonishingly dreary," he announced while he was still eight feet away. "Couldn't we think of *anything* more middle class? All we need is a tailgate party in the parking lot, and a nice mug of beer, and I'll hit high C, and aren't *you* the tall one? Where's your basketball, or do you only play at night?"

"Craig-Robert Loftus," Tatiana said. "This is Junior Bender. And Junior, the girl sort of lost in Craig-Robert's blinding aura is Ellie Wynn."

"*Oh, my God*," Craig-Robert said, placing a splayed hand in the center of his chest. "You're that *criminal*. Well, I have to say it: Crooks do furnish a room. You've certainly dressed *this* dump." He sat next to me. "Scoot over," he said. Then he said, "Not *that* far."

"Ellie works with me," Tatiana said, as the young woman sat down. "And she's also Thistle's double. Craig-Robert, in case you hadn't guessed already, is the costume designer."

"Costum*er*," Craig-Robert corrected her. "Nice plaid shirt, by the way, Tatty. Did it belong to one of the members of Nirvana?"

"Fuck off, C-R. We've just had an hour of Rodd, and we're in no mood for more drama."

"*Rodd*," Craig-Robert said in italics. "Such an inappropriate name for someone who's probably hung like a mosquito."

"*Are* you a criminal?" Ellie Wynn asked. She was slight, almost childish, with foxlike features that had something vaguely feral about them, something that suggested a small animal that hadn't learned to trust people. There are people who radiate well-being and people who radiate misery. Ellie Wynn radiated insecurity.

"Oh, please," Craig-Robert said. "Weren't you listening yesterday? Miss Trey—swell outfit this morning, by the way—Miss Trey said she'd be bringing in a *specialist* to deal with The Problem. And we're all aware that Trey, for all that she'd look good wearing a bookshelf, is a crook. I mean, is there someone here who does *not* get a paper?" He choked the flow long enough to look at me. "I must say, though, that I was expecting something more lethal looking, maybe with sallow skin and dead eyes— you know dead eyes? Like this." He dropped his lids halfway.

A young waitress who had ignored us thus far came over to the table, pad in hand, mainly to get a better look at Craig-Robert, and Tatiana said, "Keep the coffee away from this man."

"Uh, sure," the waitress said, and her accent briefly filled the air with the scent of Georgia peach blossoms. "What y'all want to—"

But Tatiana was already talking.

"Bring us five chef's salads, all in a big bowl in the middle of the table. That way, Ellie can eat around the meat and Craig-Robert can hog the avocados."

"Um, gosh" the waitress said, "Ahm not sure ah can—"

"Sure you can," Tatiana said. "You're not on Walton Mountain any more. You know the chef's salad? Eight-ninety-five on the menu? You know those big bowls in the kitchen your illegal immigrant staff uses to mix things up in? Put five chef's salads in one of those bowls and bring it here. Write five chef's salads on your little pad. Bring us five plates. What could be easier?"

"Um, okay."

Craig-Robert said, "Don't you want to tell her what order to put the utensils in?"

"Why bother?" Tatiana said. "You'll eat with your fingers anyway."

"And, uh, drinks?" the waitress said, speaking only to Tatiana. "Y'all want—"

"Diet Coke for me and the lady next to me, regular Coke for the Queen of Spades there, and Junior?"

"Coffee, black." To Tatiana, I said, "Is there someone here I can't see?"

"Sorry?" She was watching the waitress retreat.

"Five plates. Four people."

"I arranged for Doc to come by as soon as he gets back."

"Back from where?"

"From Thistle's place."

"Ah. And you," I said to Ellie. "You're a vegetarian?"

"Um," Ellie said. She was clearly flustered by the question, which had seemed relatively harmless to me. "I try, you know, not to eat anything that's got, like, a spinal cord? Except fish, I guess. They've got a spinal cord, don't they, Tatiana?" She was blushing.

"They do," Tatiana said, a bit wearily. "But they are too dumb to know they've got one, so that makes it okay, wouldn't you say, Junior?"

"*Junior?*" Craig-Robert said, looking terrifically interested. "What ghastly secret does that mask?"

"None," I said. "It's my name. My father was named Merle and he wanted his son named after him, but he'd had a skinful of being named Merle and he wasn't about to hang it on me. So he just named me Junior."

"Mmmmm," Craig-Robert said. "So what are your qualifications? Aside from the obvious ones, I mean."

"Got me. I have some history with Trey, I guess. And she seems to think I might be her little trouble-shooter. But to tell you the truth, I've got almost no idea why I'm here."

"The human condition," Craig-Robert said. "*None* of us know. You need someone sensitive to explain it all to you."

Tatiana rapped on the table. "Craig-Robert, if you could put all the fabulous on hold for a few minutes?"

"Certainly," Craig-Robert said in a deep radio announcer's voice. He crossed his hands on the table in front of him in a businesslike manner and said, "You're probably wondering why I called you here tonight."

"My life is passing before my eyes," Tatiana said.

"It's to clear up the age-old question: Why are gay men so fascinating and gay women so grim?"

"Maybe because you're imitating the *interesting* sex," Tatiana said. "We're stuck with acting like men."

"We really don't have a lot of time?" Ellie Wynn said, phrasing it as a question. "We need to eat and get back? Everything, and I mean everything, has to be ready for tomorrow."

"What's gone wrong so far?" I asked.

"Little things," Tatiana said. "But obviously intentional."

"Costumes," Craig-Robert said. "Ergo, *moi* being invited to this confab. Four costumes disappeared. And you may say, *so what?*, but there was something *very interesting* about the choice of costumes."

"And you're going to make him ask what it is, aren't you?" Tatiana said.

"What it *is*," Craig-Robert said, "is, A, they were all for Thistle, and B, they had all been worn by little Miss Ellie here in second-unit shots." Ellie blinked at the sound of her name as though someone had thrown a dinner roll at her.

"Which means?" I said.

"Which means they all had to be replaced with identical stuff," Tatiana said. "Otherwise, you'd see Thistle from behind wearing a gray dress as she pushes open a door and then, when you cut to inside the building and she comes in, she'd be wearing, I don't know, a pink one for example."

"Pink doesn't work for Thistle," Craig-Robert said.

"Oh, who gives a fuck?" Tatiana said. "I said, *for example*. It's not going to endanger your Golden Pecker or whatever they call the adult film Oscar."

"*Le Peqoir d'or*," Craig-Robert said. "And I have a place all ready for it."

"And those were the only costumes taken," Ellie said, looking vaguely surprised at the sound of her own voice. "The ones I'd worn on film, pretending to be Thistle. Which meant that we either had to re-shoot, or remake the costumes. Right, Craig-Robert?"

"So you remade them."

"It wasn't *quite* that easy," Craig-Robert said. "We're scheduled down to our hineys. It put us back by a full day."

"Trey said two days," I said.

"We'd actually be three days behind if people hadn't busted their butts to catch things up," Tatiana said. "Tell him, Ellie."

"Oh." She took a second to organize her thoughts. "Umm, two days ago, I got a call at seven-forty-five A.M., just as I was about to head for the set. It was a girl, telling me that the location had changed? We weren't going to be shooting in Hollywood, she said, we'd moved it to a shopping mall in Chatsworth. I should leave immediately, because the crew was on their way there."

"And?" I said.

"And, um, the crew was right where they were supposed to be. You know, in Hollywood. But by the time they wondered where I was and called me, I was all the way out in the Valley and I'd gone into the mall to find the closed store we were supposed to be shooting in. And then, when I got the call on my cell phone and went back outside, someone had slashed my tires."

"Cost us a day," Tatiana said. "Then yesterday, it was Lauren, the camera operator, who got the call. Toted herself halfway down to Torrance before it occurred to her that it might be bogus. And by then she was in total rush hour, just gridlock all the way back up. Just like whoever it was planned it. Half a day gone."

"Here y'all go," the young waitress said. She leaned forward with a grunt and put a massive bowl in the middle of the table. Behind her was another girl with five plates. "Will that do it?" the waitress asked.

"Fluids, dear," Tatiana said. "We would all like to take in some fluids."

"The Cokes, huh?" the waitress said, crestfallen.

"And one coffee," Tatiana said brightly. "There's a good girl."

"She fancies you," Craig-Robert said as the waitress retreated.

"She's straighter than Nebraska," Tatiana said. Ellie's eyes went back and forth between them, her mouth half-open as though she wanted to join in but didn't trust herself to say anything interesting.

"So, not to be boring," I said, "but whatever's up, it's being caused by someone who has access to the costumes, who knows which outfits have been filmed already, who knows where the crew is shooting each day, who has or is able to get everybody's phone number, and is also capable of slitting four tires in broad daylight in the parking lot of a busy shopping mall. Does that sound right?"

Tatiana thought for a moment and then nodded.

"And," I asked, "who has that kind of access?"

"Sweetie," Craig-Robert trilled, "*all* of us."

# 13

## Achilles Heel

"I'm looking at this the wrong way," I said. Craig-Robert had departed in a swirl of psychic drama with Ellie trailing along in his wake like a towed rowboat. That left Tatiana and me facing about twenty-six pounds of avocado-free chef's salad. Tatiana had been right; Craig-Robert had located, and eaten, every single piece. Ellie had concentrated on lettuce and the anchovies, once Tatiana had told her they were too small to have a spine.

"*What's* the wrong way?" Tatiana said, making a little lettuce house on her plate.

"Points of access. There are too many of them, and too many people can walk right through them. By the time I checked out everybody, the movie would either be abandoned or in the can."

She mashed the roof with her fork. "So what's the right way?"

"Before I get to that, there are two other questions to ask. First, how far is this person willing to go? Are we talking about people being in danger? And second, if we decide people aren't in danger now, at what point will they be? And then we get to the big question. Since the stuff we've seen so far hasn't worked, and it's been sort of frittering around the edges—missing costumes, mixed-up crew calls—where's the *real* pressure point? Where would damage be fatal to the movie?"

"As far as danger is concerned," Tatiana said, "The way I

understand it, half the crooks in the Valley—nothing personal—want the picture to tank so they can get rid of Trey. I think those people could be considered dangerous. I mean, they're sort of dangerous for a living."

"Okay," I said, "let's do something that's rarely useful. Let's divide the world into two groups of people. Over on one side you've got a bunch of guys whose necks are thicker than their thighs, and they want the movie to fail so Trey will go down and they can go back to boosting cars and breaking legs. Yeah, those folks are dangerous. And over here you've got a bunch of movie people who presumably want the filming to go on so they'll continue to get paid. And they're, theoretically, at least, less dangerous. And somewhere between those two types of people is one of three things: a movie person who wants the movie to fail, which I think is unlikely; a crook who can work his or her way in among the movie people, which is almost equally unlikely; or a movie person who's been promised a big bouquet of money if the movie shuts down. That's likely, and that person is not very dangerous."

"Until," Tatiana said.

"Exactly right. When, if ever, will it become dangerous? Everything that's been done so far looks like it was the work of a movie person under pressure, except maybe the tire slashing. So figure a movie person made the phone call to Ellie, who seems to be suggestible, to say the least—"

"If I were casting the role of Second Lemming, it would go to Ellie."

"Okay, so a movie person phoned Ellie, and the crook in charge—whoever promised all that money—dispatched some thug with a knife to slash the tires. The *until* is obviously the point at which the person behind the scenes feels he or she has to take direct action."

She nodded. "And that would be when?"

"If Trey's diagrams this morning were straight, I'd say the

dangerous period will begin tomorrow morning. Up until now
they've been focused on screwing up the process so the company
wouldn't get to the point when Thistle starts to shoot her scenes,
but here you are. You've gotten there. And that takes us right
to the other question, the one about the movie's Achilles Heel,
which is—"

"Hold the thought," Tatiana said, getting up. "Here's Doc."

I turned to see Milburn Stone, the guy who played Doc in the
iconic TV series "Gunsmoke," limp into the coffee shop. Same
white hair, same drooping white mustache, even the string tie. It
wasn't until he was practically sitting down that I realized I was
looking at someone who bore a passing resemblance to Milburn
Stone and had decided to push it.

"This is Doc," Tatiana said. "Doc, Junior Bender. Junior's
working with Trey."

Doc nodded at me and said, so help me God, "Howdy."

"Howdy," I said. I raised my hand for the waitress. "Wet
your whistle, partner?"

"Sure thing, stranger," Doc said, and then grinned at me.
"Pretty good," he said. "Some people think I'm doing Walter
Cronkite."

"Y'all didn't finish your salad," the waitress said.

"You have a keen eye, Daughter of the South," Doc said.
"Gimme a beer."

"What kind?"

"Whatever leaps into your hand. I'd be a fool to turn my
back on fate when it comes in such a pretty package."

"Golly," the waitress said, and blushed. She backed away
from the table until she bumped into an empty chair.

"I may be an old fart," Doc said, "but, by God, I've got it."

"Oh, come on," Tatiana said. "She's still got grits in her
hair."

"And a discerning eye for men," Doc said.

"You've been with Thistle?" I asked.

"I have indeed, poor child."

"In what way?"

"In every way you could think of. Physically, she's under-weight, anemic, got half a dozen low-grade infections, several dangerous vitamin deficiencies, and a complete spectrum of full-on addictions. Emotionally, she's isolated, depressed, possibly suicidal, terrified of everything that moves. Spiritually, although that's not my normal territory, I'd say she's the sole inhabitant of Planet Zero, where the sky is black and the rivers are full of dead animals."

Tatiana looked stricken. Doc spread his hands and said, "You asked."

"Is she—Jesus, I hate to even ask this," Tatiana said. "Is she going to be able to work tomorrow?"

"It won't be anything you'd expect from having seen her on TV," Doc said. "She's going to get a good night's sleep because I gave her enough Xanax to knock out the mule our waitress rode to California. Tomorrow, I'm going to top her up with some mild amphetamines and a couple of tranquilizers. So she'll be awake and able to go where she's pointed. She'll probably be able to hit a mark if it's a really big mark. Dialog is going to have to be on cards, and whoever's holding them may have to wave to get her attention. I don't think old Rodd's going to get a lot of long takes. But I'm told it's an easy day, so she'll probably get through it."

I asked, "What kind of a doctor are you?"

"A disbarred one," Doc said, "with a practice that special-izes in the criminal community." He looked up as the waitress, blushing all over again, put a bottle of beer in front of him.

"I, uh, I brought you a glass," she said.

"In the middle of this chemical and mechanical wasteland," Doc said, "how refreshing to meet with a moment of unexpected grace. My dear, you make me think of village greens and little white courthouses."

"We had one of those," the waitress said. She looked at the rest of us. "Anything else I can do for y'all?"

"We're fine," Tatiana said. "Bye."

"With a lynching tree in front of it," Doc said after she was gone. "The courthouse, I mean. The South is so green and lush that you forget it's from the nitrogen in all that blood." He poured the beer carefully, tilting the glass to control the head, lifted it, and drank half of it down. "Before I lost my license," he said to me, "I was a pediatrician. That's good training, because you treat everything. And that's pretty much what Thistle's got, everything."

"Why'd you lose your license?"

"What do you care?"

"Just thinking about Thistle," I said. "You're pumping her full of dope, and I don't know—"

"Young man," Doc said. "Thistle's system is cleaner right now than it's been in years. One of the reasons I sedate her is to keep her from going out and scoring some *really* deleterious shit. And don't go getting all protective about Thistle. She's not that amazing little girl you saw on television. She's a fucking mess. I'm going to get her through this, and then I'm going to sit her down with a couple of friends to try to get her straight, because if I don't—" He blinked heavily, finished the glass, and poured more. "If I don't," he said, "she's going to get paid at the end of the filming, and I think she'll go right out and kill herself. Some of the stuff she's been using, she might as well have been drinking Drano."

I said, "Mmm-hmm."

"I lost my license because I was an addict," Doc said, sounding irritated. "And that's another item on my resumé that makes me the right doctor for Thistle." He picked up the glass of beer. "See this? This is standing in for cocaine, barbiturates, methedrine, and horse. I walked away from all that, even though it turned me inside out and left me to dry, red and wet, in the sun.

Now I drink the occasional beer. A little cognac now and then. I know what she's going through. And I loved that little girl on TV, too. I'm not going to let anything happen to her."

"Other than this movie," Tatiana said.

Doc's hand stopped with the beer inches from his mouth. After a moment, he said, "Nothing I can do about that."

Tatiana said, "I really ought to quit."

"You should not," Doc said. "You should stay right where you are. Try to keep that child in one piece."

"Not to be insensitive, but we've all seen people who fucked themselves up," I said, "and it's very dramatic. And we've all got friends who are healthy now, when there was a time we didn't think they'd live through the week. How fragile is she, really?"

"Thistle Downing," Doc said, "is held together by cobwebs."

**"Doc's okay,"** Tatiana said. We were in her car, driving back to the studio. "He likes to talk, wants to write the great American novel, and he reads too much Faulkner. But he's okay."

"I'll take your word."

"You were saying something. When he came in, I mean. About the Achilles Heel or something."

"The right way to look at the problem," I said. "You're not going to like it."

She flipped up her indicator for the turn. "I don't much like any of it."

"It's all very well to steal costumes and send people to places where the crew isn't. But if you want to bring this movie down once and for all, there's only one thing you need to knock a hole in, and that's Thistle."

Tatiana said, with great feeling, "Oh, fuck."

"And you," I said. "You were going to tell me what scares you senseless."

"It's Thistle, again," she said. "I'm not sure she understands what kind of movie this is."

# 14
### Dead Wet Girls

"I need to hire someone to sit outside her apartment tonight," I said. "I know a guy who's perfect for the job. It'll run maybe three hundred fifty bucks."

"And you think this is necessary," Trey Annunziato said. She'd dumped the yellow outfit in favor of a one-piece, high-collared garment in black that looked like something that might be worn to a *Star Trek* funeral.

"Necessary? Only if you want to make your movie."

The head-tilted-to-one-side pose. "Because . . ."

"Because she's ground zero. If anything happens to her, you haven't got two sticks to rub together."

Trey was wearing long dangling earrings, little gold chains about four inches long with a good-size diamond at the end of each. One of the stones had tangled in her hair, and I watched the lazy expertise of her long fingers as she freed it. "Whom do you have in mind?"

"You don't need to know. Someone I trust. Someone who has nothing to do with your family or its operations. I can guarantee it."

"How can you guarantee that?"

"Because he's fully employed by a Chinese firm."

"Ah," Trey said.

We were back in the conversation area, having a conversation.

The password at the gate had been "buttercup," and I wondered if Trey was just having some fun. I had things to do, but I figured that fidgeting would just inspire her to prolong the chat, so I sat back and smiled.

"Fine," she said, once the earring was dangling free. "Do it."

"Do you know anything about a couple of girls? I mean really girls, one of them maybe fourteen, and the other under ten."

"No." Her lack of interest was palpable. "Why?"

"They followed me out of here yesterday."

"You were followed by children? And you couldn't lose them?"

"If I'd lost them," I said, "I wouldn't have gotten close enough to know they were children."

"Point taken. No, no idea. Maybe that's all they were, just kids, following you for fun."

"Maybe. Probably. Listen, do you really think Thistle can do this?"

The look I got went through me and continued right through the wall behind me. "Do what?"

"This movie."

For a moment, I didn't think she'd answer. Then she said, "Of course. Would I be shelling out money like this if I didn't think she could deliver?"

"Fine." I got up.

"Would you like to tell me what prompted that question?"

"The doctor says she's a mess. A couple of people on the production don't think she even realizes she's going to have to do sex."

"She's had the scripts," Trey said icily, "for six weeks."

"Having them and reading them aren't the same things."

"She'll do it," Trey said, and her face was practically rigid, "or I'll personally see that she's sitting on some curb in Hollywood with one hand out for change and the other trying to pick invisible bugs out of her skin."

My throat was suddenly tight. "Whereas if she does the movie, she can use both hands on the bugs and pick at them on the couch in some flophouse."

"How Thistle Downing chooses to live her life is not my responsibility. She could also take the money she's going to make and go clean herself up. And I have to say that I don't much like your tone."

"Sorry," I said.

"You haven't even met her, and you're already buying the *poor Thistle* legend. Would you be so consumed with pity if she were male? I doubt it. You'd think, what a jerk. But since it's a woman, you get all teary and turn her into a helpless little waif, battered by the big bad world. You know something? Crooks are the world's biggest sexists."

"I'm asking a question you should be asking yourself," I said. "Your movie depends on her."

"Do you think I haven't thought about this? I've done everything I can to make it easy. She starts with two days of dialogue, no nudity at all, much less sex. I'm willing to use a body double for some of the worst bits. She's got women all over the sound stage, and Rodd might as well be a woman for all the interest he has in the female sex. I've—we've—talked to her about the movie. I've done everything except tattoo the script on her arms, and I'd do that too if it wouldn't show on camera."

"Got it."

Now she was standing, too. "Remember which side you're on, Mr. Bender. Your job is to prevent this movie from getting derailed, and if that means keeping that little junkie on the beam, you'll do it. I don't know what Lyle and Wattles are squeezing you with, but I can't imagine it's very pleasant."

"I've enjoyed our chat," I said.

"I don't care one way or the other. What's your man going to be looking for tonight?"

"Trouble. Anyone who might want to borrow Thistle the

night before she's supposed to start working. And I'm going with Doc tomorrow morning when he picks her up."

After a moment, she said, "Good thinking. Wait a minute." She turned and said, "Eduardo."

And there he loomed: black-clad, servile, and dangerous, all at the same time. "Yes, Miss Trey."

"I need an X-acto knife."

"One second." He wheeled and left.

I watched him go. "Who says you can't get good help?"

Trey looked at me but her mind was elsewhere. "Your friend, he's competent?"

"He's a professional look-out man."

"Good." She favored me with a smile that didn't have much behind it. "Sorry if I got a little snappish. I've got a lot on my mind."

"You going to do the flower shops?"

"Too much wastage. The damn things die before you can sell them. Too fragile." One hand came up, palm out, in a *stop* gesture. "No parallels with Thistle Downing, please. No wilting blossom or fragility metaphors. Thank you, Eduardo."

She plucked a wicked-looking, silvery X-acto from his hand and went to the painting. It took her about five seconds to slice the face of the handsome, Byronic man out of the canvas. She did it quickly and expertly, leaving a face-shaped hole in the painting.

"Give this to your friend," she said, handing it to me. "Tell him to memorize this face, and if he sees the man who owns it, he should kill him."

I took it, said I'd pass the word along, and went to see my daughter.

**On Tuesday afternoons,** if I hadn't done anything to offend Kathy, such as calling too often or not calling enough, I got to take Rina out for a couple of hours. The fact that I got to see her at all was, in essence, an act of charity on Kathy's part. Throughout the separation proceedings, she never once played the card that I was a career criminal. She got custody, but she could also have had a restraining order to keep me away from Rina. The fact that she hadn't was something for which I was deeply grateful.

When I pulled up, my daughter was waiting in front of the house we all used to live in, just south of the Boulevard, which meant that I didn't have to see Kathy if she was there, or know that she'd left Rina alone, if she wasn't there.

"You've grown an inch in a week," I said as she climbed into the car.

"It's your genes," she said, settling in. "Mom's like normal size."

"She's actually short," I said, "but she makes up for it with the force of her will."

"I need ice cream," Rina said. She usually shies away from discussion of her mother, which shows that she's smarter than I am. I hope she also shies away from discussing me with Kathy.

"I think ice cream is achievable." My old neighborhood slid by, full of memories, some of them good. "Anyplace special?"

"Somewhere close. I have a lot of homework."

I signaled for a right without replying, and Rina said, "I really do. Don't get your feelings all hurt."

Of course, my feelings weren't hurt. I'm an adult. "What kind of homework?"

"Genetics."

"In sixth grade?"

"I'm accelerated, Dad. You know that."

"When I was in sixth grade we were looking at maps."

"When you were in sixth grade," Rina said, "most of the world hadn't even *been* mapped."

"Humor is a dominant trait," I said.

"Brown eyes, too. That pisses Mom off, that I got your eye color."

"Hard to imagine."

"What?" She reached for the radio and I gently intercepted her hand. I loved my daughter but I hated her music.

"Your mother being pissed off," I said, and then added "about eye color. But she's dominant in other ways."

"Mom's lawyer would call that alienating the child from the custodial parent," Rina said. "No music?"

"I meant it genetically, not emotionally."

She made a sound I could only interpret as a scoff, sort of a burst of air. "You did not."

"I did. Except for your eye color, you look just like her." And she did; every time I looked at her I saw the girl I'd fallen in love with for life when I was sixteen and she was fifteen. Kathy and I had stayed together through high school and through her college and my sort-of college, and then we'd gotten married. And stayed married until it became inescapable that one of us was going to have to change, and that it was going to be me, and that I couldn't. And none of it was anything I was proud of.

"You're as beautiful as she is," I said.

"Oh, I'm *so* beautiful," Rina said. "How come nobody except you notices?"

"If by 'nobody,' you mean the boys at school, I'm glad to hear it. You'll be fighting them off soon enough."

"So why no music?"

"If we could find something we both agreed was music, it'd be fine."

"No music, then." She lifted the metal flap on her seatbelt and let it snap closed. Then she did it again. "What are you up to?"

"Freelancing," I said. "Trying to stay out of houses with large dogs in them."

"One way to do that," she said, "would be not to go into houses that don't belong to you."

"Jesus," I said. "I'd probably end up watching television."

Rina said, "Millions of people do."

I turned right on Ventura, heading for 31 Flavors. Rina stole a look at me and said, "What happened to your face?"

"A chandelier exploded."

"You were under it?"

"Actually, I was swinging from it."

"See, this is one of the things that makes me different from my friends," she said. "When I ask them what their fathers do, they say something like banking or real estate. I say he swings on chandeliers in other people's houses and comes home looking like he donated blood with his face."

"Interesting guy."

She slumped down in her seat, the sit-on-the lungs posture of teenage discontent. "That's one way to look at it."

"Is there another?"

She rolled her window down and rolled it up again. Then she said, "Never mind."

I'm always happy to sidestep a real issue. "All right."

"Why'd you have to be so honest with me when I was little? Why couldn't you tell me you were a chef or something?"

"Well, I only work about two nights a month, for one thing. And it seemed like a good idea to tell you the truth."

"Maybe that's overrated."

"Telling the truth?"

"Let's drop it," she said. "You know what I'm talking about." She reached over and took my hand. "We don't see each other enough. I promise not to pick a fight."

"In that case," I said. "You can listen to whatever you want."

It took her less than five seconds to find something that sounded to me like a fender assembly plant being attacked by a bunch of guys with nail guns, but she nodded along with it. I decided to show her how much I loved her, so I reached over and turned it up.

Rina laughed, and I felt better than I had in days.

○ ○ ○

**"Remember how you** once told me that the most interesting questions about a society are the ones they don't ask?" Rina had a double-thick double-chocolate double-malt in front of her, so viscous she couldn't get it up the straw.

"The thought wasn't original with me, but I probably said it."

"So explain to me about Japanese horror movies."

"Not really one of my fields," I said. "But which ones? The old radioactive monsters—"

She shook her head as she dredged the straw through the shake and licked off the clump of glop that came up with it. She was wearing rimless glasses that I hadn't seen before, and it almost broke my heart that I hadn't known she had them. "No, those are easy to figure. The newer ones, you know, *Ring* and *Ju-On* and those."

"What's hard to figure? They're ghost stories."

"Yeah, sure, but what's with all the dead wet girls?"

"Ah. Dead wet girls. Well, first, they're ghost stories, right? The dead wet girls are ghosts."

"Dead wet girl ghosts."

"Lots of Asian cultures, the Chinese and the Japanese, anyway, believe that the ghost of someone who was wronged before death is especially dangerous. Women and girls in Japan are sort of repressed. They're relatively powerless. They can't take revenge during their lifetime, so they're more likely to bear a grudge after they're dead. So the ghosts are female. And as for dead, well, they're ghosts, so they're dead by default. And my guess is that they're young, meaning *girls*, because the audience for the movies is pretty much your age. So that gets you to dead girls."

"That's two out of three. And wet?"

"Well, that's probably something else. The movies are made

by men, and lots of men like to look at wet girls. You'll notice there aren't any movies about dead wet *ugly* girls."

"No. They're all dead wet pretty girls." She gazed out the window at the traffic on Ventura, and I studied her mother's bone structure, magically transferred to my daughter's face. She caught me looking when she turned back and gave me a smile that was all in the eyes before she returned her attention to the goop in her glass. "Do I ask you too many questions?"

"I dread the day you stop asking me questions. Why are you watching Japanese horror movies?"

"Mr. Miller, he's my drama teacher, he tells us to watch all sorts of stuff. Movies, old TV shows, even commercials. We're supposed to look at a lot of different ways people approach acting, and see if we can figure out what works and what doesn't, and why."

"Old TV shows?"

"Millions of them. TV's like a time machine. You can see how people acted all the way back in the fifties or the sixties. You know, like Lucy. Would Lucy get hired today?"

"If she wouldn't," I said, "I'm in a world I don't want to live in."

"Me, too. And the woman upstairs, Ethel. I wish we had a neighbor like Ethel."

"I'll bet if you stir that thing, you'll be able to drink it through the straw."

"That's no fun," she said, dragging the straw through it again.

"Have you ever watched a show, I don't know the name of it, with a little girl in it named Thistle Downing?"

"Oh, my God," Rina said, her face lighting up. "'Once a Witch.' Thistle Downing is like the queen of the world. We're doing a unit on comedy right now, and Mr. Miller assigned us to watch her and see why comedy is funnier when it's played completely seriously."

"And you liked her."

"Well *yeah.*" She just managed not to roll her eyes at the question. "She makes it look easy even when you know it's like the hardest thing in the world. And she was a really serious girl."

"You think so?"

She considered it for a moment, her eyes on the malt. "I think she was serious, yeah, but that's not exactly right. It was more like she was sad. You can see it sometimes, in the shows when she got a little older. When she was really little, it was like she didn't even know she was acting. Later, she sort of got a bunch of technique and she stopped showing you who she was underneath, but she looked sadder. I think I liked her best when she was younger. But I'll bet she was sad, even when she was a big star."

"You're a perceptive kid," I said.

Rina shook her head. "You know, Dad, only adults think of kids as kids."

"Yeah? What do kids think of kids as?"

"People," Rina said.

## 15
### Camelot Arms

In 1996, Li Bai Chen, an eighteen-year-old in Fujian, China, gave a few hard-earned *yuan* to a street vendor to buy a DVD that he thought was a bootleg of *Rush Hour*, starring Jackie Chan. When he got it home, it turned out instead to be a movie from the 1950s about a kid whose parents didn't understand him. The kid smoked cigarettes, wore a red jacket, combed his long hair back with his fingers, and at one point screamed at his parents, *"You're tearing me apart!"*

And he ripped out Li Bai Chen's heart. The kid in the movie had everything a Chinese teenage boy could want: the courage to rebel, an endless supply of smokes, that red jacket, cheekbones that could cut glass, and Natalie Wood.

Twenty-six months later, Li Bai Chen was in Los Angeles. He'd gotten work with a snakehead outfit that smuggled Chinese immigrants into *Meiguo,* or America, and then he'd gone ashore to deliver the human cargo and prevent them from running away. Once everything was in order, he ran away himself. He had no English and no marketable skills, so he decided to hide in plain sight. He changed his name to Ding Ji Ming and joined a Chinese gang in New York. Chinese names are written with the surname first, but if you wrote Bai Chen's new name in the Western fashion, first names first, it would be Ji Ming Ding, which was as close as he could get in Mandarin to *Jimmy Dean*.

Ji Ming, who preferred to be called "Jimmy," applied himself in the energetic manner of so many Chinese immigrants and rose quickly through the ranks. He spent five hours a day learning English during the time when most people would be sleeping, and got himself promoted to what, in a different kind of business, would probably be called the L.A. office. I ran into him in 2004, when we accidentally burgled the same house. In part because I gave him right of way, so to speak, and in part because I'm something of a James Dean freak myself, we became friends. We'd sit around together smoking, drinking beer, and reciting lines from the handful of movies Dean filmed before he crushed himself to death in his Porsche roadster. One evening I found—in the house of a producer whose burdensome load of material possessions I'd been sent to lighten—a videotape of one of Dean's first television roles, as a farmer's son in a 1953 drama called "Harvest." I gave it to Jimmy. Two days later, I woke up to find a vintage Porsche parked in my driveway with a bow around it and a red jacket neatly folded on the front seat. I was still living with Kathy then—Rina was only five—and this was precisely the kind of episode that made my wife wonder whether she'd made a wise marital choice.

I met Jimmy in Hollywood a couple of hours after taking Rina home, and the two of us jammed into the inevitable Porsche and took three or four turns around Thistle's apartment house. The Camelot Arms was a half-timbered, half-derelict, pathetically wannabe Tudor building with a few broken windows. It was in an area off Romaine that couldn't decide whether it was going up or down, although I'd have bet on up. It couldn't go much farther down.

"Only one way out," I said, looking at the door.

"Man," Jimmy said in the hipster English he insisted on using. "When you're living in a place like that, ain't no way out."

"Stifle the film-noir metaphysics, okay? See that door?

Practically speaking, if she's going to come out, she's going to come out there."

"And if she does?" Jimmy lit a cigarette. He thought smoking made him look more like the other Jimmy Dean. He'd learned to let the butt dangle from his lips and grin around it in a way that made his cheekbones jump out. With his hair combed back and that ciggie-centered grin, he looked about as much like James Dean as it was possible for a young Chinese gangster to look.

"She comes out, you call me," I said. "If she's alone, stick with her and stay on the phone. I'm going to sleep in Hollywood tonight, so I can be with you in eight or ten minutes. If it looks like trouble, if she's resisting or something, go point your gun at them."

"Seven-fifty if I have to do that."

"Fine. If it's anything you don't think you can handle, just stick with them until I'm there, and I'll work it out." I gave him the scrap of canvas Trey had cut from the painting. "If you see this guy, call me instantly, before he even gets into the building. Clear?"

Jimmy looked down at the picture and gave me a James Dean shrug, full of pained cool. "What's not to be clear?" he asked.

**One of my** storage facilities was in Hollywood, so I swung by and dropped off Bunny's necklace. Even with Rabbits still out of town, I was more comfortable without it in my pocket.

Storage facilities are indispensable to burglars. You need someplace to park stuff while it cools off or while you look for the right fence. Most of the time, I didn't have to deal with fences because I worked on assignment, but from time to time something extra fell into my hands, much as Bunny Stennet's necklace had. This storage space was a small one, just a four-by-six, in the name of Wyatt Gwyon, who is the hero, or at least the central character, of *The Recognitions*. I had a phony driver's license in Wyatt's name, which I figured was appropriate, since he's an art forger, and I'd given it to the manager of the facility when I leased the space.

Here's a trick in case you ever need to lease a storage space under a different name. First, master the simplest of all sleight-of hands maneuvers, the card switch, where you hold two cards in your hand, one hidden below the other so that the mark thinks you have only one. The entire trick consists of swapping the top one for the bottom one while you divert the mark's attention. A lobster could do it, and they don't even have palms. Second, when you make up your fake ID, buy a really stupid-looking wig and wear it in the photo. Third, for the second fake ID (you're going to need two), choose someone on Flickr or another image site who looks a little like you, and photo-shop the stupid wig onto him or her. When you lease the space, wear the wig. The manager will ask for identification, and you flash the ID with your real photo, with the other license hidden behind it. Then do the swap before the manager photocopies it. If he glances at the photocopy, all he'll see is the stupid hair. Someday you might hit a streak of bad luck and the cops could show up. What they'll find is a storage unit that was leased by someone with a different name and a different face than yours. And stupid hair.

My king-size bed for the night was in The Hillsider, an anonymous mid-scale motel on Highland, north of Hollywood Boulevard, at the foot of the long uphill to the Cahuenga Pass. The room I got didn't have a rear exit, but there was a back window I could have squeezed through in an emergency. The driveway opened directly onto Highland, and it was about a six-minute drive, even in traffic, to the Camelot Arms. It was only about 8:00 when I checked in, and I was hungry. I drove down to Hollywood Boulevard and parked behind Cherokee Books. Ten minutes later I had a well-worn copy of *Oracle Bones*, Peter Hessler's wonderful book about China, under my left arm and was on the sidewalk, dodging panhandlers and heading for Musso and Frank, one of the oldest and most dependable restaurants in Los Angeles. I'd already read about half of Hessler's book, but the copy I owned was all the way out in the Valley, at the Snor-Mor, and I couldn't take a chance on being that far from Thistle's apartment.

*Oracle Bones* was one of the books I'd been led to by *The Dream of the Red Chamber*, and it was proving to be one of the best. I managed to stretch dinner into a couple of hours, barely noticing what I was eating as I followed the sweep of Chinese history over 5,000 remarkably rocky years. The whole time I was in the restaurant, I never once thought about Thistle Downing.

Well, almost never.

Since Kathy and I broke up, this has pretty much been my life: sleep in motels and eat in restaurants, with books for company. It wasn't as bad as it probably sounds. I felt a kind of lightness about having gotten my possessions down to a suitcase's worth, just some clothes and my three touchstone books. I had a fine-quality first edition of *The Recognitions,* complete with dust jacket, autographed by Gaddis himself, that had cost me fifteen hundred and was now worth about $10K, and a beautiful 1930 edition of *Moby-Dick* with illustrations by Rockwell Kent. My copy of *The Dream of the Red Chamber* was more prosaic, a five-volume set of Penguin Classic paperbacks in the extraordinary translation by David Hawkes, which he titled *The Story of the Stone.* I didn't feel starved for human companionship, not when I had the enormous, tumultuous Chinese family in the *Stone,* especially the pampered and extravagantly romantic boy, Bao-Yu, who was born with a magical piece of jade in his mouth, and the two girls who love him.

But now I was caught up in something involving real people, and it didn't look like it was going to end well. None of my Big Three books has a happy ending, but when I read them I took some consolation from the fact that I had no opportunity to affect the way things worked out. Here, on the other hand, was a fluid situation with a bunch of living, breathing folks in it, all of whom were going to end up either in better or worse shape than they'd been in when the story began. Assuming that it was possible for Thistle Downing, or anyone, to be in worse shape than the lost soul Doc had described.

Back on the sidewalk, I persuaded myself that it was all going to be okay. I'd make all Trey's problems go away, and Wattles would swap the surveillance tape, and I'd move on as though none of this had happened. Maybe I'd just bury Bunny's necklace.

And maybe Thistle would be okay, too. Maybe she'd get through the shoot intact, or at least as intact as she was when she went into it. Maybe Doc would keep his promise and do something about the drugs, and she'd live happily ever after.

Maybe. But if it were a book, I wouldn't bet on it.

# 16
## Greater Than

As Rina had said, it was called "Once a Witch," and it seemed to be on all the time.

I hadn't known anything about Thistle's show when I watched those bits of it at the Snor-Mor, that one long scene and the end credits. By midnight, I was an expert.

Thistle played a character called Wanda, which I thought was a little on the cute side, since Wanda was a witch and had an actual wand. In a cosmic mix-up among dimensions, she'd been swapped with a normal baby, leaving her to wreak innocent havoc in the middle-class (read: all-white and all non-witch) suburb into which she'd been mistakenly dropped. A parallel plot line, following the normal little girl who'd been accidentally given to a family of witches, had been filmed but was dropped at the end of the first season, by which time it was apparent that the only reason anyone was watching was Thistle.

The other little girl—who was adorable but, compared to Thistle, lumpen—was apparently allowed to return to normal toddlerhood obscurity, where the odds were good she'd grow up nursing a lifelong grudge against Thistle Downing. Or might have, if things hadn't gone so spectacularly wrong in Thistle's life.

By twelve o'clock I'd seen four shows and three actors playing Wanda's father, all of whom might as well have been furniture. It wasn't fair, because when Thistle's spells went awry, they often required some expert physical comedy on old Dad's part, and at least two of the Dads were equal to it. But, unfortunately for them, Thistle was usually onscreen when their best bits came up, and it just wasn't possible to take your eyes off her. When these scenes were written, they had been about the father's dilemma, but when they were filmed they became about Thistle's *reaction* to the father's dilemma. It really wasn't fair. Here's Dad, trying to play ping-pong while hanging upside down with his shoes stuck to the ceiling, and Thistle's just standing there, and you *still* looked at her. And the Dads weren't helped by the fact that, by season three, there was almost never a shot in which Thistle didn't figure.

The actress playing Mom learned early to give the screen away with a kind of ego-free good humor that put her on the audience's side. Her attitude seemed to be saying to the viewer, *I'm with you. Let me get out of the way here, so you can sit back and see what she comes up with.* Dads had come and gone, but Mom had lasted through the show's entire eight-year run.

By the beginning of the fourth show I watched, I had distanced myself far enough to begin to wonder how Thistle could be destitute, no matter how much dope she was gobbling. The residuals from the show had to be substantial. Five or six episodes daily were fed into the maw of the cable channels. Her take had to be hundreds of thousands a year.

I wondered who would know why she wasn't getting any of it.

The shows I saw were apparently chosen at random by some programming computer. There was no attempt to stick with any single season or even cluster of seasons. As a result, I saw Thistle at eight and ten, then at eight again, and then at fifteen. It was amazing that she could hold me for two straight hours of uninspired sitcom machinations, ninety percent of which was filmed in that eternal, unchanging living room with the same damned bouquet of flowers on the table in front of the couch. She just outshone the material so strongly that everything else faded away. It was like seeing a diamond in a pile of manure.

But Rina had been right. As Thistle aged, she changed. At eight, she was all energy and uncanny instincts; she barely seemed to know the cameras were there. When she was ten, she still had the energy although the instincts weren't as clearly visible, and she had learned some technique that allowed her to build the jokes gradually and then ride them until the audience was helpless. There was, as far as I could tell, no electronic enhancement of the laughs she drew. They all sounded messy, spontaneous, and ragged, just like the laughs a real audience would create.

At fifteen, she didn't have so much energy. She was working hard, *trying* for the first time. Her technical skill had grown, but there didn't seem to be much of herself behind it. And she looked tired. Caught at certain angles, she had circles under her eyes. In one or two especially unfortunate shots, possibly preserved by an editor whom she'd treated badly, she looked exhausted. At fifteen, there were moments when Thistle Downing looked thirty.

And sad.

I turned off the television and booted my laptop, logged onto Google, and read what I could. Family life was unremarkable, at least from the outside, but then the Borgias probably looked normal from the outside. Father died when Thistle was little, mother had the kind of big-toothed smile that said she could probably bite a Chevy in half, and there was a brother, Robert, just an amorphous, pudgy, resolutely ordinary kid a couple of years older than Thistle. The kind of kid you could meet twenty times with no memory of him. In fact, I had to look back after I'd navigated away from the page to check his name again. Robert. His name was Robert.

The biggest story in Thistle's relatively recent past broke after she sold her residual rights two days after she turned eighteen, saying she didn't want to be looking over the studio's shoulder all the time. The deal made headlines for two reasons. First, Thistle was paid one hundred and forty million dollars. Second, her mother, whom she had fired as her manager the day she turned eighteen, sued for a big chunk of it.

And won.

Noting that Mrs. Downing's guidance had made Thistle one of the ten highest-paid people in television for three years running and that her brother, Robert, had contributed emotional support in spite of looking as emotional as a dinner roll, a superior court judge awarded Mom twenty-eight million, or twenty percent. The case made headlines again when Thistle hired three moving trucks, each jammed full of one-dollar bills, to deliver the money. As crews from practically every television network in the world filmed frantically and Robert ran around flapping his hands, a bunch of guys in coveralls used pitchforks to toss money from the backs of the trucks into the Downings' front yard for several hours and then drove off. Armed guards surrounded the yard for a day and a half until the money could be counted, stacked, and carted safely away.

Mother and daughter were not reputed to be on good terms.

And that was only the beginning. Thistle's money had been a banquet for the harpies to swoop down on. Her first manager, the guy who got her the part in "Once a Witch," sued and won a few million. Her own lawyer, having lost the case, sued her for seven million and won. Her business manager, who was supposed to manage the money that was left, discovered cocaine and bolted the country with another sixteen million. Thistle ran over a paparazzi's foot, and that cost a million and a half. She drove a car into someone's living room, and the settlement was apparently substantial, even though the amount was undisclosed.

It was a familiar cautionary tale, celebrity downhill skiing, leaving a trail of unflattering photographs, nightmare encounters, and thousand-dollar bills. And then, beginning about three years ago, pretty much nothing. Two stories that she'd been arrested for drug possession but released without going to trial. The mug shots had not been released, which was probably a mercy.

At midnight I started to shut down and then decided instead to Google Rabbits Stennet.

Not much there, and nothing that would lead you to believe that Robert R. Stennet was in the habit of feeding business associates to his Rottweilers. He was pleasant—even intelligent—looking, with a long collie face and a tame flop of silvery hair over a high, Sherlock Holmes brow. The overall effect was that of a college professor in some placid backwater of the Humanities rather than a ranking thug with a rep for brutality. He was active in community affairs, which I've always thought is kind of a dicey phrase, and there were a couple of pictures of him and the Missus at events. One of the shots, of the two of them on the red carpet to the Grammy Awards, with her glittering at the camera like a Christmas tree ornament in the diamonds I'd boosted plus a lot more, stopped me cold.

I'd forgotten that Bunny Stennet had looked familiar when I'd seen the photos on the bedroom wall. But there was no question about it. I had seen Bunny Stennet before. I couldn't pull it out of the snarl of yarn in my head—the end of the strand broke off every time I located it and tugged. But she was familiar, and what's more, she was familiar in a *recent* way. Whenever I'd seen her, it hadn't been long ago.

I couldn't remember meeting anyone new—anyone who looked like Bunny Stennet, that is—in months. And months.

I turned off the computer, climbed into bed, and set my cell phone to bleat at me around seven, since I was supposed to meet Doc at 7:45. I closed my eyes and settled into the pillow, tried to bring Bunny's features to mind again, and the phone rang.

I picked it up and flipped it open.

"Ummm," Jimmy Dean said. "Something's, um—maybe you'd better. *Oh.* Oh. *Wait!*"

A gunshot punched a hole in my eardrum.

**The Porsche was** at the curb, five cars north of the Camelot Arms. I passed it without slowing, went halfway around the block and parked, and then hiked back. I could see him when I was ten feet away.

Li Bai Chen, aka Ji Ming Ding, aka Jimmy Dean, had been shot once through the throat. The bullet had entered the left side of his neck, obviously fired through the open driver's window, and plowed into the back of the passenger seat. A spray of blood and brains had spattered across the window on the passenger side. Powder burns stippled Jimmy's cheek. He'd let whoever it was get close.

I smelled scorched cloth. Jimmy's cigarette had dropped from his mouth onto the thigh of his jeans, where it had burned through the denim to the skin. His right hand rested in his lap, palm up. His left was extended, the wrist caught in an opening in the steering wheel.

I followed the left arm and the hand with my eyes. In his own blood, on the inside of the windshield, Jimmy had drawn what looked like an uneven "greater than" character:

He had come fifteen thousand miles, drawn by Hollywood's vision of a young man who died in a Porsche, and here he was, a young man in Hollywood, dead in a Porsche. I closed my eyes for a moment and said goodbye, then begged his pardon as I slipped a hand inside his jacket and rifled his shirt pocket. Luck was with me, and I found it in the first place I looked: the face Trey had cut from the painting.

Jimmy's gun was holstered under his left shoulder. The jacket hadn't even been unbuttoned. The buttons were snaps so he could open them almost instantly, but they were still closed, not all the way because the evening hadn't been cool enough, but high enough to make it awkward to get to the gun.

And I couldn't find his cell phone.

I did everything I dared: leaned in as far as I could, checked the backseat, peered through the windows. Then I did what I didn't want to do—I opened the driver's door, turning on the interior light, which seemed very bright, and spent fifteen extremely anxious seconds looking for the phone. Not on the floor, not under the seat, not trapped beneath Jimmy's thighs. I closed the door and did a quick survey of the street. As far as I could tell, I was unobserved.

Other than trying to find that phone, there was no reason to stay here and many reasons to leave. Cops would probably arrive very soon, and I couldn't be anywhere around. There was nothing I could do about Thistle. If she was in her apartment, there was no point in knocking, and if she wasn't, there was no way I could find her now. Moving quickly, I wiped the driver's door where I had touched it, then went around to the Porsche's passenger side and wiped the door handle and the top of the door, then, after looking around again, I opened the door and wiped the inside, smearing some of Jimmy's blood in the process. No cell phone on the passenger side, either. Then I wadded up the handkerchief, stuffed it in my pocket, put my head down, and walked off, briskly but not hurriedly. As I got to my car and climbed in, I heard the sirens.

Coming for Jimmy.

**Part Two**

**CAMERA**

**17**

Closure

Crooks don't get much opportunity to mourn, and that's regrettable, since we probably lose friends more often than most demographic groups—water delivery men, for example, or the insurance actuaries who tell us which professions have the highest mortality rate. This is one reason that some of us are reluctant to make friends. You never knew when one of them might get hauled to the hospital with an incurable lead tumor or put away for life and a week.

But that night I did what I could. I spent most of an hour sitting on the bed at the Hillsider Motel, sending off whatever energy I could to accompany Jimmy wherever he was headed. At first I pictured someplace like Trey Annunziato's yard, but bigger and less corny, with lots of incense, and then dismissed it as faux-Asian claptrap. Jimmy was headed East of Eden, where he could hang out with the other James Dean.

And I couldn't call Theresa, Jimmy's wife, because the cops would be knocking on her door in an hour or two, and they couldn't see she'd been crying. Cops being cops, they'd regard her as a suspect, or someone who was shielding a suspect. She was going to have a rough enough time as it was.

And, of course, if the cops eventually got her to talk to them, she'd have to tell them that I was the one who'd called.

Back when I was a semi-pro, just a *patzer* who broke into

houses on weekends and took things that interested him, I got
to know a guy named Herbie, who became a mentor to me. At
the time I met him, Herbie was already deep into a long and
illustrious career, specializing in the houses of psychiatrists. He
really had a burr under his saddle about psychiatrists. The operation was simplicity itself: he'd get their patterns down so he
could identify the signs that announced that the house was really
empty, as opposed to *apparently* empty when there was actually
someone inside with ready access to a shotgun. When the place
was verifiably vacant, Herbie would go in and take everything
small enough to fit into a doctor's valise—and he had a really
exquisite eye for value, so he wasn't bagging a kid's stamp collection and a bag of garnets—and then he'd go through the doctor's files, if they were kept at home. He was looking for two
specific things: first, some sensational case notes, real headline-
quality stuff, the kind of thing it takes a while for a patient to tell
even his or her therapist; and second, evidence that the shrink
was underreporting income to the IRS. To hear him tell it, two
out of three were doing exactly that.

Then he'd blackmail them. He'd make a single phone call to
announce what he had and to inform the doctor that the patient's
secrets would be made public and the IRS would get an anonymous package in the mail, followed by the reassuring news that
these problems could be made to go away by a substantial wire
transfer into a numbered bank account in Aruba. The payment
was a whopper, and once he got it, Herbie shredded everything,
and the doctor never heard from him again. Blackmailers get
caught, Herbie said, because they don't stop.

It was obvious to me that Herbie had been through a lot of
therapy. He talked about *complexes* and *conflicts* and *childhood
traumas* and *invalid self-images* and *self-punishment* and *acting
out*, and all those other terms that shrinks use to mystify the way
pretty much everyone acts. And one of the terms Herbie used
most was *closure*. Sure, Herbie was getting rich when he held

these therapists over the fire, but he was also obtaining ongoing closure for some unrevealed wrong that had been done to him while he was stretched out on an analyst's couch.

One evening in Reseda, a blood brother of Herbie's, a hapless, judgment-free skell named Willis, robbed a liquor store in the company of some meth-addled tweaker he'd met that night. They got away with $362, a bunch of full bottles, and a string of curses in Korean from the store's owner, but they didn't get *all* the way away; the next morning Willis was found in a vacant lot with a broken bottle stuck in his neck. No money, of course. A couple of days later, the tweaker went down under a dark sedan with no license plates that didn't even slow down to let the driver take a look, and that night Herbie said something to me that I actually went home and wrote down.

*If you can't get closure*, Herbie said, *get even.*

Before I turned off the bedside lamp for the second time that night, I made a promise to Jimmy, Ji Ming, Bai Chen, or whatever name he was going by now. I promised to get even.

I closed my eyes, and my cell phone rang. When I looked at it, it displayed Jimmy's number.

# 18
## The Point of Paranoia

I watched it ring.

This was a problem. Like a total amateur, I was carrying my real phone, the number Rina and the people in my straight life had, not some throwaway bought with cash for one-time use on a job, with no name attached to the number. I just hadn't anticipated, when I drove into Hollywood, that my cell phone would be a line to me for someone I would much rather not meet.

So, I thought, let's say it's the cops. One of the first things they would do is look at the log in the phone, and they'd see that Jimmy had called me just about the time the shots were reported. Then they'd get a name for the number. Then, using a different phone so they wouldn't run the risk of destroying any trace evidence on Jimmy's, they'd call me.

The phone stopped ringing. I realized I'd shrugged off the blankets and sat up, and was now perched on the edge of the bed with my bare feet on the Hillsider's faintly tacky carpet.

The cops would definitely call. But probably not on Jimmy's phone.

So who? Only one real possibility.

Jimmy, I thought again, had let whoever it was get pretty close. Jimmy was not a trusting soul. With half the gangsters in China, plus the Immigration and Naturalization Service, the

LAPD, and assorted personal enemies eager to take his scalp, Jimmy was careful to the point of paranoia.

Either Jimmy knew the shooter, or the shooter looked helpless, or the shooter was very, very good. And I thought I could dismiss the third possibility. Jimmy was a lookout, one of the best. He kept his eyes open, took in the big picture all the time, and had installed convex rear-view mirrors on the Porsche for a wide-angle view. He used them constantly. In all the time he'd been in Los Angeles, he'd never blown a job. He'd never been arrested. On the job, Jimmy had more eyes than a spider.

Nobody had come up on him from behind. He'd seen them. He'd seen them cross the street or step off the curb to come around to the driver's side. And he hadn't even unsnapped his jacket.

If *Thistle* came out, he'd let her get close.

If a highly attractive girl approached, he'd probably let her get close, but he'd have his gun in his hand, out of sight. His gun had still been in the shoulder holster.

If a little kid approached, he'd let him or her get close.

If someone he knew well—

The phone rang again.

I picked it up and said "Hello."

No one answered. I heard a motorcycle or something go by in the background. The person on the other end of the phone was on the street somewhere.

"I'm not saying it again," I said. "Talk or let me go to sleep."

No reply, and suddenly I was blindly, hotly, pulse-poundingly furious. "I'm at the Hillsider motel on Highland, in room 210. I don't have a gun. I'm getting up right now and opening the door. I'll leave it wide open. Come over here, you asshole, and let me get a look at you." I slammed the phone closed, got up, opened the door, and got dressed, in the same coveralls I'd been wearing for two days. Then I turned off the phone, since I didn't plan to go to sleep and I didn't need the alarm, and I didn't want whoever had shot Jimmy to call me again. I was giving him or her only one way to talk to me.

I sat in the armchair, facing out through the open door, and waited. I waited for two or three of the slowest, darkest hours of my life.

And then I found myself talking to Jimmy with steep blue-green mountains in the background, definitely a Chinese land-scape with lots of mist, and he had that cigarette in the middle of his mouth, and the cigarette was putting out an enormous amount of smoke. It got harder to see Jimmy through the smoke, and then everything just seemed to go white. And I was some-place cold, sitting in the white on something hard.

Out of the white, something prodded my shoulder.

I bolted up, coming out of the chair so fast that I almost knocked Doc over.

"Do you know your door is wide open?"

"Yeah," I said. I rubbed at my face, which seemed to be all there. "It was too hot in here."

"Seven-thirty," Doc said. "We should get over there."

"Sure, sure. Did you bring coffee?"

"No, but I've got this." He held out a little flask. "Cognac," he said. "Pretty good, too."

"No, thanks. Maybe they've got coffee in the office. Let me get my stuff."

"I'll check the office for you," Doc said. He got halfway through the door, and then said, "Did you drop this?"

I went over and looked. On the cement walkway to the immediate right of my door was Jimmy's cell phone.

"No," I said, picking it up. "It belongs to a friend of mine."

We had to slow when we made the turn onto Romaine. A uni-formed cop was there, detouring people to the first right turn. Doc rolled down the window and explained that we had to pick someone up at the Camelot Arms, and rattled off the address.

The cop eyed him for a moment. Then he said, "Are you on television?"

"You spotted me," Doc said modestly.

"Tell you what," the cop said. "Give me an autograph for my daughter, and I'll let you through. Just tell the officer at the corner that Willett said it was okay."

"That's right nice of you," Doc said, in Milburn Stone mode. He grabbed a pad that was fastened to the center console with a suction cup, took a pen out of his pocket, and said, "What's your daughter's name?"

"Um, Dennis," Officer Willett said. He was very young.

"Fine, fine." Doc wrote, "For Dennis, a big howdy," and signed it "Milburn Stone." When he handed it to Willett, he said, "That's a rare one. I haven't been signing much lately."

"Thanks." Willett pocketed the signature. "Straight ahead. Remember, the name's Willett."

"Got it," Doc said, raising the window.

"*Rare*," I said, sipping the coffee he'd grabbed in the Hillsider lobby.

"Well, the new ones are. Milburn Stone died in 1980."

A block ahead, another cop tried to wave us off, but Doc lowered the window and said the magic words, and we were allowed to make the turn onto Thistle's street. A knot of cops, including three black-and-whites, a bunch of uniforms, and some detectives in suits almost as awful as Hacker's, snarled the street around Jimmy's car. Both doors were wide open and the car was empty; Jimmy had been hauled away with the night's other dead.

Doc had no problem finding a place to park. The people who went to work early had vacated their spaces, and no one had been allowed into the street to replace them. "I'll go get her," he said. "I want to give her a little wake-up injection, and I don't want to surprise her with you, standing there all tall and threatening."

"Fine," I said. I really didn't want to get out of the car anyway. You never know when you might run into a cop who'd recognize you. After Doc climbed out and closed the door, I leaned over and angled the rear-view mirror so I could see what was going on around the Porsche. But I overshot it and had to turn it back—and then froze. I thought I'd seen something.

"Nah," I said out loud.

But I readjusted the mirror anyway, and about thirty yards away, some five or six spaces behind Jimmy's Porsche, there it was. A dented white Chevy with some halfhearted primer applied at random. And the last time I'd seen it, I'd watched it dig up a bunch of lawns on Windward Circle.

# 19

### All I Remember Is the Waiting

Get out and check the Chevy, or sit here?

I angled the mirror back toward the Porsche and studied the activity. With a sinking feeling I recognized Detective Al Tallerico, a hard case from Hollywood Division, who'd almost arrested me twice for jobs I hadn't done. He must have been promoted to Homicide. I would have to walk past him to get to the Chevy. Tallerico looked busy, but not so busy he wouldn't look at anyone who approached the crime scene on foot. And if he looked at me, he'd recognize me. And if he recognized me, he'd detain me on general principles, a crook in the vicinity of a homicide. And if he detained me, Rabbits Stennet would see the wrong videotape. And, and, and.

So stay in the car.

Except.

Except that Doc was standing in the door of the Camelot Arms, gesturing with a certain amount of urgency for me to get *out* of the car and get my ass across the street. He was flapping a hand at me, and it was only a matter of moments before one of the cops noticed. I held up my hand in a *stop* gesture and got out of the car into a morning that was entirely too bright, too bright for the aftermath of what had happened in the Porsche last night, and far too bright for my own personal comfort with Al Tallerico less than twenty yards away.

The key to being inconspicuous is to look like you know where you're going and why. So I made a show of glancing at my watch and then turned my head away from the cops, like someone making sure he isn't about to step in front of a speeding bus, and crossed the street, just another citizen on a perfectly upright errand. Every step, I expected to hear Tallerico's voice yelling for me to stop, and every step I didn't, and after a certain number of steps, I was inside the doorway of the Camelot Arms and Doc was grabbing my sleeve.

"She got her hands on something," he said. Beads of sweat dotted his forehead. "I need help." He tugged me inside, toward a stairway.

"*You* need help?" I said. "What skill set do you think I possess?"

"You can walk," he said, pulling me along. "She needs to be walked."

"Walking I can do. How could she have gotten anything? I thought you knocked her out last night."

We were most of the way up the stairs now, and the second story yawned in front of us. "I did," Doc said. "All I can figure is that somebody delivered. Come on, pick it up. I'm afraid she'll heave and then aspirate it. It's remarkable she hasn't already done that, the way she's been living."

The second-floor hallway was dim, barren, and windowless: just filthy linoleum, finger-marked walls, and doors on either side, most of them absolute arsenals of locks. It smelled of damp wood, with a sharp note of urine. The door three down, on the right, stood open. Doc towed me the rest of the way down the hall, and we went through the open door into Thistle Downing's world.

The door opened into what I supposed would be called the living room, although there wasn't much on view to recommend the life that was being lived there. It was cramped, maybe ten feet by twelve, and haphazardly furnished with a threadbare, blood-red Oriental carpet in an abstract pineapple pattern, set crookedly on the linoleum floor, and a sagging couch, missing one front leg, all of it covered, except for the arm nearest me, with a dirty bedsheet. The carpet, the bedsheet, and the exposed arm of the couch were pockmarked with cigarette burns, as though butts had been laid down anywhere and everywhere to smolder forgotten. Big water stains surrounding some of them announced the places where fires had been doused. More water stains created a map of ghost continents on the ceiling. Grit scraped beneath my feet and dust rats huddled in the corners. It felt like the room had been sealed for a long time. The air smelled like cheese gone wrong.

Other than the sofa and a badly abused coffee table, the only pieces of furniture in the room were four old-fashioned standing floor lamps, probably rescued from dumpsters. They stood in the corners or leaned in exhausted poses against a wall. Scarves of red and orange had been draped over the shades, along with bright, cheap plastic beads that looked like the ones thrown from floats in the Mardi Gras. Between the scarves and the beads, the lamps reminded me of old Gypsy women. On the wall opposite the door, two small windows had been sloppily covered with aluminum foil.

"Through there," Doc said, pointing at a doorway to our right. The room on the other side was darker than the one we were in, and I realized that Doc or someone had turned on one of the floor lamps in the living room. I followed him through the door and found myself in an even smaller room. This one had no furniture at all except for two more standing lamps and a mattress on the floor against the far wall. On the mattress I saw a crumpled form wrapped in something white and shapeless.

One hand hung over the edge of the mattress, dangling palm-up from an almost childishly slender wrist. Doc ripped a scarf off one of the lights and turned it on, and the blue veins in the wrist leapt into sharp relief. The figure did not move.

White and tightly curled, she looked like something that had been wadded up and tossed. "You're sure she's not, um—"

"Nope." Doc pulled out the flask and took a nip, then screwed the top back on. "If she were dead, we'd be long gone. She's out, though, and I mean *out*. Right through the transparent wall. You could set off firecrackers and she wouldn't hear them. Heartbeat is steady, nothing wrong with her breathing. Skin's not cold, so the circulation is all right. Her pupils are dilated, but it'd be a surprise if they weren't. If she were conscious, she could probably see through the floor." He bent over her and wrapped a big hand around the small wrist. "This is either gonna work or it isn't and if it doesn't, we'll have to get her stomach pumped." He looked up at me. "You gonna stand there, or you gonna help?"

"Right," I said. "Walk her."

"Get her other side." I hesitated, reluctant to step onto the mattress wearing my shoes, and Doc said, "For God's sake. When do you think was the last time these sheets were washed? Don't be so fucking delicate. Just get her."

So I got in between her and the wall and took her other arm, which was folded under her face, straightened it, and imitated Doc's actions, putting the arm around my shoulders and grabbing the dangling hand. Throughout all of this, the unconscious woman never moved, groaned, or gave any sign that she knew she was being manhandled. I crouched there, her arm around my shoulders, and Doc said, "Up on three. Careful to come up with me, or I'll put my back out, sure as the sun rises. You set?"

I allowed as how I was set.

"One . . . two . . . *three*," Doc said, and the two of us straightened in unison. Doc grunted with the effort, but I had been anticipating much more weight and I came up too fast, so that for a moment it felt as though she and I were going to topple over onto Doc.

"Jesus," Doc said. "You want to carry both of us? Now

come on, just haul her off the mattress and get her into the middle of the floor." One of her feet squealed on the linoleum, and I winced. "Toughen up," Doc said. "You're not going to do her any good if you treat her like she's some kind of goddamn fawn. She's tougher than you are. If she wasn't she'd be dead."

The two of us now stood in the middle of the small bedroom with Thistle Downing dangling between us, limp as a Slinky. She was tiny. I was at least fourteen inches taller than she, so she couldn't have been much above five feet, and she was light enough to be porous. Her arms and wrists were so slender I could close my hand around her forearm, with room to spare. The white garment she was wearing proved to be a terrycloth bathrobe that had long ceased to be dirty and was now certifiably filthy. It said PLAZA HOTEL in a crimson cursive script on the left, beside the lapel, and its bottom hem brushed the floor. Both it and Thistle had come a long way from the Plaza.

"Walk," Doc commanded. "Not fast, but steady. And don't lift her so much. Let her feet drag, or she won't try to move them."

And so the two of us walked, Thistle's feet trailing behind, her head hanging down, veiled with hair. The hair was snarled but fine, slightly curly, a little past shoulder-length and the reddish-gold color of flax. It had been chopped any old how—I guessed she'd done it herself—and it smelled of cigarettes. I hadn't actually seen her face yet. Her hand was cold and damp in mine. Doc kept up a stream of words, encouraging, cajoling, challenging Thistle to start walking, but her feet just dragged along the floor, no livelier than the robe's hem, until we hit the edge of the carpet in the living room, and some impulse—probably an automatic reaction to a possible stumble—brought one of her feet forward, and she took two steps and sagged again.

"Turn around," Doc said. "Drag her off the carpet again and then back onto it." We did, and when we hit the carpet this time Thistle managed four steps. We reversed direction to get back onto the bare floor and repeat the procedure.

"That's it, darlin'," Doc said. "I knew you could do it. Boy, whatever you took last night, you ought to put it on your *do not do* list. Another couple of whatever they were, you'd have gone out of here in a bag. You know what they were? You know how many you took?" No response. "That's okay, it'll wait till later. *That's* right, sweetheart, walk, you're not a goddamn mermaid. You've got a big day ahead of you, lots of people waiting for you, half a dozen of them sitting around with mirrors and brushes, just can't wait to make you beautiful. This'll be an easy day, honey, five or six little shots, a few lines, and you can come home. Nothing compared to what you used to do. In the old days, you'd have done all of that and more before breakfast. You know Lillian Gish? Maybe a century before your time, but the first great American film actress, right? Wonderful story about Lillian Gish, somebody told me yesterday. She'd been working on a movie with D. W. Griffith back in the twenties, when they just went outdoors and shot in sunlight and nobody had to talk, although the great ones always did, always played their scenes like everyone would hear them. Even the indoors sets were just three walls and no roof, so the sunlight could come in, did you know that? So Lillian Gish had been working her elegant ass off for months, all over California, and then they had the big premiere and she went with Griffith, since he was her director. And when the movie was over, you know what she said to him? She said, 'Did I do all that? All I remember is the waiting.'"

Thistle made a choked sound and it took me a moment to recognize it as a laugh.

"That's good, baby," Doc said. "Keep those feet going, and let's see if you can't get your eyes open for a couple of minutes. By the way, the tall ugly guy on the other side of you is named Junior. Hey, Junior, do you know any movie stories? I just told the only one I know."

I wasn't exactly a film encyclopedia—none of my books had led me to it—but I knew a few things, one of which I had picked up that morning, courtesy of Rodd Hull. "Um, Claudette Colbert," I said.

Thistle said something that was all sibilants, and Doc said, "What, sugar? What did you say?"

"Shaid . . . she'sh . . . good," Thistle said, very slowly.

"She, um, hated the left side of her face," I said, trying desperately to remember Rodd's story, "and she always—"

"Timing," Thistle said. "Had, uhhhhhh, timing."

"Yeah, timing," I said, and glanced over Thistle's head, still hanging on her chest, at Doc, who made a rolling gesture with his free hand that meant, *Keep talking.* "So," I said, "her face," and Thistle said something. "What?"

"Side . . . moon," she whispered.

"Right, dark side of the moon." I considered and rejected a bunch of stories that suddenly came to mind, and then remembered something else about Colbert. "She had one of the funniest lines I ever heard," I said. "In a movie made in the middle thirties. I don't remember the name of it, but she's a poor girl who's working in a hat shop and having an affair with an unhappily married older man, and the man's unpleasant wife comes in to try on some hats. Colbert chooses one for her and helps her put it on, and studies her for a minute, and then says, 'That hat does something for you. It—it gives you a chin.'"

This time Doc laughed, too, and Thistle managed a couple of unclassifiable sounds, more damp little whuffles than guffaws, but progress. I was ready to talk about Bogart in *Casablanca*, how George Raft turned the part down, but I remembered how young Thistle was, and my chat with Rina the prior afternoon came to mind. I did ten or fifteen reasonably interesting minutes on dead wet girl ghosts, on the derivation and iconography of dead wet girls in Asian film, and by the time I'd used that up, Thistle was almost keeping up with us, although she still hadn't lifted her head, and without us she would have fallen in a heap.

"Keep it up," Doc said. "You're doing great."

"That's it," I said. "I can't think of anything else."

"So make something up. Talk about whatever comes to mind," Doc said. "How'd you get your face so banged up? Have you seen his face, Thistle? Looks like somebody thought it was a piece of beef and tried to grind it. Go on, take a look. You can do it."

The head turned a few inches, and the flax-colored hair parted just enough for me to see an eye, surprisingly deep green, uptilted at the end, and heavy-lidded. Then she let her head drop again and stumbled, but we had her in our grasp, and a few steps later her feet were moving again.

"Isn't he ugly?" Doc said. "Tell her, Junior. Tell her what happened to your face."

So for the third time in two days I described my encounter with Rabbits's chandelier and Rottweilers. Doc got so interested he almost walked us into the couch, and I had to pull us left to avoid a stumble. I could feel the energy returning slowly to Thistle's body; she was bearing more of her own weight and walking less erratically, so I stretched the story out, elaborated on it, exaggerated the number of marital aids and the size of the dogs, turned the swing on the chandelier into the kind of adventure Tarzan might have had if Tarzan had been an interior decorator. She laughed two or three times, although they could have been coughs. By the time I finished, she was walking relatively well, and we stopped in the center of the carpet.

Thistle removed her arm from Doc's shoulder, wobbled once, grabbed my hand to steady herself, and turned her body slightly toward me. Her head came up slowly and the hair fell away from her face.

I bit my tongue.

Drug-battered, stoned, muzzy-eyed, exhausted, debilitated, undernourished, Thistle Downing was still fundamentally ravishing. The elfin qualities in her face, the tilted eyes, the high cheekbones, the puckish mouth with its surprisingly full lower lip—they were all still there, older and more blended, and maybe even more beautiful than before. Clean up her system, feed her, put her to bed for six weeks, give her a haircut and a reason to live, and she'd be stunning.

She smiled at me, and the whole awful room brightened.

"You're funny," she said, and then her eyes rolled to the ceiling and she went down like a stone.

"Okay," Doc said. He took in a deep breath and blew it out. The flask made another appearance. "Shower time."

# 20

## For Thistle With Love

She squealed when the cold water hit her and then fought back with startling strength, kicking and sputtering. Soaking wet, the thick terrycloth bathrobe must have weighed twenty pounds, and it was a good thing it did because she came at both of us with her claws out. Dragged down by the robe, she didn't have the strength to step over the edge of the tub, and Doc pushed her down onto the bottom and aimed the shower straight at her. Over his shoulder, he said to me, "Better call the studio and tell them where we are. Talk to Tatiana. She's the only one with any sense. Oh, and see if there's any coffee around."

I went back into the living room and made the call.

"This is not going to make Trey happy," Tatiana said.

"She's probably dealt with bigger issues."

"Why don't you just haul her over here? We'll get a bunch of coffee going and bring her around. She might be more comfortable with girls."

"The street is full of cops," I said. "Some sort of investigation. I don't think it's a great idea to drag a semi-conscious woman into a car when half the badges in Hollywood are looking. We're going to get her walking first."

"How's she look?"

"Pretty good. I was expecting Miss Havisham or whoever

it was when they took her out of Shangri-La, but she's still beautiful."

"Give her a couple more years and she'll wear holes in her skin. What about the sore on her lip?

"I didn't notice."

"Uh-oh," Tatiana said. "Don't get interested."

"Don't be silly. But I have to say, now that I've seen her, I think for the first time that Trey's not crazy to be doing this movie."

"No, she's not crazy," Tatiana said. "Inhuman maybe, but not crazy. I'll tell everybody it'll be another hour or so."

I closed the phone, thinking, no one hangs up phones any more. Another linguistic artifact, like dialing a number. From the noises coming out of the bathroom, Doc had his hands full. I decided he was better qualified than I to deal with it. A quick check for coffee revealed none, which wasn't surprising since there was no stove in the kitchen, not even a hotplate— just an expanse of greasy wall and some closed-off gas lines where a range had once stood. I did find five open and partly consumed bags of cookies, four of which were Oreos, which I took to mean that Thistle had company from time to time. No single person would open all those bags without finishing at least one first. This was the detritus of multiple cases of the munchies.

There were also two half-empty, screw-top bottles of three-buck red wine, and—next to the end of the couch that faced away from the door—three chipped glasses with dried red wine dregs in the bottoms. Definitely company. I tried for a moment to imagine red wine and Oreos together and gave up. Maybe that was why she drugged: it killed her taste buds. I went into the bedroom to find some clothes Thistle could get into once she had fully rejoined us.

It was too dim in there, so I turned on the second lamp and looked around. The place couldn't have been more anonymous if she'd only been there an hour. There was absolutely nothing in the room to indicate who she was or who she had been. No photos, no albums, no clippings—nothing to suggest that the young woman who lived here had been the most famous twelve-year-old in the country. In the absence of a chest of drawers, some waxy cardboard produce cartons had been lined up against one wall. They still stank of cabbage and broccoli, and I realized that was what I had smelled when we came through the front door. A stack of journals almost filled one of the boxes, identical hardcover books of blue-lined paper, bound in a faded sky blue, cheap, and probably purchased in a university student bookstore. There was nothing on the front covers except dates, and there seemed to be a new one every two or three months, so she was writing a lot. Or maybe drawing, or cutting out pages to create abstract origami, or diagramming the neural pathways blazed by illegal chemicals. Another box was filled with all the stuff no one knows where to keep: eyeglasses; old, empty cases for eyeglasses; keys; flashlights and loose batteries; candles; two unmatched shoes; a few paperback books. The title of the book on top was *Finding the True You,* and that discouraged me so much I didn't look at the others. The books triggered a train of thought that straightened me up for a moment, and I took a short walk through the rooms to see whether I'd missed it, but I hadn't; there was no television set in the apartment.

Back in the bedroom, I dug into the third box and managed to find a couple of clean T-shirts and one pair of jeans that didn't look like it could walk by itself, and I folded the items over my left arm. I was turning to go when I saw something pink wedged between the mattress and the wall.

It was a small box, about three inches square and an inch deep. A bright yellow bow, amateurishly made from cheap gift-wrap ribbon, had been glued to the top, along with some sparkly stuff, the kind of glitter that bad magicians scatter in the air to distract the audience. Someone had written FOR THISTLE WITH

LOVE on the top in metallic gold ink. The "i" in *Thistle* was dotted with a heart.

I opened it and found myself looking at six rectangular tablets, olive-green in color. When I picked one up, I saw a number incised into the flat surface: 542. The tablets had been laid on a fluffy piece of cotton, pristine white. The bow, the heart, the cotton: It all looked so harmless.

I went into the living room and listened. No screams, no water running.

"You both alive in there?"

"More or less," Doc called. "Don't open the door. She's drying her hair."

"Tell me about green tablets with 542 written on them."

"Rohypnol," Doc said. "Roofies. The ever-popular date rape drug. Where'd you find them?"

I told him, and he opened the door a crack and stuck out a hand. I handed the box through, and I heard Thistle say, "*Mine.*"

"You'll get it back, sweetie," Doc said. "How many did you take?"

"Don't know." She sounded sullen, but the words weren't too badly slurred.

"Look, it's a present. Got a pretty bow and everything. Who gave it to you?"

"Don't know," she said again. "Sommuddy nodded, uh, *knocked* on my . . . my door. You know? And when I went to, uh, to look, those were there."

"Last night?"

"Ummmm . . . maybe."

"And you have no idea who would have left them?"

"Uh-uh. Gimme one."

"Not yet. Do you always take stuff, even when you don't know where it came from?"

A pause as Thistle processed the question, as if looking for a trap somewhere. Then she said, "Sure."

"It's a miracle you're not dead. Honey, if you're going to take stuff like this, you've got to tell me, and I won't give you all that other stuff."

"But I *like* it," she said. She sounded ten years old.

"And I like to give it to you." A certain amount of exasperation was peeking through Doc's Milburn Stone affability. "But I need to know what else you're taking."

"I won't, any more," she said. "Can I have it now?"

"Tell you what," Doc said. "We'll leave them right here, and you can take some when you get home tonight, okay?"

"No." I heard a slapping sound that might have been a wet bare foot being stamped.

"Well, that's what we're doing. I'll put them in this drawer before we leave, and tonight you can have a party, all by yourself."

"I want it now."

"Junior," Doc called through the door. "Can you get Thistle some clothes?"

"Get my own clothes," Thistle said.

"Here," I said, and I reached through with the arm that had the clothes folded over it.

"Don't want," Thistle said.

"Young lady," Doc said. "You're going to shut up and put these clothes on, and then we'll see about some medicine for you. But I'm telling you, until you're dressed and ready to go, you are going to meet the world as God made you, with no help at all. Not a shot, not a pill, not even a pair of sunglasses. So right now I'm going to leave you here to get dressed, and I'll take this little box with me, and then we'll talk about it when you come out. Got it?"

The door opened, and Doc came through it. He was soaking wet. He had the gift box in his hand, clenched hard enough to buckle the sides. "Get used to it," he said. "This is what it's going to be like until we're finished. If we ever finish."

"What about the pills? How bad could it have been?"

He shook his head. "There's only one real question, and that's whether whoever left them knew they could kill her. What I don't understand is why there are any left. That's not like her. All I can figure is that she passed out before she could take them all, which was a break for us. If she'd gotten them all down, she'd be on her way to the morgue."

"What else is she going to need when we leave?" I asked.

"Other than a good friend and a complete blood change, nothing except what's in my bag," he said. "Unless you saw a purse in there. Women always want their purse."

"I'll look." As I started to turn, the bathroom door opened and Thistle came out. Her walk was hesitant but acceptable. The pale wet hair had been combed back from her face, exposing the fine, undamaged bone structure. The sore everyone had been talking about was on her lower lip. Her eyes went to Doc. "I'm out," she said. "I got dressed, see? Give me something." Then she brought the green eyes toward me and squinted as though I was reflecting too much light.

"Who the hell are you?" she said.

# 21
Mr. Question Man

For the first five or six minutes, she might as well have been a pile of leaves. She sat slumped over, her forehead practically touching the dashboard. Every now and then she let out a syllable or two, but nothing I could translate into words.

This was a surprise, because she'd been almost lively, at least relatively speaking, when Doc had driven the two of us into the parking lot of the Hillsider so I could get my car. I'd climbed out of Doc's car and started to close the door, but a squeal had stopped me, and I'd turned to see Thistle with one leg on the asphalt, holding the door open with an extended hand.

"Jeez," she'd said, wincing in the sunlight. "*Careful,* you know?"

"Where are you going?" Doc had asked her.

"Wanna . . . wanna ride with *him,*" she said. "Tired of you."

"Aww," Doc said. "You're going to break my heart."

Thistle snickered. "*Your* heart? Don't think so. Hard. Your heart, it's hard." And then she'd pulled herself out of Doc's car, steadied herself with both hands, and said to me, "Where?"

"The white one," I said. "Right there."

"'Kay," she said, and she lowered her head, leaned in the direction of the car, and staggered in its general direction until she bumped into it. "*See?*" she said, leaning all her weight against it, "I'm fine."

I'd opened the door for her and prevented her from bumping her head when she got in. I glanced back over at Doc, and he rubbed thumb and forefinger together in the universal sign for *money* and shook his head. A moment later, both cars managed the left onto Highland and slammed straight into rush hour.

Thistle remained bent forward.

"You okay?" I asked.

She said, "Uuuuhhhh."

"Good," I said. "Good to hear it. Let me know if there's a turn for the worse."

We picked up speed a little, heading for the onramp to the Hollywood Freeway.

"Here we go." She put out a hand and pushed herself away from the dashboard. "Okay," she said, sitting a little straighter. "Okay, okay, okay."

"Something's okay?" I asked.

"Here it comes," she said. "*Whoooooooo*, that took a long time." She shook her head sharply, opened her mouth as though she were going to yawn, and then changed her mind, brought both hands up, and massaged her face. "Did I bring my sunglasses?"

"I don't know. Your purse is on the seat."

"Boy, oh boy," she said, making no move for the purse. "I didn't know what to think."

"About what?"

"That shot. It should have hit ten minutes ago. I didn't know whether, whether—"

"Whether."

"Whether he'd shot me with water, or whether I was dead."

"You're not dead," I said. "No thanks to you."

"Yeah, yeah. Must have been those pills. You know? The ones in the box."

"How many did you take?"

"Six? Seven? Who knows. I was already loaded from what

Doc gave me. Oh my golly, here comes some more." And she sat up straighter and looked over at me.

"I remember you now," she said. Her eyes were darting back and forth between me and the road ahead, and her words were only slightly slurred. "You're the one who talked about Claudette Colbert."

We were on the freeway by now, but not moving so fast that it was dangerous for me to glance over at Thistle. Her transformation was nothing short of miraculous, even if it was pharmaceutically induced: a shot of amphetamine, a couple of Percocets, fifteen minutes for her system to re-tune itself, and she was a new woman. Chemically elevated, then sedated to give her enough mass to keep her from detaching and floating away, she looked fit, alert, and ready for the balance beam. Feeling my gaze, she gave me a wary look and reached into her purse, bringing out the biggest, blackest pair of shades I'd ever seen. They were so big it looked like they should have a nose and mustache attached to them. When she put them on, they dwarfed her face. She turned away from me, looking over her far shoulder at where we'd been.

"You like Claudette Colbert?" I asked. "I'm surprised you even know who she was."

There was an interval, perhaps a good, slow count of five, during which I thought she wouldn't answer. But then she looked back over at me. She lowered her shades with an index finger and continued to stare at me, long enough to make me uncomfortable. Then she pushed the sunglasses back up, turned back to the windshield, and cleared her throat. It didn't sound like anything significant, just somebody getting her voice ready.

"I used to love her," she said. "I watched all her movies. Her and Carole Lombard and Katharine Hepburn."

"Pretty old for you."

"Actresses," she said. "I watched actresses. I used to be an actress."

"I know," I said.

"I wanted to be good," she said. "So I watched good ones. Bette Davis, too, but she didn't like to be funny. She believed she wasn't beautiful is what I think, and she thought people only took her seriously when she was being dramatic, so she was afraid to be funny. I liked the ones who weren't afraid to be funny."

"You were good," I said. "I've seen you."

She waved the remark away. "That line you liked? About the hat? That was from *Midnight*. I saw that about fifty times. I used to be able to get anything I wanted, you know? When I was on the show, I mean. *Anything.* I'd just ask somebody for it and they'd get it for me. I didn't even have to say please. So I asked one of those people, the ones who were always around then, for those old movies, and I got a lot of them. I used to watch them at night, when I got home, when I was through being Thistle."

"What did you like about her? About Colbert, I mean." We inched toward the onramp for the Hollywood Freeway.

She twisted a strand of the pulled-back hair to see how wet it was and then folded her hands in her lap. It was an odd posture, demure and too young for her. "She was having so much *fun*. More fun than anybody. Everybody else was working really hard, knitting their brows and clenching their jaws and trying to look like they were used to wearing their costumes and everything. You know, you can always tell when an actor feels silly in his costume, like they don't know where their pockets are or they wish they were wearing socks. So everybody else is all wrapped up in a sheet and feeling dumb but pretending to be Julius Caesar or whoever, really putting their backs into it, you know? And she was thinking, *I'm a big movie star and this is just like fatally cool.* There was always this glee in her eyes. You know glee?"

"I have a nodding acquaintance with it." The morning sun

was dazzling on the roofs of the cars, and I envied Thistle her sunglasses.

"People don't talk about glee much any more. Why?" She turned to me, the hands still folded in her lap. It seemed to be a serious question. "Do you know? Do you know why are there so many more ways to say you're unhappy than there are to say you're happy? Maybe that's why nobody's happy any more."

"What's why?"

"The *language*" she said, as though it were the most obvious thing in the world. "You know, *English*. It doesn't give happiness equal time, does it? It's like the hundred words for snow everybody talks about with the Eskimos, except we've got it for *complaint*. We've got it for *misery* and *boredom* and *too cool to smile*. And so you've got all these drips dressed in black and imitating each other, talking about how beamed it is to be *down* all the time. Talking about *irony* and *black comedy*. Starting fan clubs for serial killers. Making fun of happy endings. Like the world is just cinders and tin cans and there's nothing to be happy about."

"Are you happy?"

She pushed past the question without a glance in its direction. "If there was no word for *sky*," she said, "I wonder whether anybody would look up."

"*Are* you happy?"

She had been facing me, but now she shifted to give me her profile and look through the windshield. She put her feet up on the dash so her knees were practically at her chest. Then, making herself even smaller, she crossed her arms. After a full minute, she said, "When I've got what I want."

"And what do you want?"

"Who made you Mister Question Man?" Her voice had scaled up slightly into the thinner, more querulous register I'd heard when she was talking to Doc in the bathroom. "We were having a good time talking about, umm, Claudette Colbert, and all of a sudden I'm in therapy."

"Sorry."

"Jesus. I was feeling okay, too. Just drive the car, isn't that your job?"

"You can feel good again."

"Yeah?" It was a challenge. "You got anything?"

"You can feel good on your own."

"Uh-oh. Quick, somebody. Make a poster. *You can feel good on your own.* With a picture of the Olsen Twins, maybe. Put it next to the one that says *I won't come in your mouth.*" She started picking at the sore on her lower lip.

"Don't do that. It'll get infected."

"Yeah, and it'll swell up and then my head will fall off. Leave me alone."

"My daughter says you were sad when you were a little girl."

"She did, huh? Where'd she get *that* insight? Some blog about ragged-out former celebrities? *Snort.com,* or something?"

"She got it from watching you. The show. She watches you all the time."

"She should go out and play. Stop watching junk. Do kids still go out and play? Did kids ever go out and play?"

"Was she right?"

"Oh, who knows?" She drummed her fingers on one of the jack-knifed legs. "She was watching Thistle, not me. Maybe she was sad some of the time. Seems like she was. If she'd been happy, she wouldn't—" She broke off and looked out the passenger side window.

"Wouldn't what?"

Her face was averted. "You got anything or not?"

"No."

She shifted onto her right haunch, turned three-quarters away from me and touched her forehead to the window. "Then leave me alone."

I said, "It's a long drive."

"Go away."

"You want some music?"

"There's no such thing as music."

"Fine."

The traffic had picked up its pace, especially in the left lanes, and Doc turned on his indicator. I prepared to follow.

"*He's* got something," Thistle said, looking forward again. "Get him to pull over and give it to me."

"You've got a long day ahead of you."

"Yeah, and I just can't tell you how much I'm looking forward to it. Honk your horn at him."

"Forget it," I said. And then she reached across me and leaned on the horn.

The car swerved and I grabbed her arm and threw it back at her, and she banged her elbow on something, maybe the central console. She let out a wordless wail, rubbing her elbow hard enough to polish it.

I said, "I'll sympathize in a minute, after I change lanes."

"You *hurt* me. I didn't do anything to you, and you hurt me."

"I'm sorry. But grabbing the horn was stupid."

She didn't respond. Then I heard a sniffle.

"Oh, for Christ's sake, stop it," I said. "You weren't hurt that badly."

She stopped sniffling and went perfectly silent. I couldn't even hear her inhale. Just as I was about to tell her to breathe, she made a choked sound, and it turned into a laugh. "They gave me a *cave man*," she said. "They could have given me a Thistle fanatic who'd gush about how great she was and talk about shows I don't even remember. They could have given me a sensitive poet in a beret, or a paranormal who would have looked into my soul. They could have sent a drug dealer, which would have shown some consideration. But they gave me a cave man. A Neanderthal therapist. Sensitive questions and clenched fists." She laughed again. "Who *are* you, anyway?"

"I'm Junior Bender."

"No. That's what your parents named you, or some variation on it. Who are you? Who have you made yourself into in—what—thirty-eight years? Thirty-eight, thirty-nine, something like that?"

"Thirty-six."

"Well, whoops. I over-guessed. Maybe it's because your face looks like it was attacked by a cloud of parakeets. Wait, I remember, a chandelier. Look, if you're having trouble telling me who you are, if this is, as you therapists like to say, a *difficult area*, let's start with something easy. What do you do? When you're not driving people like me, as though there were people like me, what do you do?"

"I'm a burglar."

"Oh, go find somebody who'll believe it. Try the bus station. Lots of dumb people come in every day on the bus."

"It's true. Like it or not, I'm a professional burglar."

"You mean, like full-time?" She stretched the words out derisively.

"Well, you see, that's one of the nice things about being a burglar. You only work a couple of times a month."

"What do you do the rest of the time?"

"Read."

"Yeah. A bookworm burglar who punches women and does therapy on the side. What'll you say if I ask you tomorrow?"

"Same thing. I'm a crook with a book."

"Then what are you reading?" She snapped her fingers. "Right now, and don't take any time to think about it."

"*Oracle Bones* by Peter Hessler. *The Dream of the Red Chamber* by Cao Xueqin—"

"Gesundheit."

"*Waiting*, by Ha Jin, and *The Rape of Nanjing* by Iris Chang."

"Huh," she said. "Isn't Nanjing a city or something?"

"Yes. 'Rape' is figurative. The Japanese killed maybe three

hundred thousand people when they were occupying it during World War Two."

"So things could be worse, you're saying, in your oblique booky-burglar-therapist fashion. We could be in Nanjing, getting killed by the Japanese. With swords, maybe."

"Actually, I was answering your question. But things could always be worse."

"Oh, listen to you," she said. "What the fuck do you know about things being bad, or worse, or hopelessly, end-of-the-world, chew-a-hole-in-the-wall miserable? You're a cave man who breaks into houses two nights a month and gets all sensitive with stoned women."

"Don't be a jerk."

"Okay," she said. "I won't." She straightened her legs out and extended her arms in front of her in a stretch. I glanced over and saw the clarity with which the long muscles of her arms were defined. She was far too thin; she'd burned away most of the subcutaneous fat. "You got any money?"

"Of course, I have money. I'm a burglar. When we run out of money, we steal more."

"Give me some."

"For what?"

"To buy a bus ticket to Omaha, what do you think? Dope costs, and I'm not willing to do what it takes to get it free. Not yet, anyway." She put a hand on my arm. "How about it? Save me from that. It's awful, what they make a girl do. Please, mister? I'm a good kid, really. Don't make me . . . don't make me—" She laughed. "This isn't working, is it?"

"Nope."

"Aww, come on. I don't need much."

"No." Doc's right-hand signal was on again, and I looked up and saw the offramp for Woodman Avenue coming up. I muscled in ahead of the car behind me and slowed slightly to let Doc move over in front of me, getting a nice long honk for my pains.

"Why not?"

"It's a principle. I don't fund drug habits."

She removed her hand from my arm and punched me on the shoulder. "How fucking high-minded."

"And how about you?" I asked. "The question you asked me. Who are you? Who have you turned yourself into in the past twenty-three years?"

"Oh, my God," she said, bringing the back of her hand to her brow like Joan Crawford about to scream. "I'm so *ashamed*. You have no idea how much I've needed to hear that question."

"Then answer it."

"Are you familiar with the concept of irony? Remember, I was just talking about it? I was being ironic. I am who I've always been. A total fuckup. But now I'm a *drugged* fuckup. And you know what they say."

"No. I don't."

"A drugged fuckup is a happy fuckup."

"You weren't a fuckup," I said. "You were brilliant. I've watched you."

"That wasn't me," she said, putting her feet back on the dash. "That was never me, until the end, when it wasn't any good any more. *That* was me. Before, when it was good? The first three or four years? That was *Thistle*. That was the adorable, irreplaceable Thistle." She looked out the window again. "The little bitch."

## 22

### Knife Through Butter

After that announcement, we sat more or less in silence for another twenty minutes as she rode out the ups and downs of her high. During one of the peaks, she asked a couple of questions about the books I was reading, and I told her a little about my approach to education.

She thought about it for a moment and then said, "Jeez."

"I saw your journals," I said. "A lot of them. When I was getting some clothes for you. What do you write about?"

"It's not really writing," she said. "It's circling the drain. It's one long enormous spiral going down, down, down, and I'm following it around and in, closer to the center, and down, closer to the hole."

"And what's the hole?"

"My soul." She laughed. "Isn't that dramatic?"

"I guess," I said. "It's not very good, but it's dramatic."

"It's not *that* bad," she said. "It's better than that thing I said about what they make girls do for dope. Why's he stopping?" Thistle pointed at Doc's car. He had made the turn into the studio driveway and come to a sudden halt. Then he opened the door and climbed out, limping toward us as fast as he could. He got to my window, his face red, and said, "Turn around. Back up. Get her out of here."

And then from behind him, around the corner, a crowd of

people hurtled toward us: mostly drab folks carrying things, and here and there a few members of the on-camera "talent" pool, people with bright clothes, streaked hair, and orange faces.

Thistle said, "Oh, *no*." She kicked the dash. "Go, go, go, *go*."

And then Doc was elbowed out of the way and people had surrounded the car, hammering on the windows and holding up cameras and shouting questions. There seemed to be only one word: spoken, called, shouted, over and over again by the crowd: "Thistle, *Thistle*, Thistle," and every now and then, "Over here, Thistle. Take off the glasses, Thistle. Over *here*, Thistle." A blond woman wearing makeup the color of a tequila sunrise slammed a fist on Thistle's window and said repeatedly, as though it were the modern equivalent of *open sesame*, "Entertainment World News, Entertainment World News."

Thistle put both hands over her face, grabbed a breath, and started to scream, a sound high enough and sharp enough to slice a hole in the roof of the car.

"*Don't*," I said. "Don't give them what they want." I reached over and put a hand on her arm gently, as flash cameras went off like fireworks. She was shaking violently. I pinched her to get her attention. "You can ruin their day," I said. "Screw up their pictures. Don't let them affect you."

She shook her head, fast, "You don't know what you're—"

"They *want to see you fuck up*. That's why they're here. Don't fuck up. You just behave better than they do. It's easy. They'll hate it."

She went still. "How?"

"Outclass them. Class bewilders the hell out of them."

"Out*class*—"

"You have more class when you're asleep than these people will have on their wedding day."

"I have—"

"These people are liver flukes. They're tapeworms. They

have no talent whatsoever. They come at the smell of blood and drink some and then they go back to the studio and spit it up on camera. Are you telling me you can't outclass this bunch?"

She pulled away the hand over the side of her face closest to me and looked at me, one-eyed. "Take care of me?" she asked.

"I will."

"Promise? Absolutely promise?" Her teeth were clenched. "If you break it you'll die?"

"Promise. Now take your hands away from your face and sit back. Relax your face. Don't look at them. Don't take off your sunglasses. Don't even look like you're listening to me. Don't give them anything to photograph. They don't exist. Do you hear me?"

"They're not here," she said, putting her hands in her lap again, like a little girl about to receive communion.

"We're out in the middle of the desert. You don't see anybody, you don't hear anybody."

"You're sure you haven't got any pills."

"Completely sure." I looked up and saw Eduardo and three of Trey's black-suited threateners shoving their way toward us, literally picking people up, moving them, and putting them down elsewhere. They were almost to the car. I signaled them over to the driver's side.

"Slide over here," I said to Thistle. "These guys are going to bull their way through this, with us behind. You get out with me and stay right next to me. Tight, okay? I'm going to have my arm around you all the way. Don't look down, like you're hiding your face. Don't look at them. Don't say anything, don't react, no matter what they say. Just walk with me, head up, face front, with the shades on. Got it?"

"I don't know," she said. "I'm not sure I can—"

"You can. We can. Come on, I'm a cave man. I can get you through this bunch of city softies. Look at them. They wouldn't even know how to go to the bathroom outdoors. They'd wipe themselves on poison oak. They're afraid of bugs. We'll cut through them like butter."

"Like b-butter," she said, stammering slightly. Her lower lip was trembling, and I saw that the hands in her lap were knotted.

"Good. Come on, get over here."

She slid across the seat, lifting her legs for the console, until she was sitting thigh to thigh with me. The woman with the orange face was fighting her way around the front of the car, her eyes fierce and her teeth bared, as big and white as Chiclets. She was following her cameraman, who was swinging his expensive camera to clear a path.

Eduardo was at the door. He looked at me, eyebrows raised. I held up one finger.

"This is it," I said to Thistle. "You and me, okay?"

"Okay." She grabbed a breath and gave me something that was trying to be a smile. "Okay."

"Here we go." I nodded at Eduardo and opened the door. The crowd surged forward, but Eduardo and the other three guys formed a semicircle and pushed everyone back so I could get the door all the way open. There was an explosion of noise and a barrage of flashes. Thistle and I slid off the seat and into a standing position beside the car, and Eduardo's crew started forcing their way through the throng with us practically hanging onto their belts. I had an arm around Thistle's shoulder, and she was clutching my shirt with both hands.

"Over here, Thistle!"

"Thistle, give me a smile."

"What about the drugs, Thistle?"

"Is it true you're broke?"

"Thistle, look, I've got some dope."

"Over here. God damn you, look over here."

"Thistle—what about your mom? You talking to your mom yet?"

And then there was a blast of light to my right, and I saw the sun gun on top of the Entertainment World News camera, and the orange-faced woman pushed her way in with a concerned expression, glanced at the cameraman to make sure she was in the shot, leaned forward, and said, "Thistle. How do you feel about doing porno?"

Thistle shuddered against me and said, "*Aaaahhhhh,*" more a breath out than a word, and for a moment I thought she'd go limp. The woman worked her way closer and began to ask her question again, and I reached over Thistle, palm open, put my hand on the woman's face, and shoved. She went straight back and then down, her cameraman backing up to follow her trajectory to the pavement. I said, "No comment." There was another burst of flashbulbs, mostly aimed at the reporter on the asphalt, and we plowed on through the crowd. At some point, Doc fought his way over to us. "How's she doing?" he asked me.

"Ask her."

"Thistle. How are you?"

"Like a knife through butter." She was pale, and her face shone with sweat, but her voice was steady. "But when we get inside," she said, "you're going to give me something."

We made it through the gate, which slid closed behind us to shut out the horde, and Eduardo and the thugs led us to a door. One of them opened it and we went in, into a dark space, and then lights snapped on and something bright flew toward our faces, and Thistle screamed again and grabbed me. Then the bright mass broke apart into thousands of flower petals that fell around us, covering the floor at our feet.

## 23
### My Burglar

"Ms. Annunziato wants you," Eduardo said.

"That's very flattering, but not now." I'd hustled Thistle into a makeup chair and grabbed her a cup of water. Tatiana and the makeup people had been huddled around the chair, waiting to soothe Thistle, but Doc had shooed them all out and now stood with his back to us, a needle inserted into an ampule.

Pale in the lights surrounding the makeup mirrors, Thistle watched his movements, her mouth slightly open. She'd been shaking, but the sight of Doc at work seemed to calm her.

"Now," Eduardo said.

"Go away. I'll be there in a few minutes."

"Young man," Doc said over his shoulder. "As this young woman's physician, my medical opinion is that you should beat it. And Ms. Annunziato pays me big bucks for my expertise. Scram. Mosey along. There's the door."

"She's not going to like this," Eduardo said, but he turned to the door.

"It's good for her," I said. "It builds character." Eduardo closed the door somewhat loudly behind him.

"A well-bred slam," Doc said.

"Come *on*," Thistle said. "My skin feels raw."

"This one is on the light side," Doc said, the needle vertical as he pushed out the last of the air. "After a few minutes, you're going to get over the rush of that pack of wolves out there, and you'll realize you're still high from the first one. This is just a little booster."

"What about the down button?"

"Percocet. Only one."

I said, "You were great."

Thistle rolled up the sleeve of her T-shirt. "You got me through it."

Doc swabbed her arm and injected her, the process reflected in four makeup mirrors simultaneously. Thistle watched herself as though the person in the mirrors was a complete stranger. I wished she wasn't wearing the dark glasses. I wanted to see her eyes. But then her chin dropped an inch or two, and she looked down at her lap. She dragged in a deep breath and blew it out.

"Listen," I said, "I'm sorry about that woman—"

She brought the head up as though she was startled, but then she began to laugh. "You really did it, you know? World headlines. I might have been the third or fourth story of the night, but you decking Miss Entertainment World while I'm right next to you, that's going to be the lead everywhere. We'll be on the fucking BBC." She laughed again, pitched a little too high, and took off the sunglasses and wiped her eyes. "*Just walk,* you tell me. *Don't descend to their level. Don't give them anything. Show them some class.*" She laughed again. "And then you paste that horrible bitch in front of every camera in Los Angeles. You know what? About six o'clock tonight, you're going to be the most famous burglar in the world."

"Yeah, well, I'm sorry."

"Are you kidding? I haven't seen anything that funny in years. That was Buster Keaton funny. My burglar. That's going to be the title of a chapter in my autobiography."

"How you feeling?" Doc said.

"Like a cloud of gnats. I feel like you can see through me. It's okay, kind of a new place."

"Good. One pill, coming up."

The door to the dressing room opened, and Trey Annunziato came in. Today's suit was a teal blue that, floating on a pond, would have attracted every female duck for miles. I guessed it at twelve hundred on special, and I doubted she'd bought it on special.

"I want you, and I want you now," Trey said to me, and then her eyes slid past me and she smiled and said, "*Hello*, darling, don't you look pretty today? So fresh and clear-eyed. Your lip is healing nicely."

"This is really, really class dope," Thistle said. "And what's the title of this movie, *Thistle's Lip*?" It's all anybody talks about." She glanced at herself in the mirror and tugged the lip down. "While we're at it, don't yell at my burglar."

"Your—oh, you mean Mr. Bender here."

"He got me in here," Thistle said. "Don't you forget it."

Trey stepped forward, claiming the small room as hers. She was maintaining the smile, but it had very sharp corners. "Let's all just modulate our tone. This is a big morning, and we don't want to get off on the wrong foot.'

"We already have," I said. "That mob scene outside—"

Trey held up a peremptory hand. "Thistle was told there would be reporters here," she said. She leaned a little on the smile. "Weren't you, dear?"

I turned to Thistle. She raised her shoulders to her ears, pulled down the corners of her mouth, and let her shoulders drop.

"Somebody should have told me," I said.

"I can't think of a single reason why," Trey said in the brightly empty tone of someone who is determined to be pleasant no matter what.

"Because Thistle either wasn't told or doesn't remember. If she wasn't told, I should have known about it. If she forgot, someone should have anticipated that she might, and told me. I was in charge of getting her here."

"You *put* yourself in charge," Trey said. "You put yourself in charge of her last night, too, but that didn't keep her from doping herself into a coma, did it? Sorry to talk about you in the third person, darling."

"You were there last night?" Thistle asked, her face screwed up. "I don't remember you."

"I wasn't there. You and I need to talk," I said to Trey.

"Yes, and I've been sending Eduardo to you all morning to tell you that," she said. "But before we close the subject of the media, let's make sure that Thistle hasn't also forgotten the press conference that starts in"—she looked at a watch that was thinner than hope—"about fifteen minutes."

"No," Thistle said, mostly breath. Her eyes went to me.

"It's in your contract. You agreed to do it,"

"No."

"Let's not waste time. You need a little makeup and hair, and I've got a team outside—"

"You are not hearing me," Thistle said, more loudly. She swallowed twice before continuing. "I said no. Go away and leave me alone."

"All right," Trey said with resignation. "I suppose it's just as well to get this over now." She came the rest of the way into the room, edging past Doc, and leaned her backside against the edge of the makeup counter. "I want to get along with you, I really do. I loved you when I was a child. I'm sure a million people have told you this, but I had a lot of problems with my own parents, and all I wanted in the world was to be you, with magic powers that could fix everything—"

"You're right," Thistle said. "A million people have told me this."

"Well, dear, you're going to hear it again. We actually have a lot in common, did you know that? We both had our whole families depending on us all the time, watching us, making sure we were who they wanted us to be. And I don't know about you, but I *wasn't* who they wanted me to be. I was the daughter of a gangster who only wanted a son. I was given a male name, did you know that?"

"Poor you," Thistle said. "I was named after a weed."

"But as much as we have in common and as much as I admire your talent, you are contractually obligated to keep your commitments to me. You're a competent adult, more or less, who has made an agreement to deliver services in exchange for remuneration. California law is very clear on this: you are nailed to this project. I have a lot of money riding on these movies, dear, quite a bit of which is going to you. You are going to show up and do your job, and when you're finished you'll be given two hundred thousand dollars, in cash, which you can do anything you want with. If you cross me—and by that, I mean, if you don't keep your promises, *all* your promises—you won't get a penny. Is that clear? It's all in your contract, which you have signed and initialed profusely. This press conference is in that contract. If you're going to go back on your word, if you're going to breach the contract, now is the time to do it, before I waste any more money."

Trey crossed her arms, and the diamonds in her watch sparkled. "So, dear, it's really up to you. Quit right now or play the game." She pushed herself away from the counter and took a couple of steps closer to Thistle, so she was looking down at her. "You can do it," she said more softly. "You're a smart, talented girl. You just go out there and tell them the truth, and we'll be fine." She reached out and smoothed Thistle's hair and removed the sunglasses, and Thistle stood for it, didn't move her head a fraction of an inch. Her eyes were locked on Trey's sternum. "What do you say? Let's get along for a few days and get this done, and then you'll have all that money. You can go back to your life."

Thistle turned her face away and said, "You were doing great until then." She recaptured her shades but didn't put them on. To me, she said, "What do you think?"

Trey involuntarily raised one eyebrow a millimeter at the question, and her eyes went speculatively from me to Thistle.

"Do I think you *can* do it?" I asked. "Or do I think you *should* do it?"

"Can," she said. "We both know I shouldn't."

"I think you can. But I agree that you shouldn't."

"Miss Thing here has made it clear that I should. That I have to, if I want grocery money. I want you with me."

"I think the press has seen enough of Mr. Bender today," Trey said.

"Hold on," Thistle said, without looking at her. "Just hold on one fucking minute. You're used to being agreed with, so this might be hard for you, but here it is." She swung her head around to face Trey. "I may have to do the things I said I would, but that doesn't mean I can't do them my way. You want this to happen, right?"

Trey was glaring at me, as though I were to blame for Thistle's resistance. "Of course."

Suddenly something happened to Thistle. It took only an instant; there seemed to be no transition at all. Her face mirrored Trey's expression precisely, and her spine straightened in exact mimicry of Trey's stance. When she spoke, her voice sounded uncannily like Trey's. "Of course," she said. "Of course you do. You have money invested. Then go away. Go manage someone."

Startled, Trey took a step back.

"You won, okay?" Thistle/Trey continued. She even had Trey's hand gestures, the way she held her head. "Junior will help me do this, just like he helped me get in here. And it won't be in fifteen minutes, it'll be in half an hour. Or a little more. You go away and make money, and let the makeup people get in here. Doc," she said, turning, " I'm feeling that little elevator, so I want an extra smoothie. Or maybe a couple, all things considered." She looked back at Trey. "Are you still here?"

Trey regarded her for a moment, then nodded. "That's a cute

trick," she said. "Let's hope you're that good on camera." Then she turned to me, and her voice when she said, "Mister Bender?" could have frozen meat.

"Coming." Trey was out the door. "I'll be back," I said to Thistle.

With Trey gone, she was herself again. She slumped back into the chair as though she'd run a hundred yards. "Good, because if you're not, they're going to have to carry this whole chair onstage."

I followed Trey out of the room and into the hallway. Tatiana, leading the makeup and hair crew into the room, gave me a questioning glance and then looked at Trey's rigid back as she marched down the hall. "If you were a stock," she whispered, "would you advise me to buy or sell?"

"Sell," I said. "But I don't think you could get anything for it."

Before trying to catch up with Trey, I made a ninety-second telephone call. Essentially just the studio's address and a question that might prove useful in half an hour or so.

## 24

### Sew This Back Into Your Leonardo

"I want an explanation," Trey said, her hands folded in front of her, her back plumb-straight. We were back in the classroom set, facing each other over the teacher's desk, and she was the image of the strict third-grade teacher who's just found a bad word on the chalkboard. I suppose I was expected to feel chastened, but it was hard for me to look at her without seeing Thistle's extraordinary impersonation.

"Is there anything in particular you'd like explained? I'm reasonably well-informed on a relatively broad spectrum of subjects."

"Let's begin with what's going on between Thistle and you."

"That's easy. There's nothing going on between Thistle and me."

"She looks at you every time I ask her a question. She *consults* with you. I'm paying her, and she's turning to you for advice. I want to know why."

"She's got nobody in the world," I said. "I made her laugh this morning. I dragged her through that pack of parasites when we arrived. I'm the temporary hero. She's not exactly aces in the self-confidence department, and she needs to turn to somebody. Right now, I'm it."

"For someone with no self-confidence, she told me to fuck off rather effectively."

"She used to be a star. Stars are good at that."

"Well, I don't like it, you siding with her like that. You're working for me, not her."

"I've got two answers to that. The first is that she needs a friend or she's not going to be functional, and she's chosen me. The second is that you have a much bigger problem than Thistle telling you to fuck off." I reached into my pocket and took out the snippet of painting. "Here. You can sew this back into your Leonardo."

She looked down at it but made no move to take it. "I told you to give that to your lookout."

I dropped it onto the desk. "He won't need it any more. Somebody shot him."

One hand went to the surface of the desk although her face didn't change. "Excuse me?"

"Last night, outside Thistle's apartment house, someone put one through his throat at close range."

She took a mechanical step back, pulled the chair out from under the desk without looking down at it, and sat. She seemed to be giving her movements no attention whatsoever. She finally said, "Murdered?"

"If you know a nicer word, share it with me."

"Was he a friend, or just someone you hired?"

"A friend."

She turned her head an inch to the right and then brought it back. It was almost a sympathetic shake of the head. "I'm sorry." She licked her lips. "How—don't take this badly—how good was he?"

"The best I knew."

Her right hand did a little side-to-side movement, disagreement she might not have known she was expressing. "But you said it—the shot, I mean—was fired at close range."

"That's what I said."

"Then how good could he have been?" I had a feeling I was hearing her father's voice.

I said, "He had his weaknesses. Like most of us. Somebody who looked like you could have gotten close."

"Like—like *me?* Are you serious?"

"I didn't say you, I said someone who looked like you. Attractive, in other words. He liked women too much, more than I do, anyway. Or a kid could have gotten close. He wouldn't have felt threatened by a kid."

Two fingers went to her left eyebrow and smoothed it while her eyes searched mine. "You mean a child?"

"Or Thistle," I said, just to be thorough. "He was there to protect her. If she'd come out of the apartment house and approached him, he'd have just sat there and watched her come. Which is apparently what he did. His gun was still in his holster."

Trey shook her head, not so much disagreeing as having trouble processing the information. "But you know Thistle better than—I mean, you obviously don't think she shot your friend."

"I have no idea whether I know Thistle. This is someone who talks about herself in the third person. I like her, the bits of her she lets me see, which isn't much."

"How can you be sure? What you see is mostly chemicals."

"There's somebody under all that fog, somebody interesting. So I like her, and I feel sorry for her. But even if I didn't like her, I'd be sure she didn't kill him, because I'm pretty sure someone tried to kill her, too."

Trey brought up both hands, palms out. "Wait, wait. Time out." She got up, walked around the desk, and went to the edge of the set. She peered behind the wall to the left, apparently making certain no one was there, and then she checked behind the other wall. When she was certain we were alone, she came back to the desk and sat. She pointed to the nearest student desk and made a little come-here gesture. Since the desk wasn't paying attention to her, I grabbed it and hauled it over to her and sat down. Once I was down, she pointed at the walls and then touched her ear. She leaned forward conspiratorially. "You're going to have to back things up," she said very quietly. "This is the beginning of the day, and I came into it with a couple of dozen things on my mind. Now I have to toss most of them and focus on this. I want you to take a breath and tell me everything in some sort of order. Try chronological. Maybe we can make some sense out of it."

So I gave her all of it, including the little gift box of Rohypnol someone had so thoughtfully left on Thistle's doorstep. The only thing I left out was the banged-up white Chevy, because I had no idea what to make of it, and Trey had denied any knowledge of the two girls who had been driving it. When I'd finished, we sat there in that parody of a schoolroom like two students who'd been sentenced to silent detention for twenty years.

She reached up and rubbed the bridge of her nose. "Why didn't they just shoot Thistle?" she asked. It was almost a whisper.

"I don't know. She may not have been alone. There were three dirty wineglasses on the floor. Maybe whoever it was heard voices through the door, didn't want to have to kill a bunch of people. Maybe they figured killing Thistle Downing would start a firestorm in the media, so they'd let her do the job herself with the pills. But the truth is that I don't even know why they shot Jimmy."

"Because he saw them?"

"He was just a guy in a car," I said. "How would they know what he was looking for? At first, I figured he'd spotted your husband and maybe he'd reacted somehow. But then he'd have had his gun out, and he didn't. And if he didn't give them some sort of reaction, then why shoot him? They were there to leave those pills for Thistle and sneak away, not to shoot people out in the street. So that leaves another possibility, which is that someone told them Jimmy would be there."

"Did you tell anyone?"

"No."

"Well, certainly you don't think that I—"

"Did you?"

"That's both unintelligent and offensive." She pushed the chair back a couple of inches. Her hands were on the desk, all the fine bones visible beneath the skin. She was at least ten pounds underweight—not as thin as Thistle, but whip-thin, and I thought again of Thistle's imitation. Trey, I realized, was one of the people Thistle might have grown up to be, if she'd remained a star and held the drugs at bay.

"I find it offensive that he's dead," I said. "And I didn't talk to anyone."

She closed her eyes for a moment, and willed her face to soften. When she opened them, she said, "I'm sorry about your friend. I know how it is to lose people. But you have to realize that what I want most right now is to get these movies made. We can avoid another exchange like this if you'll keep that in mind. I wouldn't do anything, not anything, that would endanger this project."

It didn't cost anything, so I said, "I'm sorry."

She nodded once, just acknowledgment. She said, "There are times one doesn't want to be right, and this is one of them. I said yesterday that this was the critical period, but I never thought it would get to murder."

"I can't imagine why you didn't. You're surrounded by people who shoot other people the way most of us choose a breakfast cereal. And you said it yourself: there are a lot of them who don't like your new direction." I pushed the scrap of canvas toward her. "You cut this out. How serious are you about it?"

"You mean, do I actually think my husband is involved?" She put her face into her hands and rubbed it for a second, looking briefly like the young woman in her twenties she actually was. Then she pulled her hands back and raked her hair off her face. "I think he could be. He's a big enough shit, and he doesn't like the position I've put him in."

"Which is?"

"He married me in the firm belief that he would be the master, that I would love, honor, and obey, by which he meant I'd get up and cook breakfast and wear an apron all day and have kids who looked just like him, and leave all the hard stuff, all the *guy* stuff, to him. Stuff like running my father's family. He was going to be King Tony the First. He did everything except go out and buy a crown."

"What's his full name?"

"Tony Ramirez. Antonio, actually, but he likes Tony. It's easier for him to remember. He's not exactly Mensa material. And he doesn't expect anybody else to be, either. I think his first unpleasant surprise came when I didn't change all the monograms so I could become Trey Ramirez. And it's a good thing I didn't, since I'd be changing it back now anyway."

"Divorced?"

"All but." She picked up the scrap of painted canvas and looked at it as though from a great height, then put it face down on the desk. "A few weeks more, and the paper sword will fall on the knot binding us together. Then he'll really be out in the cold. Just another unemployed hunk of muscle with a good profile. So, yeah, I think he might be behind this. Among the more macho guys who do chores for us, there are some who figure that working for my father's son-in-law beats the hell out of working for his daughter."

"*Could* he run the business? You say he's not smart, but how smart would he have to be?"

"He operates at about the same level of intelligence as a microwave oven. But some of the guys who'll back him are counting on that. They're figuring that he'll be so busy counting his money and looking at himself in a mirror that they'll pretty much have things their way. And to answer your second question, to run an operation as complex as the one my father put together, you have to be *very* smart."

"Personal question?"

She shook her head, and then offered me the sliver of a smile. "Oh, why not?"

"You're too intelligent to marry a household appliance. Why?"

"Would you buy it if I told you I was girlishly swept off my feet?"

"Not by a tailor's dummy."

"Okay," she said. "Tony is really good. He has two skills. The first one is to stand there and let people look at him. He's pretty enough to preserve in amber, and he knows how to use it. The second thing is talking people around. You've dealt with sociopaths?"

"Who hasn't? In our line of work, I mean."

"Well, Tony qualifies. It's not just that he doesn't have a con-science, although he doesn't. I think he could shoot you and his major worry would be the price of the bullet. But mostly it's the way he can read you, play to your weaknesses, make you feel like—like whatever your question is, he's the answer. He read me down to my gene sequence. I was twenty-two and dumb and in full revolt against everything my father wanted for me. Like most kids in criminal families, I was brought up on the straight and narrow, Catholic school and everything. Tony was so far off the path my father had planned for me he might as well have been on another continent. And he played that for all it was worth. Defying my father, who didn't like Mexicans and would have been horrified at me marrying some mid-level knuckle-duster. And aiming that face straight at all that pent-up Catholic schoolgirl lust. I'd never felt so brave and alive in my life."

"Danger is addictive."

"Sure, but I knew I wasn't really the one who was in the line of fire. My father might just have resolved the situation by hav-ing him killed. Dad favored direct solutions. Tony said he was willing to risk that, and I have to admit that my reaction was pretty much, *For little me?* I figured it proved he loved me." She sat back, hearing herself. "I'm telling you this because I suppose there's a chance you're going to come up against him."

I knew the next remark might take me straight off the map, but I needed to say it, if only to begin to figure out how much trouble I was in. "But your father *didn't* kill Tony."

Trey's eyes were on me, and they didn't waver a hundredth of an inch. She held my gaze, and then said, "That's right. He might have, in a week or two, but he didn't. As you know, his plans, whatever they were, were rudely interrupted."

I said, "Yes," and let it hang.

After a moment, she said, "I don't actually know that Tony did it. Not for a fact."

This was pretty close to exactly what I didn't want to hear. "But you suspected it."

"I tried not to. Tony and I were already married. That's why my father was so furious. We eloped. I was in New York on business, staying at the Carlyle, and one evening there was a knock on the door, and surprise, surprise, guess who. We had a ridiculously romantic week, real gigolo stuff. And I fell for it. We stopped in Las Vegas on the way home. I thought my father was going to have a heart attack. Me, trading my last name for *Ramirez.*"

"You're aware," I said, "that people think you had your father done."

"Sure," she said. "And I let them. I'm a girl, remember? Everybody figured I was going to be Miss Valentine, the sweetheart of the underworld. So I took the blame, and it made a lot of people afraid of me, people who wouldn't have been afraid of me otherwise. It was useful."

"And I might be up against the guy who had your father killed."

She drew a square on the surface of the table with a carnelian-tipped index finger. "Believe me," she said, "I never thought it would get to this point." She erased the imaginary square with her palm and offered me a slender smile. "And maybe it won't."

"Whether it does or not, here's the problem. I'm only one guy. I haven't got a squad I can deploy. I can check out your ex, or I can stick with Thistle. I can't do both. And I can't protect this whole movie, although I'm pretty sure that Thistle is the obvious target."

"She's the only indispensable element." Trey said.

"But you've got resources," I said. "It's just you and me here, and nobody else is listening. Why don't you kill somebody?"

She didn't look surprised, although she let a three-heartbeat pause go by before answering. "Kill whom? If I put Tony under, I'm the first place the cops will look. Lots of public rancor there, wrangling over assets, the whole mess."

"Somebody close to him. Somebody you think might be working for him, helping with this. Send a message right back, let them know that the film is not to be fucked with."

"Aren't you the cold one? Kill this one, kill that one. I thought you were a burglar, not a hitman."

"They killed a friend of mine. Somebody's probably going to die for that, anyway."

"I see," she said. "But it'll wait until you have some time on your hands."

"It might, it might not. So what about it? There's nothing like a well-placed bullet for getting people's attention."

"I don't know," she said. "I'm supposed to be turning my back on all that. Kicking it off with a murder seems inconsistent, to say the least."

"Just a thought." I got up. "By the way, as long as we're talking, you know that this movie isn't good for Thistle."

"That's on my conscience, not yours." She stood as well. "And listen. Underneath all the dope and the psychic wreckage, Thistle may be a perfectly nice girl. I admit that. You might be right about her. And you know what? That's too bad. For my purposes, she's irreplaceable. She did to the whole world what Tony did to me. Hundreds of millions of people bought into what she was selling, and she blew them off. She's my primary asset here. I'm deadly serious about protecting her, up to the point where it endangers her making the movie. Don't make any mistakes about that."

"Noted," I said.

"And as you said, *as long as we're talking,* I think you have a problem with women. You sympathize with Thistle in a way you wouldn't if she were male. And you don't take me as seriously as you would if I'd been my father's son instead of his daughter. But I'm telling you now. I am every bit as dangerous as my father was. And if you find yourself torn between taking care of Thistle or taking care of me, just remember that I'm an Annunziato, and we don't deal well with betrayal. Is that clear?"

"Transparent."

"Your job is to help me get this movie done, no matter what you think about it. Understand?"

"No one would accuse you of ambiguity."

"When it's all over, we'll sit down and discuss things." She smiled and put a hand on my upper arm. "We can probably wind up friends, as hard as that may be to believe right now."

"Oh, good," I said. "A man can always use a friend."

## 25

### The Truth, Unless a Lie Works Better

Her hand in mine was a surprise.

Trey had commandeered a large screening room for the press conference. It seated maybe forty people, and from the sound of it, it was jammed. We could hear the hubbub the moment we opened the door into the backstage area, a jumble of voices like a crowd scene in an old radio show.

The moment she heard them, Thistle reached over and grabbed my hand. Her palm was damp and her hand was as small as a child's.

It was dark backstage, but there was a spill of light from the proscenium, which was brighter than the equator at high noon. We came in stage left, about ten feet from the brilliant stage, and the first things I saw were two sixty-inch flat-screen TVs with a tall wood-and-canvas director's chair dead center between them. The chair was on the monitors, too. And then I saw the five gigantic blow-ups of Thistle, taken when she was fourteen or fifteen, propped up on easels. Judging from their underexposure and general graininess, they were probably blowups from video. Technically they were a mess, but their message was clear, and it was sick enough to stop Thistle in her tracks.

"How could she?"

"She's smart, Thistle. She knows what her visual is. You, talking about doing this kind of a movie, in front of those pictures."

She was shifting from foot to foot, still hanging onto my hand. "I can't. I can't go out there. Not with *those*."

I thought, the hell with it. I gave her hand a tug. "Good. Let's go."

"But she'll fire me. I need—I need that money."

"She can't fire you. If she fires you, she hasn't got a movie."

She put both hands over mine, squeezing hard. "She will. She's using this to figure out whether I'm going to do what she wants me to do. If I don't go out there, I won't get anything."

"Thistle. Listen to me. I'm *working* for her. It's my job to make sure she gets this movie done. But I'm telling you that this isn't worth a couple hundred thousand. Let's go."

"I can't. It's not . . . you don't know. I can't even pay my rent."

"I'll pay your fucking rent."

"What, for the rest of my life? Are you hearing yourself?" She dropped my hand and turned away from me, the carefully brushed hair catching fire in the light from the stage. She put both hands on top of her head, one atop the other, palms down. "Ohhhh," she said. "Oh, I am so *fatally* fucked." One hand dropped to her stomach. "I don't feel good."

"Come on. We'll get out of here and think about this later."

"Later. *Later*. There isn't any later. This *is* later. *Before* is over, it ended a long time ago, and this is where I am. Oh, God, look at those dickheads out there. I need a wastebasket."

I didn't see one, but there was a fire bucket against one wall, and I said, "Over there," and Thistle ran to it, bent over, and vomited. She heaved until there wasn't anything left, and all I could do was watch the spasms rack her narrow shoulders and listen to her cough as she tried to bring up more. The cough turned into a sob and then two and then three, her body forcing them out as though something massive was squeezing her, and I thought she was going to lose it completely, but she choked it off somehow and remained there, bent over the bucket, as the chatter continued from the screening room and erupted into laughter. Her fists were clenched, her arms straight down with the elbows locked. Then, when she knew she had it under control, she relaxed her back and arms, straightened, and wiped her mouth.

She turned around and looked back at the light pouring off of the stage area, as though she wouldn't be surprised to see an arena full of lions, lazily waiting for her. Then she closed both eyes tight, squared her shoulders, and breathed out, hard. Her eyes opened again, and she was looking at me.

"Relax," she said. "I used to do that before the first take every day. Is my chin clean?"

"Immaculate."

"How's my makeup?"

I looked closely. "It's okay. Your mascara ran a little bit."

"I always tear up when I vomit." Her eyes dared me to contradict her. "Can you fix it for me?"

"Not one of my specialties, but I can try." I put my left hand on her shoulder and used the tip of my right little finger to wipe away the errant black tracks. Beneath my hand, she was shuddering as though she was moments from freezing to death. "You're okay," I said.

"I doubt it," she said. Her voice was steady. "But it should at least be interesting. I just heaved Doc's pills, all the downers and smoothies, everything that was supposed to slow me down, and he gave me a second shot. Oh, and one of the makeup girls had some coke. So I'm going nowhere but up." Her face was slick with sweat, and she mopped it with the back of her hand, then slipped her hands into the neck of her T-shirt and put them under her arms. She pulled her hands out and wiped them on her jeans. "I'm *sopping*," she said. "Dead wet girls. I remember you talking about dead wet girls. Claudette Colbert and dead wet girls. What a frame of reference."

I took my hand off her shoulder. "I'm telling you for the last time, don't go out there."

Her eyes came up to mine. "Why? You're working for Trey, right? What do you care?"

"This sounds corny, but beautiful things shouldn't be wrecked. It's nothing to cheer about when trash gets wrecked, but you have something only one person in ten million has. You need to take care of it."

"You still don't understand," she said. "I don't have *any-thing*. That wasn't me. I'm trash, and I need two hundred thousand dollars. Trash buys dope. Are you coming?"

"I said I would."

"People say a lot of things." She turned to face the stage, just in time to see Trey step into the light on the other side. "I didn't mean that," she said without turning back to me.

"What the hell are you going to tell them?"

"Trey said, *tell them the truth*," she said in Trey's voice. "So I will. Unless a lie works better."

"You're absolutely certain."

"I'm waiting for the alternative."

"Okay, I'm with you. Give me your right shoe."

"Ladies and gentlemen," Trey said. "I'm Trey Annunziato, the executive producer of *Three Wishes*. Thank you so much for coming."

"My shoe? Why do you need—"

"I just need it. Right now. Hurry."

She put a hand on my arm for balance, bent down, and pulled off her right sneaker. I took it and used the little penknife I always carry to worry a hole in the toe. "I'll buy you a new pair," I said. "Get this back on."

". . . one of the most talented actresses ever on American television, and the youngest Emmy winner ever," Trey was saying. She looked across the stage and saw me standing over Thistle, who was on one knee pulling her shoe on. Trey raised both eyebrows at me, clearly in the imperative and meaning *Get her ready right now.*

"I think this is your cue," I said.

"Wooo, that's a lot of dope," Thistle said, standing back up. "*Going up*. Wish I hadn't heaved those Percocets. Listen, if I say too much, put your hand on my shoulder, okay? If I keep talking, squeeze. I might not notice if you don't."

". . . my great pleasure," Trey said, "to introduce you to Thistle Downing."

"Fuck you and *hello*," Thistle said, smiling at Trey.

She stepped out on the stage with me two paces behind her, and every light in the northern hemisphere flashed at us. A few people clapped, but it didn't catch on. Cameras exploded all over the room, and the lights on half a dozen TV cameras did their electric supernovas. The light was so thick I felt like we were wading through it.

The director's chair I'd seen on the monitors was dead center on the stage, positioned in front of the earliest of the photos of Thistle. This close to the picture, I revised my guess at her age downward to thirteen. Thistle hoisted herself up into the chair and the image was echoed on the monitors. I stood next to her, and the bulbs all went off again as I blinked against them. I caught a sudden whiff of something sharp and acidic and realized it was Thistle's fear.

"Could you move away?" a photographer shouted at me. I started to step aside, but Thistle sunk nails into my wrist. I stayed where I was.

"Who is he?" someone else called out.

People were shouting questions, and Thistle didn't respond, just sat perfectly still, her eyes floating somewhere above the crowd as though there were a ball of light drifting there, maybe bringing the Good Witch of the East to her rescue. Trey watched nervously. To her it may have seemed as though Thistle was in command of herself, waiting calmly for order, but her grip on my wrist actually hurt, and the knuckles of her other hand, clasping the arm of her chair, were about to burst through the skin. Eventually, the noise died away.

"That's better," Thistle said. Her voice was very small. People in the four rows of seats leaned forward to hear her and some of them held up small tape recorders. The film crews standing at the back of the room fiddled with their equipment. "Someone asked—" She cleared her throat and started over, louder this time. "Someone asked who this man is. He's my personal burglar. Every girl needs a burglar, and he's mine." They started to shout again, and Thistle held up both hands. When it was relatively quiet again, she said, "I have very sensitive hearing. Especially right now. If you keep yelling, I'll have to leave. Just put up a hand, and I'll call on you one at a time."

From her side of the stage Trey said, "I thought I might choose the questions."

Without turning her head, Thistle said, "Did you really?" Trey gave her a smile that should have sliced her in half, and stepped back in retreat.

"What's his name?" a photographer called. "For the captions."

"My name is Pockets Mahoney," I said.

"Pockets is a nickname," Thistle said. "You should put it in quotation marks, those of you who bother to punctuate." She pointed to a woman in the middle of the first row and said, "You. You get to shoot first."

"Thistle," the woman said, oozing empathy. "You were a big star. Why are you doing this?"

Thistle said, "I need money. Don't you ever need money?"

"But you sold your residuals," the woman said. "You got hundreds of millions of dollars for them. What happened to all that?"

"I made bad investments," Thistle said.

Other people were waving their hands, but the woman persisted. "Investments in what?"

Thistle said, "Pharmaceuticals," and pointed at a short man with a toupee so bad I could spot it past all the lights.

"You have a whole generation of new fans," he began.

Thistle said, "If you say so."

"Most of them are young girls. How do you think they'll feel to know you're making an adult film? Do you think that you're a good role model for them?"

The girl who did Thistle's hair had put some sort of guck on her bangs to make them look spiky, and she took one of the spikes and twirled it between her fingers, her hand hiding part of her face. "Do you want a serious answer?"

"Sure," the reporter said.

"Okay. I don't think young girls should need role models. I think they should grow up on their own. But if they do need role models, it's dumb to use somebody who's on television. They should use someone they know. A teacher, maybe, or an older sister. Maybe their mother. Not my mother, obviously, but their mother. *My* mother wouldn't be a good role model for a serial killer, much less—" I squeezed her shoulder, and she broke off. "Look, nobody who saw me on television knows anything at all about me. I was never that little girl. Anyway, what kind of role model is a witch? How dumb is that? 'My role model solves problems with magic.' So what's she going to do when she's seventeen years old and she gets pregnant by some asshole with a stocking cap and a bolt through his lower lip? She going to wave a wand at her stomach? Suppose she marries some jerk who hits her. She's going to dematerialize before he connects? Actually, if you don't mind my saying so, that's a stupid question." She pointed at someone else. "Your turn."

"You were the most famous little girl in America for seven years—"

"Eight," Thistle said.

"Sorry. How has it felt to live in obscurity for the last eight or nine years?"

"*Obscurity*?" Thistle said, leaning on the word heavily enough to make it sag in the middle. "I guess that's one way to put it. It took me a while to adjust to *obscurity*, to use your word, not to mention poverty and a closer relationship with the world of large insects living under sinks. As you can probably guess, it was very different. Not that it was all bad. You know, in my old life I'd gotten used to having vultures circling around all the time, waiting for me to pick my nose or smoke a cigarette in public so they could deliver it into people's houses that night. So I didn't have bugs, but I had vultures. I'd started to think it was normal to have cameras shoved in my face all the time and hear people shout rude questions at me and then, when I was tired of being worked to death or had a stomachache and didn't answer, they'd say that I wasn't *grateful* or something, like *they'd* made me famous, when all they were really trying to do was take a bite out of me so they could get their forty-five seconds of face time on some shitty cable channel." She glanced up at me. "Coming because they smell blood and then spitting some of it up on camera. I'd gotten used to having these people live on me, sort of like mold on bread." I put a hand on her shoulder, but she shrugged it off. "I can't really say I missed being part of all that, where people like you make a big deal out of people like me just so you can turn around and start grinding us into sausage." She stopped and drew a couple of quick breaths. "So, yeah, I had to adjust, but I can't say I cried myself to sleep every night. Basically, I like the bugs better than I liked the vultures."

"But here you are again," the reporter said nastily.

"And so are you," Thistle said. "And a few dozen exactly like you. At least there's only one of me."

I caught a glimpse of motion on the far side of the stage and saw Trey stepping back out of sight. She kept her eyes on Thistle as she pulled out a cell phone and started to dial.

Thistle pointed at someone else, a female I recognized from

local news, where she did stories about how even regular people are interesting, and isn't that great? "You," Thistle said.

"You mentioned your mother a minute ago. Are you speaking to her?"

"I'm sorry," Thistle said. "I didn't hear you." She started to point at someone else, but the reporter pushed on.

"Your *mother*," she said. "I asked if you—"

"Can't hear a word," Thistle said. "Next."

Trey was talking on the phone, saying something sharp if her expression was any indication. Her eyes were still on Thistle. It looked like Trey was reconsidering her resale value.

"Why are you so hostile?" was the question.

"*Hostile*?" Thistle said. "This isn't hostile. This is just recess, we're playing together nicely. I mean, come on, let's at least be honest. You've all come here to make an omelet, and I'm the egg you have to break."

Trey hung up the phone and came back into the light.

"Why do you say that?" the reporter asked. "Why do you assume we're not on your side?"

"Okay." Thistle held up two fingers in a V formation. "First, let's forget personal experience, which I've had a lot of. But today, today there are two possible stories, right? Let's not be hypocrites. You're all going to leave with one or the other. The first one is, *Look, everybody, that cute little kid grew up to be a slut*. That's like the moral high ground angle. Whoever delivers it will probably work up a righteous frown. The second one is, *Gee, isn't it tragic, that cute little kid grew up to be a slut*. That's the compassionate angle, accompanied by a sad shake of the head, and probably mostly from female reporters whose hair won't move. Maybe one or two of you will take it further and go for a local Emmy, talk about the death of innocence in America or some puke like that. You know, *The crooked road out of childhood*. Any way you do it, I'm a slut, and probably a drug addict, and how much would you enjoy being up here while all of you pretend to be so fucking sympathetic?" She waved the question away. "Next," she said, aiming a finger at someone.

"We've all heard rumors about your drug use," said a reporter from some print outlet, armed with nothing but a little notebook.

"Is there a question there?" Thistle asked. "And when's somebody going to ask whether my feet smell?"

"Well, is it true? There were stories that Hollywood Division had arrested you a couple of times and then let you go without pressing charges."

"Mmmm-hmmmm." Thistle gave him an exaggerated nod. "And why do you think they might have done that?"

"Well . . ." The man hesitated. "Because of who you were, was the way I heard it."

"Don't we live in interesting times?" Thistle asked. "Imagine. I'd rather be with a bunch of cops who are busting me than hanging around with the guardians of free speech. And you know why? Because *cops need evidence.* You guys, you guys can turn a whisper in the fucking woods, fourth-hand hearsay, into a minute of gospel truth that makes everybody go *Oh my God,* and then they miss it when you retract it three days later. Is it any wonder I prefer cops?"

"But about the drugs," the reporter said.

"I never put *anything* harmful into my system," Thistle said, "without a qualified medical opinion." She pointed at a guy at the back of the room. "Over to you."

"I have two questions," said the woman with the orange makeup whom I'd pushed over in the parking lot.

"And you can keep them, pumpkin-face," Thistle said. "I wasn't pointing at—"

"The first question is how you'll feel when I sue you because your thug punched me."

"I'll be proud of him," Thistle said. "I wish *I'd* punched you."

"Hang on," I said. "You put your goddamn spike heel on her tennis shoe. She had to get through that crowd and you pinned her down. She may have a broken bone in her—"

"I did *not*," the woman said. "I never—"

"Thistle," I said. "Show the awful orange lady your shoe."

Thistle yanked off the shoe and held it up. She slipped her hand into it, poked a finger through the hole I'd made, and wiggled it. Then she said, "By the way, ow."

"I did not do that," the woman from World Entertainment News said.

"You'd say that, of course," Thistle said. "*I did not do that*," and suddenly she sounded and looked exactly like the woman she was talking to. It was even more striking than the way she'd done Trey. She continued, in the woman's voice: "It's not much of a surprise, is it? I mean, since you wouldn't recognize the truth if someone handed it to you on a chest x-ray." A murmur ran around the room.

"How does it feel," the woman said, between her teeth, "to be doing porn?"

"I haven't done it yet," Thistle said in precisely the same voice. Then she became Thistle again. "So you'd know as much about it as I do." She gave the woman her sweetest smile and added, "Or maybe more."

I leaned down and whispered in her ear. "Okay," she said. She turned to Trey. "Just a couple more. Let's see whether anybody can be more awful than her."

"Fine," Trey said, obviously relieved to have gotten this much. Headlines were guaranteed.

Thistle did what I'd told her to do, pointed at a short guy in the second row. All the print guys had neat little reporters' notebooks, but the best Louie the Lost had managed in the minutes since I'd called him was a bright yellow legal pad as big and conspicuous as a semaphore.

"You," Thistle said. "The handsomest man here."

"My question is for Miss Annunziato," Louie said. He made a sweeping gesture that encompassed the entire stage. "Look at those pictures, would you? That's a little kid up there. So here's my question. Your family has been in organized crime for decades, but not like this. How do you think your father would like you taking his organization into kiddie porn?"

## 26
### Like Imitating a Hand Puppet

"Well, *that* went well," Thistle said as we stepped into the hallway. "Do you think there was one person there I didn't piss off?"

"I'm pretty sure Trey was happy," I said. "Until about ninety seconds ago."

I could hear the reporters shouting questions at Trey. The volume dropped as the door swung closed behind us and then grew louder again as it opened, and Thistle's eyes darted past me and widened into circles, and two arms wrapped themselves around my neck, clamped tight, and lifted me off my feet.

I got both hands over the upper arm and pulled, kicking back with my heels at his shins, but no go: whoever it was, he'd grabbed the sleeves of his jacket—a plaid that looked familiar—with both hands and was hanging on tight. Then, as I began to choke, he pivoted so I was facing the door that had just swung closed again, and ran me, face-first, into it.

I saw some neurologically expensive special effects and said something along the lines of "Owww," and then the guy who was strangling me topped me by saying, "*OOOOOWW-WWW!*" and dropped me. I put a hand against the wall for support and swiveled to see Hacker backing away in his awful plaid suit, his hands cupped over his groin, as Thistle pulled back her foot and launched another kick. This one missed, and she staggered back, flailing her arms to keep from going over backward, but I caught her. The three of us stood there, Thistle panting in my arms, Hacker red-faced and trying not to groan, and me suddenly weak-kneed, a late reaction to near strangulation.

"What the hell was *that?*" I demanded.

"You're . . . finished," Hacker said. He sounded like he had a stone the size of a loaf of bread lodged in his throat. "Wattles and me . . . we're going to feed you to the dogs ourselves."

"That's a figure of speech, right?" Thistle said. "Tell me that's a figure of speech."

"This asshole isn't smart enough to use a figure of speech. What's got you upset, Hacker? Some kind of clampdown on police corruption?"

"You . . . you just wait."

"What would make more sense than me *just waiting* would be you starting at the beginning and telling me what the hell you're talking about. Presumably, you're here to deliver some sort of message. And unless you've got something really fundamental wrong, which wouldn't surprise me, feeding me to the dogs is the *or else* part of it. See, *or else* should come second."

Thistle said, "What dogs?"

"Tell you later, but they're not that much worse than those piranhas you just finished with. What about it, Hacker? Aren't you supposed to be trying to get me to do something?"

"I saw that, in there," Hacker said, still breathing hard.

"Gee, I guess they let just anybody in."

"I saw Louie, and don't you try to tell me you didn't bring him in."

I said, "Louie who?"

"You even *told* her," he said, lifting his chin at Thistle, "to call on him."

"He did not," Thistle said. "He told me it was time to get out of there. I was getting too loaded."

"He's a cop," I told her.

Thistle brought her hands to the center of her chest and wrung them. "Oh, my poor little heart, it's pounding so hard."

"Keep it up, you little junkie bitch," Hacker said. "When this movie is over, you won't be so fucking immune."

". . . is over, you won't be so fucking immune," Thistle said, doing Hacker to perfection.

For a moment, Hacker froze. Then he said, "And if you think I'm kidding—"

". . . think I'm kidding," Thistle said, half a syllable behind him.

"Cut that *out*," Hacker said.

"Cut that *out*," Thistle said. Her tone matched his exactly, and her voice was almost as low as his. Her arms hung loose, the fists semi-balled, shoulders high, chin forward, feet planted wide, corners of the mouth pointed down. Hacker to the quarter-inch.

Hacker's right arm came up, a pointed index finger at the end of it, and Thistle's movement mirrored his precisely. He stopped, mouth half-open, and so did she.

"See how stupid you look?" I said.

"Tell her to stop—" he said, and almost in unison, Thistle said, "Tell her to stop—" Hacker choked it off, glaring at her, and got exactly the same glare in return. He opened his mouth. Thistle opened hers. Hacker's tongue flicked the center of his lower lip, and Thistle's did the same. For five or six seconds the two of them stood there, immobile as frescoes, and then Thistle said, "Aww, you're too easy," and relaxed.

Hacker waited to make sure she'd really quit. He put his hands on his hips, but she didn't follow suit. "I still know about Louie," he said to me. "One more double-cross, one more hint you're not being straight with us, and you'll be all over Rabbits's backyard." His eyes flicked nervously to Thistle, but she was through playing.

"See?" I asked. "See how much easier it is when you do things in the right order? There's the message, errand boy: *Do what you're supposed to or it's doggie time.* Tell you what: You don't mention Louie to anybody, and I won't tell Wattles how you screwed this up. And I'll make sure she stops imitating you."

"He's no fun anyway," Thistle said. "It's like imitating a hand puppet."

"Just so's you remember," Hacker said to me, his eyes going involuntarily to Thistle. He turned to go, and when he was half-way down the hall, he looked back and said to me, "You don't want that kid of yours to lose her daddy, do you?" I took a couple of steps toward him, and he backed away, saying to Thistle, "And you, chickie, you're going to have a much bigger day than you think." Then he turned the corner and was gone.

"A bigger day?" Thistle asked. "What's that mean? Are you somebody's daddy? Where do you think he got that suit? And what was that thing about dogs?"

"I'm under a certain amount of duress," I said. "It's kind of picturesque, but you don't need to know the details."

"If you say so. But, I mean, dogs? That's like a metaphor, right?"

"Sure," I said. "You know, go to the dogs."

"That's real convincing," she said. "So tell me if there's something I can do to keep whatever it is from happening to you, I mean, I sort of owe you. And also, let's find Doc and see if I can't get taken down a few feet."

"Where'd you learn to do that? What you did to Hacker and Trey?"

"I've always been able to do it," she said. "I used to do it on the show all the time. It's about the only thing I've got left."

At that moment there was a burst of male voices, and six guys rounded the corner Hacker had vanished behind. Thistle turned in their direction, and the two of us watched them come. Four white, two black, all in their late twenties or early thirties.

I'm not generally much on snap judgments, but one sprang to mind then, a word Thistle had recently used: *trash*. Dressed in jeans, T-shirts, outdated Seattle grunge-rock plaid, leather wristbands, tattoos, and dangling steel bracelets. Chin-patches and sideburns, the ghosts of hairstyles past. Chains jingled at the heels of boots. None of them sparkled with conspicuous cleanliness or intelligence. As they swaggered down the hall, they eyed Thistle openly, even speculatively. They showed no indication of wanting to avoid a collision with us, so I tugged Thistle out of the center of the hall and over to the wall. As they passed, one of the guys closest to her reached out without slowing and touched her lower lip and said, "Hurts, I'll bet."

"Hands to yourself, asshole," Thistle said.

"Okay," the guy said, "no hands." They all laughed. They walked on down the hall in a cloud of testosterone, one or two of them looking back at her.

Thistle said, "I'm not feeling good about this."

"*There* you are, sweetie," someone trilled, and I turned to see Rodd Hull come around the corner, trailed by Tatiana and the girl who had doubled for Thistle—what was her name?

"Our little star," Rodd said. He had a clipboard clasped to his chest, but other than that he looked pretty much the same: vest full o'pockets, viewfinder dangling. "Oh, I forgot, you don't know me from Adam, do you? I'm Rodd Hull." He waited a moment, apparently anticipating some reaction from Thistle. "Your director," he added a bit more sharply.

Thistle said, "Uh-huh."

"And here we have Tatiana and, um, I forget your name, darling," he said to the other girl.

"Ellie," she said, as though she was used to it. "Ellie Wynn."

"And they're here to get you ready," Rodd said. "We've had a little schedule change. Since you were so, um, *lively* in the press conference, we're going to start with something just a wee bit more ambitious." He leaned forward and looked at Thistle's lip, then put his hand under her chin and gently turned her head. "Not bad," he said. "Maybe keep you in three-quarters."

"Ambitious?" Thistle said.

"Scene twenty-one," Rodd said. "Why not get one of the big ones out of the way? Make it a little easier later on."

"What's scene twenty-one?"

"Tatiana and, um, Ellie will explain it all to you. You do have a script, don't you, Tatiana?"

"No, Rodd," Tatiana said wearily. "I always report for work without a script."

"Wait, wait," Thistle said. "This was supposed to be an easy day, just a few setups."

"This will be much better for you," Rodd said. "As I said, get one of the big ones—"

"I'm going to need cards," Thistle said "Cue cards."

"Not that much dialog," Rod said, glancing at his watch. "Mostly action." He began to turn away.

"Just a minute," Thistle said. "Action. What action? What *kind* of action? What are you trying to—"

"I'll let the ladies explain it to you, darling," Rodd said. "I've got to get the set ready." He gave her a critical look. "You're going to need some lighting," he said, and then he turned and went down the hall, his feet splayed out like a duck's.

"Come on, honey," Tatiana said, taking Thistle's arm. "We'll talk you through it."

"But, what" Thistle stopped. She started to say something, failed to find her voice, and tried again. "It's those guys, isn't it? Those guys who just came in?"

Tatiana looked at me and then at Thistle, but said nothing. It was Ellie who said, "It's, um . . . sorry, Miss Downing. It's them."

## 27
Digital Mode

"Sweetie," Tatiana was saying. "You've got to face it. You're in digital mode now. It's either on or off, yes or no. There isn't anything in between."

Thistle was caught in an eyelock with her own reflection. She shook her head, about a sixteenth of an inch, the movement so small I wouldn't have seen it except that one of the two makeup girls, the one who was dabbing foundation on Thistle's forehead, lifted her sponge for a second. When Thistle's head was still the girl went back to work, saying to the other, "Maybe some shading under here?" indicating the space below Thistle's cheekbones.

"The light will do it," the other makeup girl said. "Can you look up, Thistle? Just with your eyes, honey, not the whole head." She began doing something to the lower lids of Thistle's left eye.

"I can do it," Thistle said.

"I'm sure you can," Tatiana said. "They're all pros. The guys, I mean. For what that's worth. They're not people you'd run into at the public library or anything, but they know what they're doing."

"I meant my *eyes*," Thistle said between her teeth. "I can do my own eyes. I've never liked having people do my eyes." She extended a hand, and the makeup girl gave her the pencil.

"Are you going to be okay here?" I asked her.

"Here's fine," Thistle said. She tugged down the skin below her left eye and applied an expert line. Her hands were not shaking, as far as I could see. "It's *there* that terrifies me." Her eyes went to Ellie, who was standing with her back against the wall as though she wished she could melt through it and out of the room, maybe out of the day altogether. "How about it, double? Wanna go to work today?"

"Ohhh," Ellie said, blinking fast. "I'm not—I mean, I'm not that kind of double, just, just for rear shots and exteriors, and . . ."

"I'm kidding," Thistle said. "Sort of. How about I give you some of the money they're going to pay me? *Maybe* pay me."

Ellie's head was going back and forth at surprising speed. "I couldn't . . . Ms. Annunziato would never—"

"No," Thistle said. "She wouldn't." Then she lowered her head and seemed to study the hands folded in her lap. Both makeup girls stepped back, and Thistle looked very much alone. She said, "Oh, my God."

"Hold on," I said. "I'll be back."

I managed not to slam the door behind me, but just barely. The hall was full of people, most of them carrying stuff: lights and equipment, but also odds and ends of furniture. I followed them down the hall and out of the building. The first thing I passed was a jumbo trailer full of mirrors and chairs. The six guys who had barged down the hallway were sitting there, stripped to the waist, smoking and talking as they got makeup sponged on their chests and shoulders. Beyond the trailer, some twenty feet away, was a sort of oversize quonset hut with an airplane door standing open. Inside, it was dark except for a brilliantly illuminated corner at the far end. That was where everyone was going, and I tagged along.

Another three-walled room, this one a bedroom that was obviously supposed to be in some sort of penthouse; large color photographs of a nighttime big-city skyline filled the windows. A king-sized bed with a peach-colored spread on it had been positioned in front of the windows, and above the bed someone had hung a big mirror, about the same size as the bed, facing directly down. Rodd was standing next to a woman who was busily aiming a camera at the mirror. He said, "Are we horizontal?"

"We're in tight," the woman said. "It'll fill the screen exactly."

"That's an artsy touch," I said. "The mirror, I mean."

Rodd glanced at me and then ignored me, but the woman said, "It's just coverage. It gives us a different view to cut to when we need an edit. And it's a little disorienting, so we'll be able to cut between setups that don't really match." She stuck out a hand. "I'm Lauren Wister."

"Junior Bender," I said.

"You're working with Trey, right?"

"I guess."

She gave me a very quick look. "The idea here is to have four cameras going the whole time. Two of them—this one on the mirror, and the master shot that takes in the entire bed—will be stationary, meaning that the cameras don't move. The other two, the Steadi-Cams my assistant and I are holding, will move all over the place. The whole idea is to try to get as much as possible in one take. We're not sure how long Thistle will last."

"One take of what?"

"Her and the—the guys," Lauren said. She had the grace to look embarrassed.

"Exactly how does this concern you?" Rodd said, a bit waspishly.

"I seem to be Thistle's sounding board. I can guarantee you I'm the person she'll talk to about this scene. I don't know whether you're even going to get her out here, once she knows what she'll have to do, but if anyone can explain it to her, it's probably me."

Rodd gave me a long look and then sighed. "In this scene," he said, "Anna—that's Thistle's character—tests the limits of her newfound sexuality. It's really the pivotal sequence in the first film. It's also probably the hardest—if Thistle can get through this, everything else should be relatively easy. You see, Anna begins as a totally repressed person, just completely closed off, living in a shell, too shy even to say hello to people. One evening, on her way home to the apartment she lives in alone, she encounters a homeless person who confronts her. She tries to sidestep, like she always does, but no go. He just won't let her walk past him without acknowledging his existence. She's a very nice person beneath all the anxiety, and she finds the courage to talk to him. She even gives him some money. We've already shot those scenes with the camera behind Thistle's character, using that mousy girl, what's-her-name—"

"Ellie," I said. "Ellie Wynn."

"Yes, using Ellie. We've shot the reverses—those are the shots where you're looking over Thistle's shoulder, so you don't see her face—on a number of scenes, using Ellie. *Anything* to minimize the length of time Thistle has to work. We'll shoot the other setups, the ones where the audience actually sees Thistle, later. Three of her twelve days, in fact. So she—Anna, I mean, Thistle's character—helps the homeless person, and he reveals that he's actually a kind of, uh, spirit, and he gives her three wishes and tells her to use them well, and then he goes all sort of twinkly and disappears before her eyes, in the one and only visual effect in the film. Anna's first wish is for the courage to act on her impulses." Rodd was more focused than I'd previously seen him, walking his own way through the story as he told it. "Her first trial of her new power was to go out with one guy, someone in her office that she'd never had the nerve to talk to, and that worked out fine, I mean, he's calling her all the time now. But in this sequence of scenes, culminating in the one we're about to shoot, she takes a giant step. She goes to a bar, and all these men cluster around her, and she decides to take them all home. The bar is over there," he said, thumbing over his shoulder at a dark set diagonally across the stage.

"She's supposed to have sex with these guys?"

"A couple of them. Some of it can be simulated, but not all of it. She's going to have to do some of it, before the day is through. If there are shots she just can't do, we can shoot some inserts later with a body double and cut them in—"

"A body double," I said.

"Some girl with the same build as Thistle, someone who's done, uh, this kind of movie before. Those will be close-ups of the real thing. The audience for a movie like this expects a few genuine money shots. "

I said, "Jesus Christ."

"Actually," Rodd said, "I pretty much agree."

"Call it any fancy name you want," I said, "but what it is, it's a gang-bang."

"Now that we're actually on the verge of filming it," Rodd said, "it would probably be disingenuous to call it anything else. But not in front of Thistle, please."

"You have some good credits," I said. "Why are you here?"

"Darling." Rodd put an open hand beneath his face, palm up, as though presenting it to an audience. "I'm fifty-eight years old. In Hollywood, that's too old to qualify for an *obituary*. Do you remember those signs they used to have at amusement parks for the kids' rides? If you were too tall to walk under it, you weren't allowed on? Well at the networks now they have a picture of a teenager over the door and a sign that says, *if you're older than this, don't knock*. Last job I actually went out for, the network executive wore braces."

"If it's any comfort," Lauren, the cinematographer, said, "he'll probably be a soda jerk on Sunset in six weeks. Most of those guys don't keep their job long enough to get the chair warm."

"Over there," I said, pointing across the stage. "You said that was the bar set, right?"

"Right." This was Lauren again.

"Wouldn't it be better to start with the bar scene? I mean, at least give Thistle a chance to, to *talk* to these guys before she has to—you know."

"Yes," Rodd said. "It would be better. It would, in fact, be the way I had it sequenced in the first place. That's why the bar's built and ready to go. But it is exactly *not* what Ms. Annunziato wants to do. She wants Thistle to cross the great divide, as she herself put it, before one more penny of the Annunziato millions is spent on this film. First the press conference, then this scene. With those out of the way, she figures she'll have no way of losing her movie. If Thistle can do this, she'll be able to do anything."

"For what it's worth," Lauren said, "we're going to talk her through all of it. We'll clear the set except for the essential people, the minimum crew to get the sequence. Most of them are women. We'll shoot the action silent and dub it later, so she can call off any activity that she *absolutely* can't do, and we'll find a way to film around it. Inserts, as Rodd said. But she's going to have to do some of it, or Trey will shut the movie down."

"I don't know," I said.

Rodd said, "Join the club."

"God damn it," I said. "I'm going to talk to Trey."

I went back outside, blinking in the sunlight, and bulled my way through the people carrying stuff until I was back in the building where we'd had the press conference. I looked everywhere—the screening room, the classroom set, the cafeteria, anyplace I'd seen Trey, but couldn't find her. I was on the way to the makeup room when Tatiana called my name. She was obviously distressed, twisting the tail of her plaid shirt in both hands as she came down the corridor. At the same time, Ellie appeared, coming from the other end of the hall, cell phone to her mouth, talking behind a cupped hand.

"Where is she?" Tatiana said. "Tell me you know where she is."

"I'm the wrong guy to ask where anyone is," I said. "Who are you talking about?"

"Thistle," Tatiana said. "She's gone."

**28**

Little Black Dress

"Tell me," I said.

"Well, she got through with her makeup and then put on the costume for the scene, just a kind of nothing dress, a little evening dress, black with—"

"I don't need to know about the dress. And?"

"And she hadn't said anything for five or ten minutes. It was like she was miles away, or memorizing something. You know what I mean? Just not there. Anyway, she asked for a few minutes alone. So I told everyone to leave the room, and then we, I mean Ellie and I, we went to the cafeteria and got a couple cups of coffee. Just, you know, giving Thistle some time to pull herself together. Then we went back and knocked on the door, but she didn't answer, and when we opened it, she was gone."

Ellie came up from behind me, putting the phone away. "Not on the sound stage," she said to Tatiana.

"How long was she alone?" I asked.

"Fifteen minutes?" Ellie said, aiming the question at Tatiana.

"Maybe twenty," Tatiana said.

"Say twenty," I said. "Enough time for anything."

"Anything?" Tatiana said. Her fingers flew to her mouth. "Oh. Oh, my God. You said it, if they're really serious about shutting this thing down, it's Thistle they'll target."

"Let's not go there yet. Did you both go into the room?"

"Yes," Ellie said hesitantly. "I went first."

'How long ago?"

"Oh, gosh, hard to—I've been so upset."

"Eight, ten minutes," Tatiana said. "And I didn't actually go into the room."

"Okay, when *you* went into the room," I said to Ellie, "was the dress in there?"

"The dress—"

"The *costume* dress. The one she had on. Did you see it in the room Thistle had been in?"

The two women looked at each other, and Ellie said, "No."

"The clothes she arrived in. Were they in there?"

"Yes," Ellie said.

"Okay," I said to Tatiana. "*Now* you can tell me about the dress."

"Little basic black number, sort of tarty," Tatiana said. "Cut to bare one shoulder—"

"The left," Ellie said.

Tatiana frowned. "Are you sure?"

I said, "It doesn't matter. There's no way Thistle would leave the lot wearing a dress like that. If she's got that on, she's here somewhere. Tatiana, get six or eight good people and divide up the lot. I want everyplace searched by at least two people. Clear?"

"Sure. What are you going to do?"

"I'm going to see whether I'm wrong."

**There were three** ways in and out of the studio. The gate we'd come in through was used mainly by vehicles, and it consisted of an eight-foot section of chain link that had to be opened and closed by the guy in the guard shack. He hadn't opened it for anyone on foot in hours, although he'd let a few cars out in the past fifteen minutes. The only car he recognized was Trey's chauffeured, bulletproof limo, which had pulled out five or ten minutes earlier.

It was also possible to walk out through the gatehouse, but it was only about four feet square, and anyone who left that way would practically have to bump into the guard. He said no one had come through on foot.

"Do you check the cars that leave?"

His brow furrowed beneath his imitation cop's hat. "Check them?"

"You know, look inside, open the trunk, anything like that."

"Geez," he said, "this ain't Checkpoint Charlie."

It wasn't Checkpoint Charlie in the Palomar Studios lobby, either. Two weight lifters in rental uniforms sat behind the desk, one of them wearing mirrored sunglasses that made me dislike him instantly.

"Has a young woman in a black dress gone past you guys in the past ten, fifteen minutes?"

"Who's asking?" said Sunglasses.

"Good to know you're awake," I said. "Hard to tell with those Top Gun way-cools sitting on your big fat nose."

"Hey," he said, getting up.

"Think about it," I said. "Somebody as rude as I am is probably eager to kill you. Can you think of another reason?"

"Um," he said, but the other guy said, "No, nobody like that. I mean, one woman, but she works here. We see her every day."

"Thanks," I said. To the other guy, I said, "Any time. Just take a swing at me any time. It'll be a pleasure."

The third gate was at the back of the lot, and it opened onto a narrow, eucalyptus-lined street that bordered the wide, white concrete trench of the Los Angeles River. There was no guard, just a metal gate with a handle that anyone could open from the inside. To re-enter from the outside, you needed to punch a numeric code into a keypad. It was the logical place for Thistle to have chosen if she'd known about it, but I doubted she did. As far as I knew, she hadn't worked at Palomar before.

I stood there, looking at the gate, at the tall rows of eucalyptus bending slightly in a breeze I couldn't feel, and kicked myself. Despite the little black dress, despite the fact that no one had seen her leave, I didn't think Thistle was still on the lot. She'd either gotten out on her own somehow, or someone had spirited her away. And there were a lot of potential someones. I remembered my question about all the things that had gone wrong before I got involved. I had said, *Who has access like that?*

And Craig-Robert had answered: *Sweetie. All of us.*

I jogged back toward the main building.

**"Somebody saw her,"** Tatiana said the moment she spotted me. "Just about five minutes ago."

"Who? Where?"

"Eddie and Lorraine. They're grips. They went into Studio A, the one we're not using, to get some lighting clamps, and she ran out of the studio and into the administration building."

"They're sure it was her?"

"Right dress, right hair, right size. You know, she was running, and she didn't look back and wave at them or anything, but it was Thistle."

"Get everybody. I want all the doors to the administration building watched by at least two people while we search every foot of the place. Have somebody tell the rent-a-cops to keep their eyes open. Nobody who could conceivably be Thistle goes out of the building until we've been through it. And I mean *conceivably*—if somebody sees a short guy with a beard, I want to know that the beard is real. She could make herself look like anything with the stuff that's available here."

"We're on it." Tatiana ran toward the stage Thistle had been going to shoot on to round up the crew. I kept my eyes on the back door to the administration building, fighting a feeling that this was going to be a waste of time.

And it was. Two hours later, the building had been turned inside out. All the exits had been monitored. The basement and a small crawlspace attic had both been checked. The people who'd been searching were tired, frustrated, and cranky. The people whose offices we'd ransacked were irritated, self-righteous, and cranky.

"Go back," I said to Tatiana. "Go through every wastebasket. Every trash receptacle in every rest room. Empty them completely. Turn the fuckers upside down."

"What are we looking for?" Tatiana asked.

"You'll know it when you see it."

Thirty minutes later, she came out with the black dress in her hands.

## 29
### Destructo the Furious

"Do you have any idea how much this is costing me?" Trey Annunziato demanded on the cell phone. "I'm paying for a full day's shoot."

"About twenty-one thousand," I said.

A short pause. Then she said, "That's right. I told you. So you don't know whether she left or was taken. What's your feeling?"

"That there's something wrong either way."

"What does that mean?"

"The dress doesn't make sense."

"Why not?"

I checked my mirror and followed the exit lane onto the off ramp into Hollywood. "Okay, she ducks out of the makeup room wearing the costume. Maybe she was freaking out, maybe all that dope peaked, and she wanted to be somewhere dark and quiet for a while. Maybe she realized she didn't have any choice except to do the scene, and she just couldn't face it. So she hides out for forty-five minutes or so, and then somebody comes into the stage she was hiding on, and she runs. She runs into the admin building and disappears into thin air. We turned the building upside down. And two hours later, we find the dress in a waste bin in one of the women's bathrooms."

"And? I'm not following you."

"Well, what did she do? Put something else on? What? Her own clothes are still in the dressing room. No costumes are kept in the administration building. She wasn't carrying a change of clothes when she ran into the building. And no one saw her come out, no matter what she was wearing. She ran in, she left the dress, she disappeared."

"Into thin air," Trey said flatly.

"That's the point. I know there's a rational explanation, but I can't find it yet."

"While you're searching for it, what do you intend to do?"

"I'm going to operate on the assumption she left under her own will. I'm going to try to figure out where she would have gone, and I'm going to look there. Then, if none of that pans out, I'll assume someone took her, and I'll start looking for that."

"Why not look for that first?"

"Because as hard as it is to figure how she got out of there alone, it's impossible to imagine her being dragged out without anyone noticing. And also, I don't know where to look yet."

"*Damn* it. I suppose I should call off the shoot."

"Rodd said something about shooting inserts, close up—what did he call them?—*money shots* to cover the things Thistle wouldn't or couldn't do. You've got the set, you've got the guys. They need to do something with those thumbs. Why not shoot those?"

"I haven't got a body double."

"You got the guys there pretty damn fast when you made that spur-of-the-moment decision to film the gang-bang."

There was a moment's silence. "Better than nothing, I suppose."

I said, "You're welcome."

"You want thanks? Get her back."

Trey hung up and I breezed across Hollywood Boulevard on Highland, the traffic mysteriously light for mid-day. Good Lord, I thought, *mid-day*? I checked my watch: one-forty. It felt like it should be getting dark already.

o o o

**If Thistle had** left voluntarily, I needed to find her for her own
sake. Feeling the way she did, all alone, pumped full of dope and
face to face at last with the reality of the deal she'd made, there
was no way to know what she'd do. I found myself somewhat
taken aback by the intensity of my anxiety. I'd met her only that
morning and she'd been stoned on a potpourri of psychotropic
substances the whole time I'd been with her. She was hopeless,
aimless, self-loathing, self-destructive, probably not long for the
world. The wreckage, I supposed, of someone who had briefly
possessed a remarkable talent and hadn't been able to adjust to
life without it.

Except, I asked myself as I slowed for a red light, who loses
a talent like that? It was innate; she'd had it at seven. Something
like that doesn't just decide to change ZIP codes, wander away,
and desert the person it animated.

What had she said about her genius for mimicry? "It's about
the only thing I have left."

The light changed, and I forced myself to confront the alternative. If she hadn't left voluntarily, if she'd been taken—well,
that was exactly what I'd been hired to prevent. I'd assumed
from the beginning that someone on the crew was involved in
the disruption, and now—if she'd been snatched—in her disap-
pearance. And behind that person, I was certain, was someone
much more dangerous. Someone who'd proved that by shooting
Jimmy. Someone who would probably be capable of writing full
stop to Trey's project by killing Thistle.

So, one way or the other—alone, on her own, loaded and
probably self-destructive, or taken by someone who wished her
ill—Thistle Downing was in trouble.

**I made the** turn onto Romaine, forcing myself to focus on nothing but what was in front of me. Nothing out of the ordinary,

as far as I could see. No lingering cops, no obvious hoods hanging around. If Thistle had run and word had gotten out, then whoever was trying to wreck the filming would be doing exactly what I was doing, but for a different reason. She finds her way here, they're waiting, and just like that, no movie. Maybe they kill her, maybe they just lock her up for a month, maybe they put her in the trunk of a car and drive her up to Canada or down into Mexico, then keep her stoned and happy until Trey's either given up or has been surgically removed from the situation. Then let her wander back on her own.

I knew a couple of people who would have handled it exactly like that. Unfortunately, I also knew a couple of people who would have just put a bullet in her head and sunk her into the Pacific off Catalina. Well-weighted and soon forgotten, just another fallen star.

No one seemed to be loitering around the Camelot Arms, no one was sitting in a parked car on either side of the street. The white Chevy was gone, and Jimmy's Porsche had been hauled and was probably being taken to pieces by now in some forensic garage. I wondered whether he'd been carrying any identification, whether the car had been registered to him, whether there was any way the cops could have put a name to him. Whether, in short, his beautiful wife, Theresa, was still pacing the floor wondering when he'd stroll through the door, wrapped in his Jimmy Dean cool.

Talk about fallen stars.

Okay, as far as I could see, there were no watchers at the moment. So. Park on a parallel street and walk, keeping my car out of sight of anyone who might come by while I was inside? Or just grab the closest space, in case I had to leave in a hurry?

Habit dies hard. I pulled around a corner and parked a couple of blocks away. I figured if anyone was going to try to come into the apartment while I was there, it would probably be marginally better if they didn't know I was inside. It might give me the ten to twenty seconds of surprise I'd need to leave the place standing up.

Up the dirty stairs for the second time that day, quietly, just in case, and slowly so I could sort out my lock picks. I paused a few steps from the top and singled out the two I thought I was most likely to use, and then climbed the rest of the way and made the right into the hallway. And then stopped dead, trying to figure out whether to stay or run. One thing was clear. I wouldn't need the picks.

Halfway down the hall, Thistle's door sagged inward on a single hinge. The top panel had been hit by something heavy enough to splinter and buckle the entire door, yanking the latch of the lock right out of its socket. I found myself thinking that the noise must have been thunderous.

I stood still, breathing shallowly through my mouth, the same way I do when I think I hear someone moving in a house that's supposed to be empty. It's the quietest way to breathe, but it doesn't let you smell much of anything. We humans have lost maybe ninety-nine percent of what was probably once a pretty keen sense of smell, but the impulse is still there, and even the human sniffer, if the human who's using it is sufficiently attentive, can occasionally deliver some information: perfume, cigarettes, someone we love, the presence of death.

And, surprise: I learned something. I learned that someone had spilled a large quantity of cheap red wine in the vicinity. The fumes had an acidic edge that went straight to the back of the nose and stayed there. But whoever spilled the rotgut, if he or she was still around, wasn't making a sound.

My imagination is actually too active for the career I've chosen. It's always too easy for me to visualize someone else, standing just as quietly as I am, waiting for me to give myself away. Waiting for the whisper of furtive movement that says *look out*.

So be Mister Neighbor. People walked up and down this hall all the time. Time for one of them to come along, and he wouldn't be on tiptoe. In fact, he'd probably be whistling. So I started to whistle and headed on down the hall, my eyes on the open door. The rank stink of the wine thickened as I approached. When I was opposite it, I slowed, just another curious yobbo, and looked in.

Devastation. The couch was tipped forward, the rug half pulled aside. Junk was everywhere on the floor.

I kept whistling and walked the rest of the way down the hall, to the fire door at the end. I pulled it open and then closed it, loudly enough to be heard by anyone who might be in Thistle's apartment. Then, moving very quietly, I worked my way back down the hall, my back hugging the wall. I was wishing for the second time in two days that I carried a gun.

At the edge of the door, I stopped, my back still touching the wall, and counted very slowly to ten. Not a sound. I pivoted around and took the three quick steps that put me inside and against the wall, just beside the door. Invisible from the hall, but a nice, close, resolutely life-size target to anyone who might be inside. The smell of the wine was strong enough to choke me, and I breathed through my mouth again, mainly for self-defense. Before I moved another inch, I surveyed everything I could see.

The couch had literally been tossed halfway across the room, as though it had been doll-house furniture. Some serious muscle had been here. The table that had stood in front of the couch was splintered on the floor, beneath a deep dent in the wall, where it had obviously been thrown. One leg had snapped off, and the whole thing leaned against the base of the wall at a vertiginous angle, balanced improbably on a single corner. The carpet was soaked with wine, and the three dirty glasses had been shattered and ground into the rug. Dark shards from the bottle gleamed here and there. The damage extended into the kitchen, where everything small enough to lift had been thrown to the floor, spilled, and broken. The refrigerator lay face-down. Even the open packages of cookies had been trampled to crumbs. As ugly and violent as all of it was, that particular detail relaxed me. I was looking at the uncontrolled malice of fury, not the results of a successful search. Whoever had been here hadn't found Thistle, and he'd trashed her world, or what remained of it, as punishment.

And he was gone, I was certain of that. I had no sense of anyone being near, and I'm good at that. Still, I moved to the bedroom door on the balls of my feet, as my burglar-mentor had taught me all those years ago, and peered in. The mattress had a huge ragged X slashed into it and it had been thrown against a wall, the boxes of belongings were upended and their contents scattered and broken underfoot. The clothes had been cut up, the notebooks thrown everywhere, some of their pages ripped out and crumpled into tattered little balls.

Just to be thorough, I checked the bathroom. Empty and pretty much intact, spared for some reason by whoever had rampaged here. Maybe he'd been making too much noise; maybe he'd been interrupted. Thistle's brush was beside the sink, fringed with long flax-colored hair that caused a surprising tug on my heart. There were still damp spots on the floor from the fight with Doc under the cold shower, a fight that felt like it had taken place two days ago.

On the way across the living room, I pushed the front door closed as best I could and shoved the little table against it, just so the noise would give me some warning. Not that I really thought whoever had done all this would be back. But it occurred to me how little I actually knew of Thistle's life. Who, for example, were the guests who had drunk from the bottle of red wine that now saturated the carpet?

It took me about eight minutes to put the bedroom into some sort of order and to discover that there was no address book. Either Thistle didn't keep one, or Destructo the Furious had taken it with him, or perhaps eaten it. When I had the mattress back in place and Thistle's miscellany of possessions returned approximately to the boxes they had come out of, I sat down on the floor and sorted through her notebooks, journals, whatever they were.

I handled them first without opening them, just arranging them chronologically by the dates on the covers. There were twenty-three in all, and the earliest was a little more than two years old. The newest had been begun only a week ago, and I overcame my reluctance to open the covers and flipped through its pages. Only ten or twelve sheets had been used, covered with a tiny, crabbed writing obviously done with a very fine-tipped pen. The writing demonstrated a reckless, aristocratic disregard for the blue lines printed on the pages. She'd written some pages at a diagonal and others horizontally, so the book would have to be held sideways to read the words. Spidery lines framed some paragraphs, and long zigzag squiggles, like a child's drawing of lightning, linked them to other paragraphs lower on the page. On some pages, Thistle's writing was a spiral.

Here and there I saw a picture, in the margin or in the middle of a page surrounded by text, just an arrangement of a few lines, all identical: a girl's face, broadly similar to the younger face Thistle had shown the world on television, eyes downcast. The same face, over and over, eyes always down. A couple of times she had drawn a hand in front of it, fingers spread, as though in the first stage of reaching for something, some item nearly forgotten. Sometimes the spiky words slashed through the face. But it was always looking down at something.

*Circling the drain*, she'd said.

Silently begging Thistle's pardon, I opened the oldest of the books and began to read.

## 30

### Barefoot on Sharp Rocks

*. . . a hole somewhere you can't see, not one of the holes that everyone has that let out the bad stuff but a secret invisible hole thats just for good stuff, that lets everything good leak away, whatever there was that had light in it and could change, and the hole just drains all of it until theres nothing left except the body and i have to do what the body wants, give it what it wants and then go away until it wants more and then give it more until i almost die and that's what i call sleep now.*

There was a picture of the girl's face, eyes downcast.

*and i stay asleep wherever i was when it took me away and then the body wants more and it wakes me up so i can go out and get the thing for the wanting and*

Those were the final words in the first book, and they set the tone for everything that followed. Doc had called it Planet Zero, and he'd been right.

I flipped through the rest of them, looking for a section that had names, addresses, phone numbers, anything that might tell me where she'd be likely to run. In the next-to-last book I'd found a kind of list of short lines that mixed letters and numbers but it was unreadable, in some sort of code:

*lnl0:2091643688*
*lnl1:7076725414*

Half a dozen entries in all. The number strings had ten digits,
which qualified them as telephone numbers, but the area codes
were certainly not local, even if I could read the names. Both area
codes were sort of middle-California: two-zero-nine belonged
to Turlock and Modesto, among others, while seven-zero-seven
was up near Sacramento. Among the strings of numbers I didn't
see a single area code within three hundred miles.

Which meant that I had to scan the pages to see whether
there was something there that would unlock the code.

They were difficult to read in every possible way. The writing was cramped, the letters elongated and jammed together,
as though the pages were made of something elastic, and had
been stretched out while she wrote. Now they had returned to
their original size, and the words had become collisions of letters, crowded so closely they almost seemed to resent it. And
when you got past that, you had to deal with whatever structure she'd built with the words on whichever page you were
looking at, and once you'd solved *that*, there were the words
themselves, and reading them was like walking barefoot on
sharp rocks.

*. . . not like lissa, jesus lissa just opened up like a window and
let herself show and that was enough because of what was in
there and that was why she could do it all day and every day and
i never opened anything i was just a bunch of reflecting surfaces
so if lissa was a lighthouse i was a disco ball and i didnt have any
light of my own so why wouldnt mine leave and why wouldnt
lissa's stay forever like it did. Why would mine stay with me no
one else has stayed with me except daddy and he died to get
away from her and sometimes i think she punched the hole in
me, the hole that meant i had to reflect light instead of showing*

*my own like lissa could and i hate feeling sorry for myself but if
i dont who will and who gives a fuck anyway.*

There was something familiar about the name *Lissa*, but I
couldn't find it in my memory.

I looked at my watch and was surprised to find it was almost
three, which meant I'd been there more than an hour, dragging
my eyes across something no one in the world should have read.

*. . . and the dope it orders me around like in that movie
where the computer orders the astronauts around and tells them
lies the same way the dope tells me lies, like this time it'll be
different because you'll get that click that means you finally got
enough and you never do, you can just keep filling yourself with
it until you die and the dope doesnt care just like the computer
didnt care when the handsome dumb guy Gary something was
caught outside the airlock, it just locked the door and let him
drift away waving his arms like a baby and getting littler and
littler and everything else was black except for stars and what
good are stars anyway. do stars give a shit, look at all the blood
and guts that gets poured out on the dirt down here while the
stars just float around up there jerking off while kids and women
and even men get stabbed and shot and drowned and fill themselves with poison and tell each other lies and say i love you i
love you i love you and mean gimme gimme gimme.*

The computer had to be HAL, the one in *2001: A Space
Odyssey*, a movie I'd never liked, because if human beings were
that cold, who cared what they got transformed into? When I
saw it, I'd found myself rooting for HAL as he attempted to get
rid of the space ship's crew.

And I knew what Thistle meant about stars. I've always
hated the buggers myself. Unattainable beauty ties me in knots.

There were a lot of references to Lissa, whoever Lissa was,

but Thistle seemed to have reserved most of her love for her father, who had died, according to what I'd read on Google, when she was eleven or twelve. About her mother there was almost nothing.

*. . . the thing about daddy was that he was clean like most people arent if you could shine a light straight through him it would have been all white and clear on the other side because there wasn't anything he was wrapped around that was dark and secret and hated the light or was ashamed of it like most people have, whatever they look like on the surface some of the most beautiful people are as poisonous as pepper trees as poisonous as rat bait but, daddy was daddy all the way through . . .*

I found myself wondering what Rina would write about me. Was I clear at the center, or was I dark at the core? Was I forcing her to love me in spite of who I really was?

*. . . the same way lissa was lissa all the way through and the camera could see that, and the best thing i can say about mommy is that she was rotten on top and rotten clear down to the middle and at least she didnt pretend to be anything except rotten. i dont know why i didn't know she wanted to be me and hated me because she wasn't me, she always thought all the cameras and the lights should have been pointed at her all the time and i had stolen them from her. But daddy just loved me and he would probably even love me now. Probably*

All pretty awful, but getting me nowhere, at least in terms of figuring out where Thistle might have gone. Although the references to the cameras reminded me who Lissa was: she was the actress who had played Thistle's mother on "Once a Witch," the one who had stood aside to let the child shine. But figuring things out wasn't reward enough to force me to read any more of this than was absolutely necessary. Maybe the thing to do was read the very last entries, the ones in the book she'd barely begun.

*. . . tomorrow will be different because i'll make it different because i have to make it different because this movie thing even if it's just junk or some kind of art movie nobody will see maybe it will bring her back maybe she'll feel the lights and all the people looking, waiting for her and she'll come and help me do something that surprises them all and makes them applaud and love me and want to see more, but she won't come back if theres no room for her and now everything is filled with all this shit all these pills that someone keeps giving me and that i take like some machine that needs oil oil oil but today has to be different and so does tomorrow because it's like i have to make a room for her to move back into someplace thats got some light and air in it and that's not full of bugs and ratshit, i mean a place i can be proud of. Inside me, but i dont know if can and even if i do she might not come back, why would she come back nobody ever comes back but look i'm in a movie again and maybe that will bring her back if she's missed being . . .*

Oh, for Christ's sake, I thought. HAL, The computer in *2001.* Arthur Clarke named it HAL as a dig at IBM. It was just one letter off—he used H, A, and L, the letters preceding I, B, and M.

Flipping through the books, I found the next-to-last one and paged to the list I'd seen earlier. The first thing that jumped out at me were the area codes. Add one to each number and 707 became 818, the code for most of the Valley. Two-zero-nine was 310, if you took nine as the digit before ten and figured ten was represented by a zero. Then I replaced each of the letters in the names with the one that followed it in the alphabet.

When I was finished, I had six readable names and telephone numbers, but the first two were the most interesting. They said:

mom1: 310-275-4799
mom2: 818-783-6515

Thistle, I thought, had to be the last person of her age in the world to write down phone numbers. I immediately corrected myself; junkies had to be the last people in the world to write down phone numbers. To a junkie, a smart phone is just waiting to be turned into a bag of dope. I was writing down the numbers, and the addresses below them, when I heard something in the other room.

It was just a little scuffing sound, like someone sliding something an inch or two, and I knew immediately what it was. It was the table I'd propped against Thistle's front door. Someone had pushed the door open just far enough to put an eye to the crack and look in.

The table, I realized in retrospect, was a terrible idea, a dead giveaway that someone was inside, exactly what I'd been trying to avoid by parking so far away. So I was surprised when I heard it slide again, from the sound of it just a little farther this time.

Whoever it was, he or she was trying to come in.

Nothing I could see in the room had any value as a weapon. The only thing I would have had was surprise, and I'd squandered that, short of jumping out and yelling "Boo."

The more I considered that idea, the better it seemed. Among the arguments in its favor was the fact that it was absolutely the only thing I could think of. A moment of complete disorientation would at least give me a chance to get close. I looked around the room again. It seemed to come down either to "Boo" or trying to bludgeon to death whoever it was with a pair of Thistle's jeans.

So I got up and edged toward the door, putting my feet down on the very back edge of the heel and then lowering the rest of the foot to the floor. The back of the heel, on a man's shoe at least, is usually the softest part of the sole.

The table moved again, just as I reached the edge of the door. I took a deep breath, centered myself in a flimsy conviction that what I was about to do was not idiocy, no matter how much it felt like it, bent my knees slightly, whirled, and jumped through the door with the most horrifying bellow I could manage.

Through the partially open front door I saw a little girl's face turn into a collection of perfect, and perfectly horrified, circles, and then she screamed back at me—a sound high enough to put a gouge in the ceiling—turned, and ran. The smaller of the two girls from the white car.

I barreled after her, grabbing the table and tossing it aside to get the door open, but by the time I hit the hallway she was already rabbiting down the stairs. As fast as I could move, she was a *lot* faster, and even though I took the stairs practically head first, essentially in a perilously controlled fall, she was through the door to the street before I made the landing, and when I threw open the door, still swinging from her exit, she was clambering into the back of that dented, beat-up Chevy. The girl at the wheel pushed the accelerator most of the way through the floor, and they took off in an eye-stinging, lung-searing trail of dark smoke.

My car was two blocks away.

# 31
## Mom Number One

Luella Downing had left the Valley far behind.

The house was in the flats, but it was still in Beverly Hills, set back from the street by thirty or forty feet of green lawn, bordered by azaleas in a pink so pure it looked like the first time God had tried out the color, before it got diluted with overuse.

The basic theme was used brick: the house was used brick. The driveway and the walkway to the door were used brick. The bricks had been painted different colors in their previous lives and then acid-scrubbed or sandblasted back into a semblance of brickiness. It might have looked like a quaint economy to someone who didn't know that used bricks were a lot more expensive than new bricks.

But, of course, the house hadn't been designed to impress people like that.

The guy who answered the door was pale and puffy enough to have solidified from the billows of cigarette smoke that accompanied him. He glanced down at my coveralls and said, "Pool's around back."

"How long since you checked the pH level?" I asked.

He blinked heavily and screwed up his left eye in complete incomprehension. He was drunk. "Isn't that, like, your job?"

"You'd be brother Robert," I said. "Still living at home, I see."

Robert said, "Uhh, the pool?"

"I'll just take a short cut," I said, and pushed him out of the way.

"Hey," he said. "Wait."

I went down a short, dim entry hall with the walls covered in those mirrored squares with gold veins running through them that I've always seen as an attempt to recapture some age of grandeur when the grand had really bad taste. Two marbletop tables, amateurishly antiqued, sported big, slightly dusty arrangements of silk flowers. The place smelled like Rush Limbaugh's pillow.

A turn to the left took me into the living room, which ran half the width of the house and culminated at the far end in what were probably sliding glass doors to the back yard. The doors were heavily curtained in some light-repellent fabric. It was bright outside but dim in here. The only illumination came from a brass fixture hanging over the green felt-covered card table at the near end of the room. Four chairs circled the table. The empty one probably belonged to pasty old Robert. Three people turned to look at me from the other chairs.

One was a woman in her early fifties, working hard to look seventy. Her face was lined and bloated, a cigarette dangled from her lips, and she'd combed her hair very carefully, probably no more than four or five days ago. The other two were men, and I recognized both of them. The one nearer to me I had seen trying to get dinner platters off his hands on TV. He was older and heavier now but had maintained the residual undercurrent of cluelessness I'd spotted on the small screen. The man in the middle was a third-rank, lounge-level comic whose catchline, "Do I look like *that* kind of guy?" was always answered with a resounding *Yes* by the wandering members of the mysteriously idle class who show up at game show tapings, inhabit bars in the daytime, and go to Vegas for the Muscular Dystrophy telethon.

The men had cigars, and not, to judge from the mountains

in the ashtrays, the first of the day. Each of them seemed to be nursing a glass of amber liquid that was probably bourbon on the rocks. The cards on the table were arrayed in a classic Texas Hold'em configuration: two face-down in front of each player and four face-up in the center of the table. The guy who had played Thistle's father on TV picked up his hole cards and checked them for a second, as though he'd forgotten what they were, then replaced them.

"He's the pool guy," Robert said from behind me.

"Honey," Luella Downing said to me around the cigarette, "The pool is outside. How many houses you go to, where they got the pool in the living room?"

"None," I said, "but that's probably because I'm not the pool guy. Do you know where Thistle is?"

Luella Downing said, "Ahhhh, shit." She pushed her chair back to look at me better. "She's disappeared, right? What day of the week is it?"

"Tuesday," said Thistle's fictional father.

"I'm asking him," Luella Downing said.

"Tuesday," I said.

"Then she's on schedule. She usually disappears for the first time every week on Tuesday. She's busy on Monday, getting loaded enough not to be able to find her way home. She'll wander in on Thursday and disappear again on Friday."

"This is different," I said.

"They're *all* different," Luella Downing said. "Every single one is a unique little human tragedy. You're what? The latest masked man to ride down from the hills to try to rescue her, right? Well, let me give you some advice, masked man. Put that horse in reverse and leave her wherever the hell she is. Edith is like trouble in a concentrate, you know? Add a few drops to some water, you got gallons of it."

"Edith?" I said.

"That's her name. Edith. That's the name me and her father

gave her. I never heard the name *Thistle* until she tried out for that show. 'What's your name, sweetie?' the casting guy said, and Edith said, 'Thistle.' Didn't even look at me. What was I supposed to do, contradict her? Anyway, it's *her* name, right? If she wants to call herself Clyde, she's Clyde."

"So you don't know where she is."

"What's the current hot dope street in Hollywood? That's where she is. Has to be cut-rate, though. She's run through the money pretty good."

"I notice you haven't," I said, just because she made me feel nasty.

"Honey, I earned every nickel of it. I know you probably think she's the poster girl for victims everywhere, but let me tell you, she's a fucking nightmare, and she's been like that since she was thirteen. If it wasn't for me, there wouldn't have been a show. Who do you think got her out of the house every morning and onto the set? Who went and found her every time they needed her and dragged her out of her trailer? Who had to watch her go through a quarter-ounce of cocaine at lunch and then get her into some sort of shape to work for the afternoon?"

"When she could," said her TV dad.

"Yeah, when she could. When she could still stand up, when she could hit her marks, when she could find the light, when she could say her lines, when she could remember not to look at the camera, when she didn't decide to fuck up the take just for the fun of it, when she—"

"When she could keep everybody employed," I said. "When she could lay the golden eggs for you to scramble."

"Without me—" Luella Downing began.

"Got it," I said. "You were the hero. And basically, you don't give a shit."

Luella Downing tapped her cigarette into an ashtray, amputating an inch of ash. "That's about right," she said. "If I got upset every time she decided to disappear—"

"It would wreck your card game," I said. I turned to go. "By the way, Thistle's pop there has a pair of aces in the hole. But what do you care? It's Thistle's money."

A second after I slammed the door, hard enough to shake the frame, I heard glass break, and then I heard some more. The gold-veined glass squares, I figured, hitting the floor and taking all that grandeur with them.

# 32
## Mom Number Two

Hidden Valley is tucked away in the mountains between LA and Van Nuys, reached by an anonymous-looking road that drops suddenly and steeply off of Coldwater Canyon. Once you're down, you find yourself in a grassy expanse of eight million-dollar ranch-style houses, each on an acre or so of what I suppose the residents think of as ranch. Here and there you see a stable, nicer than lots of houses in the Valley, with horses looking over the doors of the stalls with that serious, dreamy expression that horses always wear.

I pulled into the driveway of Lissa Wellman's house just as a silvery Lexus SUV started to back out. The woman driving it stopped, leaned out of the window, and looked back at me. Her hair in the sunlight was a rich coppery color found nowhere in nature, and bright enough to make me wince.

I got out and walked up to the driver's door. The woman at the wheel wore big sunglasses that emphasized bold cheekbones and a jaw that was surprisingly square in a face so feminine. She was wearing the kind of makeup that was designed for the old Technicolor process—vivid, expert, and none too subtle.

"Oh, dear," she said. "Are you going to rob me?"

"Not today, Miss Wellman. I need to talk to you about Thistle."

"I don't talk to the press," she said. "Especially not about Thistle."

"I'm a friend of hers. She's disappeared."

She shook her head slowly. "Oh, my. Still, that's more or less the story, isn't it? She's been trying to disappear for years."

"Well, there's some question, in my mind at least, as to whether she disappeared on her own this time, or whether it was someone else's idea."

Lissa Wellman let out a sigh. "I hate to hear that, but I haven't seen her."

"I didn't think you had. I'm just hoping for information. Something that might tell me where to look."

She glanced in her rear-view mirror. "Move your car so I can get out, and come with me," she said. "I'm on my way to see Henry." She put the car back into reverse and said, "But we can talk in front of Henry with no problem. Henry's dead."

**"My husband,"** Lissa Wellman said, carefully negotiating a curve. She drove as though a fortune-teller had warned her about the day. "Nicest man I ever knew. Not necessarily the most exciting or the most amusing—actually, Paul Lynde was probably the most amusing—but Henry was nice all the way to his bone marrow. Niceness goes a long way."

"It's got staying power, too," I said.

"You know something about it, don't you? I'm afraid that puts you in the minority. It seems to me to be getting rarer and rarer. We value other things now. Intelligence, I guess, or wit, or the ability to stay half an hour ahead of what everyone else is thinking or doing. Or even wearing. But I'll take niceness. I grew up in a small town in Kentucky. In a small town, it's important to be nice because you see the same people every day. In LA, you can be all kinds of awful because people generally only go by once. I read somewhere that the act that tells you most about someone is how they look at themselves in a mirror, but I'd say it's how nice they are to someone they know they'll never see again."

"How long were you and Henry married?"

"We're still married. Just because he's dead doesn't mean we're not married. But we were married in the flesh, so to speak, for thirty-three years."

"What did he do?"

"Nothing much. Oh, he worked when I was getting started. Sold real estate. But then I began to make some money, and he decided to take care of me. He took what I made and invested it in property and built it all into a very tidy little empire, which he called LissaLand. Apartment houses and regular houses and acreage up north, some kind of shopping mall, and, oh, I don't know, all sorts of places I never even saw. But they all brought in money every month. And a week after he died, I sold all of it, every square foot. I didn't want to be a landlord, have all those people's lives in my hands." She turned on the indicator for a left. "So here I am, old, previously famous, and rich."

"Not all that old," I said.

"Keep it up, dear," she said. "You're doing very well for someone who's not in show business." The left led us up a gentle hill, and then under an archway, heavy with climbing roses, that said ROSEHAVEN on a large metal plaque.

"By genetic standards," she said, "I don't suppose I'm very old. And the women in my family have always gone on just forever, I mean we continually live almost a century. But even if I disregard your flattery, there was no reason to expect I'd ever be famous, much less rich. The nicest thing anyone ever wrote about me was that I had a 'modest but congenial talent.'" She shook her head, and the orange hair grabbed at the sunlight. "And he meant it as a *compliment*. But an angel took a hand and made me rich and semi-famous, and you know who she was."

"I do. And I know that she thinks your talent was something special."

"Really. How do you know that?"

"This is embarrassing to admit, but I had to read her journals to figure out where she might be. She said you had a light in your center, and that's what the camera saw. She was just reflective, she said, but you were a lighthouse."

"That poor child. If I was a lighthouse, I did a rotten job of keeping her from hitting the rocks."

Lissa guided the car along a narrow road that took us between banks of roses, not so much a formal garden as an almost impromptu arrangement of beds, all different sizes and shapes, with lawn stretching like green aisles between them. Here and there a stone bench sprouted, a double bench, actually, with seats facing in both directions and sharing a single backrest between them. Then a high wall appeared in front of us, nothing fancy, just rough, weathered redwood, grayed by exposure to the elements and absolutely perfect for the site. Lissa pulled around it, and I saw half a dozen parking spaces.

"This is beautiful," I said.

"Isn't it." She undid her seat belt and got out of the car. "Like a lot of the good things in my life, it came from 'Once a Witch.'" We were walking by now, heading back around the wall toward the roses. "Years ago, back in the 1980s, I had a part in another sitcom, 'In the Family Way.' You don't have to pretend to remember me. I played the next-door neighbor, and I had brown hair and nothing but straight lines. We had this darling makeup man, Buddy Mendoza, who'd been forever with his friend Charles. Charles was an agent who'd done very well, and he and Buddy were just rolling in money. I once asked Buddy why he continued to work, and he said, 'All my life I've been playing with makeup, Lissa, so why would I stop now?'"

She led me along a strip of meticulously mowed grass between beds of roses that stood four and five feet high, most of them in full bloom. The air was thick with scent, and I could hear the lazy drone of bees. "Anyway, during our second season on 'Family Way,' Charles died. When Buddy read his will, it turned out that he wanted to be cremated and have his ashes placed in a hole and have a rose bush—he specified a damask rose, one of the very old varieties—planted on top of him, so he could supply nitrogen to the flowers. He'd bought a few acres up here but he and Buddy had never built on it. We go right, here."

I followed her as she turned. The green path we were now taking led to a circle of roses perhaps thirty feet in diameter, with a smaller circle of grass in the center. "So Buddy brought Charles's ashes up here and did what Charles had wanted, and that rose just exploded. You could practically see it grow. This was the time, I'm sure you'll remember, when men like Buddy and Charles were dying by the dozen every day. And Buddy had brought some of his friends up here when he planted Charles's rose. The idea sort of took hold in their hearts."

We entered the circle of roses. At the center was a round bench, and Lissa sat down and indicated a rosebush, not very tall but profusely adorned with blooms of a red so dark it was almost black. There was a small pewter plaque in front of it that said *Henry Wellman*. "There he is," she said. "My Henry. He chose the rose, which is called 'Othello,' because of its color, thank you, not as a comment on our marriage, which was mostly free of jealousy. By the time Henry passed on, there were almost fifty people buried up here, mostly gay men, but not all of them, and Buddy was fighting tooth and nail with the city, which wanted to close the place down. Anything new, anything beautiful, just brings out the worst in bureaucrats. By that time, I was rich from 'Once a Witch' and Henry's real estate, and I bought all the property on both sides and hired lawyers. It took a bunch of lawsuits and newspaper stories and some stuff on television, but the little gray men eventually went away. The funny thing is that two of the men who fought the hardest to stop Buddy have their own roses here now."

"How many people are up here?"

"Twelve, thirteen hundred, and more every week. Buddy doesn't charge fees, but everybody has to bring the rose, naturally, and for the first ten years they're expected to pay twenty or thirty dollars a month for upkeep. Of course, everybody does. Some people have left the place thousands of dollars. And why not? Who wouldn't want to see their loved ones continue to bloom? Properly cared for, a rose bush can live fifty or sixty years."

"You're a very nice woman," I said.

"It's easy to be nice when you've been blessed. Isn't Henry blooming, though? He was never what you would have called a handsome man, although he had his angles, so it's especially nice that he's so beautiful now. It's more like how he was inside." She folded her hands in her lap and sat quietly, looking at the new incarnation of Henry for several minutes. Then she said, "Thistle's father is here."

I said, "Oh."

"*She* fought it of course, the mother, I mean. Luella the Cruel. *It's all faggots up there*, she said. She wanted to plant him in Forest Lawn, probably under a life-size sculpture of herself, paid for by Thistle, of course, with a stone saying something like, *Can you imagine leaving someone like this behind*? I'm sorry, I'm being terrible."

"I've met her," I said.

"Then you know. The poor child, as if she wasn't having enough trouble by then. Oh, good heavens, you came to see me to talk about Thistle, and all I've done is rattle on about everything under the sun."

"I could listen to you rattle for weeks."

"Well, that's sweet of you, but it's not going to help you find out what's happened to our girl." She got up and blew Henry's rose a kiss and said, "Come on, I'll introduce you to Howard." With Lissa leading the way, we left the circle and followed a path that led around a large gray boulder. On the far side of the stone was a bed of roses planted directly against the rockface, their colors especially intense on the gray background. "He's the

Sterling Silver," she said, "the sort of lavender one. A very delicate rose, subject to mildew and other problems. In that way, I'm afraid it was an appropriate choice." The pewter plaque read *Howard Downing.* "He was a pleasant man, but no match for Luella."

"Vlad the Impaler would have been no match for Luella."

"You know, it never ceased to amaze me that she felt no concern for that child. Later, I mean, when things began to go wrong. All the misbehavior, all the acting out and the drugs. It was just an *inconvenience* to Luella, an irritation. And, of course, it threatened her lifestyle. That little girl was a miracle at the beginning, but then . . ." She broke off, looking down at Harold Downing's plaque. "But then," she said, "it was just heartbreaking."

## 33
### Slipping Away

"It really began in season four," Lissa said. We were sitting in the front seat of her SUV with the doors wide open to admit the fragrance of the roses. "I'm sorry to date everything in terms of the show, but that's how I remember those years. And, of course, Thistle *was* the show. In more ways than one."

"I never actually saw her until recently," I said. "I guess what I saw was filmed in the middle nineties, and it looked like it, except for her. *She* looked like her performance was ninety seconds old."

"The really good ones don't date. And the really awful ones don't, either, they're just as horrid today as they were fifty years ago. It's the rest of us who get frozen in a moment, a style, a way of being—in my case, I guess, a woman, what everybody's idea of a woman was then. The hairstyles don't help, of course, but that's not what's really wrong. What's really wrong is that tastes change. Nobody eats baked Alaska any more, nobody wants their refrigerator to be avocado green, and no actor overplays on camera, but there was a time when those things were the *ne plus ultra*. And film, of course, unlike avocado-colored refrigerators, never goes away. On the other hand, some things don't date at all. A simple white refrigerator, a perfect apple pie, great acting. They appeal as much now as they did fifty years ago."

"Some child actors are instinctively perfect," she said.

"Thistle was one of those. It's not so surprising, I guess. Give a boy a towel to tie around his shoulders and he can fly. Give a little girl a doll—I'm aware that my attitudes here are not exactly breaking news—give a little girl a doll and a toy set of cups and saucers, and she'll have a tea party. But eventually they stop playing, while Thistle could turn it on all day long, ten hours a day, and it went way, way beyond simply believing what she was doing. She was phenomenally inventive. The thing I heard her say most often on the set was, 'I did it that way before,' and what *that* meant was that she was about to come up with a completely different approach to presenting, say, shock or surprise or guilt or incomprehension. She'd ask for a minute, and she'd sit on the couch if we were in the living room or on one of the kitchen chairs if we were shooting in there, and she'd close her eyes. Sometimes she'd laugh while her eyes were still closed. Then she'd get up and say, "Okay," and nail it in one take. And woe betide the director who was new to the show and who didn't want to give Thistle one of her little timeouts. Everyone in the studio jumped on him."

"And so they should have."

"We were the biggest problem, because we laughed. She'd catch us off guard and we'd just stand there, laughing, and the scene would grind to a stop. How she loved it when that happened. You know how much she looked like an elf? At those moments, she looked like the naughtiest elf in the swarm, if that's what you call a bunch of elves, like she'd just gotten the idea to put the donkey ears on old Bottom."

"This was in the early days?"

"Yes." She put both hands on the steering wheel and looked at her wedding ring, which had caught fire in the sun. "Really the first three years. They were magic, in so many ways. The trouble is that *Thistle* thought it was magic, too, and believed to the center of her being that it was. And that left her defenseless. Oh, how can I explain this without it sounding crazy? You know, lots of creative people feel like someone else is actually doing the work. Some of the best writers I know say that the words come *through* them, from somewhere else, that the characters talk and all the writer does is try to get it down before it fades. It's not like they're making things up. It's like someone is *telling* them the story, and they're just, I don't know, taking dictation."

"I've read pieces where writers say things like that."

"Well, Thistle believed that there actually was *someone named Thistle*, someone talented who lived inside her and did all the good work. Her real name was Edith, did you know that?"

"Yes."

"After we got to know each other—after we realized we had a hit and we were going to be working together for a while instead of being broken up after three or four months of filming—she told me what had happened. She said that Thistle just appeared, just came out of nowhere, at her first reading for the show. Even told her what her name was, and that was the name Edith gave the casting director. And, look: she got the part. All she had to do was relax and let Thistle do whatever she wanted. So she did, just read the lines the way Thistle wanted them read and added some physical business Thistle thought of. The casting director left the room and came back with the three executive producers, guys who don't laugh at anything, and asked to see the scene again, and this time Thistle did something completely different, something even better. Even the producers were laughing, but the casting director quieted them down and said, 'Once more. Differently this time.' And she got what she asked for, the best one yet. And of course, she got the part. They made an offer that evening."

"And Thistle—I mean, Edith—didn't believe she was the one who had done it."

"She never did. She, Edith I mean, would take the script home and learn the lines, and when she got to the set in the

morning, all she had to do was open up and let Thistle in, and
Thistle would move Edith around like a hand puppet."

*A hand puppet*, she'd said to Hacker.

"That's what she was doing when she sat with her eyes
closed. She believed she was opening up to Thistle. And that's
what she did, scene after scene, show after show."

"What did you think about it?"

She shook her head, a gesture packed with regret. "I didn't
give it the thought it deserved. Like everybody else, I was just
happy to be part of the show, happy that Thistle could keep it
up, keep the people tuning in, keep the damn ratings up. Keep
the money coming in. And, of course, everyone was afraid of
screwing up Thistle's process. Afraid for our own sakes, not
hers. We were like an army that was being led from victory to
victory by someone who believed he was Napoleon. The cities
are falling one after another, all this booty is landing in our laps,
and who's going to go into his tent and tell him he's really Harold Mednick? Who's going to tell him he's suffering a delusion?
So we all went along with it, with the Thistle idea, even though
we knew perfectly well that she was simply the most talented
child—oh, hell, one of the most talented *actresses*—we'd ever
worked with. We listened to her talk about Thistle and never
said a word.

"I remember telling myself—guess I was actually comforting
myself—that the whole thing was just a phase she was going
through, like an imaginary friend, and that she'd grow out of it,
and realize that the talent was hers, that she was really the one
doing all the work."

"But," I said.

"But I didn't *tell* her that, and there was no one else who
could, no one who mattered to her. God knows her mother
didn't. I really think the reason Edith made Thistle up in the first
place was that her mother had always told her how ordinary
she was, how unattractive she was. So if the child was suddenly

capable of all *that*, getting laughs, getting applause, becoming a *star*, there had to be a reason. Thistle was the reason. And then her father died, just as Thistle started slipping away."

"Slipping away?"

"That's how she described it. She'd been having harder and harder weeks, weeks when the sitting sessions got longer, and the work wasn't as fresh. You could see her grabbing for inspiration, thrashing around like someone who's afraid she's drowning. And she came up with things, eventually, but not on the same plane. Before, she'd been startling, and now she was just good. She was relying more and more on technique."

"I saw that," I said. "In the shows I watched."

"I think she was just tired. She'd worked nonstop for three years, with all of us riding on her shoulders, but she didn't think that was the reason. She told me she could feel it. Thistle was leaving. This child was literally growing up on television, doing what she did in front of seventy or eighty million people every day, and she felt like she was failing. She felt the talent, the spark, whatever it was that Thistle represented to her, slipping away. Going out, like a candle. And there she was, under those lights, under all those eyes, surrounded by people whose paychecks depended on her, her father just dead and her mother glaring at her whenever things weren't perfect, and she was *failing*. We all fail, all actors, we all have bad takes and sometimes whole bad days, but she'd never had a bad minute, and suddenly here they were, one after another after another. And she was just a kid. So what she believed was that she'd never had talent, really, it had all been Thistle, and Thistle was leaving."

"I heard her say it a couple of times. She said, *That wasn't me, it was Thistle.*"

"Exactly," Lissa said. "And it just got worse and worse. Because, of course, who she was, when Thistle was gone, was a failure. She was a phony, someone who was pretending to do things she couldn't really do, and everyone was beginning to see that she couldn't do it. I'll never in my life, not if I live to be a hundred, forget the morning in season five after the *TV Guide* review came out that panned her. I remember every word of it. It said, 'The problem with the show is that Thistle Downing seems to have lost what used to be the surest touch in television. Before, she dominated the scripts, but now she's just trying to live up to them. And the scripts aren't much to live up to.' And then the press piled on. The child was twelve or thirteen years old."

I couldn't think of anything to say.

"Everyone on the set was so *kind* to her that day," Lissa said. "I think it would have been better if we'd all made jokes about it, or just surrounded her and hugged her, even though I think Californians overestimate the healing power of a hug. But that would have been better than what she got. Everyone was just so, *please sit here Thistle; lovely take, Thistle; that was wonderful, Thistle; let's do it one more time, Thistle.* It was enough to make you sick. About four o'clock, she disappeared. The call went out for her, we were all in place on the set, and she just wasn't there. We looked absolutely everywhere for her—I honestly think some of us were afraid she'd done herself harm—but it turned out she'd gone out to the street, gotten into a cab, and just taken off. A week later, she told me she'd come up here, up where her father was." She fell silent for a moment. "She had nowhere to run, so she ran to a rose bush."

Lissa Wellman took off the big glasses and touched the sides of her index fingers to her lower eyelids, a blotting motion. She put both hands on the wheel and sat there, chewing on her upper lip, her sunglasses forgotten in her lap, and looked at the featureless weathered redwood wall in front of us as though something were written there. "I could have helped more than I did," she said. "I always told her I loved her. And she believed me, God help her. She didn't know how little it meant. Everybody in show business loves everybody else so much, it's darling this and darling that, people fall in love and drink together and swear eternal friendship and then the shoot ends and we all lose each other's phone numbers. I loved Thistle, but it was something like that, sort of talk-show love, not the kind of all-out, no-holds-barred, no-questions-asked, I'll-love-you-forever-no-matter-what love she needed. Probably still needs. And, of course, no one was giving her *that* except the millions of fans who never got anywhere near her and who were beginning to wonder what was wrong with her anyway. Who were beginning to change the station. Abandoning her by the tens of thousands every week. So the problems started. The tantrums, the lines she didn't learn because she didn't believe she could do the scene, the days she was late because she couldn't sleep at night and then couldn't get out of bed because she was terrified of failing again." She sighed. "And the drugs."

"The drugs could kill her," I said.

"If they haven't already. Killed whatever was inside her, I mean. Doing something creative is tough, but it comes from a fragile place. I can name lots of people who killed their talent with less cause than Thistle. I think Hollywood's continuing fascination with zombies comes from the fact that there are so many of them among us. They look the same, they sound the same, but they've been unplugged. The thing that made us want to look at them, listen to them: it's gone. They're still here, but they're just waiting to be embalmed. I'd do anything, I'd give years off my life, to turn the clock back for that girl."

"She's still in there," I said. "She doesn't believe anything good about herself, but she's still in there."

Lissa Wellman put a hand on my wrist. "Listen. In your life, there must have been one horrible, unforgettable, humiliating moment, maybe when you were ten or eleven, at the most sensitive time in your life, there must have been one moment when you wished you could disappear forever. *More* than that, not only wanting to disappear, but wishing you'd never existed at all. A moment that can still make you cringe, twenty or twenty-five years later."

"There was," I said.

"Well, multiply that moment by a million, imagine it happening to you on national television, and make it last for *four years*." She put the sunglasses back on and looked away from me, toward the life and color of the roses, rooted in people's dead loved ones. "That's what happened to Thistle Downing."

## 34
### My Little Murderer

By the time I was back in my own car, making the long climb out of Hidden Valley, the sun was close to the day's finish line. The expensive homes in the basin beneath me were being swallowed up in the mountains' shadows, the rooftops just darker rectangles against the darkness of the earth, but the sky was still a thinly scattered blue, and high above me the tops of the Santa Monica mountains gleamed in the last of the sunlight. I had the windows down, feeling a new cooling in the air. Sometimes, in the middle of the hottest summer, the Los Angeles nights will suddenly turn cold, as though to remind us that this place was the next thing to a desert before the old men stole all that water and piped it down here to the thirsty city.

6:10 by my watch. Almost six hours since anyone had seen Thistle. And I still had no idea where she was.

Something Lissa Wellman had said to me was picking at a corner of my mind, something about the relationship between Thistle and Edith, but try as I would, I couldn't focus on it. There was an answer there somewhere, if I could get a clear view of it. And I was growing increasingly uncomfortable with my own position. No matter how ridiculous they were at times, Hacker and Wattles were not comic figures, and Rabbits Stennet was undiluted murder. And yet I was finding it difficult to see myself actually doing anything that would put Thistle Downing in front of the cameras with those five gym rats.

With nothing else to do, I decided to head back to the Camelot Arms. It was possible she'd finally made it home, that she was there alone now, bewildered by the destruction of the few things she'd called her own. She'd need someone with her. She'd probably need someone to hide her, at least for the time being.

I replayed what I'd just thought. I was going to hide Thistle? I wasn't taking Rabbits seriously enough.

Well, first, see if she's home. So I made the left on Coldwater and joined the long line of cars that headed over the mountains to the Valley at the end of every business day. I'd pick up the Hollywood Freeway and go back to Thistle's apartment.

And then something else popped into my mind. A question I should have asked hours ago.

Since I was barely moving anyway, I looked at the touchpad on my cell phone rather than trying to punch in the number by feel. One ring, then two, and I was saying, "Come *on*" when Tatiana picked it up and said, "Have you found her?"

"No. Is Craig-Robert around?"

"Why would I know? He may have left. Hold on, I'm walking down there now. Where have you looked?"

"At her apartment, which somebody trashed. At her father's grave. In her past."

"Nothing?"

The car in front of me came to a complete stop. "Something in her past, and it's kind of tickling me. But am I any closer to knowing where she is physically? No."

"Hang on, I'm at the costume lab. Here's the dramatic part, I'm opening the door now. Oh, well, you *are* in luck. By now Craig-Robert is usually at home trying to figure out which Supreme he'll be for the evening. Craig-Robert, talk to Junior for a second."

"With *barely* suppressed pleasure at any time of day or night. Hello, hello."

"Hello, hello yourself. Listen, are you missing any costumes? It wouldn't be anything fancy, just—"

"How did *you* know? I was just writing it up."

"What was it?" We were moving again, a tire-screeching three or four miles per hour up the hill.

"Strictly Ross Dress for Less, but with Miss Trey, the balance sheets are expected to balance. So here we are, on paper, in my finest cover your precious ass style: *Missing: One pair of jeans, one long-sleeved blue cotton blouse, one pair of sneakers.*"

"Women's clothes, right?"

"*Mein Gott,* I should have put that in, shouldn't I? Yes, for the fairer sex, as they like to style themselves."

"Thanks." Traffic started moving again, and the car behind me gave me a discreet toot.

"Is this important?" Craig-Robert asked. "Should I feel the plot thickening or something?"

"It answers some questions." Now I knew why I'd been picking at the thing Thistle told Lissa.

My phone beeped to tell me I had an incoming call. I took a look at the caller ID and saw it was Kathy. My ex-wife rarely calls to chew the fat, unless the fat she wants to chew is still attached to my body. I told Craig-Robert I had another call, took a deep breath, punched the button, and said, "Hello."

"Junior," Kathy said, and she sounded like it was taking most of her energy to keep her voice level. "I might as well come right to the point. You are *this far* from having me challenge your visitation rights. And I mean a total ban, no contact with Rina whatsoever. Do you understand?"

"I understand that you're severely pissed off," I said. "It's a little hard to respond when I have no idea what the context is."

"You *don't?*"

The cars ahead of me, which had been at full stop, started to move, and I followed along. "I just said I don't."

"Burglary was bad enough. But pornography—"

"Stop. Stop right there."

"We saw the news, Junior. We saw it together, Rina and I. I had to watch Rina's face as she saw it. You and that poor girl. And you even talked to Rina about her, yesterday. You know perfectly well that she's one of Rina's heroes, and here you are, practically carrying her into the studio where she's going to film, I don't know what *you'd* call it, probably something fancy, but in my father's day, it was a stag movie."

"I don't have anything to do with the movie," I said. And I listened to my own lie echo down the phone line. Of *course*, I had something to do with the movie.

"That's not what it looked like to us. I'm telling you, Junior, if Rina weren't fighting me tooth and nail on this right now, I'd be on the phone with my lawyer, not you, and you wouldn't see your daughter until she's of legal age to make these decisions for herself."

"Kathy," I said. "It's really not what it looks like."

"That poor baby. She looked so *lost*, all that bravado and those terrible people."

"She is lost," I said.

"The only good thing you did was knock that bitch on her ass."

"Listen, Kathy, this is more complicated than it seems—"

"It's always complicated with you, Junior. Because you don't understand that the only thing that's not complicated is doing the right thing. Telling the truth and doing the right thing."

"I'm trying."

"You could have fooled me. You looked so big on TV. It looked like you were there to keep her from running away."

"That's not true. It's not even close."

"Whatever's true, you need to call me by about noon tomorrow and tell me how you're going to resolve this in a way that satisfies me. Because I'm telling you, if you don't, you can kiss your daughter goodbye until she's eighteen."

"Let me talk to her."

"Are you listening to me *at all*? Of course, I'm not going to let you talk to her." In the background, I could hear Rina arguing with her mother, and Kathy said, "You hush." Then, to me, she said, "By noon tomorrow, do you hear me?"

She hung up.

I slid the phone into my pocket and focused on inching my way up the hill, shutting everything else out. When in doubt, put one foot in front of the other until the view clears. I was approaching the top of the canyon now, because there were periods of forty to sixty seconds where we'd actually get up to ten or twelve miles per hour, which meant we were nearing the stoplight on Mulholland that's the last thing before the long downhill.

The phone rang again. Rina.

"Hello, sweetie," I said.

"Daddy. How could you not tell me?" She sounded younger and less certain of herself. She sounded hurt.

"Honey, I didn't know . . ."

"Didn't know *what*? You *asked* me about her. You let me talk about her, and all the time you were doing, doing this—this *thing* with her. It was—it was just the same as lying to me."

"I wasn't trying to lie—"

"Don't tell me that," she said, sounding exactly like her mother. "Don't tell me what you were trying to do. We sat there and talked about her, and you never said *one thing*—"

"Wait. Wait just a second, okay? Let me try to tell you something."

There was a silence on the line.

"Haven't you ever been in a situation where you don't know what to do? Where you've been told to do one thing and there are good reasons to do it, like maybe you'll get into some kind of trouble if you don't, but deep inside you know you don't want to do it? And you don't know how you're going to resolve it?"

A long pause, and then an extremely grudging, "I suppose."

"Well, that was me. Yesterday, that was me. I didn't want talk to you about it until I knew what I was going to do."

We crested the hill at last and the Valley spread itself out below me, tens of thousands of houses, offices, buildings. Lives in process. The sun was dropping fast now, and I could see it glaring off of west-facing windows, and, in much closer houses on the side of the mountain I was driving down, lights were coming on. Lights behind windows.

"And now?" Rina said. "Do you know now what you're going to do?"

"Yes," I said. "I know exactly what I'm going to do. And it's nothing you'll be ashamed of."

"What? Can you tell me what it is?"

I was driving past the lighted windows now as more lights snapped on behind tens of thousands of windows below, whole square miles of them, on the Valley floor. Just once, I thought, just once, I was going to put myself on the right side of that illuminated glass.

"Yes," I said. "I'm going to make absolutely sure that Thistle doesn't make that movie."

"Daddy—" Rina said.

"It's a promise. Don't tell your mother. I'll tell her tomorrow, when I said I would. I love you, and I've got to go."

I broke the connection and let the car free-wheel downhill. Trey, Hacker, Wattles. I would have to deal with all of them. But, on the other hand, I knew why the black dress had been in the wastebasket, and why we couldn't find Thistle in that building. And, thanks to Thistle's remark, I probably knew who had shot Jimmy.

When I got to Ventura Boulevard, I didn't cross it to pick up the freeway to Thistle's apartment. Instead, I turned left, toward Palomar Studio. Where my little murderer probably was.

Part Three

ACTION

## 35
### The Character for *Woman*

They came out together in Tatiana's car, Tatiana and Ellie in the front seat, Craig-Robert in back, leaning forward and talking as fast as the other two put together. They waited for the gate to swing open.

"This one's mine," I said into the cell phone. "Yours should be coming out any minute, assuming he hasn't left already."

"Looks like Doc in 'Gunsmoke'?" Louie the Lost said.

"Shouldn't be a problem," I said, "not for someone who watches as much TV as you do."

"What about my girl?" Louie asked.

"That's what all this is about. Your girl."

"So you don't want a Caddy," Louie said, returning to an earlier theme. "I got a nice BMW, real clean."

"I'm happy with what I've got."

"That piece of shit? Looks like everything on the road. You get a landslide on Laurel Canyon, five of the six cars get smashed, they're going to look just like yours."

"That's more or less the point." The gate was mostly open, and Tatiana started edging the car around it, too eager to wait. Craig-Robert said something and they all fell all over themselves laughing. "Toyota Camry has been the best-selling car in America since anybody started counting. You tell the cops it was a white Camry you saw, and you don't have a license plate, they throw it in the *inactive* file."

"Huh," Louie said. "This him?"

I looked through the chain link gate, now closing behind Tatiana's car. "Sure is. Just stay with him, don't get too close, don't let him see you."

"Don't let him see me?" Louie said. "Jesus Christ, would you tell Sherlock Holmes, *don't trip on the clue?* Then how about a Jag? They actually run now, you know, go forward and back-ward, not like before."

"You're not going to tell me how clean it is?" I had pulled out behind Tatiana, and some big Meezer in a Lincoln behind me leaned on the horn. "Meezer" is what my old burglar men-tor Herbie used to call guys who drove like they'd just finished buying the road. He said they should all have horns that said MEEEEEEE, MEEEEEEE.

But the horn didn't attract any attention from the passen-gers in Tatiana's car. They were having so much fun it was hard to believe that one of them was a murderer. But one of them almost certainly was: even if it weren't for the fact that one of the people in that car was the only one who could have been responsible for the problem with the black dress, there was also the figure Jimmy had drawn on his windshield, which I should have recognized, since he obviously meant it for me and it was the only Chinese character I knew. Put it together, and you had two questions—the black dress? and who killed Jimmy?—with the same answer.

"What's with all the sales pitches?" I asked Louie. "You opening a used car lot?"

"It's like a sideline," Louie said. "I got all this inventory I need to turn over from time to time, I might as well make some money selling it. But there's something wrong with my technique."

"With all due respect," I said, "you couldn't sell aspirin to a woodpecker."

"Ow," Louie said. "He's coming out now. Hey, he's going left."

"Does your car turn left?"

"Yeah."

"Then is there something I'm missing?"

"Jeez," Louie said. "Take my fuckin' ear off, why don't you." He hung up.

The mystery of the motor pooling was solved two blocks away when Tatiana pulled into a baking expanse of asphalt with a sign that said PALOMAR STUDIOS OVERFLOW LOT and went on to warn all sorts of dire consequences to anyone who parked there without being part of the Palomar Studios overflow, which didn't sound like a particularly exclusive club to me. Hollywood is nothing if not status-conscious, and nothing defines status like a parking space. Tatiana, as production supervisor, rated; Ellie and Craig-Robert did not. So I pulled over and waited for the two members of the overflow club to depart, and once all three cars were on the road I hitched myself to the murderer's tail and followed in her wake.

It's always the little things, I thought. Cops know it; that's why there's no such thing as a detail to a really good detective. I was once acquainted with a con man, a guy with the impeccable plausibility that Trey had described in Tony—her soon-to-be ex-husband—the quality that marks a real sociopath. The con man made quite a lot of money selling houses he didn't, in any recognizably legal sense, own. He put ads in the papers offering amazing deals on probate properties and simply showed the marks houses that were on the market and vacant, meeting them there only moments after he'd picked the lock and opened the place up. Very complicated situation, he'd say; probate was likely to be challenged, and if the challenge was successful, the deceased owner's son or daughter would take the property off the market. But right now, it was still in probate, and it was priced about forty percent under the comps for the neighborhood, a printout of which he happened to have in his jacket pocket. But if an offer was made quickly, an offer he had the sole power to accept, there would be no grounds for challenge because the house would no longer belong to the estate.

Most of the customers would very sensibly walk away from the deal, but he "showed" four or five houses a day, six days a week, and two or three times a week he'd get a check for $2500 or $3500 to prevent him from showing the house to anyone else while the suckers thought about it. The money was fully refundable if, twenty-four hours later, the buyers came to their senses. Of course, ten minutes after they drove away, their check was cashed.

But this story was about details. This guy dressed like Cary Grant. I mean, he had really beautiful clothes, *Vogue*-for-men clothes, all wool and silk, hand-tailored, pleats all over the place, shoes too nice to wear outdoors. As a finishing touch, he liked to sport a pocket handkerchief, which for most men has gone the way of the hairline mustache, and since the handkerchiefs were the finest silk and very expensive, he showed just about a quarter of an inch too much. And that quarter of an inch was what got him: it turned up in too many descriptions, and one day the customer he showed up for was a cop with such a sharp eye he didn't even need a ruler. A quarter of an inch got our sociopath six years.

And the detail here was a little black dress.

**She wasn't driving** very fast. She drove with the blithe obliviousness of someone who was early, who had time to kill and a really insatiable curiosity about the contents of store windows. Doing the tail was a character-building exercise in patience; if I'd been behind her by accident instead of on purpose, I'd have probably had my horn welded permanently into *honk* position by now. But, of course, I couldn't do that. The people behind *me*, however, were free to abuse both her and me in any way they felt was appropriate, and they did. If there was any comfort to be taken, it was that the exercise gave me some time for thought.

The way it looked, I had five problems.

1. Staying alive, as opposed to spending a very vivid final five or six minutes as dog chow.
2. If I *did* stay alive, not making a permanent and possibly lethal enemy out of Trey Annunziato.
3. Finding a way to neutralize Hacker, who, as a cop, I regarded as a separate problem from Rabbits, Wattles, and Trey.
4. Keeping Rina and Kathy out of the line of fire.
5. Doing something about Thistle.

I had a feeling that the last point was a lot easier to put into a simple declarative sentence than it would be to implement. First, there was the issue of finding her, although I didn't think she was in the hands of anyone who meant her harm. The state of the apartment announced the searcher's failure to find her in the most likely place, and I doubted they knew any of her other hidey-holes, of which there must have been several. After all, her bone-grinder of a mother had said she disappeared on a regular basis. My best guess was that she'd gone to ground somewhere and she'd reveal herself whenever her internal clock said it was time.

Even if I could have located her in the next quarter-hour though, Thistle had more problems than most saints have blessings, and there was nothing I could do about some of them. She was going to have to deal with the drugs by herself, although Doc had said something, back in the coffee shop the first time we met, about helping her out. She was going to need some money, especially if she didn't do Trey's "art film," as Thistle had described it in her journal. And since I was going to try to make sure she didn't, it might also be nice if I could find some way to put some bucks in her pocket. Not to mention giving her an opportunity to rediscover the talent she believed had abandoned her.

And maybe, while I was at it, I could arrange for two Sundays in every week, too.

But I've always figured that aiming high is just as easy as aiming low, so what the hell. And actually, now that I'd opened my mind to it, there was a slim chance I actually could so something for Thistle's moribund career, if my educated guess about Wattles's customer for that ugly Klee I'd stolen was correct. Assuming, of course, that I survived past Friday night, when Rabbits and Bunny came back.

And this, I remembered uncomfortably, was Wednesday.

Following my murderer as she navigated her browser's course down Ventura, it was impossible not to focus on the item I'd left off of my list.

I was going to avenge Jimmy.

It all came down to the dress. I'd said that Jimmy liked women too much, but until the dress, I hadn't been certain that his weakness had been responsible for his death. But when the dress suggested a physical impossibility, the dematerialization of a living woman, I'd thought *woman* and suddenly seen in my mind's eye the symbol Jimmy had drawn with his own blood on the inside of his windshield:

He'd been making the first two strokes of one of the most common Chinese radicals, the character *nü,* or "woman." Jimmy had taught it to me as indispensable if I ever went to China if only as insurance against stumbling into a women's bathroom. He'd helped me to remember it by pointing out that the first two strokes resembled a breast. And after the breast, only two simple strokes remained to complete it.

女

But it had taken the dress to prod me to that recognition, and I'd almost missed it. It had nearly slipped past me because the whole thing had been unnecessary, a diversion to give the other side a one- or two-hour start on trying to find Thistle before I started searching for her. And so they made something impossible happen. A woman went into a building and never came out, and wasn't there when it was searched.

The murderer put on her right-turn signal and braked, although she was already a good ten miles per hour under the speed limit. She made a right into the parking lot of a three-story, poison-green office building that had once been a Cadillac dealership and now played host to entertainment-business fly-by-nights, the kinds of companies whose most substantial asset was their logo, plus one very substantial thug, a thug whose business address I'd already researched.

Thistle never came out of the administration building because she had never gone in. She had left Palomar Studios on her own, probably hiding in the back of some car, wearing the jeans and blouse she stole from wardrobe, about five minutes after Tatiana and Ellie left her in the dressing room. And the person wearing the black dress who had run into the administration building was, of course, the young woman who had reported the dress as missing, who had already doubled for Thistle in a few dozen shots, a woman who looked enough like her, from the back at least, to fool the camera even when it was up close. And almost certainly the young woman who had shot Jimmy.

So I sat at the curb and watched yet another link fall into

place as mousy little Ellie Wynn got out of her car, her face alight
with love and tenderness, and fell into the arms of an impossibly
handsome lunk whom I recognized, with no surprise at all, as
Antonio Ramirez, aka Tony Ramirez, aka Mr. Trey Annunziato.

## 36
### This Was For Hitting, Not Cooking

Back in the days of my apprenticeship, Herbie always said, *When in doubt, find out.*

So I was back at the Snor-Mor for the first time in almost forty-eight hours, preparing for an informational burglary with the well-equipped modern burglar's tools, which include the amazing portable Canon IP90v printer and a stack of business card stock, when the phone rang.

"He's just staying in there," Louie the Lost said. "For all I know, he's climbed into the freezer. He could be in there all night."

"And by *in there*, you mean . . ."

"The Encino address you gave me. His house."

I was watching a business card emerge from the printer and I said, "What time is it?"

"Maybe I should forget the cars and sell you a watch," Louie said. "It's a little before nine."

"Are you sure he's alone in there?"

"He's not," Louie said. "There's a very nice-looking lady in, I'd say, her middle fifties, got that kind of face says she bakes a really good apple pie and the kind of waistline says she eats a lot of it. But nobody else."

"I don't know," I said. The card was nice, but it wanted to be a darker green. "Maybe I'm wrong."

"Call the *LA Times*," Louie said. "We can probably make the morning edition."

"Give it another hour. She's been depending on him for her dope supply. She's going to come down from those three shots sooner or later, and I'd guess she'll call him." I tweaked the color and added a drop shadow to the company's name. Drop shadows provide substance. Pushed *print*.

"Sure," Louie said. "Another hour. Why not? It's not like this is the only life I'm gonna get." He hung up.

The card popped out and said Hi, and it was fine. Might have been better if it had been engraved, or professionally heat-transferred so the letters were raised, but it would work. It's not like the guy who was going to look at it was a career printer. I printed five more so I had a convincing little stack and slipped them in my wallet. They said *Wyatt Gwyon* on them, and they announced that I was Regional Manager, a useful, all-purpose, essentially meaningless title. They matched the name on the bad driver's license, and once I put on the stupid wig, I'd match the picture on the bad driver's license, too.

I rummaged through the valise and pulled out the bare minimum. Carrying a bag didn't seem appropriate, since I was going to have to get past a security guard. I'd seen the lock, so I knew what kind of picks it would take. The filing cabinets were nothing to worry about; I hadn't paid attention to them, but there are only four or five manufacturers who sell widely, and the locks they use are pretty much just there for show. I could probably open most of them with a pipe cleaner.

Video surveillance was an open question because I hadn't been looking for it when I was there, but I'd learned my lesson at Rabbits's house, so I brought along a ski mask. Tonight, both sides of my profile were the dark side of the moon.

**Thirty-five minutes later** I was pulling into the office building's underground garage, my adrenaline building to a nice natural high, when the phone rang and Louie said, "He's moving."

"Which way?"

"Toward the Hollywood Freeway. If you want a professional guess, he's either going into town or else he realized he's out of vodka."

"He doesn't drink vodka." I hung a wide U, cutting through the empty parking spaces. There were only five or six cars in a garage that had been built to hold maybe sixty.

"Well," Louie said, "there you are."

"There I am what?"

"He's on the onramp."

"Here I come," I said, hitting a speed bump on the way out. I turned right onto Ventura. "You guys are about three miles north of me, so I'll be ahead of you as we head into town. Stay on the phone, okay? You've got to keep me clued so I don't overshoot."

"As a professional driver and everything," Louie said, "let me make a suggestion."

"What?"

"Stop the fuckin' car. Take some deep breaths. Get a burger in a drive-through. What's your nearest onramp?"

"Woodman."

"I'll call you when we pass Van Nuys Boulevard. You take your time, don't drive like a crazy person, and you'll be right behind us. That way we can do this right."

"Got it." I was too nervous to be hungry, but I idled along Ventura, much as Ellie Wynn had done a few hours earlier, and got the same audible wishes for peace and joy from the cars behind me. I made the left onto Woodman just as the phone rang again and Louie said, "Just passing Van Nuys."

"I'm with you." And, in fact, I was. As I pulled from the top of the ramp into the right-hand lane, Doc's car whizzed past. Louie was four cars back, in a 1997 Oldsmobile that badly needed waxing. I caught a glimpse of the cherry-red coal on his cigar, and then I was behind him.

Straight on into town, doing about sixty all the way. Off at Highland and down past the Hollywood bowl, then across Hollywood Boulevard, freak city at this time of night. Two more turns and we'd be at the Camelot Arms, and I wondered whether Thistle had come back home after all, seen the wreckage, and called Doc for a little something to adjust her mood. But Doc slid on past Romaine and dropped south toward Santa Monica Boulevard before making a left into a little area of stucco boxes built in the thirties and forties and originally put on the market at about $5000. Another left took him, and us, back up toward the Camelot Arms. I was beginning to think Doc had accidentally overshot when he pulled the car to the curb and got out.

He stood behind his car, hands on hips, looking back at us. I passed Louie and pulled up next to Doc. He leaned in through the open passenger window and said, "Quite a coincidence."

"Seven million people in this city," I said, "and here we are. If that don't beat all."

He nodded. "Would you like to explain your thinking?"

"I was busy. I had Louie—that's Louie, back there in the Detroit dinosaur—stay with you in case Thistle called you to do a delivery. I'd like to find her, make sure she's okay."

"And it didn't occur to you to ask me to call you if I heard from Thistle."

"You want the polite answer or the honest one?"

"I think the honest one," he said. "See whether I've got the *cojones* to handle learning I'm not trusted."

"I've figured out a lot of stuff today," I said. "And the more I figure out, the less I know about what's actually happening. I know some of the *whos* of what's going on, but I'm weak on the whys. And I've made a personal commitment about Thistle, which makes it a little trickier to know who's actually on my side."

"What commitment is that?"

"Well, that's a problem. Since I'm not really sure who's danc-ing with whom, so to speak."

"Oh, for Christ's sake," Doc said. "Look at me. I'm a doctor. I fucking *radiate* moral fiber. If you think what you're doing is the right thing, I'm probably on your side. In fact, how about this: I'll *tell* you what you're doing. You're not going to let This-tle make this movie. Is that right?"

I said, "Yeah."

Doc stuck a hand through the window. "Shake," he said. "I'm *also* not going to let Thistle make this movie. Now why don't you park that thing and let's see whether we can't find out where she is."

**"She hasn't called,"** he said as I followed him along a cracked-con-crete driveway past a dilapidated little frame house, its windows thankfully dark, heading for what had originally been a garage. The driveway was an example of the old design made up of two narrow, parallel strips of concrete, one for each tire, created for much better drivers than I. Grass had probably been planted between the concrete tracks several neighborhood demographic changes ago, but it had long since given way to hip-high weeds, which I was knocking down with a certain amount of negli-gent brio as we went. "Of course," he added, "she hasn't got a phone."

"What's here?" I asked.

"Friends."

"Didn't know she had any."

"Counting you and me, I can think of four," Doc said. "The other two live here."

He led me around to the right of the garage. In the center of the wall was a crappy-looking door, warped, blistered wood and four panes of glass, which had been painted an opaque color that looked like Wedgewood blue, with a lot of gray in it. Doc waved me to the left-hand side of the door, put a finger to his lips, and knocked.

No answer.

He knocked again, in a pattern this time: three fast, two slow, then two fast. A moment later, a high female voice said, "Who?"

Doc said, "Doc."

"Hold on," said the female voice, and in a few seconds the door opened. "I brought a friend," Doc said, and I came around the edge of the door, just in time to see it start to slam closed. I got a foot wedged in there, and looked down at the eight- or nine-year-old whom I'd chased out of the Camelot Arms that afternoon.

Up close, she was even smaller than I'd thought. She had fine, flyaway blond hair that had been chopped into some semblance of an intentional haircut, a high, narrow nose, and wide, very startled blue eyes, which were staring up at me as though Charles the Child-Eater had just materialized in front of her.

"It's okay," I said. "I'm a friend of Thistle's."

"Uh-*uh*," she said. "You liar. You're working for that, that—"

"No," I said. "I was, but now I'm not. Look, do you think Doc would bring me here if I wasn't Thistle's friend?"

"If you told him a bunch of lies," she said.

"Who is it?" another voice said from inside.

"The big bad guy," the little one said. "He's with Doc."

"Well," said the other voice, "there's no way to keep him out. If he leans on the door it'll probably fall over."

The little one's face twisted as she pulled her mouth to one side, as though it was chasing her left ear. "I don't like it, though," she said for the record. She stepped back and let Doc push the door open.

"Junior," Doc said, "this is Wendy." He knelt down so they were eye to eye. We hadn't yet taken a step over the threshold. "Wendy, this big clown is named Junior, and he's not as dumb as he looks."

Wendy said, "He couldn't be."

"May we come in?" Doc asked.

"Jennie said it was okay," Wendy said.

"Is it okay with *you*?"

The mouth twisted again as she considered the question. "I guess," she finally said.

"Wait," Doc said. "Have you girls eaten?"

Wendy didn't say anything, but her tongue flicked her upper lip. I could have counted to ten by the time the other one, Jennie, said from wherever she was, "No."

"Come on, then," Doc said, standing up. "We'll let the big ugly guy buy."

Jennie came around from behind the door with a cast-iron frying pan in both hands, gave me a quick but thorough look, and said, "This was for hitting, not cooking."

**Five minutes later,** we were sitting in the nearest McDonald's, which had come in first, second, and third on the list of places the girls wanted to go. Before we left I'd seen the inside of the garage apartment, a single room of absolutely astonishing messiness: clothes, shoes, boxes, and cooking implements everywhere, whole odd lots of stuff piled in corners. The basic organizational principle seemed to be, *if this won't tip the stack over, put it on top.*

"Where's your mom?" I asked as Jennie bit into the first of the two quarter-pounders in front of her.

Jennie was chewing, so Wendy said, "She went shopping."

"When?" I asked.

Wendy said, "February."

Doc kicked me under the table, but I asked anyway. "So you're all alone?"

"Not zhe firsht time," Jennie said around three or four ounces of meat.

"Mommy likes boys," Wendy said.

"Men," Jennie corrected her. She considered the burger, looking for the next point of attack.

"And we don't like the men Mommy likes," Wendy said. She picked up a fry and nibbled the tip. "So Mommy takes them someplace."

"They're doing fine," Doc said, giving me a Meaningful Look. "A lot better than they'd be doing if those pinheads in Child Protective Services got involved." He pushed Wendy's burger a tactful half an inch toward her. "They're together, for one thing."

"I'll eat it later," Wendy said, looking at the burger.

"No, you won't," Doc said. "You'll eat it now, and later you can eat the one we'll buy to go."

Wendy said, "A whole nother one?"

"Or two," Doc said. "Maybe two for each of you. Junior's got lots of money, don't you, Junior?"

"I can hardly walk, my pockets are so full."

Wendy said, "Maybe your pants will fall down," and laughed, and Jennie joined in, sneaking one of her sister's fries during the general merriment.

"Where do you get all your money?" Jennie said once sobriety had been restored. "We can hardly get enough for macaroni and cheese."

Wendy said, "And we don't even *like* macaroni and cheese."

"I steal it," I said. "I'm a burglar."

"Nuh-uh," Wendy said. Then she said, "*Are* you?"

"How old are you?" I asked Jennie.

"Fifteen." Wendy's head came around, and Jennie said, "Almost."

"I started when I was your age," I said. "I broke into my first house when I was fourteen."

Wendy was looking at me uneasily. "What did you steal?"

"Nothing. I did it to get even with the guy next door. You know anybody who's only happy when somebody else is miserable?"

"Come on," Jennie said. "We live in Hollywood."

"Right. Well, Mr. Potts was like that. And the summer I was fourteen, Mr. Potts made himself happy by opening the gate to our back yard and letting my dog out, and then calling animal control. The fifth or sixth time he did it, I decided to send him a message. I put a set of tools together and then waited one morning until he'd left for work. Then I let myself in through a back window—"

"Weren't you scared?" Wendy asked.

"Are you guys scared living alone?"

"No."

"Okay. You're good at living on your own. I'm good—I was good even then—at breaking into houses."

"What did you do to him?" Jennie asked, her chin on her hand while her other hand fished another of her sister's fries off the plate.

"A bunch of things. I put cayenne pepper in his jar of cinnamon and sand in his salt shaker. Ajax cleanser in his sugar bowl. Some cat poop into the Tupperware containers in his refrigerator."

Wendy said, "Ick" and slapped her sister's hand, which was once again straying toward the fries.

"And I used Superglue to seal every one of the little holes in the burners on his stove. And since I had the Superglue in my hand, I glued the TV remote to the coffee table."

"Facing which way?" Jenny immediately asked.

"Away from the screen, of course."

"Was the coffee table heavy?" Jenny was displaying some unexpected talent.

"Massive," I said. "And it was on a hardwood floor, so I glued the legs down, too."

"What did he do?"

"My guess is that he moved the TV. But if he had, it would have been in front of the fireplace. And then I went back out through the window and spent the next four or five days just keeping an ear cocked. Every time he started to scream, I ran over and knocked on his door and asked him if he was okay, and was there anything I could do? The fourth time, when he opened the door, something came into his eyes, and he looked down at me for about a minute and then closed the door."

"Did he ever do that again? With the dog, I mean?" Wendy asked.

"No."

"That is so *beamed*," Jennie said. "I'd like to do something like that to a couple of Mom's guys."

"Beamed?" I said.

"That's Thistle's word," Jennie said proudly "She makes up her own slang. Did you ever see her on TV?"

"Quite a bit, lately. When did you see her last?"

"Last night," Jennie said. "We were at her apartment."

"Really," I said. "Who else was there?"

"Nobody. Just Thistle, Wendy, and me."

"Um," I said. "Who drank all that wine?"

The look Jennie gave me was rich in pity. "Thistle, Wendy, and me." she said patiently.

"You kids aren't old enough to—"

"We smoked cigarettes, too," Jennie said. "We do whatever we want."

"It's okay," Wendy said in all seriousness. "We didn't drive."

"Fine," I said, mentally throwing up my hands. "Good, that's good. Drinking and driving don't mix. Especially when you can barely see over the steering wheel."

"Eat something," Doc said to me. "These kids are okay. Better than you were at their age."

"And it's not like *you* drive so great," Jennie said, a burger less than an inch from her mouth. "You drive like an old lady. You signal with the flicker, you use your arm. You do everything except get out of the car and say, 'I'm going to turn now.'"

"I know," I said. "I've always been too careful."

"Boy," Jennie said. "It's like a driver's ed movie."

"Did anybody knock on the door when you were there?"

Wendy thought about it for a minute and said, "Uh-uh."

"What time did you leave?"

"Eleven?" Wendy asked. "Jennie's the one with a watch," she explained.

"About eleven," Jennie confirmed.

"Was she taking pills when you were there?"

"Not in front of us," Jennie said. "She doesn't. She always goes in the other room. She does that when she sniffs stuff, too."

"Did you see a little box, like a present?" I described it, but both girls shook their heads.

"Probably came later," Doc said.

"Not too much later," I said. "Jimmy called me a little after midnight, and she'd had time to take some of them by then."

Jennie said, "Some of what?" and Wendy said, "Who's Jimmy?"

"Somebody delivered some bad dope to Thistle last night. Knocked on the door and ran, left the package for her to find. Jimmy's a friend of mine."

Jenny looked away, slightly uncomfortably, at nothing in particular.

Wendy shook her head. "We don't know anything about that."

"So," I said, looking at Jennie, "any idea where Thistle might be?"

"She fades in Hollywood sometimes," Jennie said, her eyes coming back to mine. "It's like, you know, a dope pad." She picked up a packet of ketchup, tore the end off with her teeth, and squeezed the contents directly onto her tongue, then took another bite out of the burger.

"Gross," her sister said.

"It's all going to the same place anyway," Jennie said with ketchup on her chin. Doc made a little mopping motion on his own chin, and she followed suit. "But she'll come over sometime soon. After she sees what that big guy did to her place—"

"You saw who did that?" I asked.

"Sure," Jennie said. "*Boy,* was he pissed."

"Because Thistle wasn't there?"

"Well, *yeah.*" I got the wide eyes the young reserve for idiots. "Why else?"

"Would you know him if you saw him again?"

"I'd know him anywhere," she said. "I'd know him in the dark. He was like the Hulk."

All of a sudden, for the second time in two days, I wanted to be somewhere else. Florida, maybe. "Big, was he?"

"He was just a bunch of muscles," she said. "And he was wearing black clothes."

"Tell me about his shirt," I said.

"His shirt?"

"You know," I said. I tugged at my sleeve.

"I know what a *shirt* is," she said with a massive amount of patience.

"What about . . . ?" I took hold of the near point of Doc's collar and yanked it, and he pulled away as though he thought I might be wiping my hands on it.

Jenny closed her eyes for a moment, and when she opened them, she looked puzzled. "How did you know?" she said. "He didn't have a collar."

## 37

### My Sweet Inflatable You

By the time we dropped the girls at their garage, we were all on first-name terms. Jennie told Doc and me that she had read, with horror, the scripts Trey had sent to Thistle. Trey's address was on the envelope, and Jennie and Wendy had spent a couple of days following people out of her driveway. One of them seemed to have been Rodd Hull ("He just kept fluffing his hair in the rear-view mirror," Wendy said, "like a *girl*.") and another was certainly Craig-Robert, who Jennie thought was pretty.

I was the third one they'd trailed, and the only one who turned around and bit them.

"We flipped you off pretty cool," Jennie said.

There was widespread agreement that it had been pretty cool, and the two of them started laughing about the expression on my face. "Dumb" was the descriptive term of choice. They were still laughing as they made their way up the driveway, toting a take-out sack of quarter-pounders.

"One of the world's least-celebrated joys," Doc said, watching them go, "is being a cause of mirth in children."

"You can have it," I said.

"Am I going to be allowed to drive home without an escort?"

"Oh, sure. Louie's probably all tucked in by now."

"Good, good. Nice to know that the criminal element gets to bed early. I always think of them as nocturnal."

"If you had to take a guess, where would you say Thistle is?"

He mulled it for a second. "Hollywood. She knows some of the sidewalk entrepreneurs well enough to score small on credit. She probably bought something and crashed in some squat. She's too smart to have gone home. She would have figured that's the first place Trey would have checked."

"About Trey," I said. "How well do you know her?"

"*Know* her?" We were standing next to Doc's car, parked beside the driveway the girls had gone down. He tilted his head back at me, and the streetlight filled the lenses of his glasses. "Well, I didn't deliver her or anything. I can't claim to have carried her around like a papoose. But I think I know her pretty well. She accidentally shot herself when she was ten or eleven and they brought her to me because they knew I wouldn't report the gunshot wound. I've treated her on and off ever since."

"Accidentally?"

"Unless she was trying to kill herself by blowing off a toe. The house was bristling with guns. She picked one up and fooled around with it."

"And they had you treat her after that."

"I was a pediatrician, remember?" A little steel came into his tone. "She was a child."

"Lower your head," I said. "I want to see your eyes."

Doc brought his head down, and there were his eyes again, warm and kindly as ever. "Am I under suspicion again?"

"I've told you about my commitment to Thistle," I said. "And now I've got my doubts about Trey, and I want to know for sure who I'm talking to. It's helpful to see your eyes."

"Well, then," Doc said, and took off his glasses. It made his eyes look smaller.

"Here's one edge of the problem. The person who trashed Thistle's apartment today was Trey's guy. Eduardo."

"Steroids, probably," Doc said. "He was sent to find her, he didn't, and it hit the rage button. These guys are always a couple of seconds away from tearing a Buick in half."

"It's not so much his reaction that gives me pause. It's the timing. He was there about an hour *before* I told Trey that Thistle was missing, and she put quite a bit of effort into being surprised by the news. So was she lying to me, or is it possible she didn't know Eduardo was there?"

Doc said, "Ah."

"Here's where things get shaky. Oh, and just to make things clear, I'm trusting you here, and it would be good policy for you to bear in mind that, despite the fact I inspire mirth in children, I'm a career criminal. And as much as I may like you personally, if I find out you're fucking around with me, I'll take you to pieces and scatter the bits from here to Tijuana in a pattern that spells out *he shouldn't have*."

Doc nodded. "Noted."

"Background, okay? Just to set things up. Since all this started, which I guess was only the day before yesterday, I've been operating on the thesis that the problems with the production were being caused by a member of the crew, who was, in turn, reporting to someone who wanted to cripple the movie, someone who wanted to bring Trey down. A crook, in other words."

"Sounds plausible."

"Well, I know who the person on the crew was. And I know that she and at least one of the crooks murdered somebody last night."

The avuncular Milburn Stone facade slipped a bit. "Murdered?"

I told him about Jimmy.

"Oh, criminy," he said. "I had no idea."

"Nobody did, except Trey and me. So it worries me that Trey may have lied to me about knowing that Thistle disappeared. Because *why* Jimmy was murdered isn't an issue: he was killed,

I'm about ninety percent sure, because he saw who delivered that little present to Thistle, after the girls left. And *who* isn't an issue, because I know who it was. But *how* is an issue. How did they know who he was? He was just a Chinese guy sitting in a car, in front of the apartment house."

"Unless they knew somehow that . . ." Doc said and then trailed off.

"That's right. And Trey and I were alone in her living room when she authorized me to put Jimmy out there. And, of course, there's every chance in the world that Eduardo heard it, since he's attached to her by an invisible rope."

"And if he heard it, then what?"

"Then one of two things. Either he sold Trey out and told the people who killed Jimmy and then went to ransack the apartment on their behalf. Or, and this is the one that worries me, he did it all on Trey's orders."

"Slow it down," Doc said. "Are you suggesting that Trey is sabotaging her own movie?"

"I'm suggesting that it's one possible explanation for everything that's happened."

Doc hooked his thumbs in his suspenders and gave them a snap. "But why? She needs the money. It's part of her plan."

"Money would be the answer," I said. "Something that would make more money than actually finishing the movies. But the only thing I can think of that would pay her anything substantial is a huge insurance loss."

Doc nodded. "I hadn't considered that."

"Well, forget it. Tatiana made it very clear to me. Thistle is completely uninsurable."

He turned his head and looked down at the sidewalk. I didn't think he was going to reply, but then he said, "And you believe Tatiana."

The question stopped me. I *had* believed her, certainly. There was something plausible and solid about her. As there was, I thought, about so many crooks. "I'll find a way to check it," I said. "But I don't know. The way Trey held Thistle's feet to the fire yesterday, threatening her with her contract and everything. Seems like she could have had her default right then."

"This is your area," Doc said. "I'm a simple pediatrician."

"Okay, one more question, purely about Trey. How do you think she really feels about her ex-husband?"

"That one's easy," he said. "She hates the ground his shadow falls on. She'd pay scalper's rates for a front-row seat at his execution."

"Not likely, then, that they'd be working together."

"Here's how unlikely it is," he said. "I'll bet you five thousand dollars right now that he's dead within eighteen months."

I shook my head. "A lot earlier than that."

**"Omaha," I said** to the guard.

"Long way," the guard said, although it sounded like a guess.

"That's why they need me. Hard to run an office that far away without having a man right there."

"Johnny on the spot," the guard suggested. He was a liberally weathered fifty-five or so, with a richly veined nose and enough alcohol on his breath to float an olive. His name tag said CARL.

*"Johnny on the spot,"* I said admiringly. "Exactly. Boots on the ground. Local talent. ZIP code savvy. You gotta know the territory." I was, just conceivably, over-extending.

"You the man," Carl contributed, offering proof, if further proof were needed, that here was one more expression that needed permanent retirement.

I resisted offering Carl a knuckle-bump and said instead, "So anyway, Jack said to me, 'Just show all this stuff to Carl, and he'll let you go on up.'" I paired the homemade business card with the bogus driver's license and held them nice and steady in front of Carl's eyes. It took him a second to home in on them. "I just need to drop something off," I said.

"Kind of late," Carl said.

"Damn airplanes," I said. "You know how it is."

"Do I ever." Carl snorted. "Damn airplanes," he said.

"Thanks," I said, heading for the elevators. I half expected him to call me back, but all he said was, "Damn airplanes," and then he snorted again. Apparently, he flew a lot more than I'd guessed.

The company on the card I'd made was called Earl Distribution and it was run by someone named Jack Earl. That, and the fact that it was on the same floor as Wattles, Inc., was one hundred percent of what I knew about it, since that was all that the office directory in the lobby had on offer when I'd read it on my way out with Hacker. I'd been worried that old Carl might have asked me something about what we were distributing, but I'd underestimated the vehemence of the universal frustration with the airline industry.

I turned my back to the camera on the elevator and waited until the doors opened before I put on the ski mask. If there was a camera in the hallway, I couldn't see it, but I kept my head down anyway. And I was wearing the stupid wig to match the driver's license, so any camera above me would be getting a nice clear shot of someone who looked like he'd kept his head in a jar since 1968.

I took one look at Wattles's door and felt like he was letting down the team. He was a crook, and he should have been ashamed of himself for relying on those locks. If I'd had a few more minutes, I probably could have sweet-talked them open, just a little judicious lock flattery. As it was, it took less than forty-five seconds before the door swung wide.

I slipped in, closed the door behind me, turned on the lights, and jumped half a foot straight up into the air.

I'd forgotten all about Dora, the inflatable receptionist, who sat behind the desk, looking at me expectantly. I was leaning against the door, trying to get my knees to stop wobbling, when

I looked at her more closely. I blinked a couple of times, but it didn't go away. A cherry bomb went off in my head.

I knew who she looked like. How could I have been so stupid?

Laughter was an appropriate response, and I gave her quite a lot of it. If she'd been sentient, she probably would have approved of it, if only as a change from the steady diet of necessarily humorless lust she'd been created to endure. One thing about guys who buy blow-up dolls: there's probably a pretty good chance they aren't hypersensitive to the funny side of things.

But Dora wasn't just funny. I had to look at her three times to be sure, but there was no question about it. Wattles had screwed up on a planetary scale. Dora was a chance at deliverance.

I went through the closet in the reception room and found half a dozen of her, neatly packed into their garish cardboard boxes, made in China, of course. It was easy to picture the assembly line of Chinese peasants, yanked from the mud of their little Puritan villages so fast their shoes were probably still stuck there, trying to figure out exactly what it was they were making. The company name Wattles had come up with was *My Sweet Inflatable You,* and the box copy waxed sub-poetic to describe Dora's infinite willingness to be penetrated in a variety of ways and her deluxe feature, a voicebox that said, "Oh, baby," and/ or "Don't stop now" when the eager lover pressed her left ear. I guessed the phrases came at random, although "Don't stop now" seemed a little risky, especially if lover boy had just wrapped it up, so to speak. These guys are probably fragile enough without being urged to exceed their sexual capacity by a blow-up doll.

Anyway, I had a vitally important use for Dora. It wasn't the one Wattles had planned on, but it met my needs so perfectly that I guessed things averaged out.

I put two Doras, all boxed up, just beside the door, and went to the files. In the locked drawer for My Sweet Inflatable You, I found that Wattles kept two sets of books, one for himself and one for the government, with remarkably little in common. The one for himself contained a tidy little spread sheet that told me that Dora had been purchased by more than 24,000 presumably blissful consumers, who had paid $79.95 each for her latex companionship and conversational skills, which meant that Wattles had grossed about a million nine on her. Suddenly his choice of models didn't look quite so dumb, at least not from a commercial perspective. I wrote down the precise number of sales for that persuasive touch of verisimilitude. Sometimes, when you want to make a point, a detail really nails it, and I thought this number would make a truly lethal difference.

The file I had come for wasn't in a filing cabinet. There were four cabinets in all, with four drawers in each, and I went through all sixteen of them before I gave up. The sale of a hot Paul Klee canvas was too sensitive to be kept in anything as obvious as a filing cabinet.

And then I remembered Wattles's admiration of Rabbits Stennet's technological approach to security. Rabbits had good tech, he'd said, or something like that. So, if I were a tech enthusiast like Wattles, I'd rely on a little tech to hide the things I really didn't want anyone to see.

The remote.

The remote Hacker had used to reveal the flatscreen was in the top drawer of Wattles's desk. I pointed it at the wall and pushed a bunch of buttons, and nothing happened, but I heard something behind me and turned to see a section of drywall behind Wattles's desk slide obediently to one side.

Inside the cupboard behind the sliding wall were two manila folders. One of them told me that my guess about the new owner of the ugly Klee was correct. There just isn't that big a market in Los Angeles for people who are rich enough and crazy enough to buy an extremely expensive painting they'll only be able to show a few very close friends. The proud new owner of the painting that had gotten me into all this trouble was Jake Whelan, legendary film producer and world-class narcissist, a human cocaine scoop with a year-round tan who would have been an automatic and unanimous choice to lead Team America in the Olympic Flaming Jerk competition. Now semiretired, mostly because even Hollywood wouldn't put up with him any more, he nevertheless retained some influence in the industry, in small part because he had done some people favors back in his day, and in large part because he knew enough about the currently employed to end an enormous number of careers.

The second folder in the cabinet stopped me cold. It was a photocopy of a bank statement documenting a wire transfer from Jake Whelan to an account in the Cayman Islands. It told me what Whelan had paid for the painting. And it also told me I was the sap of the century.

I'd been promised $20,000 to take it off the wall in the face of a pack of man-eating Rottweilers and a vengeful gangster who would undoubtedly enjoy feeding me to them. Wattles, who had spent the entire time with his gut resting comfortably on his desk, had been paid $1,750,000 for it.

I felt decisively stiffed, especially since I still hadn't seen the money. But, as I put the folders back, I found myself thinking that it was good news, too.

So when I left the office, I had two blow-up dolls and a bunch of new information. Now all I needed was a lot of luck, a couple of sixty-hour days in the forty-eight hours before Rabbits and Bunny got back on Friday, and a very special gun.

## 38
### Bleak Receptors

Since Jenny and Wendy didn't appear to be any more dangerous than the average Brownie troop, I spent the night at the Snor-Mor, but I took the minor precaution of moving from room 204 to 203 and locking the connecting door. Not much of a tactic, but not much was called for.

The night I'd been forced into this thing, I'd slept badly because I hated the idea of dragging someone as talented as Thistle into a porn film, even an extra-fancy porn film with arcs and sequels and Rodd Hull and everything. The second night, I'd barely slept at all, sitting in that chair at the Hillsider Motel hoping that whoever killed Jimmy would show. So here I was, one night later; I had committed to keep Thistle out of the movie, I knew who had killed Jimmy, and I was pretty clear on what I was going to do about it.

And I *still* couldn't sleep.

The early morning hours are the Valley of the Shadow of Death for the fearful. For some reason, people's Bleak Receptors are yawning wide at that time, waiting hungrily to clamp onto every doubt, unanswered question, possible reversal, potential disastrous outcome, and negative self-assessment that might be floating around in the local ether. I had every one of those items, a museum-quality collection, a veritable royal flush of worries, dreads, and night-terrors. With them in charge of my perspective, it seemed inescapably clear that I had built a rickety bridge from *here* to *there* constructed from dubious assumptions, character miscalculations, underestimations of the amount of malice and cunning on the other side's team, and a fundamental misunderstanding of the laws of probability. What had looked to me, when I left Wattles's office, like a relatively good hand of cards that might prevail with skillful play now looked like muck.

And I wasn't just frightened for myself. I was frightened for Thistle, for Doc, for Louie, for anyone who had done or was going to do anything at all to help me try to get out of this mess with my skin and my ethics, such as they were, intact. And, of course, I was worried about the spatter effect, especially where Rina and Kathy were concerned. I couldn't let anything endanger them. And Hacker, that multifaceted son of a bitch, had, at least obliquely, threatened Rina.

Another reason to put Hacker in a different category.

Around three-fifteen, I got honest with myself and stopped pretending I was going to drop off to sleep just any minute now. I got up, turned on the lights, and wandered around the room. The rooms at the Snor-Mor offer a minimum of wandering area, complemented by a minimum number of items of interest. Finally, out of desperation at the sheer absence of anything useful to do, I turned on CNN and spent about forty-five minutes watching the coverage of Thistle Downing's emergence from obscurity to star in a porno flick, tastefully referred to as an *adult film*. I got to see myself deck the lady reporter a couple of times—that was what they'd chosen as the promo—and watched myself standing next to Thistle at the press conference. I could see why Kathy had gotten so upset; I looked like some human trafficking enforcer who'd been stationed there to break her spine if she got out of line.

Thistle had predicted the angles precisely. CNN went with what she had characterized as the compassionate approach: "Isn't it tragic? That cute little girl turned out to be a slut."

The surprise was that they spent quite a bit of the segment on excerpts from the press conference in which Thistle excoriated the ladies and gentlemen who had turned out, and then cut to some brief street interviews of people who, by and large, agreed with her. The general consensus seemed to be that the press was a bunch of scumbags, that they were interested only in bad news and cheap angles, and that they should leave the poor kid alone. These compelling tidbits were followed by a *very* carefully worded piece, a piece many lawyers had reviewed, about the possibility of there being crime-family money behind the enterprise. When the CNN all-night anchorwoman, who was attractively weary-looking, or maybe it was just me, promised an upcoming editorial on *The Media: Are We Out of Control?*, I turned off the set and looked for something else, anything else, to do.

And there, jammed provocatively into her four-color box, was Dora.

I unwrapped her and blew her up, which turned out to be a lot harder than it sounded. By the time she was sitting propped up in the armchair opposite the bed, looking at me with a certain passive interest, I had spots floating in front of my eyes. I checked the package for a health warning, something like DO NOT ATTEMPT SEXUAL ACTIVITY WHILE HYPERVENTILATED, but it seemed as though Wattles hadn't had his legal team evaluate the language on the box. If he had, I thought, there would be more of those infuriating cautions for the clueless that have become such a permanent part of the American landscape: DO NOT FILL WITH MOLTEN LEAD. DO NOT USE ON LIGHTED STOVE. DO NOT SHARE WITH STRANGERS. DO NOT INFLATE AND TAKE TO DENTIST.

There was one nice lawyerly touch: in small print on the back of the package were the words MODEL WAS EIGHTEEN YEARS OF AGE OR OLDER AT TIME OF MANUFACTURE. I knew for a fact that *that* was true. So Wattles, whatever other kinds of nefarious activity he might be engaged in, wasn't promoting plastic pedophilia. I found myself wondering whether there might not be a worldwide underground traffic in used department-store mannequins of children. Somewhere, I figured, there was probably a catalog.

*Catalog,* I thought. Good idea; here was something useful I could do. I went online, brought up Google, and typed MY SWEET INFLATABLE YOU, hoping this query wasn't being electronically filed in an indelible record of my online activities by some gray government bureau. Wham! With the absolute moral neutrality that makes Google so perversely fascinating, it filled my screen with a whole bouquet of hits. And the very first one had everything I needed, and more: a picture of Dora at her most alluring (high-definition version available), the price, some truly unsettling prose about her capabilities, a couple of even more unsettling endorsements from happy customers, and—almost too good to be true—Wattles's mailing address for those who wished to pay with checks or money orders rather than having Visa or Mastercard know they were buying inflatable companionship.

I printed five copies of the page, using glossy paper for the full effect. Then I killed half an hour writing the letter I planned to roll up in Dora's open mouth when it came time for her to take center stage. It was good, even by my strict editorial standards.

"You're going out there a limp bag of latex," I said to Dora. "But you're coming back a star."

I thought it would be polite for her to answer me, so I pressed her left ear, expecting either, "Oh, Baby" or "Don't stop now," or maybe both of them together to show I was someone special, not just another guy with a good pair of lungs. Nothing. I pressed the right ear, and I have to admit that pressing either ear was mildly creepy-feeling. Not a word, not a syllable, not a perfunctory appreciative moan. In addition to being a second-rate

burglar, a bad planner, a danger to those around me, and someone whose personal clock was set on fast forward, I couldn't get
a cheap rise out of a blow-up doll.

I picked up the package, and my spirits lifted: in print that
was smaller than most punctuation marks were the words, BAT-
TERIES NOT INCLUDED.

Okay. It wasn't me. I went to sleep.

**"Geez, I'm sorry,"** Louie said in the doorway. "Didn't know you
had company."

I'd shot halfway across the room, traveling eight inches
above the carpet, at the sound of the door opening, and I stood
there now, panting, trapped somewhere between the adrenaline
rush of panic and the post-sleep fog of no-coffee-yet. "Jesus," I
said. "Don't *do* that. And look a little closer before you apolo-
gize to the lady."

"Holy smoke," Louie said, peering at Dora. He'd come in
from a bright morning and the room was as dim as I'd been
able to make it. He looked concerned. "You know, Junior," he
said slowly, "you're not what I call handsome, but you're not
a *bad*-looking guy. I mean, Alice knows some girls she could
introduce . . ." His voice trailed off. "She looks a lot like somebody," he said.

I said, "Doesn't she."

Louie said, "You're fuckin' kidding me" in the tone of someone who has just seen the Virgin Mary in a swirl of powdered
coffee creamer. He came the rest of the way into the room and
tugged a lock of Dora's Dynel hairdo. "I mean, same hair and
everything."

"We should try to be gentlemen," I said. "Neither of us
knows about the *everything* part."

"Oh, man," Louie said. "This is dynamite."

"Take it from me," I said. "It's harder to blow up."

He looked around the room. "You thought about the maid?"

he asked. "She's gonna take one look at that and run all the way back to Venezuela."

"You're right. I probably need to stash her." I unplugged the little valve on her back and started to press on her to push the air out. "You want to help?"

"Not on your life," he said, sitting as far away as the room allowed.

"Just asking." I found that I was trying to avoid pressing on her, um, sensitive areas. I put her on the floor and sat on her and was rewarded by a nice long hiss.

"Got your gun, I think," Louie said, watching me. "The thing you want, it uses CO2 cartridges, right?"

"I don't know. Sounds right. Not noisy anyway."

"Makes a little noise like *phut*," Louie said.

Dora was shrinking nicely. "Like what?" I wanted to hear him say it again.

"Like phut you," Louie said. "I don't mind being laughed at, but I like to get paid for it."

"If this works out," I said, "I'll have ten K for you day after tomorrow."

"Ten K counts," Louie said. "What if it doesn't work out?"

"You can sue my estate. What about the car?"

"It's the old LAPD black-and-white," Louie said. "What do you want Willie to write on the door?"

"*Pacific Security.*"

Louie made a mouth. "Not much of a ring to it."

"I know, but I've got a shirt that says that, and they might as well match."

"You're the only guy I know," Louie said, "gets a car to match his shirt." He made a sound that probably passed for a laugh at his house.

"Where's the guy with the special gun?" Dora was almost flat enough to fold.

"Where are *all* the freaks?" Louie asked. "Hollywood."

"Good. We'll go together. I've got another stop to make."

"What are we, running errands?"

"Got to see a girl about a phone," I said.

"Am I going to like her?"

"I don't know," I said. "But she's got a sister."

## 39
### A Tunnel Behind His Eyes

Wendy's eyes widened in panic when she saw what was in my hand. She stuck her tongue between her teeth, bit down on it, and took a step backward. For a second, I thought she was going to close the door in my face. She yelled, *"Jennie."*

Louie said to me, "Why isn't this kid in school?"

"She's a full-time student in the School of Life," I said.

"Kid like this," Louie said righteously, "she oughta be learning stuff."

"I am," Wendy said. Then she called, more loudly this time, *"JENNIE."*

"I'm peeing," Jennie shouted. "Is that okay with you? Am I supposed to get permission or something?" I heard a door open, and Wendy glanced to her left and said, "Pull your pants up. Junior's here with some little guy."

"Little?" Louie said.

"She means like cute," I said.

"Hey, Junior," Jennie said, coming around the door. Then she saw the phone in my hand and stopped like some character in Ovid, turned into a stone fountain or something.

"You guys left something out last night," I said. I waved the phone back and forth. "And it's sort of important."

"I don't know what you're—" Jennie began.

"I saw your eyes in the restaurant when I mentioned Jimmy,"

I said. "And you should have seen your sister's face just a second ago. Don't look at Wendy like that. You weren't exactly Miss Cool, either."

The two of them stood there, their eyes drifting downward, identical expressions of thought on their faces. "Why don't we come in," I said, "and you can tell me about it."

**"I was worried,"** Jennie said. "Thistle had been really scared about doing that movie. She was taking too much stuff, and I got scared that maybe she'd try something stupid, you know, something to, uh, hurt herself. So I went back over."

"What time?"

"A little after midnight." Louie and I were sitting on the double bed, Jennie having cleared a spot for us simply by throwing onto the floor everything that had been in the space we now occupied. She and Wendy sat on the floor, or what would have been the floor if it hadn't had a couple of inches of stuff on top of it.

"You kids were up at *midnight*?" Louie said.

"Louie," I said. "Just bottle all the paternal outrage and let these young ladies tell me what happened."

"So I was worried. I took the car and went back over. When I was looking for a place to park, I saw the Porsche. We'd seen it before, when we went to see Thistle the first time that day."

"She means *she* saw it," Wendy said. "She thought the guy was hot."

"So I came back and parked a couple of spaces away, and I saw that his cell phone was on the street, just under the driver's door. It had broken apart, you know how they do that? So the little door on the back pops off and the, the battery comes out?" She licked her lips and swallowed, coming up on the hard part of the story.

"I know," I said. "Happens to mine all the time."

"So I picked it up, and I, um . . . I—" She passed a hand over her hair, although it was already neatly brushed. "I went to, like, hand it to him." She broke off, blinking hard.

"And you saw him."

She nodded. "I was just really, really scared," she said. "I suddenly thought, oh, Jesus, he was there to watch Thistle. I mean nobody else interesting lives there, just trailer trash and dopers and stuff like that. Who else would this really cool-looking guy, in a Porsche, and all, be . . . But he was all *bloody*. And his eyes were open. It was almost like he could see me, like there was still something in him that could see me but it was just miles and miles away, whatever it was, like there was some long dark tunnel behind his eyes and he was looking down it at me." She swallowed, hard. "And then I thought, Oh my god, what about Thistle? I mean, maybe she was dead, too."

Her voice had climbed up a couple of notes, and Louie surprised me by leaning over and putting a hand on her shoulder and saying, "It's okay, sweetie. It's okay. We're all here now."

Jennie nodded once, then twice, and looked over at Wendy. Wendy put an arm around her waist.

"So I went up to Thistle's apartment and I used the key she gave me."

"You're a brave girl," I said.

"Thistle's my friend. So anyway, she was there. I mean, she was out and everything, but she was there. I'd seen her worse. I put her white robe over her like a blanket and came back down. I looked at the Porsche again and just got really scared, and ran all the way home. I even forgot my car. I didn't know I still had the phone in my hand until Wendy asked me where I got it."

"Because we don't have one," Wendy said. "So she told me how she got it, and we tried to figure out what to do with it."

"You called me," I said.

"I didn't know it was you. It was the last number he dialed, and the time, you know how you can see the time the call was made, well, it was only about fifteen minutes before I—I found him. And I figured, probably, you know, he was trying to call some kind of friend. I thought if I dialed it and didn't say anything, whoever it was would know something was wrong. There was nothing anybody could do for him, but, I mean, it seemed like somebody should at least *know*."

"And I yelled into the phone and probably scared you to death."

"Yeah," she said. "And I was going to dig a hole and bury the phone. But then I started thinking, and it seemed to me that you probably weren't yelling at him, the boy in the car, whatever his name—"

"Jimmy," I said.

"Not at Jimmy, because he called you. I thought maybe he'd been talking to you when he got shot, because of how the phone fell out of the car and he didn't pick it up, and maybe you thought you were yelling at the person who shot him. So we waited a really long time and then we drove over to the Hillsider and we saw your open door, but we couldn't see you because the lights were off."

"So you what—just sat there?"

"Yeah." She swiveled her head around and up and down, as though her neck were stiff. "And after about an hour, Wendy tiptoed up and put it by your door. Then we went home."

"Why'd you do that?"

"Maybe there was a clue on it or something. Maybe you could use it to figure out who shot him. He was so cute." Jennie looked down at her lap for a moment. "And we couldn't keep it anyway. Probably the cops were looking for it."

"Geez," Louie said. "You're some smart kids."

Jennie shrugged.

"Not smart enough to tell me last night," I said.

"Leave her alone," Louie said.

"I didn't want to talk about it with Doc there," Jennie said. "He's such an innocent guy. And you didn't really ask."

"No," I said. "I didn't. Here." I reached into the pocket of my shirt and came out with two throwdown phones, the kind you can buy for cash at Radio Shack with hours of calling time already programmed in. "These are for you. They're both good for about ten hours of talking, if you don't call Russia or something."

"You're giving us these?" Wendy asked.

"Yeah. And when you've almost used them up, call me and I'll give you a couple more."

"Why?" That was Jennie.

"Two reasons. First, I want to know you're all right, okay? Call me every four or five hours. Don't get up in the middle of the night or anything, but do it whenever you think about it. And second, I want you to call me the minute, and I mean the actual minute, you hear from Thistle. Deal?"

Their eyes met for perhaps a hundredth of a second. "Deal," Jennie said.

"And now my friend Louie, here, and I are going to take you out to breakfast. And don't even *think* the word McDonald's."

**"I axed you** before, how many darts you want?"

"As many as you've got."

He gave me a squint, which didn't mean anything since he gave everything a squint. He was teensy and gaunt, maybe a hundred twenty angry pounds, paler than a floater, and balding in front but sporting a luxuriant ponytail that curled to mid-back. At some point in his career someone had drawn a knife down the left side of his face. The scar started at the hairline and bisected the left eyebrow and traced a fine line across the lid below it, then dug a more substantial furrow down his cheek. It ended at the corner of his mouth, the part that would have gone up when he smiled, if he ever smiled. If he did, he kept it to himself.

His name was Wain, which he spelled twice, because, I was

pretty sure, he forgot he'd already spelled it once. If NASA had ever had his phone number, they'd probably tossed it. His office was in an auto repair shop off of Western Boulevard, dirty in the way only auto repair shops can be, and stinking of old black sludge. The sky, which had been turning gray when Louie and I left the Valley, was now dark, and the air was warm and unusually humid. Some sort of tropical storm system seemed to be wheeling up from Baja, so we were all sweating, which did not add to the spirit of camaraderie.

"You know, this ain't an automatic," he said. He was talking to me as though I were a kindergarten student with a tenuous grasp of English. "It's not like you got a clip or something, you can put it on full repeat and just stand there with the gun getting hot and watch stuff fall over."

"Got it," I said. "It's okay. I plan just to stand there, shooting and loading, shooting and loading, until I'm done."

"Uh-huh. And everybody's just going to hang around while you shoot them." He looked at Louie, and Louie shrugged. "Tell you what," Wain said. "If that's your plan, I want a deposit for the whole thing, gun, cartridges, darts, and all. You come back alive, I'll give it back to you."

"What are we talking about?"

He wiped sweat off his forehead, leaving a trail of dark grease. "I got fourteen sets. You really want fourteen? I mean it's gonna take all day to fire the damn things."

"I'll take ten," I said.

"Okey-doke." He grabbed a brown paper bag that a burrito had drained onto, wiped his palm on his filthy jeans, and painstakingly wrote a column of numbers, threading a path between the oil spots, where the ball point ink wouldn't take to the paper. It was modestly impressive. "Four-twenty," he said. "And one-seventy-five for the rental."

"Why don't I just pay you the deposit, and when I return the gun and the unused cartridges, you deduct the rental?"

I got the squint. "Why don't you just do what I said. Four-twenty and one-seventy five is five-ninety-five."

"That's what I like," I said, reaching into my hip pocket. "The old give and take."

"Ain't no point in making friends," Wain said. "You probably gonna be dead by dark."

**40**

She Thinks You Sweat Perfume

I wound up taking all fourteen of the cartridges after all. I went back to the Snor-Mor, blew up Dora again, and, once the spots had retreated from my field of vision, I practiced firing the gun. It didn't make much noise, which was a point in its favor, but it wasn't very accurate, either. Six cartridges later, I had eight left, three were stuck in various pieces of furniture, Dora was deflating rapidly, and I knew that the gun threw to the left and that I'd have to sight above the target because the darts dropped pretty fast if they had to travel much more than about six feet.

So, not perfect. But under the circumstances, probably the best I could hope for.

I turned on the lights. It was getting darker outside, and it wasn't even lunchtime yet. Once in a great while Los Angeles gets a summer rainstorm, usually just the ragged end of something that was much bigger eight or nine hundred miles south, but every four or five years we catch more of it. I had the feeling that this was going to be one of those times.

The phone rang for the seventh or eighth time, Trey wanting to get hold of me, and I figured it was probably time to cool her off. I answered and lived through three or four minutes of frustration and recrimination, and when she'd gotten herself to the point where she had to inhale occasionally, I told her I hadn't found Thistle yet.

"And assuming you've actually looked anywhere, where *did* you look?"

I bypassed the dudgeon and gave her the short version: the apartment, both moms, the graveyard. "By the way," I said, "somebody tore the hell out of her apartment."

"Really," Trey said. "How could you tell?" Oh, she was in fine spirits.

I decided to treat it as a genuine question. "They broke everything, they turned the refrigerator over, threw the couch across the room. Not your normal wear and tear, not even at Thistle's."

"Oh, who cares," she said, after a long silence. "If someone's got her, they're not going to give her back. If she's run away, she's not going to come back of her own free will."

"I don't think anyone's got her," I said. "I think she's hiding out."

"Well, that's not much help, since you can't seem to find her. Or aren't interested in finding her."

"Okay," I said. "That's twice. You want to tell me what you're so pissed off about?"

"Your sympathy for poor little Miss Downing has been obvious from the beginning. I'm sitting here watching this whole enterprise go south, and all I have to depend on is someone who may not even be on my side."

"That's absolutely correct. Emotionally, I'm not on your side. You're very perceptive about that. I think the whole enterprise stinks."

"Oh, please," she said. "Speak right up."

"Not much point in my trying to lie to you. But you're just going to have to believe that my desire to continue living, with all four limbs functioning, is stronger than whatever sympathy I might feel for Thistle."

"Even the most useless," she said, "cling to life."

"I'm hoping that's a quotation that just sort of sprang to

mind," I said. "Because I may be in a tight spot, but that doesn't give you a license to fuck with me."

"You're right," she said. "It's self-indulgent and counterproductive. What's your assessment right now?

"I think we'll hear from her soon. I've turned up some friends of hers, and I think she'll contact either them or Doc pretty quickly."

"Why?"

"Dope. She probably hasn't had any since yesterday morning."

"Who were the friends?"

"Nobody." There was no way I could risk telling Trey about Jennie and Wendy. "Just a couple of people in the apartment. George and Martha. I didn't know you'd actually been there."

"Once," Trey said, "although my chat with Thistle is apparently one of thousands she's forgotten."

"Did you meet anyone she knew?"

"I got the impression she didn't know anybody in the world except drug dealers."

"That's about right. But she doesn't have any money, so it'll either be Doc or George and Martha."

"All right." Now that she'd parked the anger, she sounded discouraged and dispirited.

"What happens?" I asked. "What happens if you have to fold the movie?"

She blew air past the mouthpiece. "I'm in trouble."

"How serious?"

"It doesn't concern you. But there are a bunch of people sitting around waiting for me to hit a bump. I probably talked about this more than I should have."

"Are you insured? The film, I mean? Is the film insured?"

"Sure, but it's pennies. No one would sell me completion insurance with Thistle in the movie."

"But you can get back some of what you spent."

"Some. Rodd and the cinematographer both have play or

pay, which means they get their money one way or the other. But most of the rest of it, I can get back. The problem is that I've fallen on my ass, made promises I couldn't deliver. It was a bad judgment call. I'm not in a business where people forget bad judgment calls."

"Listen," I said. "This is probably a stupid question, but suppose I could find Thistle and bring her in, and she'd work for you, but not in that kind of movie?"

"She's a television star," Trey said, "and, sure, she was big, but it's been years since she's been on the air. There's some curiosity about her, we saw that yesterday, but I doubt she could carry a movie, not a *real* movie, anyway. The kink thing, that's what would have driven the sales. All I needed was four, five million units worldwide at twenty, twenty-five bucks, maybe sell to one out of every hundred people who thought she was so great, and I'd have been solid gold. Put her in some other movie, you're talking art house. English majors, people in sandals. And anyway, what do I know about making movies? Porn, sure. That's easy. Buy some Viagra, rent a camera, find a star in some strip club. But something good? Like with a story and everything? I'm just a girl from the Valley."

"Well," I said. "It's not over yet." I suddenly had a case of the guilts about Trey.

"It's over as of tomorrow night," she said. "We're doing inserts today, but Friday at six I'm pulling the plug unless you've got Thistle back and she's working. And if I do pull the plug because she's not around, I'm not going to go out of my way to make sure you get any kind of cushy treatment from Hacker and Wattles."

"No reason you should," I said.

"On the contrary," she said. "You're a nice person and everything, but if I really have to fold this thing, and I find out later you've actually been working against me, I'd probably shoot you myself."

o o o

**I ate lunch** at a coffee shop on Ventura. This being Los Angeles, there was a coin newsstand selling the entertainment trade papers, and I spotted Thistle's name on the front page of *Variety*, so I parted with quite a lot of change and bought it. What the damn thing costs, you'd think they print it on money.

*Variety* writers, at least the journeymen hacks, use one-name bylines, and this story was by someone who signed him/herself as *Vern*. According to *Vern*, Thistle had "emerged from seclusion" to appear in front of the press at a "local indie studio" to announce plans to star in a "multiple adult flix package." *Vern* went on to say that Ms. Downing had appeared high-strung and contentious, displaying a tendency to ramble and, at times, to forget which of the reporters had asked the question she was answering. And a lot more, all of it shorthand for *drug problem*.

But the placement was interesting: front-page, below the fold. I left my mushroom and grease omelet to cool and solidify, and went out to the news vending machines on the sidewalk and bought the *Reporter* and the *LA Times*. It was starting to sprinkle, so I got back inside at a trot. Both the *Reporter* and the *Times* "Calendar" section had put Thistle in prime position. The *Times* ran the story in the lower corner of the section's front page, with a big jump to page five, where there was a two-column story on her, with photos from "Once a Witch." The story felt like it might have been adapted from a pre-written obituary, the *Times* always being in the forefront of the vulture watch. It told the story of her discovery, of the amazing success of the series and the fall-off in ratings toward the end, and it referred to vague "problems" during the show's last two seasons, followed by Thistle's plummet out of the public eye. The reporter who had been at the press conference described Thistle's demeanor as "troubled," another code word for *stoned*. In one of the pictures from the press conference, I loomed beside her, arms crossed menacingly, looking like a gargoyle on loan from Notre Dame. The caption referred to me as "Ms. Downing's companion, 'Pockets' Mahoney." It was good to know someone had been listening when Thistle suggested the quotes around "Pockets."

The *Reporter* was less chatty, but they had what qualifies in entertainment news coverage as a scoop: they'd somehow got hold of the fact that Thistle was to be paid $200,000 for the movies. They spent a paragraph on the historic deal she'd made for her "Once a Witch" residuals and then speculated that "an erratic lifestyle" may have accounted for the fact that she was now, as far as anyone could tell, the next thing to indigent. Yet *more* code for drugs.

So, loaded or not, Thistle was big news. This was important, if the part of my plan that involved proud new Paul Klee-owner Jake Whelan was to have any possibility of working out. Hollywood reads these three publications every morning as though Moses personally brings them down from the mountain at dawn. Jake Whelan's participation, assuming he'd play, would be plausible.

I was blotting cooking oil off the top of the omelet with a napkin when the phone rang. It wasn't a number I recognized.

"Our girl ain't happy," a man said.

"That's a terrific sentence," I said. "Gets you off to a fast start, takes the audience right into the thick of the action. Raises all sorts of fascinating questions. What girl? Why isn't she happy? And who the hell is this?"

"Wattles," Wattles said. "You want to watch that lip, you know that?"

"My lip is the least of my problems."

"Listen, I don't really give a shit one way or the other, you know? This is like a friendly call, like a heads-up. But Hacker, you want to watch out for Hacker. This girl Trey is half his paycheck. Something goes wrong, he's gonna be like the Bloodmobile, but in reverse."

"Do they still have the Bloodmobile?"

"I'm dating myself, huh? Hey, you asked Janice out yet?"

"I've actually been kind of busy."

"You gotta look at your priorities," he said. "Life is short, although you wouldn't know it to look at me, and I'm telling you, that girl's ready. Buy a new shirt, get rid of some of that hair—"

"What's wrong with my hair?"

"Huh? Probably nothing. But, you know, a guy like you, you can use any edge you can get. I'm telling you, though, she thinks you sweat perfume." He hung up.

*Hacker*, I thought.

I gave up on the omelet and went into the parking lot to call Kathy. The drizzle had intensified slightly, so I stepped under the overhang above the restaurant's front door.

"Is your watch broken?" she said by way of openers.

"I am calling to tell you personally that there will be no movie."

"And I'm supposed to believe you have something to do with that."

"I can't help what you believe or don't believe. But I'm putting a stick into the spokes of this project. If this movie is made, Thistle won't be in it."

"If that's the best I can get, it'll have to do," Kathy said. "Rina's fighting me anyway. There are times I wish she didn't love you so much."

"Not a wish I can share."

"Okay, then, I wish there were times you loved me more."

"I do love you," I said. "I love you the best I can."

"And look where *that's* gotten us."

I said, "Kathy,"

"There was a time," she said, "when I thought that hearing you say my name in the morning was the way I wanted to begin every day for the rest of my life." She paused, while I tried to think of something, anything, to say. "That time lasted quite a while, too."

"Kathy," I said again. "I haven't bought a house yet."

"Oh," she said. There was another pause, and I could see her in my mind's eye, standing at the kitchen table with the little stone Buddha on it, phone to her ear. "Well," she finally said, "you've always liked motels."

"I hate motels."

"Poor us. I guess we're both someplace we hate."

"We're both a hell of a lot better off than Thistle Downing," I said.

Kathy let a few seconds pass, probably to let me know I wasn't getting away with changing the subject unnoticed, and then she said, "How bad is she?"

I said, "She's the saddest person I ever knew."

# 41
## A Little More About the Moderns

The former police car I'd gotten from Louie was a beast. It steered like a hippopotamus, pulled to the right, braked unevenly, and had springs like an Army cot. It skidded all over the wet street every time I made a turn. The windshield wipers captured the drizzle, mixed it efficiently with dirt, and spread a thin and surprisingly opaque layer of mud over the glass. I had to pull over twice and wipe it off.

But it helped me solve the mystery of why cops usually look so grim. If I had to drive something like that all day, I'd want to shoot somebody, too.

I was not terrifically happy with the precipitation, which was threatening to turn into real rain. The black PACIFIC SECURITY lettering on the doors of the car was damp enough to run. This would not contribute to the persuasiveness of my disguise. I kept seeing a chalky fluorescent flicker of heat lightning down near the horizon that suggested that something more ambitious might be on the way.

But the weather on hand was the weather I had. It wasn't as though, with less than two days of relatively safe life remaining before Rabbits and Bunny got back, I could enjoy the luxury of waiting for a sunny day. I wrestled the car to the curb in front of the Stennet mansion, braked with an attention-getting soprano squeal, got out, kicked the door twice, opened the trunk, and grabbed my bag. I was wearing white jeans and a white shirt with PACIFIC SECURITY written on it in letters so big they could be read from a helicopter. No furtive movements today. Today called for bold as brass and obvious as daylight. I was one of the good guys.

I stood in front of the door, listening to the dogs go crazy inside, and presented the broadest silhouette I could, trying to mask what I was doing with my hands. It took only a minute to pick the lock, now that I'd already done it once, and the little noises I was making raised the level of the canine frenzy inside. Once I had the lock taken care of, I didn't open the door. Instead, I pulled a tire iron out of the bag and began to tap it, somewhat carefully, against a ruby-colored pane of glass at eye level. The stained glass was made up of individual pieces of different sizes and shapes, like a puzzle, with strips of lead between them. The lead was good, because it meant I didn't have to break the whole window. The last thing I wanted was to knock out a huge hole that could be seen from the street. I wanted a relatively small opening, and I wanted it at eye level so I wouldn't have to bend over or take any stance that might raise questions in an onlooker.

The chicken wire was a pain in the ass. The glass shattered easily and thanks to the lead the breakage didn't travel to the adjoining panes, but the glass was fused to the wire, and it took more work than I'd anticipated to knock it free. Time is risk, as far as I'm concerned, and by the time I had created a neat hole five or six inches around, I was getting into thrill ride territory.

I could see into the Stennets' entry hall now, and it was more fully inhabited by dogs than you would have thought possible when there were actually only four of them. They were in constant motion, sometimes packed close together, sometimes running at the door, sometimes snapping at each other. The snapping was pretty much an equal-opportunity activity, with one exception. Nobody snapped at the big guy. Moby-Dog had his own little nation of floor space wherever he went, and nobody crossed his borders.

When most of the glass was gone, a pair of wire cutters cleared the hole and gave me better access. I put the tire iron back and got the awkward, heavy, not-very-accurate gun Wain had rented to me, popped in a cartridge, loaded a dart, and stuck the barrel through the hole in the glass.

I chose the nearest of the beasts and waited until he turned sideways to present me with the biggest target. I aimed a little high and a tad to the right to compensate for the throw, and pulled the trigger.

*PHUT.* It was a lot louder here on the porch than it had seemed at the Snor-Mor. The dart found its way to the dog's shoulder and he jumped and let out a little yelp, then turned to look at it. Dogs have amazingly flexible necks, and he demonstrated that now by craning all the way around and, with some delicacy, removing the dart with his teeth. Then he launched himself at the door again.

This was not the reaction I had planned for. I now had seven darts left and four dogs standing, one of whom was Moby-Dog, the Dog of Bad Dreams, who I'd figure would take a couple of darts at least. Time seemed to be accelerating: security uniform or no security uniform, I could only stand here so long without attracting unwanted attention. I repeated the intricate routine of preparing the gun, chose another target, and missed altogether.

Six darts and four dogs left.

My eyes registered a flash of light, and a moment later I heard a dull rumble of thunder. Behind me, the sound of the rain intensified. That would make me less conspicuous, standing here, but it increased the danger of my car's mascara running.

One of the dogs was right there, simply too close to miss, and I pulled the trigger. This time the dart was high enough on the back of the dog's neck so that he couldn't reach it with its teeth. I was so busy watching it, waiting for some sort of reaction, that I almost missed it when the first dog I'd hit went down, just toppled over sideways like a tree. He lay there with his legs stretched out as though he were still standing, sleeping like a baby. He earned himself a couple of interested sniffs from the others, and then they all turned their attention back to me.

Just as a dart hit Moby-Dog, the second dog went over. Moby-Dog growled scornfully at the dart and threw his weight against the door. I was still loading, but I got him with another one as he retreated to take another rush. He looked at me, and I could see confusion in his face. Wasn't *he* supposed to be doing damage to *me*? He sat down and scratched at the second dart with his hind leg as though it had been a flea, and he managed to knock it off, but then he very slowly went over sideways, his hind leg still raised. Lying on his side like that, he looked like he'd been stuffed.

I shot the final one right between the shoulders, aiming almost directly down as he charged the door. He backed off fast and started to turn in a circle, like he was thinking of chasing his tail, but then he changed his mind. I could see his mental processes slow down, and he looked like he was enjoying it. He shot me a glance that was almost friendly, let his tongue loll out, took another look around as though he'd never seen the place before, but, boy, it was *far out*, and decided, kind of dreamily, to go upstairs, just, you know, see what was happenin', just kind of trippin'. He got about four steps up and then went down like a bundle of rags, sprawled diagonally across the staircase.

Grabbing a much-needed breath, I opened the door. I couldn't claim to be relaxed; I suppose some part of my brain suspected that the dogs had recognized the tranquillizer darts and were only pretending to be out cold, but fortunately this was real life, and they were all several fathoms under. I stepped over two of them as though they were couch cushions and keyed in the number to disarm the alarm system.

First things first. I pulled on the ski mask, climbed the stairs, edging past the slumbering man-eater, and went into the bed-room. I grabbed the other Paul Klee, which, I was surprised to learn, I actually liked better on second look. I gave it a third look as I took it off the wall and had one of those moments, a moment when you think you might actually be changing. I liked it even better the third time. Hmmm. Maybe I should read a little more about the moderns.

At the top of the stairs I heard a sound that froze my heart and instantly put me in statue mode, every hair on my body bris-tling, and the temperature of my blood dropping by ten degrees. Then I heard it again, and I started to laugh. What I'd thought was a bunch of resuscitated Rottweilers getting back into the growl state was actually snoring. All four killers were in doggie dreamland, where they were probably frolicking among daisies in gauzy slow motion and ripping kittens to tatters.

When I got downstairs, I stood the picture near the door, next to one of the torporous beasts, and gave it another look. Definitely growing on me. I even liked the colors, sort of. Then I picked up the bag and toted it up the steps to the raised living room, where I found what I assumed was a Kirghiz carpet, pro-fusely soiled. Bunny was not going to be amused.

The box Dora was in had been sealed by some Chinese per-son who had probably found rich amusement at the prospect of Dora's predictably impatient new owner discovering that it was literally impossible to open the package. It took me five minutes and two of the blades on my all-purpose knife to get her out, and when I did, I was briefly afraid I'd punctured her. I kept checking for leaks as I blew her up, but her skin, like her virtue, was intact. When I had her all plumped up, I did a couple of minutes on her hair, working from memory. Then I rolled up my computer-printed note and put it into the perfect circle of her mouth. As a final touch, I taped the color printout of the website download to her chest.

I stood back and admired the effect. She looked like she

belonged here, which in a sense she did. At the bottom of my bag was a pocket digital camera, and I worked for a few minutes to get her best angles. Then I dropped the camera in the bag and grabbed the handle, left the box Dora had come in right where I'd dumped it, next to a Rottweiler deposit on the Kirghiz, went down to the entry hall, stepped over a few dogs, picked up my new Paul Klee, and let myself out into the rain.

I hadn't gone half a block when the phone rang and Jennie said, talking very fast, "Thistle was here, and the big man who wrecked the apartment tried to catch her. *Please.* You have to come. You have to come *now.*"

# 42

## A Funnel of Whirling Dervishes

"Meet me there," I said to Louie. "They need somebody with them."

"Gonna take me some time," Louie grumbled. "This fuckin' rain's gonna slow everyone down."

"Then get moving. I'll be there in thirty-five, forty minutes, but I can't stay long. I've got a couple of things I've got to do."

"Like your life is so much more important than mine."

"You want me to live long enough to pay you?"

Louie said, "On my way."

*He was so big*," Wendy said. The brightness of her eyes betrayed that she'd been crying. Jennie stood behind her, both hands on her sister's shoulders, marginally calmer but still obviously agitated. She had a welt under her left eye that looked like it was going to swell until the eye closed.

"Let him in," Jennie commanded. "He's getting all wet."

Wendy stepped aside, and I went in. The place had been a mess before, but now it looked like it had been invaded by a funnel of whirling dervishes. The two chairs were on their sides, dishes, pots, and pans were all over the place, and when I turned back to look at the door, I saw that the lower right panel of glass had been broken.

"He did that with his *fist*," Wendy said, her eyes absolutely enormous. "He punched our door and then reached in and opened it."

"Whose is that?" I asked. Their eyes followed my finger to a long line of blood, left by someone on the move who'd been bleeding pretty freely.

"His," Jennie said.

"What, when he broke the glass, he cut himself?"

"No," she said. "Thistle had just come in, she ran in and slammed the door, and when he punched out the glass she grabbed a piece of it and sliced his hand while he was trying to turn the knob. I think she cut him three or four times. He was shouting like, I don't know, a giant or something."

"Okay, so he got the door open. Then what?"

"We started throwing stuff," Jennie said. "Everything in the kitchen, everything we could get our hands on. But he didn't even seem to notice us. He was just chasing Thistle, and every time he got near her she took a swipe at him with the piece of glass. She cut him one more time, across the arm, and then I got behind him and hit him with the frying pan."

"He felt *that*," Wendy said.

"So he turned around and punched me," Jennie said, her hand going to the welt under her eye. "And Thistle got out the door, and Wendy had the broom and when he turned to run after her, she stuck out the broom handle and it got tangled up in his feet and he fell on his face. And by the time he got up and got out the door, Thistle was gone."

"And he came back in and said he was going to kill us," Wendy said. "But he didn't."

"Well, *duh*," Jennie said.

"I mean, you know, not then." Wendy blinked four or five times fast. "But he said he'd be back."

"Don't worry about that," I said, and something banged on the door. The girls went straight up in the air, screaming, and came down with their arms around each other. The door opened, and Louie said, "You guys ain't glad to see me?"

**Two minutes after** Louie stuck the girls in his big Detroit behemoth and took them to his house, where Alice would fuss over them until it was safe for them to go back home, I was back at the Camelot Arms. I had to check it, even though I was certain that the apartment was the last place Thistle was likely to be. The door was still leaning crazily inward, and things looked pretty much the same, although someone, probably a covetous neighbor, seemed to have nicked a couple of the vintage standing lamps.

I went through the place anyway, looking for anything to tell me whether she'd been here, and where she might have gone. I spent a few minutes wandering around in the bedroom, trying to figure out what was different, before I realized that the most recent journal, the one that had only had ten or twelve written pages, was missing.

So she had dropped by, at least. Almost certainly before she went to Jennie and Wendy's place.

And the question remained: Was Eduardo working *for* Trey, or *against* her?

**The old expression** about waiting for the other shoe to drop is too vague, because it doesn't tell you *which* shoe. Sometimes it's not important which shoe drops first or second, but at other times it's almost the only thing that matters.

I'd abandoned the horrible former police car at one of Louie's garages and was back at the wheel of my anonymous Toyota Camry, meticulously obeying every traffic law in sight, just another sheep in the automotive flock. Since the garage was near Hollywood, I dropped by Wain's, taking a certain amount of pleasure at his surprise that I'd survived whatever he thought I was doing, and got my deposit back. He nicked me for an extra ten bucks, the crook, pointing out a scratch on the gun that I certainly hadn't put there, but I didn't even argue.

I was trying to figure out which shoe to drop next.

Weighing the alternatives in my mind, I swung past my small Hollywood storage area, parked, and went inside. Out of a locked fishing-tackle box I grabbed a nine-millimeter automatic, one with no provenance of prior use in violent crimes. I knew this to be true because once in a while I staked out a gun shop, waited until someone bought a new one, followed the customer home, and waited for an opportunity to steal the gun. It had been worked on by an expert: serial numbers filed off, an acid bath to remove any lingering traces, and the kind of oiling and cleaning that a Marine drill instructor would approve. I kept three of these, two Glocks and a Heckler & Koch, one in each of my storage facilities. They're part of my disaster-prevention kit. They didn't get much use, but I was approaching the kind of territory where the weight felt good under my shoulder.

I also grabbed Bunny's diamonds, which I thought might come in handy.

When I was on the road again, it was three-thirty, and the rain was a reality. From the color of the sky, a rich charcoal gray, it wasn't going anyplace soon.

The thing I most wanted to do was find Thistle, but Los Angeles is a big city with a lot of places to hide. I could spend a month on it and get nowhere. On the other hand, there were two people I needed to see face to face pretty soon, and I knew exactly where both of them were. But which one first? Left shoe, right shoe?

Right shoe. Make the more difficult of the calls now, while there was still time to beat the deadlines for tomorrow's enter-tainment trade papers.

Every burglar in Los Angeles knows where Jake Whelan lives. The house is famous, an eighteenth-century French chateau that had been dismantled, shipped to Los Angeles, and reassembled stone by stone in the middle of fifteen hilly acres in Laurel Canyon, where it hosted some of the most memorably debauched parties in Hollywood's memorably debauched history. This had been back in Whelan's sunny years, when he had the golden touch, when every film he made took in a zillion dollars and won every award in sight, when the studios bred starlets under the warm film lights like baby chicks, and Whelan had his pick. Before the studio system fell to pieces, making guys like Whelan secondary to stars in terms of clout, and driving the price of filmmaking into the stratosphere. Before starlets began to form their own production companies. Before white powder arrived on the scene and Jake Whelan fell to pieces, losing his touch, his sense of story, and his credibility.

But Whelan had hung onto the ancillary rights to his films; and television, video, the global explosion of DVDs, and now high-definition streaming, had kept the money flowing, faster than even Whelan could spend it. Which was saying quite a lot, given his undiminished appetite for white powder and colored pictures, many of which had been bought from people who didn't, strictly speaking, own them.

Rabbits Stennet's Klee, for example.

Whelan's pictures—a small museum's worth—were one reason every burglar in Los Angeles knew where he lived. The other was the white powder. Unlike an underground Klee, which can be paid for via wire transfer, white powder is exclusively a cash commodity. Everyone had heard the stories: two inches of hundred-dollar bills beneath half an acre of wall-to-wall carpet, whole sliding walls with bricks of money where the insulation should be, a wine cellar full of currency. Cold cash, so to speak.

Every burglar in Los Angeles also knew that Jake Whelan supported a tidy posse of muscle on twenty-four hour duty, to discourage anyone from getting touchy-feely about his financial reserves. So the house was much talked about but rarely attempted, the subject of many extravagantly complicated schemes that had been hatched over bottles of whiskey or wine late at night and abandoned in the cold, sober light of day.

And here I was, ringing the buzzer outside the black wrought-iron gates and looking up at the television camera trained directly on me.

The man's voice was gruff and unpolished, as Jake Whelan no doubt intended. "Yeah? Who is it?"

I said, "Tell Mr. Whelan it's Paul Klee."

"Hang on."

I sat there, wondering whether to wave at the camera, for a minute, and then two. Time goes very slowly when nothing is happening, and half an hour or so later, it had been five minutes, and I was wondering whether to turn around and go home or back up, gun the engine, and knock down the gates.

The voice came back. "Drive in slow. Stop about twenty feet from the house, near the bushes. Get out of the car and wait."

"*Slowly*," I said. "*Drive* is a verb, and it should be modified by an adverb. Drive in *slowly*."

"Awww," the voice said, "Fuck you."

"Nothing wrong with that sentence," I said as the gates opened.

The driveway was slate, black and shining in the rain, and it curved its way uphill between ferns big enough to shelter a whole platoon of soldiers wearing camouflage. Every ten or twenty feet I saw another camera, trained right at me. More attention than a burglar generally wants.

The first bits of the house I saw were the turrets, two of them, pointing their dark stone tips at the sullen sky. Then the drive took a final sweeping turn to the right, widening as it did so, and the whole structure came into view. It was enough to make me hit the brakes and just sit there like some yahoo from Yazoo City, staring at it.

The chateau sprawled over half an acre, all rough-carved stone in shades of dark brown and deep gray, muted even further now that they were wet. The lights were on inside, since the day was so gloomy, and the light through the mullioned windows—dozens of them, it seemed—threw the falling rain into relief exactly as it would have done two hundred years ago, when the lights inside would have been torches and oil lamps. Just a combination that's looked good since people moved out of caves: light, water, and stone.

The front door was arched, made of massive beams of wood with wide bands of rusted iron across them, and it opened as I pulled the car over to the bushes, as directed. Three guys came out, two of them bulked up and hard-looking, wearing T-shirts and jeans, the third slender and nicely turned out in a dark suit. He was carrying an umbrella. They fanned out as they came, one of the muscle boys going left and the other right, and the dapper gent with the umbrella making a beeline for me.

When I opened the back door of the car, everyone froze. The umbrella-toter just stood there patiently, but the hard guys watched my hands as I leaned in and picked up the Klee, which I'd covered with an old Dodgers jacket I keep in the trunk. Everybody watched as I took it out, held it up, and turned it from side to side so they could see I wasn't hiding a cannon behind it. Mr. Umbrella smiled and covered the rest of the ground to me, extended the umbrella to share it, and walked me back to the front door. One of the muscle boys preceded us, and the other followed.

"To your right," Mr. Umbrella said, folding the umbrella as we passed through the door. "Please remove your shoes and put them in the rack."

And there it was, a wooden rack from Japan, perfectly plain and ordinary except that it was beyond the attainable perfection of the mortal world and it looked four hundred years old. I put the Klee down gently, the jacket still covering it, and leaned it against the wall. Then I took off my shoes and put them on the rack, feeling like I was committing sacrilege. In the meantime, everyone else had kicked off loafers, and one of the bodybuilders went to the right, down a couple of stone steps.

"This way," Mr. Umbrella said, and we followed the body builder into a room that Henry the Fifth would have felt at home in.

The first myth to bite the dust was the cash tucked beneath the wall-to-walls. The floor was dark stone, buffed to a dull shine by several centuries' worth of feet, and only the central quarter-mile or so was covered by carpet, an enormous all-silk Afghan that was probably older than the house. A couple of couches, two deep-looking chairs, and some dark wood tables had been arranged in front of a fireplace big enough to host the Chicago fire, with room left over for a couple of neighborhood barbecues. In defiance of the warm weather, a fire was roaring in it, nothing much, just a couple of trees' worth of wood.

"Sit anywhere but the yellow chair," Mr. Umbrella said, glancing at one that was covered in butter-colored leather. "That's Mr. Whelan's chair. Would you like some coffee? Something stronger? Something much stronger?"

"No, thanks." I sat at the end of one of the couches. "I'm fine."

"Mr. Whelan will be with you in a few minutes." Mr. Umbrella turned and went back the way we'd come, climbing the two steps to the entrance hall and going on straight across. The muscle guy who'd preceded us into the room leaned up against a wall and gave me the alpha-male stare.

"I've always wondered," I said, "how you get those muscles on the tops of your shoulders and the sides of the neck. You know, the ones that make your head look so small."

"Picking up guys like you and throwing them through windows," he said.

"I guess I'll eliminate that from my workout," I said.

I heard some fast click-clack, and two young ladies appeared in the archway that led, presumably, to wherever Whelan was. On second glance, they weren't so young, although they were fearsomely toned and buffed, if the eighty percent of their bodies that was on display was any indication. They wore tight tops and micro-skirts that were no thicker than their makeup, and the click-clack was the sound of their four-inch heels on the stone floor. They gave me a professional glance, saw directly through me to my wallet, and kept right on going, heading for the front door.

"How come they don't have to take *their* shoes off?" I asked the muscle guy.

"'Cause I like them," Jake Whelan said, coming into the room. He was wearing cream-colored silk from head to foot, the slacks in a subtle herringbone that caught the light. He'd tanned his face to the color of a cigar. "The shoes. I like those shoes." His voice was a rasp, like a striking match. "The girls are okay, too, of course." He held out a hand and gave me a smile. "I'm Jake Whelan."

When Whelan smiled, he showed you both rows of teeth, top and bottom, and with good reason. They were the most expensive teeth I'd ever seen in my life. I knew people who lived in houses that cost less than Jake Whelan's teeth. If there were an aftermarket in teeth, there would be a line of burglars standing patiently in line, all the way around Jake Whelan's head.

I gave him my hand and as little in the way of teeth as I could manage. His own were enough for both of us.

"So, so, so," he said, folding himself into the yellow chair. "Mr. Klee, in the surprising flesh." He'd crossed his leg and one foot bounced up and down in its white calfskin slipper, a telltale cocaine jitter. "You look pretty good for someone who died in 1940."

"I keep active," I said. "You know, travel, play shuffleboard, try to learn something new every day."

"And what brings you to me?"

"Good things come in twos," I said. "I thought you might have something new that would like company."

He cocked his head to one side, the smile still in place. "Who have you been talking to?"

"Actually, nobody, and that's good for you."

"Then you haven't got a name, and I'm afraid that means I have no idea what you're talking about."

"I'm talking about a Paul Klee painting, one of the geometric ones, blue background, one point seven-five million to Wattles's offshore bank."

"Mm-hmm," he said. The foot jumped around some more. "And what's your relationship to that transaction, if it ever took place?"

"If it had," I said, "I'd be the guy who went and got the painting for Wattles to sell to you."

"Do me a favor," he said. "Stand up and spread your arms. I want Wally here to perform a basic security maneuver."

"Fine," I said, getting up. "Wally should know I've got an automatic in a shoulder holster under my jacket."

"He'll relieve you of that, temporarily, although it's not really firearms I'm thinking about." He looked past me. "Wally?"

Wally patted me down, helped me out of my jacket, lifted the automatic, and generally made sure I wasn't wired. "Seems okay," he said.

"Please," Whelan said. "Sit. And forgive the rudeness. I didn't get old by being careless."

I didn't sit. "I'd like you to look at something," I said. "I think it would be best if I stepped back a bit before I show it to you. I'm telling you this so old Wally doesn't think I'm embarking on some obscure martial arts move."

"Fine, fine. Back away."

I picked up the picture, backed up five or six feet, and unveiled it by removing my Dodgers jacket from the frame.

Whelan was good. His expression didn't change at all. The only telltale was the pulse that was suddenly visible at the side of his neck.

After a minute or so, he said, "Quite nice."

"Actually," I said, "it's better than the one you just bought."

"If I bought it," Whelan said.

"Sure, if."

"And you're showing this to me because, I assume, you think I'd be interested in acquiring it."

"I know you would," I said. "Especially at the price I'm asking."

"And what would that be?"

"A little less than a third of what you paid Wattles."

"Three, four hundred?" Whelan said.

"Nice try."

"Okay, five or six?" Whelan said.

"Right in there."

"Bring it here."

I carried it to him, and he took it as reverently as if it had the head of John the Baptist on it. He turned it this way and that, looking at the play of light on the painted surface. He held it level in front of him, parallel to the floor, and examined the brush strokes. He turned it over and checked the back of the canvas. Then he lowered it, very carefully, to his lap and looked at me.

"Why?" he said.

"Why so cheap? Well, for one thing, there's no middle man. This is more money than I made off the last one."

"You said for one thing. What's the other thing?"

"It's going to require a little effort on your part."

"What kind of effort?"

"A couple of minutes' thought and two phone calls."

"Thought I can handle. Tell me about the phone calls."

I turned to Wally. "I changed my mind. I would like a cup of coffee."

Wally's eyes went to Whelan, and Whelan gave him a tiny nod. Wally left.

"Let's start with the thought," I said. "I need you to come up with the name of a director or producer who owes you a favor and has a film working right now, a film with a good small part for a woman in her early twenties. I'm not talking about a lead, just a few days' worth of work, some dialog, and a few minutes onscreen."

Whelan shook his head. "I can tell you right now, whoever it is, she'll take the part and forget about you. You'll never see her again. She'll be schtupping the cameraman. I can't tell you how many chicks I've given parts to—"

"I don't care," I said. "There's no romantic relationship."

"Really. In Hollywood? That's almost as big a surprise as the painting. What type is she?"

"Think Thistle Downing," I said.

"Oh-*ho*," he said. "I read about that myself, just this morning. Sort of sad, I guess, I mean, that was a cute little girl once. I gotta tell you, I give the lady who's making the movie more credit for balls than sense. She'll never get that kid on camera."

"You're right," I said. "Thistle isn't going to do that movie. She's going to do the one you get for her."

He shook his head. "Nobody will work with her."

"They will if you ask them to. And if you guarantee to cover the expenses if she screws up."

"Are you crazy? That could be a couple hundred K."

"That's pretty much what I figured," I said. "And I'm donating it, so to speak, out of the cost of the painting. So you offer whoever it is that sum of money in advance, in case Thistle screws up. If she does, they're covered. If she doesn't, they've just picked up a nice chunk of change."

Whelan was looking at me as though he expected me to sprout fins and gills. "So that's two hundred," he said. "And it doesn't even go to you." He shook his head. "What's the rest of it?"

"A hundred is Thistle's salary," I said. "So the producer is getting her both risk-free and *literally* free. A hundred and fifty is to buy her contract."

"To buy . . ."

"Her contract."

He shrugged. "Sure. Her contract. So, four-fifty in all."

"And a hundred for me."

"Just a hundred. Out of all that."

"That's right."

"So it's all about you, wrapped in pure motives, walking on water."

"If you like."

"You gotta be crazy. I don't do business with crazy people." He said it with a straight face, too.

I got up just as Wally came in carrying a ridiculously fragile-looking cup and saucer. "Sorry, Wally," I said. "I'm going."

"Siddown," Whelan said. "Wally, give the gentleman his coffee."

**For ten minutes,** I watched Whelan work the phone, and it was like watching Derek Jeter play shortstop. In less than a minute he burned through three assistants to reach someone named David, and in under a minute he'd ascertained that the part of the receptionist—"You know, the one whose nails are so long she can't do anything?"—was as yet uncast, and had made a pitch for Thistle that was nothing short of brilliant: the publicity value, the good-deed aspect of it, how everybody in town would be pulling for her, how it was practically a guaranteed supporting actress nomination if she was any good because everybody votes for a reformed fuckup—and get this, I'll cover the expenses and even pay her salary. Why? Because I read that thing in the trades this morning and it broke my heart, that poor little kid. You're a young guy, David, don't tell me you didn't watch her every week, well, don't you think she oughta get another chance? Yeah, me, too. No, I don't want any credit, I'm just behind the scenes, you're the one the Pope will sprinkle the water on. Nah, nah, she's as straight as a string. I'm telling you, all that's behind her, and I'll tell you what, if you don't think two weeks from now that I've done you a huge favor, you can come over here and kick me in the ass. Yeah, and I'll wear my best pants, the silk crepe you keep asking where I got them. Okay, David, you're a sweetheart, which days? And send the script to me and I'll get it to her, you're doing a great thing, bye for now.

"Okay?" he asked me.

"It's a pleasure to watch you work."

"You said two calls. Who's next?" He seemed to be enjoying himself.

"This one needs a little preparation," I said.

We talked for three or four minutes, and he said, "Piece of cake. You got a number?" I gave it to him, and he dialed.

"Ms. Annunziato, please. This is Jake Whelan. Yes, that Jake Whelan." He looked at me. "Nobody answers the phone himself any more. Call your fucking plumber, you get an assistant." He sat up as though someone had entered the room. "Ms. Annunziato," he said. "Jake Whelan here. Yes, fine, and you? Glad to hear it. Listen, here's why I'm calling. I read the trades this morning like everyone else in town, and I gotta tell you, it didn't make anybody happy, I had calls all day from people you wouldn't believe, the whole fucking A-list, it was like RSVPs for the *Vanity Fair* party, and they all sound exactly alike, what they're saying. Yeah, yeah, I know you got a business, but a lot of people, they read that story and thought the same thing I did, which is, *this isn't right*. So I'm telling you that a few of us got together and we're not going to let Thistle make your movie."

He held the phone away from his ear and made a yacking motion with his free hand. He looked over his shoulder at Wally and made a vague gesture that was perfectly clear to Wally, who went to a heavy wooden chest to the left of the fireplace, pulled out a couple of logs big enough to ride over Niagara Falls on, and tossed them onto the blaze. Throughout all of it, I could hear Trey on the other end, going a mile a minute. After he was satisfied that the logs were going to catch, Whelan put the phone back to his ear and just started talking, without even waiting for her to pause. "Yeah, I hear what you're saying and I know you got a point of view there, but here's what's going to happen. She's going to make another movie, a real movie, not like a star or anything, but it's gonna be something we can all feel good about, and we've decided to buy her contract from you. How does a hundred thousand sound?"

I started to object, but he held up a hand. "What do you mean, it's low? Okay, okay. I can sweeten it to one-fifty, but that's it. And I mean, she's not going to make your movie no matter what, so you might as well take the money and be a good sport. And also, we're gonna let you look like an angel here, instead of being on the wrong side in a media pissing match. I mean, just how good does this sound? You announce that you're delighted to learn that the news about Thistle's participation in your movie has brought her new offers, and as much as you looked forward to working with her, it's a privilege to know you've played a part in helping her get a more suitable role, and you're releasing her and you wish her all the best and blah blah blah. And we all just keep quiet about the money you're getting. See, this way you're like Lady Bountiful instead of being the bitch who's trying to force America's sweetheart into doing the dirty on film."

He winked at me and rubbed his nostrils. "That's what I thought. Sure, sure you can release it, we don't want any credit, in fact, try to get it out tonight, it'll hit bigger, and the trades are still open. You can use my PR guy if you don't have one, you got a pencil? Here's his number." Whelan rattled off a number. "His name is Skip. Yeah, I know, but that's what he calls himself." He rubbed his nose again and his eyes flicked longingly in the direction of the door he'd come in through. "We set, then? All clear on your end? Great, great. Love to meet you some time. I've thought for years that your family was one of the great American success stories, great movie idea there. Bye."

He hung up, swiped his nose with the finger again, and said, "Be right back. You want your hundred Gs in cash, right?"

"Right." And I defy you to come up with a better answer.

Whelan started toward Powder Central, then bent down and picked up the Klee. "Just in case you change your mind," he said. He gave it one more look on his way out of the room, and over his shoulder he said, "It really *is* better than the other one."

## 43
### I Can Hurt

The thing about Laurel Canyon is that it isn't really anywhere, but it's sort of *close* to everywhere. It's not the Valley, it's not Beverly Hills, it's not Hollywood or even West Hollywood, but they're all just around the corner, at least in terms of LA distances. It's a nice fifteen-minute purr in the Rolls or the Bentley, or an eleven-minute hop in the Porsche, to anywhere the canyon dwellers might be most likely to go.

And it was just a few minutes, even during rush hour, to where I was headed.

My watch made it 6:20. The world was mainly headlights and rain, plus the drama of the occasional fallen branch, supernaturally wet and leafy, in the middle of the road. Long red spectra of brakelights traveled the night, as the car ten or twelve ahead of me slowed and glowed red and passed it on to the one behind, and so on until my own foot hit the brake and left me motionless on a shining street, the car standing still while my mind moved a million miles an hour, mostly in unpleasant directions.

But I learned a long time ago not to linger on the things that might kill me. If you're not capable of figuring out how to get past all that and move toward solutions, it would probably be better not to break the law for a living, which, despite the appeal of short hours and long pay, more or less guarantees that you're going to be in constant contact with dangerous people. And once in a while, in the natural order of things, one or more of these people will want to do you harm.

But this was ridiculous. I'd been a career criminal for seventeen years, and I'd never had so many people willing to stand in line to make me dead. And what had I done? One little burglary, and a contract job at that. I'd stolen something from someone who could afford to lose it, who in the larger scheme of things was entirely unharmed; I hadn't taken the presents from under some poor kids' Christmas tree or mugged some domestic worker and grabbed her week's pay. I'd ripped off a couple of pictures from a rich man—a *gangster*, for Christ's sake—and it felt like the whole world was pointing guns at me.

It was enough to get me mad. I don't get mad often, but I get mad *thoroughly*. I was already absolutely greased about Jimmy's murder, and now I was getting mad on my own behalf, too.

I finally made it through the light at Mulholland but instead of dropping down the other side of the hill into the Valley I turned left and followed the Drive north along the spine of the hills, the clouds to my right pale and spectral with the light from the Valley floor. Up here, the rain was a little thinner than it had been at Whelan's chateau, or so it seemed. I wasn't really paying attention to it. I was sorting things in my mind: first this, then that, what if this, what if that? No matter what order I stacked things, there were still a couple of wild cards. I was barely conscious of having swung left onto Coldwater as I started back down toward the Los Angeles basin.

A few minutes later I made the right I'd been looking for and stopped the car about halfway up the hill. I didn't want headlights or noise to announce me. Feeling like I was on a fool's errand, and that I didn't know anyone better qualified to run one, I hiked on up the hill, sticking to the asphalt to keep my feet from getting any wetter than necessary until I realized I was already soaked to the bone. Where was Jake Whelan's Mr. Umbrella when I needed him?

I cut to the right, heading around the big gate, the rain coming down heavily enough that I didn't have to worry about the sound of my feet in the grass. The sky went white above me, and the landscape brightened for an instant, flat as paper and highly detailed, and a moment later heaven growled and then the growl died off to a bottom-heavy grumble.

The flash of light had reoriented me. I knew exactly where I was, and I knew that I needed to take the path to the right, following the slope of the hill. Despite the reduced visibility in the rain, despite the tall bushes everywhere, I found myself moving bent at the waist, trying to reduce my silhouette, trying to remain invisible as long as possible.

The pathway curved again and widened, and I could feel, rather than see, the bulk of the big gray stone, and just as I knew for certain it was ahead of me, the world lit up again, and I saw Thistle's dad's rosebush and, in front of it, the crumpled form, the out-thrown arms, the sopping clothes, the tangle of soaked hair, the long smears of black, no, *red,* running down the soaked blouse, and as clearly as if she had been standing behind me I heard my daughter's voice, heard her say: *dead wet girl.*

**"You're home,"** I said into the phone. At the sound of his voice it felt as if something had been lifted off my heart. We were tearing down the hill at an unwise speed.

"I am," Doc said.

"Don't go anywhere. I'm coming as fast as I can."

"Ummm," Doc said. "This isn't a good—"

"*No.* Whatever you have to do, no. I've got Thistle, and she needs attention—some stitches, maybe some blood, and God knows what else. Just stay where you are." I closed the phone and followed the curve of the canyon to the right, and Thistle toppled across the seat toward me, dead weight, and landed against my shoulder. She said, "Uuhhhhh."

"Hang on," I said. "You're okay now. You've lost some

blood, you're exhausted. We're going to see Doc, and he'll get you back together."

"No," she said. It was barely a whisper.

"No? No what?"

"No. No shots. Don't want . . ."

I said, "Fine." She put a hand down on the seat to push herself upright, and I said, "Careful, you cut that hand to ribbons. You'll be lucky if you didn't slice a tendon."

"Cut him," she said. Out of the corner of my eye I saw her bare her teeth. "I cut him."

"I know. I saw the blood."

"Jennie," she said, her spine straightening slightly. "Wendy."

"They're okay. A friend of mine has taken them somewhere else."

"I want . . . I want to see." She stopped talking and let out a rush of air. Her head was hanging down, and the ropes of wet hair caught the headlights of an oncoming car. A drop of water detached itself from one of them and began its fall, and then the light was gone.

"Don't worry," I said. "Listen, you can talk to them. I gave them phones. Do you want to talk to them?"

"Yes. Please." She turned her head, and she was smiling. "They were . . . brave," she said.

"I know, I was there. Hang on, let me get them. I punched in the speed-dial and said, "Take it with your right hand, the one that isn't cut."

"'Kay," she said, stretching out the hand, and at the sight of the slender fingers, the intricate and harmless frailty of her hand as I put the phone into it, the anger I'd been feeling about the situation I was in, about all of it, exploded in my chest. It was a thick red smoke, so real I could feel it in the back of my throat and so harsh I could taste it. I had to force myself to focus on steering the car. People were going to pay, if not for what they wanted to do to me, then for what they'd already done to Thistle and Jimmy.

"Wendy," Thistle said in a voice like ripping silk. "You, you . . . guys, you're okay."

I could hear Wendy's voice, high and excited, on the other end of the line, and after a moment, Thistle gave a ragged little laugh. "Yeah," she said. "I'm fine. Wet. Junior says . . . says you went somewhere."

Wendy talked and Thistle listened as I made the left onto Ventura, heading for Encino, for Doc's house. "Quarter-pounder?" Thistle said, telling me where Louie had taken the girls for dinner. "Oh, you luckies," she said. "I want—no, I don't want—I don't . . . I don't want anything. I'm glad you're okay." She closed the phone without saying goodbye. "I hurt," she said.

"Almost there," I said. "Doc'll give you—"

She said, "Where I was."

"Where—what? What do you mean, where you were? Rose Haven? Your father's—"

"The *movie*," she said. "I was . . . I was going to do . . ."

"You didn't," I said. "You won't have to."

"It's okay to hurt," she said. "I can learn to hurt."

I said the only thing I could think of. "You're stronger than you think."

"I'm a fuckup. But I can hurt."

"Let's take care of the cuts," I said. "Then I think you could use about two days' sleep. Hang on, honey, we're here."

I pulled the car to the curb. Doc's house was a low cinder-block one-story, what they used to call a rambler, probably built in the early fifties, with a picture window looking out on a small front yard. Someone had drastically over-pruned the orange tree to the right of the sidewalk, cutting the branches back almost to the trunk. The stripped tree made the yard seem barren. The street was wide enough for tanks to pass each other, and a street-light shone right down on us: a nice, safe neighborhood. I went around, opened Thistle's door, and leaned across to undo the seatbelt, since it fastened on the left side, beneath the ravaged hand. Then I helped her out and she leaned against me as we went up the sidewalk to the door.

"I'm okay," she said, but she was putting most of her weight on me.

"You'll be better in a few minutes," I said as the door opened and Doc stood there, and licked his lips, and just as I registered that something was wrong with his eyes, he was shoved aside, hard enough to knock him off his feet, and a long arm snaked out and circled Thistle's neck, and I found myself looking into the barrel of a gun with Eduardo standing behind it.

## 44

Focker

He hauled her in by the neck, straight through the door as though she weighed nothing, and her feet caught on Doc's legs, and she went down in a heap. Eduardo didn't even glance down at her, just took a step back, kicking her once in the hip, and said to me, "Get in here."

I thought about it for a second and said, "No."

"Then I shoot her," he said. There were bandages all over his gun hand.

I said, "Great. Point the gun down. I fucking dare you."

He blinked. "You don't think I can put one in her and still get you?"

"I don't think you could hit yourself in the balls if you had all day to aim."

"You fucker," he said. He pronounced it "focker."

"Okay," I said. "You win. You said the bad word first. How you doing, Doc?"

"I'm okay." A nice-looking woman who matched the description Louie had given me stood wringing her hands behind him. "My wife is okay. I've had better conversations."

"Fine," Eduardo said, having used the interval to work things through. "Then I shoot you first."

"Why didn't you say that at the beginning?" I said. "*What* is it you want me to do?"

"Get in here."

"Sure. Okay. Kind of a jam-up, though. Maybe one or two people should get up. You wouldn't want me to trip or anything. I might sue."

He backed away, leaving the left side of the door clear. "Through here. Just get your ass through here."

"On the way," I said. I paused partway in. "Do you want me to close the door?"

"Uhh, yeah," he said.

"Good thinking," I said. I came the rest of the way in, avoided stepping on either Thistle or Doc, both of whom were looking up at me, and pulled the door closed. "Now what?" I said.

"Now stand there and shut up." He took another couple of steps back and wiggled the gun back and forth in the bandaged hand a little to make the point that he could aim it at any of us who earned it, and then he pulled out a cell phone. With both eyes on me, he pushed a button and waited.

"Speed dial," I said. "What did guys with guns do before speed dial?"

"Fucking shut up." He practically jumped to attention. "No, Tony, no, not you. Listen, I got her. I got her right here."

Tony said something, and Eduardo said, "Encino. Like near Hayvenhurst. Umm, Doc and Doc's wife and the guy she hired, the crook. Yeah, both of them."

I said, "The *crook?*"

"He's talking too much," Eduardo said, apparently in response to a question from Tony. "Yeah, no problem, I can bring her. The house or the office? Yeah, yeah, okay." He closed the phone, tried to slip it into his pocket, and missed the pocket. He looked down for a second try, and I got the automatic out and shot him in the right shoulder.

The impact spun him around, the gun in his hand spraying bullets into Doc's paneled walls as he reflexively pulled the trigger, and I covered the distance between him and me in a single leap and slammed my own gun against the side of his skull, hard enough to leave an imprint in the bone. His legs went loose, the muscles slack and purposeless. He took two aimless steps away from me, reminding me of the dog that had climbed the stairs with the dart in him, and just as I was about to hit him again, he collapsed, taking a table and a small mirror down with him.

"Get something that will put him out and keep him out," I said to Doc. "Don't be stingy with it, either. He's got the body mass of a whale." I took his gun and patted the parts of his body that were accessible and then rolled him over with my foot and checked the rest of the likely places. Doc had gotten up and was helping Thistle to her feet while Mrs. Doc fussed around with shaking hands, brushing at her husband's jacket. "She needs some stitches in her hand," I said. "And my guess is that she's dehydrated and maybe a little bit in shock. And she's lost a bunch of blood."

"I'll see to it," Doc said.

"Great. But with all due respect, can you please get the shit you're going to shoot into this behemoth?"

"On it," Doc said, hurrying into the next room.

"Doesn't look so big now, does he?" I asked Thistle.

"Shoot him," she said. Mrs. Doc gasped.

"Honey, I already shot him. If I kill him, there'll be all sorts of boring stuff to go through with cops and other folks I prefer not to hang with. We're going to give him to people who won't be nearly as nice to him as I am."

Eduardo groaned. His eyes opened, and crossed to focus on the barrel of the gun that was about two inches from the bridge of his nose. "Just one question," I said. "House or office?"

"Office," he said. "Don't shoot me."

"You're really, absolutely, positively, without any question whatsoever *certain* that it's the office? Because if it isn't, I'm going to come back here and shoot you seven or eight times, starting at the ankles and working my way up. I'm told that bullets through the knees and the hips cause extremely interesting reactions."

"House," he said.

"Good for you," I said. "How difficult was that?"

Doc came in with a hypodermic and an ampule. Eduardo watched as he inserted the needle into the ampule and pulled back the plunger.

"This isn't going to hurt a bit," I said. "Don't you hate it when they say that? It *always* hurts."

Doc said to Eduardo, "Bye-bye." He stuck the needle right through the sleeve of Eduardo's jacket and pushed the plunger.

Eduardo winced, the big baby, when the needle went in. He looked at Doc. Then he looked at me. He put his uninjured arm underneath him as though he wanted to get up. His mouth was hanging open. He raised himself five or six inches and then it was as though the arm had dissolved, and he hit the floor face first.

"He's bleeding on my rug," Doc said.

"Was your life better before I arrived, or after?" I asked. Thistle laughed.

"There's a sweet sound," Doc said. "Come on, Junior, grab this asshole and help me get him onto the hardwood. I don't want him to die on anything expensive."

We dragged him off the carpet. "What am I supposed to do with him?" Doc asked.

"What you can, without going overboard. Fix him to the point where he won't bleed to death, get Thistle feeling better, and then call Trey. Tell her that Eduardo showed up here and pushed his way in with a gun to wait for Thistle because he figured she'd come here for drugs, and that he's been working with Tony. Tell her when he had Thistle here, he called Tony and said he was going to bring her over, but while he was on the phone, you got your hands on a gun and shot him. Tell her to get someone over here and take him off your hands."

"What about Thistle?" Doc asked.

"Hide her. Tell Trey she ran away when you shot Eduardo. Whatever you do, don't tell Trey I was here."

"Where are you going?" Thistle asked.

"I'm going to put an end to this."

## 45
### Something in Common

The house couldn't have been more perfect.

It sat well back from the street in the middle of one of the valley's tattered scraps of orange grove. High hedges hid much of the yard and all of the house from the street, and the gate had a lock I could have picked with my teeth. I barely had to pause to open it, which was okay with me because the rain was pelting down with serious intent. The nearest neighbor was fifty, sixty yards away and, thanks to the hedges that followed the property line, completely out of sight.

I thought he might have installed cameras or lights activated by motion detectors, or something, but as I stood behind one of the orange trees farthest from the house and surveyed the property one square yard at a time, I didn't see anything. Either he thought everybody loved him or else he believed he was so bad nobody would dare to mess with him.

Wrong on both counts.

I was pushing myself away from the tree, having decided the next stop in my cautious progress would be a big hibiscus with a wire frame around it, when somebody screamed.

It was a high scream, definitely female, and it came from the house. I'd like to say that the scream kicked me into heroic rescue mode, and that's why I started running across open ground toward the door, but in fact, all it did was make it seem a lot more likely that everybody inside was too distracted to be watching the yard. I was only ten or twenty feet from the door when I heard another scream, and this time it was clear that the screamer was not screaming from pain. She was furious.

"You PROMISED," I heard, and then something that sounded like someone turning a china cabinet inside out. The noise was considerable, so I just turned the knob on the front door at normal speed rather than inching it around, and it turned cooperatively in my hand. I pushed the door open, slipped in, and quietly closed it behind me. Then I stood there, getting my bearings.

A hall with a dark red saltillo tile floor stretched a good thirty feet in front of me, and a flight of stairs went up on the right. Halfway down the hall was a big Spanish archway that probably opened into the living room. Hanging here and there on the walls, which were rough-mortared in the deathlessly popular mission style, were heavy black Spanish-looking shields and swords and other implements of preindustrial mayhem, probably intended to suggest some sort of conquistador lineage. They were all really, really dusty. Tough guys don't dust.

Another scream, and then something broke, something that sounded like pottery or crockery rather than glass. Then I heard a man's voice, low and sharp: "You remember where you parked? Well, get your ass out there and drive away."

"You son of a *bitch*. You promised, you told me that you, that you—"

"I got Thistle coming here. Trey's fucked, it's over, stupid. I don't need you no more, so get going, go get a job or something. You want a couple hundred bucks? That's about what it's worth, what you done."

The woman began to shout over him, words I couldn't make out, and then there was the unmistakable sound of a slap, a real carpet-beater to judge from the volume.

As near as I could figure, I was only hearing two voices. No one else had said anything, or laughed, or applauded. The woman's voice reasserted itself, and she'd changed approaches, going from murderous to injured in less time than it would have taken me to say it out loud. She said, "Tony, sweetie, we talked about all of this, remember we said that once . . ."

I removed the automatic from my jacket, racked it, and stepped into the archway.

The living room was about forty feet long, with the same Spanish-influenced tile floors and an open-beam ceiling, nice enough if you're nostalgic for the Inquisition. The furniture was Testosterone Modern, all black leather and dark heavy wood, and quite a bit of it was lying on its side, so this squabble had been going on for a while. A shelf that had contained bowls and other ceramic treasures lay flat on the tile floor, surrounded by brightly colored fragments. There was a big glass coffee table in the center of the room, in front of a couch that had been shoved back at about a thirty-degree angle.

They were so involved with each other that they didn't even notice me. She was working up to tears, going from sad reason to recrimination at a virtuoso pace, and he was standing there with his fists balled up, obviously weighing the wisdom of simply punching her out.

I said, "Hi."

Both heads snapped around and she shut up, which was a real relief. From our previous interactions, I never would have thought Ellie Wynn had such an impressive harpy vocal range. She looked confused for a second, but then she pushed her face into a smile. "Junior," she said, as though my absence had been the only missing element in an otherwise perfect evening.

He wasn't working as hard as she was. He looked at me with that absurdly handsome face and said, "What the fuck?"

"This is Junior," Ellie said, keeping the smile in place and sounding like she was introducing the new third-grader to the rest of the class. "Trey hired him to—"

"I know who he is," Tony said. "What I want to know is what the fuck he's doing in my house."

I lifted the gun an inch or two, keeping it trained on him. "I'd think this would be some sort of clue."

"Oh, well, excuse me," he said. "Pardon me if I don't just drop to my knees here and plead for my life. And you're dripping on my floor."

"I wouldn't have believed it if I hadn't seen it," I said, "but it's true. It's possible to be so good-looking that it gets silly."

"It's nothing you're going to have to worry about," he said.

"That's okay. You're not going to have to worry about it much longer, either."

He shook his head, and his hair moved perfectly. The guy or girl who cut him was worth every penny. "I don't get it," he said. "I don't know you from nobody except you're working for my fucking wife, and you bust in here with a gun in your hand."

"And drip on your floor," I said. "Don't forger that I'm dripping on your floor."

"Yeah, so what's the beef? Tell you what, why don't I get rid of Stupid here, and we can talk man to man?"

"*Stupid*?" Ellie Wynn asked, her voice soaring back up into the migraine zone.

"Actually," I said, "what we need to talk about *involves* Stupid, so I think she ought to stick around."

"I don't believe this," Ellie said. "Junior, what have I ever done to you?"

"It's not what you did to me, sweetie."

"Then—what?" She shook her head and tried out a little laugh. "Oh, I know, you're mad about that trick with Thistle's dress. It was just a way, I mean, I was just, um, trying to give her some time to get away, you know?"

"That's pretty good," I said. "But it's sort of beside the point. I want you to think back, both of you, to a couple of nights ago."

I was still standing in the archway, a puddle forming beneath me. They were fifteen, eighteen feet away, and there were only two directions they could go in: toward me, or through the archway to my right, which led to a formal dining room.

"While you're thinking about it," I said, "both of you move to your right five or six feet. Toward the front windows."

"Fuck that," Tony said, and I blew a hole in the chair he was standing beside, which jerked backward and sent up a nice explosion of dust and stuffing. Ellie screamed, but Tony looked at the chair, and then his eyes came back to me, and his mouth was open. "Ellie," he said. "Do what he said." And the two of them edged away from the dining room.

"Outside Thistle's apartment," I said. "Around midnight. There was a Porsche parked there. With a guy in it."

"That was her," Tony said, and it was Ellie's turn to go open-mouthed. She stared at him as though he hadn't been there a second ago and said, "But, but, but—"

"Shut up," I said. "I don't really care."

But Tony kept talking. "She was just supposed to talk to him, get him to look at her so's I could go into the building, I didn't tell her to, I mean, I had no idea she'd—"

"Where did she get the gun? Do you usually carry a gun, Ellie?"

"No," she said. "I don't own one."

"So the one that Jimmy got shot with—that was his name, by the way, Jimmy. He liked James Dean, the old movie star, so he called himself Jimmy. It made him feel more American. He was proud of being American. Anyway, the gun that Jimmy got shot with. Where'd you get it?"

"It was—" she hesitated, realizing she was making an admission. "It was his."

"That's a fucking lie," Tony said. "I don't know where she got it. I didn't even know she had it. I told her to go talk to him, and next thing I know, she pops him."

"You—you *liar*," Ellie said. "You told me to—you told me you loved me, you told me that once this was over with, you and I could, we could—"

"Listen to her," Tony said. "Look at her. Do you believe any of this? I mean, is this a chick I'm going to be with? I wouldn't pick her up off the sidewalk. Looks like nothing. She's like crazy. She pops him out of nowhere, and she's all proud of herself, like I'm gonna pin some fucking medal on her, and I'm just, I'm like *why did you do that*, and—"

"This is way too embarrassing. What happened, Ellie?"

"He saw us come out of the building," she said. "And there was something about the way he looked at Tony, Tony knew it was trouble. So he handed me the gun and said I should get up close, like I needed to talk to him, and then shoot him. I didn't want to, but Tony said maybe Thistle would die from the pills we left, and the guy would tell on us, and it would be like murder, and we couldn't get married if we got caught, so I went to talk to him; even though I didn't think I could do it, I went to talk to him, and he brought his hand up and he had a gun in it, and I—I shot him." She blinked rapidly and put a hand to the side of her neck as though checking for a fever.

"I had zero idea she was going to shoot him," Tony said. "Zeee-ro."

"There was no gun in his hand," I said. "It was inside his jacket."

"Tony put it there," Ellie said. "And he fastened the guy's jacket. Said it would make things more confusing, they might figure he got shot by somebody he knew."

"It worked," I said.

Tony put out both hands, palms up. "Hey, hey. You're not buying any of this. Does that make sense to you? I mean, come on. Listen, listen, give me a minute. I know something about you, you've got a great reputation. People say you're together and everything, that you could do anything you want, but you haven't had the breaks. All you need is a couple breaks, and you could be rolling in it. Look at you, you're not just some guy, even Trey knew that. You know what I'm talking about here, right?"

I just watched him, watched him try to find the gear that would get him up this particular hill, watched him do the mind reader's trick, studying my eyes every time he laid out a new line, looking for the reaction that would tell him he'd had a strike. Watched the face, perfect in every way except there was no life behind it.

"Look," he said, and now he had one hand on his hip, the other stretched reasonably toward me. "Trey, you know, Trey's picky, but she likes you. I can tell just looking at you, women like you. You're a man, I'm a man. Look at this one. Listen to her. *Me,* marry *her*? I wouldn't touch her, you wouldn't touch her. That's loser's meat, and we're not losers. Come on, we've got more in common than you might—"

He actually *said* that. He said that he and I had something in common.

So I shot him through the center of the chest.

He went over backward, arms and legs spread, and landed on top of the heavy glass coffee table, which broke in half under his weight with a sound that I could hear even over the ringing of the shot. He went straight through and ended up on his back at the center of a V of thick glass, the far ends propped up in the air by the table frame.

Ellie screamed and stood there, looking down at him with her hands over her mouth.

"Is anyone else here?" I asked.

"Oh, oh, oh," she said. "I can't—please, please don't—"

"I asked you if there was anyone else here."

"No," she said.

"You know what happened, right?"

"I—no, I mean—what? What happened?"

"That piece of dirt on the floor told you to kill a man. A good man, who had come thousands of miles from China because he fell in love with the movies, a man with a wife who adored him. Twenty-two years old, a kid, really. For the thing on the floor there, you shot that man. And the whole time you were doing what he wanted you to, this pile of shit on the floor held you in contempt. He despised you. He thought you were ridiculous. Unattractive. The whole time, while he was telling you he loved you, while you were helping him to wreck the movie, he was sneering at you. When you killed that man for him, he was sneering at you. You loved him. You loved him enough to kill someone for him. He thought you were loser's meat. It made him sick to look at you."

Ellie still had her hands over her mouth. I holstered the gun.

"Live with it," I said.

## 46
### Knowing What People Will Love

That night, the night after I shot Eduardo and killed Antonio Ramirez, I had my first solid night's sleep of the week. No anxieties, no dreams, no pacing, no CNN. Just eight hours of sawing logs.

Part of it was because Doc had told me on the phone that Thistle was fine, and maybe better than fine. After administering some advanced first aid, Doc had called up a couple of hard-line twelve-steppers, and they and Thistle were sitting *shiva* for her habit. When she told me she could hurt, she'd meant what I'd hoped she meant.

The new day was bright. The rain had lifted overnight, and the mountains were so clearly visible they might have been painted directly onto the sky. The roads were wet and clean, and I was still lifting off from my first cup of coffee when I pulled into the largely empty parking garage. I grabbed the things I'd need and headed for the elevator.

I was sitting on the excruciatingly uncomfortable couch at 9:04 when the door to the office opened and Wattles came in, followed by Hacker. Wattles barely broke stride, but Hacker froze, letting loose something that sounded like a hiss.

"You ask Janice out yet?" Wattles asked. He lowered himself into his chair, got his belly settled against his desk, and lifted the screen on his laptop.

"I don't know whether that's in the cards," I said.

"I doubt it," Hacker said. "You fucked up. Trey's calling off the project. You're gonna meet Rabbits real soon."

"I had nothing to do with that," I said. "Don't you read the trades? Thistle's doing a real movie."

"Your job was to get *Trey's* movie made," Hacker said. "You gonna tell me you succeeded?"

"Big people got interested," I said. "And people say Hollywood has no heart."

"What am I supposed to do?" Wattles asked me. "Lyle here, he's got a point."

"I don't know," I said. "I've been giving it a lot of thought. Maybe you should start by looking at this." I leaned across and slid the eight-by-ten prints I'd made, three of them, showing Dora at her resplendent best.

After an interested moment, Wattles said, "What's in her mouth?"

"Tell you in a second. First, do you recognize the room?"

"I'm not big on remembering furniture," he said. "I barely remember my own."

"It's the living room at Rabbits Stennet's house," I said, and Wattles leaned back in his chair, looking at me. He reached inside the pocket of his jacket, without taking his eyes off me, and came out with a cigar.

"So?" Hacker said.

Wattles said, "Shut up, Lyle." He stripped the cellophane from the cigar. "The thing in her mouth," he said. "I bet I'm going to love it."

"I've found that one of the hardest things in life," I said, "is knowing what people will love. I can't tell you how often I've bought what I thought was the perfect present for someone, and then she didn't like it. You know what I mean?"

Wattles took his eyes off me long enough to give the cigar a glance. Then he sat back in the chair, slapped the side of his belly with his free hand, and emitted his one-syllable laugh. "Bet it's a peach, isn't it?"

"You decide," I said. I pushed a copy of the letter over to him.

"Hi," Wattles read aloud. "My name is Dora. I'm manufactured by Wattles, Inc., 14586 Ventura Boulevard, suite 512. Mr. Wattles has sold me to 24,393 men, and most of them sleep with me every night." He gave me the amputated little laugh again. "I live to please them in every way. I'm sure that the woman who inspired me and her lucky husband will both be proud to know how many men love me, and how often." He looked at me over the top of the page. "Do I need to read the rest?"

"Depends on your reaction so far."

"I'm persuaded."

"Good. So you'll fix the video surveillance disk and send somebody in to get old Dora before they get back this evening."

"Absolutely."

"And in case you change your mind after you get Dora out of there, I have copies of everything, and anything happens to me, they go to Rabbits."

"I wouldn't expect anything less," he said.

"Why did you do it?" I asked. "You knew what would happen if Rabbits ever found out."

"She's the hottest thing I ever saw, that Bunny," Wattles said. "Why's Rabbits ever gonna see Dora? He doesn't even do takeout any more. And I wanted a big seller. You know how much money this thing has made me?"

I said, "Yes."

"Oh, yeah," he said. "Sure you do." He laughed again. "You probably know the names of the Chinese guys who put her together."

"You're going to let him get away with this?" Hacker demanded.

"You got an alternative?" Wattles asked. "Anyway, I kind of admire the guy's style. We'll take care of it," he said to me.

"The dogs are in the house," I said. "Whoever goes in will have to deal with them."

"I got a guy, works for county animal control some of the time. He'll handle it."

"In the interests of full disclosure, I need to tell you something."

"Yeah?" Wattles said. "You win the Nobel Prize or something?"

"I stole the other Klee," I said.

Wattles turned his head to one side as though to bring into play the ear that heard better. "You stole—"

"The other Klee," I said. "The good one."

"Oh, shit," Wattles said, and this time the laugh lasted. He laughed maybe ten seconds and then wiped his eyes. "And you sold it to, uh"—he glanced in Hacker's direction—"the guy up the hill?"

"Yeah."

"Oh," he said, laughing again. "Oh, boy, I'm glad I lasted this long. Anyone says there's nothing good about getting old doesn't know shit. The *good* one, huh?" He laughed again. "You sold him the good one?"

"He seems happy with it." I waited until he'd calmed down, and then asked, "Why didn't you have me take it in the first place? You didn't even mention it."

"It's a fake," Wattles said, and started laughing again. "I had it painted for him. Rabbits didn't want to shell out as much as two of them would have cost, no matter how hot Bunny is, so I went to a guy and got that one painted. Cost forty-five hundred, plus about nine hundred for the frame."

"So it isn't a Klee," I said. "No wonder I liked it," and this time both of us laughed.

Hacker was watching Wattles, and he wasn't laughing.

"You got style," Wattles said. "We'll do business again."

"You owe me twenty thousand," I said.

"I do, I do." He said, "You stay here, okay? It's not that I don't trust you, but I don't want you following me right now." He got up and waddled to the door, opened it, and closed it behind himself.

Hacker glowered at me. "Don't get too comfortable," he said. "We're not finished."

"I sort of figured."

"When we leave," he said, "you and me, we're going to have a talk."

"Fine."

We sat there, breathing poisonous fumes, until Wattles came back in with a wad of hundreds in his hand. "Did he peek?" he asked Hacker.

"No," Hacker said. He was sulking.

"Here you go. All in hundreds, okay? I don't have smaller."

"No problem." I got up. "Nice doing business with you."

"You sold him the good one," Wattles said, and laughed again. "You know, he'll never figure it out. He can't show it to anybody who could tell him. And he's obviously not gonna sell it. I wonder how many fakes he's sitting on, up in that castle."

"Starting with his teeth," I said.

Wattles raised a finger. "You know, you're gonna be on camera. I haven't got any coverage for the second picture."

"I was masked," I said. He didn't have any coverage of me opening the safe, either, but that footage would be erased when Wattles made the swap. "I didn't like the way I photographed in high-def. Made me look like a crook."

Wattles was laughing as I left, and Hacker was all of four inches behind me. We got out into the corridor and he grabbed my sleeve, but two young women came out of another office, and the four of us stood there, Hacker quietly seething, and waited for the elevator.

The young women got out at the lobby, and Hacker and I rode down to the garage. The moment we got out and the elevator doors closed, he grabbed my throat and pushed me up against a wall. "*You owe me*," he said. "I'm going to lose Trey because of you. Do you have any idea how bad I can hurt you?"

"I think so," I croaked. "You being a cop and all."

He loosened his grip. "Installments," he said. "It starts now, and it continues until whenever I want it to. You're never going to know when I'll be there with my hand out, and you better fucking find something to put in it, you got me? Starting now." He put a hand out. "The twenty K."

I gave it to him, and he stuck it into the pocket of his jacket, shoved me, and turned away.

I said, "Wait."

He turned back to me.

"Make a deal," I said. "You give me the money back, I'll give you these." And I brought Bunny Stennet's diamond necklace out of my pocket, dangling them so they caught the light. "It's worth twice as much as what you just took."

"A *deal*?" he said. He grabbed the necklace. "You got nothing to deal with. Tell you what, this'll slow things up a little. I got all this, it'll be a little longer before you see me again. A *deal*," he said again, and he turned his back on me and went to his car and got in.

I stood where I was and let him drive past me. When he was up the driveway and making the right onto Ventura, I said, not very loudly, "Fence them carefully."

# 47

## Oh, Yeah . . .

. . . I read the *New York Times* now, just to see what's up with Thistle. Her cure took, and she was three weeks straight by the time she reported for work on the movie. I'd called Jake Whelan to ask him to make sure that the crew would applaud the first time she nailed a take. They had, and she blossomed after that. She wasn't amazing, no best supporting actress nomination, but she got good reviews and a bunch of offers, including one for a new series. She turned them all down and went to New York to study at the Actor's Studio. Right now she's playing Rosalind in an off-Broadway production of "As You Like It," getting respectable reviews, and packing them in. She used to call regularly, but I don't hear from her any more. I know she's busy.

Tony Ramirez's death was seen as a mob hit, and there was the inevitable speculation that Trey had been involved, but she had an unshakable alibi: She'd been in a conference practically that whole night, working with Rodd Hull and the writer and Tatiana to see whether there was any way to do the movie with somebody else. Around three A.M., they decided to scrap it and started drinking. No charges were brought against Trey, but privately she has allowed people in her organization to believe that she killed both her father and her former husband, which has had the Lucrezia Borgia effect. Her troops are being very careful around her. She's still going legal, but more slowly than she'd wanted to.

A few months after all this happened, Eduardo's left hand was found by a camper in the Angeles National Forest. Searchers found his right thigh about a quarter of a mile away. It had been pretty extensively gnawed by the local four-footers, but a DNA test identified it as genetically identical with the hand. So it was Eduardo, not I, who got eaten by canines, even if, in his case, it was post-mortem. It's not a fate I'd wish on anyone, but if I were forced to be frank, I'd have to say I'm happier than I would be if it had been the other way around.

No one I know ever saw Ellie Wynn again.

I buried most of Jake Whelan's hundred thousand and lived on the rest. Pretty soon now, I'll have to go dig up some more.

I finally asked Janice out again, and she told me she was just about to get married, so I guess Wattles got himself another laugh. But that's okay, because Kathy and I are getting along a lot better now.

Hacker wound up in the hospital with two broken arms, a broken leg, and a nice new three-piece pelvis. He'll be trouble when he gets out, but that won't be for a quite a while.

And my mentor, Herbie—you remember Herbie?—he burgled a psychiatrist's office and found a file that made it clear that the good doctor was treating a patient who was "conflicted," to use the doctor's term, by the fact that he'd murdered two people. Herbie made his usual phone call, and then some very unsettling stuff started to happen, and Herbie called me, and—

Oh, forget it. That's another story.

Author's Note

For most people who write thrillers and mysteries, creating crooks is more than half the fun. They're intrinsically interesting because they've rejected the standard set of values and, since we all need values of some kind, they've invented their own. It was probably just a matter of time before I came up with a series that's essentially all crooks.

In the middle of writing the third Poke Rafferty book, *Breathing Water*, I began to hear a voice in my head. It was sufficiently kind and tactful to let me write the other book, but the moment I turned off the computer each day, it came back. It was especially persistent when I was trying to go to sleep. I finally sat down at the keyboard and put down what it was saying.

As it turned out, the voice didn't belong to Junior. The character who wouldn't stop pestering me was Louie the Lost. What came out of my listening to him was a short story about a stolen koala bear that I called "Koala Mode." In it, Louie buys a baby koala bear—the cutest thing he's ever seen in his life, just ootsa-pootsa cute, almost throat-thickeningly cute—from an animal smuggler, but then the koala disappears. To my surprise, Louie turned to a friend to get his bear back, and the friend was Junior Bender. Stinky Tetwiler found his way into the narrative, too.

I showed the story to my agent, who felt it was mildly amusing but not very well developed. (He was being kind; it was twee in the extreme.) But the characters nagged at me, and finally I knocked a hole in the writing schedule for *Breathing Water* and reopened the bottle to let the genie out.

The novel began with nothing but a notion about the attempted exploitation of a former child star, but once the Rottweilers pushed their way in, there was no stopping. The first draft took about seven weeks, a record for me. Then I finished *Breathing Water* and went back to *Crashed* for another five weeks. Ultimately Soho's Juliet Grames applied a keen eye and a red pencil, and the result is this book.

This was a rock and roll book all the way. I wrote it to the music of Arcade Fire, Arctic Monkeys, Cream, Dodos, Franz Ferdinand, Jon Fratelli, Green Day, Jason Isbell and the 400, Little Feat, James McMurtry, My Morning Jacket, Oasis, Smashing Pumpkins, The Raconteurs, The Red Hot Chili Peppers, Warren Zevon, The White Stripes, The Wombats, Neil Young, and Warren Zevon, among others. Pretty much all guys, I'm afraid.

From time to time as I wrote, I read chunks of the story to my wife, Munyin Choy-Hallinan, who had the good grace to laugh in the right places. Thanks, Mun.